“Jack Reacher is the coolest [illegible] **char**[illegible]

[illegible]

Lee Child

“**Electrifying** . . . utterly addictive . . . dazzles. Not for nothing has the cover art of his recent books depicted a bull’s-eye.” — Janet Maslin, *New York Times*

“**Explosive** and nearly impossible to put down.”
—*People,* “Sizzling Summer Reads”

“Child’s **hard-boiled** meal ticket shows no signs of drying up anytime soon. Thank goodness.”
—*Entertainment Weekly* (A-)

“A breathless, ultracool novel with **relentless** pacing.”
—*Cleveland Plain Dealer*

“Lee Child [is] the current poster-boy of American crime fiction.” —*Los Angeles Times*

“Jack Reacher is **a tough guy’s tough guy.**”
—*Santa Monica Mirror*

“[An] **action-packed** thrill ride.”—*Chicago Sun-Times*

More Praise for **Nothing to Lose**

"With his powerful sense of justice, dogged determination and the physical and mental skills to overcome what to most would be overwhelming odds, Jack Reacher makes an **irresistible** modern knight-errant." —*Publishers Weekly*

"As always, Child constructs sentences like a flurry of jabs, before delivering a **knockout punch of a climax**." —*Kirkus Reviews*

"At the stage of his career when many other suspense writers fumble for new ideas or settle on ho-hum, repetitive story lines, Child still cranks out thrillers that you simply can't put down." —*Miami Herald*

Praise for **Bad Luck and Trouble**

"As always, **the action is intense,** the pace unrelenting, and the violence unforgiving. Child remains the reigning master at combining breakneck yet **brilliantly constructed** plotting with characters who continually surprise us with their depth."

—*Booklist* (starred review)

"Perhaps there are action-lit writers more recognizable than Child, but the bet is that none of them will turn in a tighter-plotted, richer-peopled, faster-paced page-turner this year."

—*Kirkus Reviews* (starred review)

"A **slam-bang** yarn filled with Child's usual terse life-and-death lessons . . . Turns out, even when Reacher gets personal, he never gets mushy."

—*Entertainment Weekly* (A-)

Praise for The Hard Way

"The best thriller writer of the moment."

—*New York Times*

"Jack Reacher, the tough-minded hero of a series of best-selling noir thrillers, has all the elements that have made this genre so popular among men for decades. He travels the country dispensing his own form of justice, often violently and without remorse. . . . Reacher is doing something surprising: winning the hearts of many women readers."

—*Wall Street Journal*

Praise for One Shot

"**Ranks in the first tier** . . . Before it's all, vividly, over, one feels confident that Reacher—smart, rootless, and brave—will not only get his man but make him suffer."

—*New Yorker*

Also by Lee Child

KILLING FLOOR

DIE TRYING

TRIPWIRE

RUNNING BLIND

ECHO BURNING

WITHOUT FAIL

PERSUADER

THE ENEMY

ONE SHOT

THE HARD WAY

BAD LUCK AND TROUBLE

and coming soon

GONE TOMORROW

NOTHING TO LOSE

A REACHER NOVEL

LEE CHILD

A DELL BOOK

NOTHING TO LOSE
A Dell Book

PUBLISHING HISTORY
Delacorte Press hardcover edition published June 2008
Dell international edition / March 2009

Published by Bantam Dell
A Division of Random House, Inc.
New York, New York

This is a work of fiction. Names, characters, places and incidents either are the product of the author's imagination or are used fictitiously. Any resemblance to actual persons, living or dead, events, or locales is entirely coincidental.

Cover art by Belina Huey and Tom Hallman

Library of Congress Catalog Card Number: 2007043735

ISBN: 978-0-440-29697-3

Printed in the United States of America

www.bantamdell.com

OPM 10 9 8 7 6 5 4 3 2

For Rae Helmsworth and
Janine Wilson. They know why.

1

The sun was only half as hot as he had known sun to be, but it was hot enough to keep him confused and dizzy. He was very weak. He had not eaten for seventy-two hours, or taken water for forty-eight.

Not weak. He was dying, and he knew it.

The images in his mind showed things drifting away. A rowboat caught in a river current, straining against a rotted rope, pulling, tugging, breaking free. His viewpoint was that of a small boy in the boat, sitting low, staring back helplessly at the bank as the dock grew smaller.

Or an airship swinging gently on a breeze, somehow breaking free of its mast, floating up and away, slowly, the boy inside seeing tiny urgent figures on the ground, waving, staring, their faces tilted upward in concern.

Then the images faded, because now words seemed more important than pictures, which was absurd, because he had never been interested in words before. But before he died he wanted to know which words were his. Which applied to him? Was he a man or a boy? He had been described both ways. *Be a man,* some had said. Others had been insistent: *The boy's not to blame.* He was old enough to vote and kill and die, which made him a man. He was too young to drink, even beer, which made him a boy. Was he brave, or a coward? He had been called both things. He had been called *unhinged, disturbed, deranged, unbalanced, delusional, traumatized,* all of which he understood and accepted, except *unhinged.* Was he supposed to be *hinged*? Like a door? Maybe people were doors. Maybe things passed through them. Maybe they banged in the wind. He considered the question for a long moment and then he batted the air in frustration. He was babbling like a teenager in love with weed.

Which is exactly all he had been, a year and a half before.

He fell to his knees. The sand was only half as hot as he had known sand to be, but it was hot enough to ease his chill. He fell facedown, exhausted, finally spent. He knew as certainly as he had ever known anything that if he closed his eyes he would never open them again.

But he was very tired.

So very, very tired.

More tired than a man or a boy had ever been.

He closed his eyes.

•

2

The line between Hope and Despair was exactly that: a line, in the road, formed where one town's blacktop finished and the other's started. Hope's highway department had used thick dark asphalt rolled smooth. Despair had a smaller municipal budget. That was clear. They had top-dressed a lumpy roadbed with hot tar and dumped gray gravel on it. Where the two surfaces met there was an inch-wide trench of no-man's-land filled with a black rubbery compound. An expansion joint. A boundary. A line. Jack Reacher stepped over it midstride and kept on walking. He paid it no attention at all.

But he remembered it later. Later, he was able to recall it in great detail.

Hope and Despair were both in Colorado. Reacher was in Colorado because two days previously he had been in Kansas, and Colorado was next to Kansas. He was making his way west and south. He had been in Calais, Maine, and had taken it into his head to cross the continent diagonally, all the way to San Diego in California. Calais was the last major place in the Northeast, San Diego was the last major place in the Southwest. One extreme to the other. The

Atlantic to the Pacific, cool and damp to hot and dry. He took buses where there were any and hitched rides where there weren't. Where he couldn't find rides, he walked. He had arrived in Hope in the front passenger seat of a bottle-green Mercury Grand Marquis driven by a retired button salesman. He was on his way out of Hope on foot because that morning there had been no traffic heading west toward Despair.

He remembered that fact later, too. And wondered why he hadn't wondered why.

In terms of his grand diagonal design, he was slightly off course. Ideally he should have been angling directly southwest into New Mexico. But he wasn't a stickler for plans, and the Grand Marquis had been a comfortable car, and the old guy had been fixed on Hope because he had three grandchildren to see there, before heading onward to Denver to see four more. Reacher had listened patiently to the old guy's family tales and had figured that a saw-tooth itinerary first west and then south was entirely acceptable. Maybe two sides of a triangle would be more entertaining than one. And then in Hope he had looked at a map and seen Despair seventeen miles farther west and had been unable to resist the detour. Once or twice in his life he had made the same trip metaphorically. Now he figured he should make it for real, since the opportunity was right there in front of him.

He remembered that whim later, too.

The road between the two towns was a straight two-lane. It rose very gently as it headed west. Nothing dramatic. The part of eastern Colorado that Reacher was in was pretty flat. Like Kansas. But the

Rockies were visible up ahead, blue and massive and hazy. They looked very close. Then suddenly they didn't. Reacher breasted a slight rise and stopped dead and understood why one town was called Hope and the other Despair. Settlers and homesteaders struggling west a hundred and fifty years before him would have stopped over in what came to be called Hope and would have seen their last great obstacle seemingly within touching distance. Then after a day's or a week's or a month's repose they would have moved on again and breasted the same slight rise and seen that the Rockies' apparent proximity had been nothing more than a cruel trick of topography. An optical illusion. A trick of the light. From the top of the rise the great barrier seemed once again remote, even unreachably distant, across hundreds more miles of endless plains. Maybe thousands more miles, although that too was an illusion. Reacher figured that in truth the first significant peaks were about two hundred miles away. A long month's hard trekking on foot and in mule-drawn carts, across featureless wilderness and along occasional decades-old wheel ruts. Maybe six weeks' hard trekking, in the wrong season. In context, not a disaster, but certainly a bitter disappointment, a blow hard enough to drive the anxious and the impatient from hope to despair in the time between one glance at the horizon and the next.

Reacher stepped off Despair's gritty road and walked through crusted sandy earth to a table rock the size of a car. He levered himself up and lay down with his hands behind his head and stared up at the sky. It was pale blue and laced with long high feathery clouds that might once have been vapor trails from coast-to-coast red-eye planes. Back when he smoked he might have lit a cigarette to pass the time. But he didn't smoke anymore. Smoking implied carrying at least a pack and a book of matches, and Reacher had long ago quit carrying things he didn't need. There was nothing in his pockets except paper money and an expired passport and an ATM card and a clip-together toothbrush. There was nothing waiting for him anywhere else, either. No storage unit in a distant city, nothing stashed with friends. He owned the things in his pockets and the clothes on his back and the shoes on his feet. That was all, and that was enough. Everything he needed, and nothing he didn't.

He got to his feet and stood on tiptoe, high on the rock. Behind him to the east was a shallow bowl maybe ten miles in diameter with the town of Hope roughly in its center, eight or nine miles back, maybe ten blocks by six of brick-built buildings and an outlying clutter of houses and farms and barns and other structures made of wood and corrugated metal. Together they made a warm low smudge in the haze. Ahead of him to the west were tens of thousands of flat square miles, completely empty except for ribbons of distant roads and the town of Despair about eight or nine miles ahead. Despair was harder to see than Hope. The haze was thicker in the west. The place looked larger than Hope had been, and teardrop-shaped, with a conventional plains downtown mostly south of the main drag and then a wider zone of activity beyond it, maybe industrial in nature, hence the smog. Despair looked less pleasant than Hope. Cold, where Hope had looked warm; gray, where Hope had been mellow. It looked unwelcoming. For a brief moment Reacher considered backtracking and striking out south from Hope itself, getting back on course, but he dismissed the thought even before it had fully formed. Reacher hated turning back. He liked to press on, dead ahead, whatever. Everyone's life needed an organizing principle, and relentless forward motion was Reacher's.

He was angry at himself later, for being so inflexible.

He climbed off the rock and rejoined the road twenty yards west of where he had left it. He stepped up onto the left-hand edge and continued walking, long strides, an easy pace, a little faster than three miles an hour, facing oncoming traffic, the safest way. But there was no oncoming traffic. No traffic in either direction. The road was deserted. No vehicles were using it. No cars, no trucks. Nothing. No chance of a ride. Reacher was a little puzzled, but mostly unconcerned. Many times in his life he had walked a lot more than seventeen miles at a stretch. He raked the hair off his forehead and pulled his shirt loose on his shoulders and kept on going, toward whatever lay ahead.

3

Despair's downtown area began with a vacant lot where something had been planned maybe twenty years before but never built. Then came an old motor court, shuttered, maybe permanently abandoned. Across the street and fifty yards west was a gas station. Two pumps, both of them old. Not the kind of upright rural antiques Reacher had seen in Edward Hopper's paintings, but still a couple of generations off the pace. There was a small hut in back with a grimy window full of quarts of oil arrayed in a pyramid. Reacher crossed the apron and stuck his head in the door. It was dark inside the hut and the air smelled of creosote and hot raw wood. There was a guy behind a counter, in worn blue overalls stained black with dirt. He was about thirty, and lean.

"Got coffee?" Reacher asked him.

"This is a gas station," the guy said.

"Gas stations sell coffee," Reacher said. "And water, and soda."

"Not this one," the guy said. "We sell gas."

"And oil."

"If you want it."

"Is there a coffee shop in town?"

"There's a restaurant."

"Just one?"

"One is all we need."

Reacher ducked back out to the daylight and kept on walking. A hundred yards farther west the road grew sidewalks and according to a sign on a pole changed its name to Main Street. Thirty feet later came the first developed block. It was occupied by a dour brick cube, three stories high, on the left side of the street, to the south. It might once have been a dry goods emporium. It was still some kind of a retail enterprise. Reacher could see three customers and bolts of cloth and plastic household items through its dusty groundfloor windows. Next to it was an identical three-story brick cube, and then another, and another. The downtown area seemed to be about twelve blocks square, bulked mostly to the south of Main Street. Reacher was no kind of an architectural expert, and he knew he was way west of the Mississippi, but the whole place gave him the feel of an old Connecticut factory town, or the Cincinnati riverfront. It was plain, and severe, and unadorned, and out of date. He had seen movies about small-town America in which the sets had been artfully dressed to look a little more perfect and vibrant than reality. This place was the exact opposite. It looked like a designer and a whole team of grips had worked hard to make it dowdier and gloomier than it needed to be. Traffic on the streets was light. Sedans and pick-up trucks were moving slow and lazy. None of them was newer than three years old. There were few pedestrians on the sidewalks.

Reacher made a random left turn and set about finding the promised restaurant. He quartered a dozen blocks and passed a grocery store and a barber shop and a bar and a rooming house and a faded old hotel before he found the eatery. It took up the whole ground floor of another dull brick cube. The ceiling was high and the windows were floor-to-ceiling plate glass items filling most of the walls. The place might have been an automobile showroom in the past. The floor was tiled and the tables and chairs were plain brown wood and the air smelled of boiled vegetables. There was a register station inside the door with a *Please Wait to Be Seated* sign on a short brassed pole with a heavy base. Same sign he had seen everywhere, coast to coast. Same script, same colors, same shape. He figured there was a catering supply company somewhere turning them out by the millions. He had seen identical signs in Calais, Maine, and expected to see more in San Diego, California. He stood next to the register and waited.

And waited.

There were eleven customers eating. Three couples, a threesome, and two singletons. One waitress. No front-of-house staff. Nobody at the register. Not an unusual ratio. Reacher had eaten in a thousand similar places and he knew the rhythm, subliminally. The lone waitress would soon glance over at him and nod, as if to say *I'll be right with you.* Then she would take an order, deliver a plate, and scoot over, maybe blowing an errant strand of hair off her cheek in a gesture designed to be both an apology and an appeal for sympathy. She would collect a menu from a stack and lead him to a table and bustle away and then revisit him in strict sequence.

But she didn't do any of that.

She glanced over. Didn't nod. Just looked at him for a long second and then looked away. Carried on with what she was doing. Which by that point wasn't much. She had all her eleven customers pacified. She was just making work. She was stopping by tables and asking if everything was all right and refilling coffee cups that were less than an inch down from the rim. Reacher turned and checked the door glass to see if he had missed an opening-hours sign. To see if the place was about to close up. It wasn't. He checked his reflection, to see if he was committing a social outrage with the way he was dressed. He wasn't. He was wearing dark gray pants and a matching dark gray shirt, both bought two days before in a janitorial surplus store in Kansas. Janitorial supply stores were his latest discovery. Plain, strong, well-made clothing at reasonable prices. Perfect. His hair was short and tidy. He had shaved the previous morning. His fly was zipped.

He turned back to wait.

Customers turned to look at him, one after the other. They appraised him quite openly and then looked away. The waitress made another slow circuit of the room, looking everywhere except at him. He stood still, running the situation through a mental database and trying to understand it. Then he lost patience with it and stepped past the sign and moved into the room and sat down alone at a table for four. He scraped his chair in and made himself comfortable. The waitress watched him do it, and then she headed for the kitchen.

She didn't come out again.

Reacher sat and waited. The room was silent. No talking. No sounds at all, except for the quiet metallic clash of silverware on plates and the smack of people chewing and the ceramic click of cups being lowered carefully into saucers and the wooden creak of chair legs under shifting bodies. Those tiny noises rose up and echoed around the vast tiled space until they seemed overwhelmingly loud.

Nothing happened for close to ten minutes.

Then an old crew-cab pick-up truck slid to a stop on the curb outside the door. There was a second's pause and four guys climbed out and stood together on the sidewalk outside the restaurant's door. They grouped themselves into a tight little formation and paused another beat and came inside. They paused again and scanned the room and found their target. They headed straight for Reacher's table. Three of them sat down in the empty chairs and the fourth stood at the head of the table, blocking Reacher's exit.

4

The four guys were each a useful size. The shortest was probably an inch under six feet and the lightest was maybe an ounce over two hundred pounds. They all had walnut knuckles and thick wrists and knotted forearms. Two of them had broken noses and none of them had all their teeth. They all looked pale and vaguely unhealthy. They were all grimy, with ingrained gray dirt in the folds of their skin that glittered and shone like metal. They were all dressed in canvas work shirts with their sleeves rolled to their elbows. They were all somewhere between thirty and forty. And they all looked like trouble.

"I don't want company," Reacher said. "I prefer to eat alone."

The guy standing at the head of the table was the biggest of the four, by maybe an inch and ten pounds. He said, "You're not going to eat at all."

Reacher said, "I'm not?"

"Not here, anyway."

"I heard this was the only show in town."

"It is."

"Well, then."

"You need to get going."

"Going?"

"Out of here."

"Out of where?"

"Out of this restaurant."

"You want to tell me why?"

"We don't like strangers."

"Me either," Reacher said. "But I need to eat somewhere. Otherwise I'll get all wasted and skinny like you four."

"Funny man."

"Just calling it like it is," Reacher said. He put his forearms on the table. He had thirty pounds and three inches on the big guy, and more than that on the other three. And he was willing to bet he had a little more experience and a little less inhibition than any one of them. Or than all of them put together. But ultimately, if it came to it, it was going to be his two hundred and fifty pounds against their cumulative nine hundred. Not great odds. But Reacher hated turning back.

The guy who was standing said, "We don't want you here."

Reacher said, "You're confusing me with someone who gives a shit what you want."

"You won't get served in here."

"You could order for me."

"And then what?"

"Then I could eat your lunch."

"Funny man," the guy said again. "You need to leave now."

"Why?"

"Just leave now."

Reacher asked, "You guys got names?"

"Not for you to know. And you need to leave."

"You want me to leave, I'll need to hear it from the owner. Not from you."

"We can arrange that." The guy who was standing nodded to one of the guys in the seats, who scraped his chair back and got up and headed for the kitchen. A long minute later he came back out with a man in a stained apron. The man in the apron was wiping his hands on a dish towel and didn't look particularly worried or perturbed. He walked up to Reacher's table and said, "I want you to leave my restaurant."

"Why?" Reacher asked.

"I don't need to explain myself."

"You the owner?"

"Yes, I am."

Reacher said, "I'll leave when I've had a cup of coffee."

"You'll leave now."

"Black, no sugar."

"I don't want trouble."

"You already got trouble. If I get a cup of coffee, I'll walk out of here. If I don't get a cup of coffee, these guys can try to throw me out, and you'll spend the rest of the day cleaning blood off the floor and all day tomorrow shopping for new chairs and tables."

The guy in the apron said nothing.

Reacher said, "Black, no sugar."

The guy in the apron stood still for a long moment and then headed back to the kitchen. A minute later the waitress came out with a single cup balanced on a saucer. She carried it across the room and set it down in front of Reacher, hard enough to slop some of the contents out of the cup and into the saucer.

"Enjoy," she said.

Reacher lifted the cup and wiped the base on his sleeve. Set the cup down on the table and emptied the saucer into it. Set the cup back on the saucer and squared it in front of him. Then he raised it again and took a sip.

Not bad, he thought. A little weak, a little stewed, but at heart it was a decent commercial product. Better than most diners, worse than most franchise places. Right in the middle of the curve. The cup was a porcelain monstrosity with a lip about three-eighths of an inch thick. It was cooling the drink too fast. Too wide, too shallow, too much mass. Reacher was no big fan of fine china, but he believed a receptacle ought to serve its contents.

The four guys were still clustered all around. Two sitting, two standing now. Reacher ignored them and drank, slowly at first, and then faster as the coffee grew cold. He drained the cup and set it back on the saucer. Pushed it away, slowly and carefully, until it was exactly centered on the table. Then he moved his left arm fast and went for his pocket. The four guys jumped. Reacher came out with a dollar bill and flattened it and trapped it under the saucer.

"So let's go," he said.

The guy standing at the head of the table moved out of the way. Reacher scraped his chair back and stood up. Eleven customers watched him do it. He pushed his chair in neatly and stepped around the head of the table and headed for the door. He sensed the four guys behind him. Heard their boots on the tile. They were forming up in single file, threading between tables, stepping past the sign and the register. The room was silent.

Reacher pushed the door and stepped outside to the street. The air was cool, but the sun was out. The sidewalk was concrete, cast in five-by-five squares. The squares were separated by inch-wide expansion joints. The joints were filled with black compound.

Reacher turned left and took four steps until he was clear of the parked pick-up and then he stopped and turned back, with the afternoon sun behind him. The four guys formed up in front of him, with the sun in their eyes. The guy who had stood at the head of the table said, "Now you need to get out."

Reacher said, "I am out."

"Out of town."

Reacher said nothing.

The guy said, "Make a left, and then Main Street is four blocks up. When you get there, turn either left or right, west or east. We don't care which. Just keep on walking."

Reacher asked, "You still do that here?"

"Do what?"

"Run people out of town."

"You bet we do."

"You want to tell me why you do?"

"We don't have to tell you why we do."

Reacher said, "I just got here."

"So?"

"So I'm staying."

The guy on the end of the line pushed his rolled

cuffs above his elbows and took a step forward. Broken nose, missing teeth. Reacher glanced at the guy's wrists. The width of a person's wrists was the only failsafe indicator of a person's raw strength. This guy's were wider than a long-stemmed rose, narrower than a two-by-four. Closer to the two-by-four than the rose.

Reacher said, "You're picking on the wrong man."

The guy who had been doing all the talking said, "You think?"

Reacher nodded. "I have to warn you. I promised my mother, a long time ago. She said I had to give folks a chance to walk away."

"You a momma's boy?"

"She liked to see fair play."

"There are four of us. One of you."

Reacher's hands were down by his sides, relaxed, gently curled. His feet were apart, securely planted. He could feel the hard concrete through the soles of his shoes. It was textured. It had been brushed with a yard broom just before it dried, ten years earlier. He folded the fingers of his left hand flat against his palm. Raised the hand, very slowly. Brought it level with his shoulder, palm out. The four guys stared at it. The way his fingers were folded made them think he was hiding something. *But what?* He snapped his fingers open. *Nothing there.* In the same split second he moved sideways and heaved his right fist up like a convulsion and caught the guy who had stepped forward with a colossal uppercut to the jaw. The guy had been breathing through his mouth because of his broken nose and the massive impact snapped his jaw shut and lifted him up off the ground and dumped him back down in a vertical heap on the sidewalk. Like a puppet with the strings cut. Unconscious before he got halfway there.

"Now there are only three of you," Reacher said. "Still one of me."

They weren't total amateurs. They reacted pretty well and pretty fast. They sprang back and apart into a wide defensive semicircle and crouched, fists ready.

Reacher said, "You can still walk away."

The guy who had been doing the talking said, "You got lucky."

"Only suckers get sucker punched."

"Won't happen twice."

Reacher said nothing.

The guy said, "Get out of town. You can't take us three-on-one."

"Try me."

"Can't be done. Not now."

Reacher nodded. "Maybe you're right. Maybe one of you will stay on your feet long enough to get to me."

"You can count on it."

"But the question you need to ask is, which one of you will it be? Right now you've got no way of knowing. One of you will be driving the other three to the hospital for a six-month stay. You want me out of town bad enough to take those odds?"

Nobody spoke. Stalemate. Reacher rehearsed his next moves. A right-footed kick to the groin of the guy on his left, spin back with an elbow to the head for the guy in the middle, duck under the inevitable roundhouse swing incoming from the guy on the right, let him follow through, put an elbow in his kidney. One, two, three, no fundamental problem. Maybe a little cleanup afterward, more feet and elbows. Main difficulty would be limiting the damage. Careful restraint would be required. It was always wiser to stay on the right side of the line, closer to brawling than homicide.

In the distance beyond the three guys Reacher could see people going about their lawful business on the sidewalks. He could see cars and trucks driving slow on the streets, pausing at four-way stops, moving on.

Then he saw one particular car blow straight through a four-way and head in his direction. A Crown Victoria, white and gold, black push bars on the front, a light bar on the roof, antennas on the trunk lid. A shield on the door, with *DPD* scrolled across it. *Despair Police Department.* A heavyset cop in a tan jacket visible behind the glass.

"Behind you," Reacher said. "The cavalry is here." But he didn't move. And he kept his eyes on the three guys. The cop's arrival didn't necessarily guarantee anything. Not yet. The three guys looked mad enough to move straight from a verbal warning to an actual assault charge. Maybe they already had so many they figured one more wouldn't make any difference. *Small towns.* In Reacher's experience they all had a lunatic fringe.

The Crown Vic braked hard in the gutter. The door swung open. The driver took a riot gun from a holster between the seats. Climbed out. Pumped the gun and held it diagonally across his chest. He was a big guy.

White, maybe forty. Black hair. Wide neck. Tan jacket, brown pants, black shoes, a groove in his forehead from a Smokey the Bear hat that was presumably now resting on his passenger seat. He stood behind the three guys and looked around. Surveyed the scene. *Not exactly rocket science,* Reacher thought. *Three guys surrounding a fourth? We're not discussing the weather here.*

The cop said, "Back off now." Deep voice. Authoritative. The three guys stepped backward. The cop stepped forward. They swapped their relative positions. Now the three guys were behind the cop. The cop moved his gun. Pointed it straight at Reacher's chest.

"You're under arrest," he said.

5

Reacher stood still and asked, "On what charge?"

The cop said, "I'm sure I'll think of something." He swapped the gun into one hand and used the other to take the handcuffs out of the holder on his belt. He held them on the flat of his palm and one of the guys behind him stepped forward and took them from him and looped around behind Reacher's back.

"Put your arms behind you," the cop said.

"Are these guys deputized?" Reacher asked.

"Why would you care?"

"I don't. But they should. They put their hands on me without a good reason, they get their arms broken."

"They're all deputized," the cop said. "Especially including the one you just laid out."

He put both hands back on his gun.

"Self-defense," Reacher said.

"Save it for the judge," the cop said.

The guy behind him pulled Reacher's arms back and cuffed his wrists. The guy who had done all the talking opened the cruiser's rear door and stood there holding it like a hotel doorman with a taxicab.

"Get in the car," the cop said.

Reacher stood still and considered his options. Didn't take him long. He didn't have any options. He was handcuffed. He had a guy about three feet behind him. He had a cop about eight feet in front of him. Two more guys three feet behind the cop. The riot gun was some kind of a Mossberg. He didn't recognize the model, but he respected the brand.

"In the car," the cop said.

Reacher moved forward and looped around the open door and jacked himself inside butt-first. The seat was covered in heavy vinyl and he slid across it easily. The floor was covered in pimpled rubber. The security screen was clear bulletproof plastic. He braced his feet, one in the left foot well and one in the right. Uncomfortable, with his hands cuffed behind him. He figured he was going to get bounced around.

The cop got back in the front. The suspension yielded to his weight. He reholstered the Mossberg. Slammed his door and put the transmission in drive and stamped on the gas. Reacher was thrown back against the cushion. Then the guy braked hard for a stop sign and Reacher was tossed forward. He twisted as he went and took the blow against the plastic screen with his shoulder. The cop repeated the procedure at the next four-way. And the next. But Reacher was OK with it. It was to be expected. He had driven the same way in the past, in the days when he was the guy in the front and someone else was the guy in the back. And it was a small town. Wherever the police station was, it couldn't be far.

The police station was four blocks west and two blocks south of the restaurant. It was housed in another undistinguished brick building on a street wide enough to let the cop park nose-in to the curb on a diagonal. There was one other car there. That was all. Small town, small police department. The building had two stories. The cops had the ground floor. The town court was upstairs. Reacher guessed there were cells in the basement. His trip to the booking desk was uneventful. He didn't make trouble. No point. No percentage in being a fugitive on foot in a town where the line was twelve miles away in one direction and maybe more in the other. The desk was manned by a patrolman who could have been the arresting officer's kid brother. Same size and shape, same face, same hair, a little younger. Reacher was uncuffed and gave up the stuff from his pockets and his shoelaces. He had no belt. He was escorted down a winding stair and put in a six-by-eight cell fronted by ancient ironwork that had been painted maybe fifty times.

"Lawyer?" he asked.

"You know any?" the desk guy asked back.

"The public defender will do."

The desk guy nodded and locked the gate and walked away. Reacher was left on his own. The cell block was otherwise empty. Three cells in a line, a narrow corridor, no windows. Each cell had a wall-mounted iron tray for a bed and a steel toilet with a sink built into the top of the tank. Bulkhead lights burned behind wire grilles on the ceilings. Reacher ran his right hand under cold water at the sink and massaged his knuckles. They were sore, but not damaged. He lay down on the cot and closed his eyes.

Welcome to Despair, he thought.

6

The public defender never showed. Reacher dozed for two hours and then the cop who had arrested him clattered down the stairs and unlocked the cell and gestured for him to get up.

"The judge is ready for you," he said.

Reacher yawned. "I haven't seen my lawyer."

"Take it up with the court," the cop said. "Not with me."

"What kind of a half-assed system have you got here?"

"The same kind we've always had."

"I think I'll stay down here."

"I could send your three remaining buddies in for a visit."

"Save gas and send them straight to the hospital."

"I could put you in handcuffs first. Strap you to the bed."

"All by yourself?"

"I could bring a stun gun."

"You live here in town?"

"Why?"

"Maybe I'll come visit you one day."

"I don't think you will."

The cop stood there waiting. Reacher shrugged to himself and swung his feet to the floor. Pushed himself upright and stepped out of the cell. Walking was awkward without his shoelaces. On the stairs he had to hook his toes to stop his shoes falling off altogether. He shuffled past the booking desk and followed the cop up another flight. A grander staircase. At the top was a wooden double door, closed. Alongside it was a sign on a short post with a heavy base. Same kind of thing as the restaurant sign, except this one said: *Town Court.* The cop opened the left-hand panel and stood aside. Reacher stepped into a courtroom. There was a center aisle and four rows of spectator seating. Then a bullpen rail and a prosecution table and a defense table, each with three wheelback chairs. There was a witness stand and a jury box and a judge's dais. All the furniture and all the structures were made out of pine, lacquered dark and then darkened more by age and polish. The walls were paneled with the same stuff. There were flags behind the dais, Old Glory and something Reacher guessed was the state flag of Colorado.

The room was empty. It echoed and smelled of dust. The cop walked ahead and opened the bullpen gate. Pointed Reacher toward the defense table. The cop sat down at the prosecution table. They waited. Then an inconspicuous door in the back wall opened and a man in a suit walked in. The cop jumped up and said, "All rise." Reacher stayed in his seat.

The man in the suit clumped up three steps and slid in behind the dais. He was bulky and somewhere over sixty and had a full head of white hair. His suit was cheap and badly cut. He picked up a pen and straightened a legal pad in front of him. He looked at Reacher and said, "Name?"

"I haven't been Mirandized," Reacher said.

"You haven't been charged with a crime," the old guy said. "This isn't a trial."

"So what is it?"

"A hearing."

"About what?"

"It's an administrative matter, that's all. Possibly just a technicality. But I do need to ask you some questions."

Reacher said nothing.

The guy asked, "Name?"

"I'm sure the police department copied my passport and showed it to you."

"For the record, please."

The guy's tone was neutral and his manner was reasonably courteous. So Reacher shrugged and said, "Jack Reacher. No middle initial."

The guy wrote it down. Followed up with his date of birth, and his Social Security number, and his nationality. Then he asked, "Address?"

Reacher said, "No fixed address."

The guy wrote it down. Asked, "Occupation?"

"None."

"Purpose of your visit to Despair?"

"Tourism."

"How do you propose to support yourself during your visit?"

"I hadn't really thought about it. I didn't anticipate

a major problem. This isn't exactly London or Paris or New York City."

"Please answer the question."

"I have a bank balance," Reacher said.

The guy wrote it all down. Then he sniffed and skipped his pen back over the lines he had already completed and paused. Asked, "What was your last address?"

"An APO box."

"APO?"

"Army Post Office."

"You're a veteran?"

"Yes, I am."

"How long did you serve?"

"Thirteen years."

"Until?"

"I mustered out ten years ago."

"Unit?"

"Military Police."

"Final rank?"

"Major."

"And you haven't had a permanent address since you left the army?"

"No, I haven't."

The guy made a pronounced check mark against one of his lines. Reacher saw his pen move four times, twice in one direction and twice in the other. Then the guy asked, "How long have you been out of work?"

"Ten years," Reacher said.

"You haven't worked since you left the army?"

"Not really."

"A retired major couldn't find a job?"

"This retired major didn't want to find a job."

"Yet you have a bank balance?"

"Savings," Reacher said. "Plus occasional casual labor."

The guy made another big check mark. Two vertical scratches, two horizontal. Then he asked, "Where did you stay last night?"

"In Hope," Reacher said. "In a motel."

"And your bags are still there?"

"I don't have any bags."

The guy made another check mark.

"You walked here?" he asked.

"Yes," Reacher said.

"Why?"

"No buses, and I didn't find a ride."

"No. Why here?"

"Tourism," Reacher said again.

"What had you heard about our little town?"

"Nothing at all."

"Yet you decided to visit?"

"Evidently."

"Why?"

"I found the name intriguing."

"That's not a very compelling reason."

"I have to be somewhere. And thanks for the big welcome."

The guy made a fourth big check mark. Two vertical lines, two horizontal. Then he skipped his pen down his list, slowly and methodically, fourteen answers, plus four diversions to the margin for the check marks. He said, "I'm sorry, but I find you to be in contravention of one of Despair's town ordinances. I'm afraid you'll have to leave."

"Leave?"

"Leave town."

"What ordinance?"

"Vagrancy," the guy said.

7

Reacher said, "There's a vagrancy ordinance here?"

The judge nodded and said, "As there is in most Western towns."

"I never came across one before."

"Then you've been very lucky."

"I'm not a vagrant."

"Homeless for ten years, jobless for ten years, you ride buses or beg rides or walk from place to place performing occasional casual labor, what else would you call yourself?"

"Free," Reacher said. "And lucky."

The judge nodded again, and said, "I'm glad you see a silver lining."

"What about my First Amendment right of free assembly?"

"The Supreme Court ruled long ago. Municipalities have the right to exclude undesirables."

"Tourists are undesirable? What does the Chamber of Commerce think about that?"

"This is a quiet, old-fashioned town. People don't lock their doors. We don't feel the need. Most of the keys were lost years ago, in our grandparents' time."

"I'm not a thief."

"But we err on the side of caution. Experience elsewhere shows that the itinerant jobless have always been a problem."

"Suppose I don't go? What's the penalty?"

"Thirty days' imprisonment."

Reacher said nothing. The judge said, "The officer will drive you to the town line. Get a job and a home, and we'll welcome you back with open arms. But don't come back until you do."

The cop took him downstairs again and gave him back his cash and his passport and his ATM card and his toothbrush. Nothing was missing. Everything was there. Then the cop handed over his shoelaces and waited at the booking desk while he threaded them through the eyelets in his shoes and pulled them tight and tied them off. Then the cop put his hand on the butt of his gun and said, "Car." Reacher walked ahead of him through the lobby and stepped out the street door. It was late in the day, late in the year, and it was getting dark. The cop had moved his cruiser. Now it was parked nose-out.

"In the back," the cop said.

Reacher heard a plane in the sky, far to the west. A single engine, climbing hard. A Cessna or a Beech or a Piper, small and lonely in the vastness. He pulled the car door and slid inside. Without handcuffs he was a lot more comfortable. He sprawled sideways, like he would in a taxi or a Town Car. The cop leaned in after him, one hand on the roof and one on the door, and said, "We're serious. You come back, we'll arrest you, and you'll spend thirty days in that same cell. Always assuming you don't look at us cross-eyed and we shoot you for resisting."

"You married?" Reacher asked.

"Why?"

"I thought not. You seem to prefer jerking off."

The cop stood still for a long moment and then slammed the door and got in the front. He took off down the street and headed north. *Six blocks to Main Street,* Reacher figured. *If he turns left, takes me onward, to the west, maybe I'll let it go. But if he turns right, takes me back east to Hope, maybe I won't.*

Reacher hated turning back.

Forward motion was his organizing principle.

Six blocks, six stop signs. At each one the cop braked gently and slowed and looked left and looked right and then rolled forward. At Main Street he came to a complete halt. He paused. Then he hit the gas and nosed forward and swung the wheel.

And turned right.

East.

Back toward Hope.

8

Reacher saw the dry goods emporium and the gas station and the abandoned motor court and the vacant unbuilt lot slide by and then the cop accelerated to a steady sixty miles an hour. The tires rumbled over the rough road and stray pebbles spattered the underside and bounced and skittered away to the shoulders. Twelve minutes later the car slowed and coasted and braked and came to a stop. The cop climbed out and put his hand on the butt of his gun and opened Reacher's door.

"Out," he said.

Reacher slid out and felt Despair's grit under his shoes.

The cop jerked his thumb, to the east, where it was darker.

"That way," he said.

Reacher stood still.

The cop took the gun off his belt. It was a Glock nine millimeter, boxy and dull in the gloom. No safety catch. Just a latch on the trigger, already compressed by the cop's meaty forefinger.

"Please," the cop said. "Just give me a reason."

Reacher stepped forward, three paces. Saw the

moon rising on the far horizon. Saw the end of Despair's rough gravel and the start of Hope's smooth blacktop. Saw the inch-wide trench between, filled with black compound. The car was stopped with its push bars directly above it. The expansion joint. The boundary. The line. Reacher shrugged and stepped over it. One long pace, back to Hope.

The cop called, "Don't bother us again."

Reacher didn't reply. Didn't turn around. Just stood and faced east and listened as the car backed up and turned and crunched away across the stones. When the sound was all gone in the distance he shrugged again and started walking.

He walked less than twenty yards and saw headlights a mile away, coming straight at him out of Hope. The beams were widely spaced, bouncing high, dipping low. A big car, moving fast. It came at him out of the gathering darkness and when it was a hundred yards away he saw it was another cop car. Another Crown Vic, painted black and white, police spec, with push bars, lights, and antennas. It stopped short of him and a spotlight mounted on the windshield pillar lit up and swiveled jerkily and played its beam all the way up and down him twice, coming to rest on his face, blinding him. Then it clicked off again and the car crept forward, tires hissing on the smooth asphalt surface, and stopped again with the driver's door exactly alongside him. The door had a gold shield painted on it, with *HPD* scrolled across the middle. *Hope Police Department.* The window buzzed down and a hand went up and a dome light came on inside. Reacher saw a woman cop at the wheel, short blonde hair backlit by the weak yellow bulb above and behind her.

"Want a ride?" she asked.

"I'll walk," Reacher said.

"It's five miles to town."

"I walked out here, I can walk back."

"Riding is easier."

"I'm OK."

The woman was quiet for a moment. Reacher listened to the Crown Vic's engine. It was idling patiently. Belts were turning, a muffler was ticking as it cooled. Then Reacher moved on. He took three steps and heard the car's transmission go into reverse and then the car came alongside him again, driving backward, keeping pace as he walked. The window was still down. The woman said, "Give yourself a break, Zeno."

Reacher stopped. Said, "You know who Zeno was?"

The car stopped.

"Zeno of Cittium," the woman said. "The founder of Stoicism. I'm telling you to stop being so long-suffering."

"Stoics have to be long-suffering. Stoicism is about the unquestioning acceptance of destinies. Zeno said so."

"Your destiny is to return to Hope. Doesn't matter to Zeno whether you walk or ride."

"What are you anyway—a philosopher or a cop or a cab driver?"

"The Despair PD calls us when they're dumping someone at the line. As a courtesy."

"This happens a lot?"

"More than you'd think."

"And you come on out and pick us up?"

"We're here to serve. Says so on the badge."

Reacher looked down at the shield on her door. *HPD* was written across the scroll in the center, but *To Protect* was written at the top of the escutcheon, with *And Serve* added at the bottom.

"I see," he said.

"So get in."

"Why do they do it?"

"Get in and I'll tell you."

"You going to refuse to let me walk?"

"It's five miles. You're grumpy now, you'll be real cranky when you arrive in town. Believe me. We've seen it before. Better for all of us if you ride."

"I'm different. Walking calms me down."

The woman said, "I'm not going to beg, Reacher."

"You know my name?"

"Despair PD passed it on. As a courtesy."

"And a warning?"

"Maybe. Right now I'm trying to decide whether to take them seriously."

Reacher shrugged again and put his hand on the rear door handle.

"Up front, you idiot," the woman said. "I'm helping you, not arresting you."

So Reacher looped around the trunk and opened the front passenger door. The seat was all hemmed in with radio consoles and a laptop terminal on a bracket, but the space was clear. No hat. He crammed himself in. Not much legroom, because of the security screen behind him. Up front the car smelled of oil and coffee and perfume and warm electronics. The laptop screen showed a GPS map. A small arrow was pointing west and blinking away at the far edge of a pink shape labeled *Hope Township*. The shape was precisely rectangular, almost square. A fast and arbitrary land allocation, like the state of Colorado itself. Next to it Despair township was represented by a light purple shape. Despair was not rectangular. It was shaped like a blunt wedge. Its eastern border matched Hope's western limit exactly, then it spread wider, like a triangle with the point cut off. Its western line was twice as long as its eastern and bordered gray emptiness. Unincorporated land, Reacher figured. Spurs came off I-70 and I-25 and ran through the unincorporated land and clipped Despair's northwestern corner.

The woman cop buzzed her window back up and craned her neck and glanced behind her and K-turned across the road. She was slightly built under a crisp tan shirt. Probably less than five feet six, probably less than a hundred and twenty pounds, probably less than thirty-five years old. No jewelry, no wedding band. She had a Motorola radio on her collar and a tall gold badge bar pinned over her left breast. According to the badge her name was Vaughan. And according to the badge she was a pretty good cop. She seemed to have won a bunch of awards and commendations. She was good-looking, but different from regular women. She had seen stuff they hadn't. Reacher was familiar with the concept. He had served with plenty of women, back in the MPs.

He asked, "Why did Despair run me out?"

The woman called Vaughan turned out the dome light. Now she was front-lit by red instrument lights from the dash and the pink and purple glow from the GPS screen and white scatter from the headlight beams on the road.

"Look at yourself," she said.

"What about me?"

"What do you see?"

"Just a guy."

"A blue-collar guy in work clothes, fit, strong, healthy, and hungry."

"So?"

"How far did you get?"

"I saw the gas station and the restaurant. And the town court."

"Then you didn't see the full picture," Vaughan said. She drove slow, about thirty miles an hour, as if she had plenty more to say. She had one hand on the wheel, with her elbow propped on the door. Her other hand lay easy in her lap. Five miles at thirty miles an hour was going to take ten minutes. Reacher wondered what she had to tell him, that less than ten minutes wouldn't cover.

He said, "I'm more green-collar than blue."

"Green?"

"I was in the army. Military cop."

"When?"

"Ten years ago."

"You working now?"

"No."

"Well, then."

"Well what?"

"You were a threat."

"How?"

"West of downtown Despair is the biggest metal recycling plant in Colorado."

"I saw the smog."

"There's nothing else in Despair's economy. The metal plant is the whole ballgame."

"A company town," Reacher said.

Vaughan nodded at the wheel. "The guy who owns the plant owns every brick of every building. Half the population works for him full time. The other half works for him part time. The full-time people are happy enough. The part-time people are insecure. They don't like competition from outsiders. They don't like people showing up, looking for casual labor, willing to work for less."

"I wasn't willing to work at all."

"You tell them that?"

"They didn't ask."

"They wouldn't have believed you anyway. Standing around every morning waiting for a nod from the foreman does things to people. It's kind of feudal. The whole place is feudal. The money the owner pays out in wages comes right back at him, in rents. Mortgages too. He owns the bank. No relief on Sundays, either. There's one church and he's the lay preacher. You want to work, you have to show up in a pew from time to time."

"Is that fair?"

"He likes to dominate. He'll use anything."

"So why don't people move on?"

"Some have. Those who haven't never will."

"Doesn't this guy want people coming in to work for less?"

"He likes the people he owns, not strangers."

"So why were those guys worried?"

"People always worry. Company towns are weird."

"And the town judge toes their line?"

"It's an elected position. And the vagrancy ordinance is for real. Most towns have one. We do, for sure, in Hope. No way around it, if someone complains."

"But nobody complained in Hope. I stayed there last night."

"We're not a company town."

Vaughan slowed. Hope's first built-up block was ahead in the distance. Reacher recognized it. A mom-and-pop hardware store. That morning an old guy had been putting stepladders and wheelbarrows out on the sidewalk, building a display. Now the store was all closed up and dark.

He asked, "How big is the Hope PD?"

Vaughan said, "Me and two others and a watch commander."

"You got sworn deputies?"

"Four of them. We don't use them often. Traffic control, maybe, if we've got construction going on. Why?"

"Are they armed?"

"No. In Colorado, deputies are civilian peace officers. Why?"

"How many deputies does the Despair PD have?"

"Four, I think."

"I met them."

"And?"

"Theoretically, what would the Hope PD do if someone showed up and got in a dispute with one of your deputies and busted his jaw?"

"We'd throw that someone's sorry ass in jail, real quick."

"Why?"

"You know why. Zero tolerance for assaults on peace officers, plus an obligation to look after our own, plus pride and self-respect."

"Suppose there was a self-defense issue?"

"Civilian versus a peace officer, we'd need some kind of amazing reasonable doubt. You'd have felt the same in the MPs."

"That's for damn sure."

"So why did you ask?"

Reacher didn't answer directly. Instead he said, "I'm not a Stoic, really. Zeno preached the passive acceptance of fate. I'm not like that. I'm not very passive. I take challenges personally."

"So?"

"I don't like to be told where I can go and where I can't."

"Stubborn?"

"It annoys me."

Vaughan slowed some more and pulled in at the curb. Put the transmission in Park and turned in her seat.

"My advice?" she said. "Get over it and move on. Despair isn't worth it."

Reacher said nothing.

"Go get a meal and a room for the night," Vaughan said. "I'm sure you're hungry."

Reacher nodded.

"Thanks for the ride," he said. "And it was a pleasure to meet you."

He opened the door and slid out to the sidewalk. Hope's version of Main Street was called First Street. He knew there was a diner a block away on Second Street. He had eaten breakfast there. He set out walking toward it and heard Vaughan's Crown Vic move away behind him. He heard the civilized purr of its motor and the soft hiss of its tires on the asphalt. Then he turned a corner and didn't hear it anymore.

An hour later he was still in the diner. He had eaten soup, steak, fries, beans, apple pie, and ice cream. Now he was drinking coffee. It was a better brew than at the restaurant in Despair. And it had been served in a mug that was cylindrical in shape. Still too thick at the rim, but much closer to the ideal.

He was thinking about Despair, and he was wondering why getting him out of town had been more important than keeping him there and busting him for the assault on the deputy.

9

The diner in Hope had a bottomless cup policy for its coffee and Reacher abused it mercilessly. He drank most of a Bunn flask all on his own. His waitress became fascinated by the spectacle. She didn't need to be asked for refills. She came back every time he was ready, sometimes before he was ready, as if she was willing him to break some kind of a world record for consumption. He left her a double tip, just in case the owner fined her for her generosity.

It was full dark when he left the diner. Nine o'clock in the evening. He figured it would stay dark for another ten hours. Sunrise was probably around seven, in that latitude at that time of year. He walked three blocks to where he had seen a small grocery. In a city it would have been called a bodega and in the suburbs it would have been franchised, but in Hope it was still what it had probably always been, a cramped and dusty family-run enterprise selling the things people needed when they needed them.

Reacher needed water and protein and energy. He bought three one-liter bottles of Poland Spring and six chocolate chip PowerBars and a roll of black thirteen-gallon garbage bags. The clerk at the register packed them all carefully into a paper sack and Reacher took his change and carried the sack four blocks to the same motel he had used the night before. He got the same room, at the end of the row. He went inside and put the sack on the nightstand and lay down on the bed. He planned on a short rest. Until midnight. He didn't want to walk seventeen miles twice on the same day.

Reacher got off the bed at midnight and checked the window. No more moon. There was thick cloud and patches of distant starlight. He packed his purchases into one of the black garbage bags and slung it over his shoulder. Then he left the motel and headed up to First Street in the darkness and turned west. There was no traffic. No pedestrians. Few lit windows. It was the middle of the night in the middle of nowhere. The sidewalk ended twenty feet west of the hardware store. He stepped off the curb onto the asphalt and kept on going. Route-march speed, four miles an hour. Not difficult on the smooth flat surface. He built up a rhythm to the point where he felt he could keep on walking forever and never stop.

But he did stop. He stopped five miles later, a hundred yards short of the line between Hope and Despair, because he sensed a shape ahead of him in the blackness. A hole in the darkness. A car, parked on the shoulder. Mostly black, some hints of white.

A police cruiser.

Vaughan.

The name settled in his mind and at the exact

same time the car's lights flicked on. High beams. Very bright. He was pinned. His shadow shot out behind him, infinitely long. He shielded his eyes, left-handed, because his bag was in his right. He stood still. The lights stayed on. He stepped off the road and looped out over the crusted sand to the north. The lights died back and the spot on the windshield pillar tracked him. It wouldn't leave him. So he changed direction and headed straight for it.

Vaughan turned the light off and buzzed her window down as he approached. She was parked facing east, with two wheels on the sand and the rear bumper of the car exactly level with the expansion joint in the road. Inside her own jurisdiction, but only just. She said, "I thought I might see you here."

Reacher looked at her and said nothing.

She asked, "What are you doing?"

"Taking a stroll."

"That all?"

"No law against it."

"Not here," Vaughan said. "But there is if you take three more steps."

"Not your law."

"You're a stubborn man."

Reacher nodded. "I wanted to see Despair and I'm going to."

"It isn't that great of a place."

"I like to make my own mind up about things like that."

"They're serious, you know. Either you'll spend thirty days in jail or they'll shoot you."

"If they find me."

"They'll find you. I found you."

"I wasn't hiding from you."

"Did you hurt a deputy over there?"

"Why do you ask?"

"I was thinking about the question you asked me."

"I don't know for sure what he was."

"I don't like the idea of deputies getting hurt."

"You wouldn't have liked the deputy. If that's what he was."

"They'll be looking for you."

"How big is their department?"

"Smaller than ours. Two cars, two guys, I think."

"They won't find me."

"Why are you going back?"

"Because they told me not to."

"Is it worth it?"

"What would you do?"

Vaughan said, "I'm an estrogen-based life-form, not testosterone. And I'm all grown up now. I'd suck it up and move on. Or stay in Hope. It's a nice place."

"I'll see you tomorrow," Reacher said.

"You won't. Either I'll be picking you up right here a month from now or I'll be reading about you in the newspaper. Beaten and shot while resisting arrest."

"Tomorrow," Reacher said. "I'll buy you a late dinner."

He moved on, one pace, two, three, and then he stepped over the line.

10

He got off the road immediately. The Hope PD had predicted that he would rise to the challenge. It was an easy guess that the Despair PD would make the same assessment. And he didn't want to blunder into a parked Despair cruiser. That event would have an altogether different conclusion than a pleasant chat with the pretty Officer Vaughan.

He looped fifty yards into the scrub north of the road. Near enough to retain a sense of direction, far enough to stay out of a driver's peripheral vision. The night was cold. The ground was uneven. No chance of getting close to four miles an hour. No chance at all. He had no flashlight. A light would hurt him more than help him. It would be visible for a mile. It would be worse than climbing up on a rock and yelling *Here I am*.

A slow mile later the clock in his head told him it was quarter to two in the morning. He heard an aero engine again, far away to the west, blipping and feathering. A single-engine plane, coming in to land. A Cessna, or a Beech, or a Piper. Maybe the same one he had heard take off, hours before. He listened to it until he imagined it had touched down and taxied. Then he started walking again.

Four hours later he was about level with the center of downtown, three hundred yards out in the scrub. He knew he must have left a healthy trail of footprints, but he didn't particularly care. He doubted that the Despair PD maintained a kennel full of bloodhounds or ran aerial surveillance from a helicopter. As long as he stayed off the roads and the sidewalks he was as good as invisible.

He sensed the bulk of another boat-sized table rock and hunkered down behind it. The night was still cold. He unwrapped his stuff and drank water and ate a PowerBar. Then he repacked his bag and stood up behind the rock and turned to study the town. He leaned against the rock with his elbows out and his forearms flat on its top surface and his chin resting on his stacked fists. At first he saw nothing. Just darkness and stillness and the hidden glow from occasional lit windows. Farther in the distance he saw more lights and sensed more activity. The residential areas, he guessed. He figured people were getting up for work.

Ten minutes later he saw headlight beams coming north. Two, three sets. Their light funneled through the cross-streets and bounced and dipped and threw long shadows straight toward him. He stayed where he was, just watching. The beams paused at Main Street and then swept west. More came after them. Soon every cross-street was lit up bright by long processions of vehicles. It was like the day was dawning in the south. There were sedans and pick-up trucks and old-model SUVs. They all drove north to Main Street and paused and jostled and swung west, toward where Vaughan had said the recycling plant was.

A company town.

Six o'clock in the morning.

The people of Despair, going to work.

Reacher followed them on foot, four hundred yards to the north. He stumbled on through the crusted scrub, tracking the road. The last truck got ahead of him and he followed the red chain of tail lights with his eyes. A mile or more ahead the horizon was lit up with an immense glow. Not dawn. That was going to happen behind him, to the east. The glow to the west was from arc lighting. There seemed to be a huge rectangle of lights on poles surrounding some kind of a massive arena. It looked to be about a mile long. Maybe a half-mile wide. *The biggest metal recycling plant in Colorado,* Vaughan had said.

No kidding, Reacher thought. *Looks like the biggest in the world.*

White steam and dirty black smoke drifted here and there in the glow. In front of it the long convoy of vehicles peeled off and parked in neat rows on acres of beaten scrub. Their headlights swung and bounced and then shut down, one by one. Reacher holed up again, a quarter-mile short and a quarter-mile north of the gate. Watched men file inside, shuffling forward in a long line, lunch pails in their hands. The gate was narrow. A personnel entrance, not a vehicle entrance. Reacher guessed the vehicle entrance was on the other side of the complex, convenient for the highway spurs.

The sky was lightening behind him. Landscape features were becoming visible. The terrain was basically flat, but up close it was pitted with enough humps and dips and rocks to provide decent concealment. The earth was sandy and tan. There were occasional scrubby bushes. There was nothing interesting anywhere. Nothing to attract hikers. Not attractive picnic territory. Reacher expected to spend the day alone.

The last worker filed inside and the personnel gate closed. Reacher moved on, staying hidden, but looking for elevation where he could find it. The recycling plant was truly enormous. It was ringed by an endless solid wall welded out of metal plates painted white. The wall was topped with a continuous horizontal cylinder six feet in diameter. Impossible to climb. Like a supermax prison. His initial estimate of the size of the place had been conservative. It looked bigger than the town itself. Like a tail that wags a dog. Despair was not a town with a plant attached. It was a factory with a dormitory outside its gates.

Work was starting inside. Reacher heard the groan of heavy machinery and the ringing sound of metal on metal and saw the flare and spark of cutting torches. He moved all the way around to the northwest corner, fifteen minutes' fast walk. The vehicle gate was right there. A section of the wall was standing open. A wide road ran from the horizon straight to it. The road looked to be smooth and solid. Built for heavy trucks.

The road was a problem. If Reacher wanted to

continue his counterclockwise progress, he would have to cross it somewhere. He would be exposed. His dark clothes would stand out in the coming daylight. But to who, exactly? He guessed the Despair cops would stay in town east of the plant. And he didn't expect any roving surveillance teams out of the plant itself.

But that was exactly what he got.

Two white Chevy Tahoes came out of the vehicle gate. They drove fifty yards down the road and then plunged off it, one to the left and one to the right, onto beaten tracks of packed scrub created by endless previous excursions. The Tahoes had raised off-road suspensions and big white-lettered tires and the word *Security* stenciled in black across their doors. They drove slowly, maybe twenty miles an hour, one clockwise, one counterclockwise, as if they intended to lap the plant all day long.

Reacher hated turning back.

He struck out west, staying in the dips and washes as far as possible and keeping boulders between himself and the plant. Ten minutes later the natural terrain gave way to where the land had been cleared and graded for the road. The near shoulder was maybe ten yards wide, made of packed sand dotted with stunted second-growth weeds. The roadbed was fifteen or sixteen yards wide. Two lanes, with a bright yellow line between. Smooth blacktop. The far shoulder was another ten yards wide.

Total distance, thirty-five yards, minimum.

Reacher was no kind of a sprinter. As any kind of a runner, he was pretty slow. His best attempt at speed was barely faster than a quick walk. He crouched just east of the last available table rock and watched for the Tahoes.

They came around much less often than he had predicted. Which was inexplicable, but good. What wasn't good was that the road itself was starting to get busy. Reacher knew he should have seen that coming. The largest recycling plant in Colorado clearly needed input, and it clearly produced output. They didn't dig stuff out of the scrub and then bury it again. They trucked scrap in and then trucked ingots out. A lot of scrap, and a lot of ingots. Shortly after seven o'clock in the morning a flat-bed semi roared out of the gate and lumbered onto the road. It had Indiana plates and was laden with bright steel bars. It drove a hundred yards and was passed by another flat-bed heading inward. This one had Oregon plates and was loaded with crushed cars, dozens of them, their chipped and battered paint layered like thin stripes. A container truck with Canadian plates left the plant and passed the Oregon semi. Then the counterclockwise Tahoe showed up and bounced across the roadbed and kept on going. Three minutes later its clockwise partner rotated in the opposite direction. Another semi left the plant and another headed in. A mile west Reacher saw a third approaching, wobbling and shimmering in the morning haze. Way behind it, a fourth.

It was like Times Square.

Inside the plant, giant gantry cranes were moving and cascades of welding sparks were showering everywhere. Smoke was rising and fierce blasts of heat from furnaces were distorting the air. There were muted noises, the chatter of air hammers, clangs of sheet metal, metallic tearing sounds, deep sonorous rings like massive impacts on a blacksmith's anvil.

Reacher drank more water and ate another PowerBar. Then he repacked his plastic sack and waited for the Tahoes to pass one more time and just got up and walked across the road. He passed within forty yards of two speeding trucks, one inbound, one outbound. He accepted the risk of being seen. For one thing, he had no real choice. For another, he figured it was a question of degrees of separation. Would a truck driver tell a plant foreman he had seen a pedestrian? Would the plant foreman call the security office? Would the security office call the town cops?

Unlikely. And even if it happened, response time would be slow. Reacher would be back in the weeds well before the Crown Vics showed up. And the Crown Vics would be no good off-road. The Tahoes would stick to their own private itineraries.

Safe enough.

He made it onward to where the rocks and the humps and the dips resumed and headed south, tracking the long side of the plant. The wall continued. It was maybe fourteen feet high, welded out of what looked like the roofs of old cars. Each panel had a slight convex curve. They made the whole thing look quilted. The six-foot cylinder along the top looked to be assembled from the same material, molded in giant presses to the correct contour, and welded together in a seamless run. Then the whole assembly had been sprayed glossy white.

It took Reacher twenty-six minutes to walk the

length of the plant, which made it more than a mile long. At its far southwest corner he saw why the Tahoes were so slow. There was a second walled compound. Another huge rectangle. Similar size. Tire tracks showed that the Tahoes were lapping it too, passing and repassing through a fifty-yard bottleneck in a giant distorted figure 8. Reacher was suddenly exposed. His position was good, relative to the first compound. Not so good, relative to the second. The clockwise Tahoe would sweep through the gap and make a wide turn and come pretty close. He backed off again, aiming for a low boulder. He got halfway across a shallow pan of scrub.

Then he heard tires on dirt.

He dropped flat to the ground, facedown, watching.

11

The white Tahoe came through the bottleneck at twenty miles an hour. Reacher heard its tires on the scrub. They were wide and soft, squirming on the loose surface, squelching small stones, shooting them left and right. He heard the hiss of a power-steering pump and the wet throb of a big V-8 as the vehicle turned. It came through a shallow curve, close enough for Reacher to smell its exhaust.

He lay still.

The truck drove on. Didn't stop. Didn't even slow. The driver was high up in the left-hand seat. Reacher knew like most drivers his eyes were following the turn he intended to make. He was anticipating the curve. Looking ahead and to his left, not sideways to his right.

Bad technique, for a security guard.

Reacher lay still until the Tahoe was long gone. Then he stood up and dusted himself off and headed west and sat down again behind the low boulder he had been heading for.

The second compound was walled with fieldstone, not metal. It was residential. There was ornamental planting, including screens of trees placed to block any view of industrial activity. There was a huge house visible in the distance, built out of wood in a chalet style more suitable to Vail than Despair. There were outbuildings, including an oversized barn that was probably an aircraft hangar, because inside the whole length of the far wall was a wide graded strip of dirt that could only be a runway. It had three windsocks on poles, one at each end and one in the middle.

Reacher moved on. He stayed well away from the fifty-yard bottleneck. Too easy to be spotted. Too easy to be run over. Instead, he looped west again and aimed to circle the residential compound too, as if both enclosures were one giant obstacle.

By noon he was holed up way to the south, looking back at the recycling plant from the rear. The residential compound was closer, and to his left. Far beyond it to the northwest was a small gray smudge in the distance. A low building, or a group of buildings, maybe five or six miles away. Indistinct. Maybe close to the road. Maybe a gas station or a truck stop or a motel. Probably outside of Despair's town limit. Reacher couldn't make out any detail. He turned back to the nearer sights. Work continued inside the plant. Nothing much was happening at the house. He saw the Tahoes circling and watched the trucks on the distant road. There was a continuous stream of them. Mostly flat-beds, but there were some container trucks and some box trucks. They came and went and the sky was stained dark with diesel in a long ribbon all the way to the horizon. The plant belched smoke and flame and sparks. Its noise was softened by distance, but up close it must have been fearsome. The sun was high and the day had gotten warm.

He watched and listened and then he headed east, for a look at the far side of town.

It was bright daylight, so he stayed cautious and moved slow. There was a long empty gap between the plant and the town itself. Maybe three miles. He covered them in a straight line, well out in the scrub. By the middle of the afternoon he was level with where he had been at six o'clock in the morning, but due south of the settlement, not due north, looking at the backs of houses, not the fronts of commercial buildings.

The houses were neat and uniform, cheaply but adequately built. They were mostly one-story ranches with shingle siding and asphalt roofs. Some were painted, some were stained wood. Some had garages, some didn't. Some had picket fences around their yards, some yards were open. Most had satellite dishes, tilted up and facing southwest like a regiment of expectant faces. People were visible, here and there. Mostly women, some children. Some men. The part-time workers, Reacher guessed, unlucky today. He moved along a hundred-yard arc, left and right, east and west, changing his point of view. But what he saw didn't change. Houses, in a strange little suburb, tight in to the town, but miles from anywhere else, with empty vastness all around. The skies were high and huge. The Rockies looked a million miles away. Reacher suddenly understood that Despair had been built by people who had given up. They had come over the rise and seen the far horizon and had quit there and then. Just pitched camp and stayed where they were. And their descendants were still in town, working or not working according to the plant owner's whim.

Reacher ate his last PowerBar and drained the last of his water. He hacked a hole in the scrub with his heel and buried the wrappers and the empty bottles and his garbage bag. Then he dodged from rock to rock and got a little closer to the houses. The low noise coming from the distant plant was getting quieter. He guessed it was close to quitting time. The sun's last rays were kissing the tops of the distant mountains. The temperature was falling.

The first cars and pick-up trucks straggled back close to twelve hours after they had left. A long day. They were heading east, toward darkness, so they had their headlights on. Their beams swung south down the cross-streets, bouncing and dipping, coming Reacher's way. Then they turned again, and scattered toward driveways and garages and car ports and random patches of oil-stained earth. They stopped moving, one after another, and the beams died. Engines stopped. Doors creaked open and slammed shut. Lights were on inside houses. The blue glow of televisions was visible behind windows. The sky was darkening.

Reacher moved closer. Saw men carrying empty lunch pails into kitchens, or standing next to their cars, stretching, rubbing their eyes with the backs of their hands. He saw hopeful boys with balls and mitts looking for a last game of catch. He saw some fathers agree and some refuse. He saw small girls run out with treasures that required urgent inspection.

He saw the big guy who had blocked the end of the restaurant table. The guy who had held the police car's door like a concierge with a taxicab. The senior deputy. He got out of the old listing crew-cab pick-up truck that Reacher had seen outside the restaurant. He clutched his stomach with both hands. He passed by his kitchen door and stumbled on into his yard. There was no picket fence. The guy kept on going, past a cultivated area, out into the scrub beyond.

Straight toward Reacher.

Then the guy stopped walking and stood still on planted feet and bent from the waist and threw up in the dirt. He stayed doubled up for maybe twenty seconds and then straightened, shaking his head and spitting.

Reacher moved closer. He got within twenty yards and then the guy bent again and threw up for a second time. Reacher heard him gasp. Not in pain, not in surprise, but in annoyance and resignation.

"You OK?" Reacher called, out of the gloom.

The guy straightened up.

"Who's there?" he called.

Reacher said, "Me."

"Who?"

Reacher moved closer. Stepped into a bar of light coming from a neighbor's kitchen window.

The guy said, "You."

Reacher nodded. "Me."

"We threw you out."

"Didn't take."

"You shouldn't be here."

"We could discuss that further, if you like. Right now. Right here."

The guy shook his head. "I'm sick. Not fair."

Reacher said, "It wouldn't be fair if you weren't sick."

The guy shrugged.

"Whatever," he said. "I'm going inside now."

"How's your buddy? With the jaw?"

"You bust him up good."

"Tough," Reacher said.

"I'm sick," the guy said again. "I'm going inside. I didn't see you, OK?"

"Bad food?"

The guy paused. Then he nodded.

"Must have been," he said. "Bad food."

He headed for his house, slow and stumbling, holding his belt one-handed, like his pants were too big for him. Reacher watched him go, and then he turned and walked back to the distant shadows.

He moved fifty yards south and fifty yards east of where he had been before, in case the sick guy changed his mind and decided he had seen something after all. He wanted some latitude, if the cops started a search in the guy's backyard. He wanted to begin the chase outside of a flashlight beam's maximum range.

But no cops showed up. Clearly the guy never called. Reacher waited the best part of thirty minutes. Way to the west he heard the aero engine again, straining hard, climbing. The small plane, taking off once more. Seven o'clock in the evening. Then the noise died away and the sky went full dark and the houses closed up tight. Clouds drifted in and covered the moon and the stars. Apart from the glow from draped windows the world went pitch black. The temperature dropped like a stone. Nighttime, in open country.

A long day.

Reacher stood up and loosened the neck of his shirt and set off east, back toward Hope. When the lit houses fell away he looped left into the dark and skirted where he knew the dry goods emporium and the gas station and the abandoned motor court and the vacant lot must be. He couldn't see the line of the road. He moved toward where he figured it must be, as close as he dared. Eventually he saw a black stripe in the darkness. Indistinct, but different from the black plain that was the scrubland. He lined himself up with it and fixed its direction in his mind and retreated sideways a safe ten yards and then moved on forward. Walking was difficult in the dark. He stumbled into bushes. He held his hands out in front of him to ward off table rocks. Twice he tripped on low football-sized boulders, and fell. Twice he got up and brushed himself off and staggered onward.

Stubborn, Vaughan had said.

Stupid, Reacher thought.

The third time he tripped was not on a rock. It was on something altogether softer and more yielding.

12

Reacher sprawled forward and some kind of a primitive instinct made him avoid landing right on top of the thing he had tripped on. He kicked his legs up and tucked his head in and rolled, like judo. He ended up on his back, winded, and hurting from having landed on sharp stones, one under his shoulder and one under his hip. He lay still for a moment and then rolled on his front and pushed himself to his knees and shuffled around until he was facing the way he had come. Then he opened his eyes wide and stared back into the blackness.

Too dark to see.

No flashlight.

He shuffled forward on both knees and one hand, with the other held low in front of him and curled into a fist. A slow yard later it touched something.

Soft.

Not fur.

Cloth.

He spread his fingers. Clamped them loosely. Rubbed his fingertips and the ball of his thumb left and right. Squeezed.

A leg. He had his hand on a human leg. The size

and heft of a thigh was unmistakable. He could feel a hamstring under his fingers and a long quadriceps muscle under his thumb. The cloth was thin and soft. Probably cotton twill, worn and washed many times. Old chinos, maybe.

He moved his hand to the left and found the back of a knee. He pushed his thumb around and underneath and found the kneecap. It was jammed down in the sand. He skipped his hand three feet to the right and slid it up a back to a shoulder blade. Walked his fingers to a neck, and a nape, and an ear.

No pulse.

Cold flesh. No warmer than the nighttime air.

Below the ear was a collar. Knit, rolled, faintly abrasive. A polo shirt, maybe. He shuffled closer on his knees and opened his eyes so wide the muscles in his face hurt.

Too dark to see.

Five senses. Too dark to see, nothing to hear. He wasn't about to try tasting anything. That left smell, and touch. Reacher had smelled more than his fair share of deceased organisms. This one wasn't particularly offensive. Unwashed clothes, stale sweat, ripe hair, dry sun-baked skin, the faintest trace of methane from early decomposition. No voided bowel or bladder.

No blood.

No perfume, no cologne.

No real information.

So, touch. He used both hands and started with the hair. It was not long, not short, and tousled. Maybe an inch and a half or two inches. Wiry, with a tendency to wave. Caucasian. Impossible to say what color. Under it was a small, neat skull.

Man or woman?

He ran his thumbnail the length of the spine. No bra strap under the shirt, but that didn't necessarily mean anything. He poked and probed the back of the ribcage like a blind man reading Braille. Light skeleton, pronounced backbone, light and stringy musculature. Narrow shoulders. Either a thin boy, slightly wasted, or a fit woman. The kind who runs marathons or rides her bike for a hundred miles at a time.

So, which?

Only one way to find out.

He found folds of cloth at the hip and the shoulder and rolled the body on its side. It was reasonably heavy. The way his hands were spaced told him it was maybe five-eight in height, and the weight was probably close to one-forty, which made it probable it was male. A woman marathon runner would have been much lighter, maybe a hundred and five. He kept hold of the bunches of cloth and eased the body past the vertical and let it flop on its back. Then he spread his fingers and started again at the head.

A man, for sure.

The forehead was ridged and bony and the chin and the upper lip were rough with maybe four days of stubble. The cheeks and the throat were smoother.

A young man, not much more than a boy.

The cheekbones were pronounced. The eyes were hard and dry, like marbles. The facial skin was firm and shrunken. It was slightly gritty with grains of sand, but not much had stuck. The skin was too dry.

The mouth was dry, inside and out. The tendons in the neck were obvious. They stood out like cords. No fat anywhere. Barely any flesh at all.

Starved and dehydrated, Reacher thought.

The polo shirt had two buttons, both of them undone. No pocket, but it had a small embroidered design on the left chest. Under it there was a thin pectoral muscle and hard ribs. The pants were loose at the waist. No belt. The shoes were some kind of athletic sneakers, hook-and-loop closures, thick waffle soles.

Reacher wiped his hands on his own pants and then started again from the feet upward, looking for a wound. He went at it like a conscientious airport screener starting a patient full-body search. He did the front and rolled the body again and did the back.

He found nothing.

No gashes, no gunshot wounds, no dried blood, no swellings, no contusions, no broken bones.

The hands were small and fairly delicate, but a little calloused. The nails were ragged. No rings on the fingers. No pinkie ring, no class ring, no wedding band.

He checked the pants pockets, two front, two rear.

He found nothing.

No wallet, no coins, no keys, no phone. Nothing at all.

He sat back on his heels and stared up at the sky, willing a cloud to move and let some moonlight through. But nothing happened. The night stayed dark. He had been walking east, had fallen, had turned around. Therefore he was now facing west. He pushed back off his knees and stood up. Made a quarter-turn to his right. Now he was facing north. He started walking, slowly, with small steps, concentrating hard on staying straight. He bent and swept his hands flat on the scrub and found four stones the size of baseballs. Straightened again and walked on, five yards, ten, fifteen, twenty.

He found the road. The packed scrub gave way to the tarred pebbles. He used his toe to locate the edge. He bent and butted three of his stones together and stacked the fourth on top, like a miniature mountain cairn. Then he turned a careful one-eighty and walked back, counting his paces. Five yards, ten, fifteen, twenty. He stopped and squatted and felt ahead of him.

Nothing.

He shuffled forward with his arms out straight, patting downward, searching, until his right palm came down on the corpse's shoulder. He glanced up at the sky. Still solid.

Nothing more to be done.

He stood up again and turned left and blundered on through the dark, east toward Hope.

13

The closer he got to the Hope town line, the more he let himself drift left toward the road. Hope wasn't a big place, and he didn't want to miss it in the dark. Didn't want to walk on forever, all the way back to Kansas. The clock in his head said that it was midnight. He had made good progress, close to three miles an hour, despite falling four more times and detouring every thirty minutes to confirm he wasn't drastically off course.

Despair's cheap road crunched loudly under his feet but the hard level surface allowed him to speed up. He hit a good rhythm and covered what was left of the last mile in less than fifteen minutes. It was still very cold. Still pitch dark. But he sensed the new blacktop ahead. He felt it coming. Then he felt the surface change under his feet. His left foot pushed off rough stones and his right foot landed on velvet-smooth asphalt.

He was back over the line.

He stood still for a second. Held his arms wide and looked up at the black sky. Then bright headlights hit him head-on and he was trapped in their beams. A spotlight clicked on and played over him, head to foot and back again.

A cop car.

Then the beams died as suddenly as they had appeared and a dome light came on inside the car and showed a small figure at the wheel. Tan shirt, fair hair. Half a smile.

Vaughan.

She was parked head-on, with her push bars twenty yards inside her own jurisdiction, just waiting in the dark. Reacher walked toward her, moving left, skirting her hood and her fender. He stepped to the passenger door and put his hand on the handle. Opened it up and crammed himself into the space inside. The interior was full of soft radio chatter and the smell of perfume.

He asked, "So are you free for a late dinner?"

She said, "I don't eat with jerks."

"I'm back, like I said I would be."

"Did you have fun?"

"Not really."

"I'm working the graveyard shift. I don't get off until seven."

"Breakfast, then. Drinking coffee with jerks is not the same as eating with them."

"I don't drink coffee for breakfast. I need to sleep in the daytime."

"Tea, then."

"Tea has caffeine, too."

"Milk shake?"

"Maybe." She was resting easy in the seat, one elbow on the door and the other hand in her lap.

"How did you see me coming?" Reacher asked. "I didn't see you."

"I eat a lot of carrots," Vaughan said. "And our video has night-vision enhancement." She leaned forward and tapped a black box mounted high on the dash. "Traffic camera and a hard disc recorder." She moved her hand again and hit a key on the computer. The screen changed to a ghostly green wide-angle image of the scene ahead. The road was lighter than the scrub. It had retained more of the daytime heat than its surroundings. Or less. Reacher wasn't sure.

"I saw you half a mile away," Vaughan said. "A little green speck." She tapped another key and spooled back through the time code and Reacher saw himself, a luminous sliver in the dark, getting bigger, coming closer.

"Very fancy," he said.

"Homeland Security money. Got to spend it on something."

"How long have you been out here?"

"An hour."

"Thanks for waiting."

Vaughan started the motor and backed up a little and then turned across the width of the road, in a wide arc that took the front wheels off the blacktop and through the sand on the shoulder. She got straightened up and accelerated.

"Hungry?" she asked.

"Not really," Reacher said.

"You should eat anyway."

"Where?"

"The diner will still be open. It stays open all night."

"In Hope? Why?"

"This is America. It's a service economy."

"Whatever, I might go take a nap instead. I walked a long way."

"Go eat in the diner first."

"Why?"

"Because I think you should. Nutrition is important."

"What are you, my mother?"

"Someone was asking about you."

"Who?"

"Some girl."

"I don't know any girls."

"She wasn't asking about you personally," Vaughan said. "She was asking if anyone had been thrown out of Despair more recently than her."

"She was thrown out?"

"Four days ago."

"They throw women out, too?"

"Vagrancy isn't a gender-specific offense."

"Who is she?"

"Just some kid. I told her about you. No names, but I said you might be eating in the diner tonight. I was assuming you would get out OK. I try to live on the sunny side of the street. So I think she might come looking for you."

"What does she want?"

"She wouldn't tell me," Vaughan said. "But my impression was her boyfriend is missing."

14

Reacher got out of Vaughan's cruiser on First Street and walked straight down to Second. The diner was all lit up inside and three booths were occupied. A guy on his own, a young woman on her own, two guys together. Maybe some Hope residents commuted for work. Not to Despair, obviously, but maybe to other towns. Maybe to other states, like Kansas or Nebraska. And those were big distances. Maybe they all got back too late to face KP at home. Or maybe they were shift workers, just starting out, with long trips ahead of them.

The sidewalks close to the diner were deserted. No girls hanging around. No girls watching who was going in and coming out. No girls leaning on walls. No girls hiding in the shadows. Reacher pulled the door and went in and headed for a booth in the far corner where he could sit with his back protected and see the whole room at once. Pure habit. He never sat any other way. A waitress came over and gave him a napkin and silverware and a glass of ice water. Not the same waitress he had met before, during his caffeine marathon. This one was young, and not particularly tired, even though it was very late. She could have been a college student. Maybe the diner stayed open all night to give people jobs, as well as meals. Maybe the owner felt some kind of a civic responsibility. Hope seemed to be that kind of a town.

The menu was in a chromium clip at the end of the table. It was a laminated card with pictures of the food on it. The waitress came back and Reacher pointed to a grilled cheese sandwich and said, "And coffee." The waitress wrote it down and walked away and Reacher settled back and watched the street through the windows. He figured that the girl who was looking for him might pass by once every fifteen or twenty minutes. It was what he would have done. Longer intervals might make her miss his visit. Most diner customers were in and out pretty fast. He was sure there was a trade association somewhere with the exact data. His personal average was certainly less than half an hour. Shorter if he was in a hurry, longer if it was raining. The longest stay he could recall might be upward of two hours. The shortest in recent memory was the day before, in Despair. One fast cup of coffee, supervised by hostile glares.

But nobody passed by on the sidewalk. Nobody glanced in through the windows. The waitress came over with his sandwich and a mug of coffee. The coffee was fresh and the sandwich was OK. The cheese was sticky in his mouth and less flavorful than a Wisconsin product would have been, but it was palatable. And Reacher was no kind of a gourmet. He rated food quality as either adequate or not adequate, and the adequate category was always by far the larger of the two. So he ate and drank and enjoyed it all well enough.

After fifteen minutes he gave up on the girl. He figured she wasn't coming. Then he changed his mind. He quit staring out at the sidewalk and started looking at the other customers inside the diner and realized she was already in there, waiting for him.

The young woman, sitting three booths away.

Stupid, Reacher, he thought.

He had figured that if their relative positions had been reversed he would have walked by every fifteen or twenty minutes and checked through the windows. But in reality, he wouldn't have done that. He would have come in out of the cold and sat down and waited for his mark to come to him.

Like she had.

Pure common sense.

She was maybe nineteen or twenty years old, dirty blonde hair with streaks, wearing a short denim skirt and a white sweatshirt with a word on it that might have been the name of a college football team. Her features didn't add up all the way to beauty, but she had the kind of irresistible glowing good health that he had seen before in American girls of her station and generation. Her skin was perfect. It was honey-colored with the remnant of a great summer tan. Her teeth were white and regular. Her eyes were vivid blue. Her legs were long, and neither lean nor heavy. *Shapely,* Reacher thought. An old-fashioned word, but the right one. She was wearing sneakers with tiny white socks that ended below her ankles. She had a bag. It was beside her on the bench. Not a purse, not a suitcase. A messenger bag, gray nylon, with a broad flap.

She was the one he was waiting for. He knew that because as he watched her in his peripheral vision he could see her watching him in hers. She was sizing him up and deciding whether to approach.

Deciding against, apparently.

She had had a full fifteen minutes to make her decision. But she hadn't gotten up and walked over. Not because of good manners. Not because she hadn't wanted to disturb him while he was eating. He suspected her concept of etiquette didn't quite stretch that far, and even if it did, then a missing boyfriend would have overwhelmed it. She just didn't want to get involved with him. That was all. Reacher didn't blame her. *Look at yourself,* Vaughan had said. *What do you see?* He had no illusions about what the girl three booths away was seeing. No illusions about his appearance or his appeal, in the eyes of someone like her. It was late at night, she was looking at an old guy twice her age, huge, untidy, disheveled, somewhat dirty, and surrounded by an electric stay-away aura he had spent years cultivating, like a sign on the rear end of a fire truck: *Stay Back 200 Feet.*

So she was going to sit tight and wait him out. That was clear. He was disappointed. Primarily because of the questions surrounding the dead boy in the dark, but also because in a small corner of his mind he would have liked to be the kind of guy that pretty girls could walk up to. Not that he would have taken it anywhere. She was wholesome and he was twice her age. And her boyfriend was dead, which made her some kind of a widow.

She was still watching him. He had moved his gaze so that he could see her reflection in the window next to her. She was looking up, looking down, kneading her fingers, glancing suddenly in his direction as new thoughts came to her, and then glancing away again as she resolved them. As she found reasons to stay well away from him. He gave it five more minutes and then fished in his pocket for cash. He didn't need a check. He knew what the sandwich and the coffee cost, because the prices had been printed on the menu. He knew what the local sales tax percentage was, and he was capable of calculating it for himself in his head. He knew how to work out a fifteen percent tip, for the college-age waitress who had also stayed well away from him.

He folded small bills lengthwise and left them on the table. Got up and headed for the door. At the last minute he changed direction and stepped over to the young woman's booth and slid in opposite her.

"My name is Reacher," he said. "I think you wanted to talk to me."

The girl looked at him and blinked and opened her mouth and closed it again and spoke at the second attempt.

She said, "Why would you think that?"

"I met a cop called Vaughan. She told me."

"Told you what?"

"That you were looking for someone who had been to Despair."

"You're mistaken," the girl said. "It wasn't me."

She wasn't a great liar. Not great at all. Reacher had come up against some real experts, in his previous life. This one had all the tells on display. The gulps, the false starts, the stammers, the fidgets, the glances to her right. Psychologists figured that the memory center was located in the left brain, and the imagination engine in the right brain. Therefore people unconsciously glanced to the left when they were remembering things, and to the right when they were making stuff up. When they were lying. This girl was glancing right so much she was in danger of getting whiplash.

"OK," Reacher said. "I apologize for disturbing you."

But he didn't move. He stayed where he was, sitting easy, filling most of a vinyl bench made for two. Up close the girl was prettier than she had looked from a distance. She had a dusting of freckles and a mobile, expressive mouth.

"Who are you?" she asked.

"Just a guy," Reacher said.

"What kind of a guy?"

"The judge in Despair called me a vagrant. So I'm that kind of a guy, I guess."

"No job?"

"Not for a long time."

She said, "They called me a vagrant, too."

Her accent was unspecific. She wasn't from Boston or New York or Chicago or Minnesota or the Deep South. Maybe somewhere in the Southwest. Arizona, perhaps.

He said, "In your case I imagine they were inaccurate."

"I'm not sure of the definition, exactly."

"It comes from the Old French word *waucrant*," Reacher said. "Meaning one who wanders idly from place to place without lawful or visible means of support."

"I'm in college," she said.

"So you were unfairly accused."

"They just wanted me out of there."

"Where do you go to school?"

She paused. Glanced to her right.

"Miami," she said.

Reacher nodded. Wherever she went to school, it wasn't Miami. Probably wasn't anywhere in the East. Was probably somewhere on the West Coast. Southern California, possibly. Unskilled liars like her often picked a mirror image, when lying about geography.

"What's your major?" he asked.

She looked straight at him and said, "The history of the twentieth century." Which was probably true. Young people usually told the truth about their areas of expertise, because they were proud of them, and they were worried about getting caught out on alternatives. Often they didn't have alternatives. Being young, it came with the territory.

"Feels like yesterday to me," he said. "Not history."

"What does?"

"The twentieth century."

She didn't reply. Didn't understand what he meant. She remembered maybe eight or nine years of the old century, maximum, and from a kid's perspective. He remembered slightly more of it.

"What's your name?" he asked.

She glanced to her right. "Anne."

Reacher nodded again. Whatever her name was, it wasn't Anne. Anne was probably a sister's name. Or a best friend's. Or a cousin's. Generally people liked to stay close to home with phony names.

The girl who wasn't called Anne asked, "Were *you* unfairly accused?"

Reacher shook his head. "A vagrant is exactly what I am."

"Why did you go there?"

"I liked the name. Why did *you* go there?"

She didn't answer.

He said, "Anyway, it wasn't much of a place."

"How much of it did you see?"

"Most of it, the second time."

"You went back?"

"I took a good look around, from a distance."

"And?"

"It still wasn't much of a place."

The girl went quiet. Reacher saw her weighing her next question. How to ask it. Whether to ask it. She put her head on one side and looked beyond him.

"Did you see any people?" she asked.

"Lots of people," Reacher said.

"Did you see the airplane?"

"I heard one."

"It belongs to the guy with the big house. Every night he takes off at seven and comes back at two o'clock in the morning."

Reacher asked, "How long were you there?"

"One day."

"So how do you know the plane flies every night?"

She didn't answer.

"Maybe someone told you," Reacher said.

No reply.

Reacher said, "No law against joyriding."

"People don't joyride at night. There's nothing to see."

"Good point."

The girl was quiet for another minute, and then she asked, "Were you in a cell?"

"Couple of hours."

"Anyone else in there?"

"No."

"When you went back, what people did you see?"

Reacher said, "Why don't you just show me his picture?"

"Whose picture?"

"Your boyfriend's."

"Why would I do that?"

"Your boyfriend is missing. As in, you can't find him. That was Officer Vaughan's impression, anyway."

"You trust cops?"

"Some of them."

"I don't have a picture."

"You've got a big bag. Probably all kinds of things in there. Maybe a few pictures."

She said, "Show me your wallet."

"I don't have a wallet."

"Everyone has a wallet."

"Not me."

"Prove it."

"I can't prove a negative."

"Empty your pockets."

Reacher nodded. He understood. *The boyfriend is some kind of a fugitive. She asked about my job. She needs to know I'm not an investigator. An investigator would have compromising ID in his wallet.* He lifted his butt off the bench and dug out his cash, his old passport, his ATM card, his motel key. His toothbrush was in his room, assembled, standing upright in a plastic glass next to the sink. The girl looked at his stuff and said, "Thanks."

He said, "Now show me his picture."

"He's not my boyfriend."

"Isn't he?"

"He's my husband."

"You're young, to be married."

"We're in love."

"You're not wearing a ring."

Her left hand was on the table. She withdrew it quickly, into her lap. But there had been no ring on her finger, and no tan line.

"It was kind of sudden," she said. "Kind of hurried. We figured we'd get rings later."

"Isn't it a part of the ceremony?"

"No," she said. "That's a myth. I'm not pregnant either, just in case that's what you're thinking."

"Not for a minute."

"Good."

"Show me the picture."

She hauled the gray messenger bag into her lap and rooted around for a moment and came out with a fat leather wallet. There was a billfold part straining against a little strap, and a change-purse part. There was a plastic window on the outside with a California driver's license behind it, with her picture on it. She unpopped the little strap and opened the billfold and riffled through a concertina of plastic photograph windows. Slid a slim fingertip into one of them and eased a snapshot out. She passed it across the table. It had been cut down out of a standard six-by-four one-hour print. The edges were not entirely straight. It showed the girl standing on a street with golden light and palm trees and a row of neat boutiques behind her. She was smiling widely, vibrant with love and joy and happiness, leaning forward a little as if her whole body was clenching with the onset of uncontrollable giggles. She was in the arms of a guy about her age. He was very tall and blond and heavy. An athlete. He had blue eyes and a buzz cut and a dark tan and a wide smile.

"This is your husband?" Reacher asked.

The girl said, "Yes."

15

Reacher squared the snapshot on the tabletop in front of him. Looked at the girl across from him and asked, "How old is this photo?"

"Recent."

"May I see your driver's license?"

"Why?"

"Something I need to check."

"I don't know."

"I already know your name isn't Anne. I know you don't go to school in Miami. My guess would be UCLA. This photograph looks like it was taken somewhere around there. It has that LA kind of feel."

The girl said nothing.

Reacher said, "I'm not here to hurt you."

She paused and then slid her wallet across the table. He glanced at her license. Most of it was visible behind the milky plastic window. Her name was Lucy Anderson. No middle name. Anderson, hence Anne, perhaps.

"Lucy," he said. "I'm pleased to meet you."

"I'm sorry about not telling you the truth."

"Don't worry about it. Why should you?"

"My friends call me Lucky. Like a mispronunciation. Like a nickname."

"I hope you always are."

"Me too. I have been so far."

Her license said she was coming up to twenty years old. It said her address was an apartment on a street he knew to be close to the main UCLA campus. He had been in LA not long before. Its geography was still familiar to him. Her sex was specified as female, which was clearly accurate, and her eyes were listed as blue, which was an understatement.

She was five feet eight inches tall.

Which made her husband at least six feet four. Maybe six feet five. He towered over her. He was huge. He looked to be well over two hundred pounds. Maybe Reacher's own size. Maybe even bigger. His arms were as thick as the palm trunks behind him.

Not the guy in the dark. Not even close. Way too big. The guy in the dark had been Lucy Anderson's size.

Reacher slid the wallet back across the table. Followed it with the photograph.

Lucy Anderson asked, "Did you see him?"

Reacher shook his head.

"No," he said. "I didn't. I'm sorry."

"He has to be there somewhere."

"What's he running from?"

She looked to the right. "Why would he be running from something?"

"Just a wild guess," Reacher said.

"Who are you?"

"Just a guy."

"How did you know my name wasn't Anne? How did you know I'm not in school in Miami?"

"A long time ago I was a cop. In the military. I still know things."

Her skin whitened behind her freckles. She fumbled the photograph back into its slot and fastened the wallet and thrust it deep into her bag.

"You don't like cops, do you?" Reacher asked.

"Not always," she said.

"That's unusual, for a person like you."

"Like me?"

"Safe, secure, middle class, well brought up."

"Things change."

"What did your husband do?"

She didn't answer.

"And who did he do it to?"

No answer.

"Why did he go to Despair?"

No response.

"Were you supposed to meet him there?"

Nothing.

"Doesn't matter, anyway," Reacher said. "I didn't see him. And I'm not a cop anymore. Haven't been for a long time."

"What would you do now? If you were me?"

"I'd wait right here in town. Your husband looks like a capable guy. He'll probably show up, sooner or later. Or get word to you."

"I hope so."

"Is he in school, too?"

Lucy Anderson didn't answer that. Just secured the flap of her bag and slid off the bench sideways and stood up and tugged the hem of her skirt down. Five-eight, maybe one-thirty, blonde and blue, straight, strong, and healthy.

"Thank you," she said. "Good night."

"Good luck," he said. "Lucky."

She hoisted her bag on her shoulder and walked to the door and pushed out to the street. He watched her huddle into her sweatshirt and step away through the cold.

He was in bed before two o'clock in the morning. The motel room was warm. There was a heater under the window and it was blasting away to good effect. He set the alarm in his head for six-thirty. He was tired, but he figured four and a half hours would be enough. In fact they would have to be enough, because he wanted time to shower before heading out for breakfast.

16

It was a cliché that cops stop in at diners for doughnuts before, during, and after every shift, but clichés were clichés only because they were so often true. Therefore Reacher slipped into the same back booth at five to seven in the morning and fully expected to see Officer Vaughan enter inside the following ten minutes.

Which she did.

He saw her cruiser pull up and park outside. Saw her climb out onto the sidewalk and press both hands into the small of her back and stretch. Saw her lock up and pirouette and head for the door. She came in and saw him and paused for a long moment and then changed direction and slid in opposite him.

He asked, "Strawberry, vanilla, or chocolate? It's all they've got."

"Of what?"

"Milk shakes."

"I don't drink breakfast with jerks."

"I'm not a jerk. I'm a citizen with a problem. You're here to help. Says so on the badge."

"What kind of problem?"

"The girl found me."

"And had you seen her boyfriend?"

"Her husband, actually."

"Really?" Vaughan said. "She's young to be married."

"I thought so, too. She said they're in love."

"Cue the violins. So had you seen him?"

"No."

"So where's your problem?"

"I saw someone else."

"Who?"

"Not saw, actually. It was in the pitch dark. I fell over him."

"Who?"

"A dead guy."

"Where?"

"On the way out of Despair."

"Are you sure?"

"Completely," Reacher said. "A young adult male corpse."

"Are you serious?"

"As a heart attack."

"Why didn't you tell me last night?"

"I wanted time to think about it."

"You're yanking my chain. There's what out there, a thousand square miles? And you just happen to trip over a dead guy in the dark? That's a coincidence as big as a barn."

"Not really," Reacher said. "I figure he was doing the same thing I was doing. Walking east from Despair to Hope, staying close enough to the road to be sure of his direction, far enough away to be safe. That put him in a pretty specific channel. I might have missed him by a yard, but I was never going to miss him by a mile."

Vaughan said nothing.

"But he didn't make it all the way," Reacher said. "I think he was exhausted. His knees were driven pretty deep in the sand. I think he fell on his knees and pitched forward on his front and died. He was emaciated and dehydrated. No wounds, no trauma."

"What, you autopsied this guy? In the dark?"

"I felt around."

"Felt?"

"Touch," Reacher said. "It's one of the five senses we rely on."

"So who was this guy?"

"Caucasian, by the feel of his hair. Maybe five-eight, one-forty. Young. No ID. I don't know if he was dark or fair."

"This is unbelievable."

"It happened."

"Where exactly?"

"Maybe four miles out of town, eight miles short of the line."

"Definitely in Despair, then."

"No question."

"You should call the Despair PD."

"I wouldn't piss on the Despair PD if it was on fire."

"Well, I can't help you. It's not my jurisdiction."

The waitress came over. The day-shift woman, the witness to the coffee marathon. She was busy and harassed. The diner was filling up fast. Small-town America, at breakfast time. Reacher ordered coffee and eggs. Vaughan ordered coffee, too. Reacher took that as a good sign. He waited until the waitress had bustled away and said, "You *can* help me."

Vaughan said, "How?"

"I want to go back and take a look, right now, in the daylight. You can drive me. We could be in and out, real fast."

"It's not my town."

"Unofficial. Off duty. Like a tourist. You're a citizen. You're entitled to drive on their road."

"Would you be able to find the place again?"

"I left a pile of stones on the shoulder."

"I can't do it," Vaughan said. "I can't poke around over there. And I sure as hell can't take *you* there. You've been excluded. It would be unbelievably provocative."

"Nobody would know."

"You think? They've got one road in and one road out and two cars."

"Right now they're eating doughnuts in their restaurant."

"You sure you didn't dream this?"

"No dreaming involved," Reacher said. "The kid had eyeballs like marbles and the inside of his mouth was parched like shoe leather. He'd been wandering for days."

The waitress came back with the coffee and the eggs. The eggs had a sprig of fresh parsley arrayed across them. Reacher picked it off and laid it on the side of the plate.

Vaughan said, "I can't drive a Hope police cruiser in Despair."

"So what else have you got?"

She was quiet for a long moment. She sipped her coffee. Then she said, "I have an old truck."

She made him wait on the First Street sidewalk near the hardware store. Clearly she wasn't about to take him home while she changed her clothes and her vehicle. A wise precaution, he thought. *Look at yourself,* she had said. *What do you see?* He was getting accustomed to negative answers to that question. The hardware store was still closed. The window was full of tools and small consumer items. The aisle behind the door was piled high with the stuff that would be put out on the sidewalk later. For many years Reacher had wondered why hardware stores favored sidewalk displays. There was a lot of work involved. Repetitive physical labor, twice a day. But maybe consumer psychology dictated that large utilitarian items sold better when associated with the rugged outdoors. Or maybe it was just a question of space. He thought for a moment and came to no firm conclusion and moved away and leaned on a pole that supported a crosswalk sign. The morning had come in cold and gray. Thin cloud started at ground level. The Rockies weren't visible at all, neither near nor far.

Close to twenty minutes later an old Chevrolet pick-up truck pulled up on the opposite curb. Not a bulbous old classic from the forties or a swooping space-age design from the fifties or a muscley El Camino from the sixties. Just a plain secondhand American vehicle about fifteen years old, worn navy blue paint, steel rims, small tires. Vaughan was at the wheel. She was wearing a red Windbreaker zipped to the chin and a khaki ball cap pulled low. A good disguise. Reacher wouldn't have recognized her if he hadn't been expecting her. He used the crosswalk and climbed in next to her, onto a small vinyl seat with an upright back. The cab smelled of leaked gasoline and cold exhaust. There were rubber floor mats under his feet, covered with desert dust, worn and papery with age. He slammed the door and Vaughan took off again. The truck had a wheezy four-cylinder motor. *In and out real fast,* he had said. But clearly *fast* was going to be a relative concept.

They covered Hope's five miles of road in seven minutes. A hundred yards short of the line Vaughan said, "We see anybody at all, you duck down." Then she pressed harder on the gas and the expansion joint thumped under the wheels and the tires set up a harsh roar over Despair's sharp stones.

"You come here much?" Reacher asked.

"Why would I?" Vaughan said.

There was no traffic ahead. Nothing either coming or going. The road speared straight into the hazy distance, rising and falling. Vaughan was holding the truck at a steady sixty. A mile a minute, probably close to its comfortable maximum.

Seven minutes inside enemy territory, she started to slow.

"Watch the left shoulder," Reacher said. "Four stones, piled up."

The weather had settled to a luminous gray light. Not bright, not sunny, but everything was illuminated perfectly. No glare, no shadows. There was some trash on the shoulder. Not much, but enough that Reacher's small cairn was not going to stand out in glorious isolation like a beacon. There were plastic water bottles, glass beer bottles, soda cans, paper, small unimportant parts of vehicles, all caught on a long ridge of pebbles that had been washed to the side of the road by the passage of tires. Reacher twisted around in his seat. Nobody behind. Nobody ahead. Vaughan slowed some more. Reacher scanned the shoulder. The stones had felt big and obvious in his hands, in the dark. But now in the impersonal daylight they were going to look puny in the vastness.

"There," Reacher said.

He saw his little cairn thirty yards ahead on the left. Three stones butted together, the fourth balanced on top. A speck in the distance, in the middle of nowhere. To the south the land ran all the way to the horizon, flat and essentially featureless, dotted with pale bushes and dark rocks and pitted with wash holes and low ridges.

"This is the place?" Vaughan asked.

"Twenty-some yards due south," Reacher said.

He checked the road again. Nothing ahead, nothing behind.

"We're OK," he said.

Vaughan passed the cairn and pulled to the right shoulder and turned a wide circle across both lanes. Came back east and stopped exactly level with the stones. She put the transmission in park and left the engine running.

"Stay here," she said.

"Bullshit," Reacher said. He got out and stepped over the stones and waited on the shoulder. He felt tiny in the lit-up vastness. In the dark the world had shrunk to an arm's length around him. Now it felt huge again. Vaughan stepped alongside him and he walked south with her through the scrub, at a right angle to the road, five paces, ten, fifteen. He stopped after twenty paces and confirmed his direction by glancing behind him. Then he stood still and checked all around, first on a close radius, and then wider.

He saw nothing.

He stood on tiptoe and craned his neck and searched.

There was nothing there.

17

Reacher turned a careful one-eighty and stared back at the road to make sure he hadn't drifted too far either west or east. He hadn't. He was right on target. He walked five paces south, turned east, walked five more paces, turned around, walked ten steps west.

Saw nothing.

"Well?" Vaughan called.

"It's gone," he said.

"You were just yanking my chain."

"I wasn't. Why would I?"

"How accurate could you have been, with the stones? In the dark?"

"That's what I'm wondering."

Vaughan walked a small quiet circle, all around. Shook her head.

"It isn't here," she said. "If it ever was."

Reacher stood still in the emptiness. Nothing to see. Nothing to hear, except Vaughan's truck idling patiently twenty yards away. He walked ten more yards east and started to trace a wide circle. A quarter of the way through it, he stopped.

"Look here," he said.

He pointed at the ground. At a long line of shallow crumbled oval pits in the sand, each one a yard apart.

Vaughan said, "Footprints."

"My footprints," Reacher said. "From last night. Heading home."

They turned west and backtracked. Followed the trail of his old footprints back toward Despair. Ten yards later they came to the head of a small diamond-shaped clearing. The clearing was empty.

"Wait," Reacher said.

"It's not here," Vaughan said.

"But it was here. This is the spot."

The crusted sand was all churned up by multiple disturbances. There were dozens of footprints, facing in all directions. There were scrapes and slides and drag marks. There were small depressions in the scrub, some fairly precise, but most not, because of the way the dry sand had crumbled and trickled down into the holes.

Reacher said, "Tell me what you see."

"Activity," Vaughan said. "A mess."

"A story," Reacher said. "It's telling us what happened."

"Whatever happened, we can't stay here. This was supposed to be in and out, real fast."

Reacher stood up straight and scanned the road, west and east.

Nothing there.

"Nobody coming," he said.

"I should have brought a picnic," Vaughan said.

Reacher stepped into the clearing. Crouched down and pointed two-fingered at a pair of neat parallel depressions in the center of the space. Like two coconut shells had been pressed down into the sand, hard, on a north-south axis.

"The boy's knees," he said. "This is where he gave it up. He staggered to a stop and half-turned and fell over." Then he pointed to a broad messed-up stony area four feet to the east. "This is where I landed after I tripped over him. On these stones. I could show you the bruises, if you like."

"Maybe later," Vaughan said. "We need to get going."

Reacher pointed to four sharp impressions in the sand. Each one was a rectangle about two inches by three, at the corners of a larger rectangle about two feet by five.

"Gurney feet," he said. "Folks came by and collected him. Maybe four or five of them, judging by all the footprints. Official folks, because who else carries gurneys?" He stood up and checked and pointed north and west, along a broad ragged line of footprints and crushed vegetation. "They came in that way, and carried him back out in the same direction, back to the road. Maybe to a coroner's wagon, parked a little ways west of my cairn."

"So we're OK," Vaughan said. "The proper authorities have got him. Problem solved. We should get going."

Reacher nodded vaguely and gazed due west. "What should we see over there?"

"Two sets of incoming footprints," Vaughan said. "The boy's and yours, both heading east out of town.

Separated by time, but not much separated by direction."

"But it looks like there's more than that."

They skirted the clearing and formed up again west of it. They saw four separate lines of footprints, fairly close together.

"Two incoming, two outgoing," Reacher said.

"How do you know?" Vaughan asked.

"The angles. Most people walk with their toes out."

The newer of the incoming tracks showed big dents in the sand a yard or more apart, and deep. The older showed smaller dents, closer together, less regular, and shallower.

"The kid and me," Reacher said. "Heading east. Separated in time. I was walking, he was stumbling and staggering."

The two outgoing tracks were both brand new. The sand was less crumbled and therefore the indentations were more distinct, and fairly deep, fairly well spaced, and similar.

"Reasonably big guys," Reacher said. "Heading back west. Recently. Not separated in time."

"What does it mean?"

"It means they're tracking the kid. Or me. Or both of us. Finding out where we'd been, where we'd come from."

"Why?"

"They found the body, they were curious."

"How did they find the body in the first place?"

"Buzzards," Reacher said. "It's the obvious way, on open ground."

Vaughan stood still for a moment. Then she said, "Back to the truck, right now."

Reacher didn't argue. She had beaten him to the obvious conclusion, but only by a heartbeat.

18

The old Chevy was still idling patiently. The road was still empty. But they ran. They ran and they flung the truck's doors open and dumped themselves inside. Vaughan slammed the transmission into gear and hit the gas. They didn't say a word until they thumped back over the Hope town line, eight long minutes later.

"Now you're really a citizen with a problem," Vaughan said. "Aren't you? The Despair cops might be dumb, but they're still cops. Buzzards show them a dead guy, they find the dead guy's tracks, they find a second set of tracks that show some other guy caught up with the dead guy along the way, they find signs of a whole lot of falling down and rolling around, they're going to want a serious talk with the other guy. You can bet on that."

Reacher said, "So why didn't they follow my tracks forward?"

"Because they know where you were going. There's only Hope, or Kansas. They want to know where you started. And what are they going to find?"

"A massive loop. Buried PowerBar wrappers and empty water bottles, if they look hard enough."

Vaughan nodded at the wheel. "Clear physical evidence of a big guy with big feet and long legs who paid a planned clandestine visit the night after they threw a big guy with big feet and long legs out of town."

"Plus one of the deputies saw me."

"You sure?"

"We talked."

"Terrific."

"The dead guy died of natural causes."

"You sure? You felt around in the dark. They're going to put that boy on a slab."

"I'm not in Despair anymore. You can't go there, they can't come here."

"Small departments don't work homicides, you idiot. We call in the State Police. And the State Police can go anywhere in Colorado. And the State Police get cooperation anywhere in Colorado. And you're in my logbook from yesterday. I couldn't deny it even if I wanted to."

"You wouldn't want to?"

"I don't know anything about you. Except that I'm pretty sure you beat on a deputy in Despair. You practically admitted that to me. Who knows what else you did?"

"I didn't do anything else."

Vaughan said nothing.

Reacher asked, "What happens next?"

"Always better to get out in front of a thing like this. You should call in and volunteer information."

"No."

"Why not?"

"I was a soldier. I never volunteer for anything."

"Well, I can't help you. It's out of my hands. It was never *in* my hands."

"You could call," Reacher said. "You could call the State Police and find out what their thinking is."

"They'll be calling us soon enough."

"So let's get out in front, like you said. Early information is always good."

Vaughan didn't reply to that. Just lifted off the gas and slowed as they hit the edge of town. The hardware guy had his door open and was piling his stuff on the sidewalk. He had some kind of a trick stepladder that could be put in about eight different positions. He had set it up like a painter's platform good for reaching second-story walls. Vaughan made a right on the next block and then a left, past the back of the diner. The streets were broad and pleasant and the sidewalks had trees. She pulled in to a marked-off parking space outside a low brick building. The building could have been a suburban post office. But it wasn't. It was the Hope Police Department. It said so, in aluminum letters neatly fixed to the brick. Vaughan shut off the engine and Reacher followed her down a neat brick path to the police station's door. The door was locked. The station was closed. Vaughan used a key from her bunch and said, "The desk guy gets in at nine."

Inside, the place still looked like a post office. Dull, worn, institutional, bureaucratic, but somewhat friendly. Accessible. Oriented toward service. There was a public inquiry counter and a space behind it with two desks. A watch commander's office behind a solid door, in the same corner a postmaster's would be. Vaughan stepped past the counter and headed for a desk that was clearly hers. Efficient and organized, but not intimidating. There was an old-model computer front and center, and a console telephone next to it. She opened a drawer and found a number in a book. Clearly contact between the Hope PD and the State Police was rare. She didn't know the number by heart. She dialed the phone and asked for thc duty desk and identified herself and said, "We have a missing person inquiry. Male, Caucasian, approximately twenty years of age, five-eight, one-forty. Can you help us with that?" Then she listened briefly and her eyes flicked left and then right and she said, "We don't have a name." She was asked another question and she glanced right and said, "Can't tell if he's dark or fair. We're working from a black-and-white photograph. It's all we have."

Then there was a pause. Reacher saw her yawn. She was tired. She had been working all night. She moved the phone a little ways from her ear and Reacher heard the faint tap of a keyboard in the distant state office. Denver, maybe, or Colorado Springs. Then a voice came back on and Vaughan clamped the phone tight and Reacher didn't hear what it had to say.

Vaughan listened and said, "Thank you."

Then she hung up.

"Nothing to report," she said. "Apparently Despair didn't call it in."

"Natural causes," Reacher said. "They agreed with me."

Vaughan shook her head. "They should have called it in anyway. An unexplained death out in open country, that's at least a county matter. Which means it would show up on the State Police system about a minute later."

"So why didn't they call it in?"

"I don't know. But that's not our problem."

Reacher sat down at the other desk. It was a plain government-issue piece of furniture, with steel legs and a thin six-by-three fiberboard top laminated with a printed plastic approximation of rosewood or koa. There was a modesty panel and a three-drawer pedestal bolted to the right-hand legs. The chair had wheels and was covered with gray tweed fabric. Military Police furniture had been different. The chairs had been covered with vinyl. The desks had been steel. Reacher had sat behind dozens of them, all over the world. The views from his windows had been dramatically different, but the desks had been all the same. Their contents, too. Files full of dead people and missing people. Some mourned, some not.

He thought of Lucy Anderson, called Lucky by her friends. The night before, in the diner. He recalled the way she had wrung her hands. He looked across at Vaughan and said, "It is our problem, kind of. The kid might have people worried about him."

Vaughan nodded. Went back to her book. Reacher saw her flip forward from *C* for *Colorado State Police* to *D* for *Despair Police Department*. She dialed and he heard a loud reply in her ear, as if physical proximity made for more powerful electrical current in the wires. She ran through the same faked inquiry, missing person, Caucasian male, about twenty, five-eight, one-forty, no name, coloring unclear because of a monochrome photograph. There was a short pause and then a short reply.

Vaughan hung up.

"Nothing to report," she said. "They never saw such a guy."

19

Reacher sat quiet and Vaughan moved stuff around on her desk. She put her keyboard in line with her monitor and put her mouse in line with her keyboard and squared her phone behind it and then adjusted everything until all the edges were either parallel or at perfect right angles to each other. Then she put pencils away in drawers and flicked at dust and crumbs with the edge of her palm.

"The gurney marks," she said.

"I know," Reacher said. "Apart from them, I could have invented this whole thing."

"If they were gurney marks."

"What else could they have been?"

"Nothing, I guess. They were from one of those old-fashioned stretchers, with the little skids, not the wheels."

"Why would I invent anything anyway?"

"For attention."

"I don't like attention."

"Everyone likes attention. Especially retired cops. It's a recognized pathology. You try to insinuate yourselves back into the action."

"Are you going to do that when you retire?"

"I hope not."

"I don't, either."

"So what's going on over there?"

"Maybe the kid was local," Reacher said. "They knew who he was, so he wasn't a candidate for your missing persons inquiry."

Vaughan shook her head. "Still makes no sense. Any unexplained death out-of-doors has got to be reported to the county coroner. In which case it would have showed up on the state system. Purely as a statistic. The State Police would have said, *Well, hey, we heard there was a dead guy in Despair this morning, maybe you should check it out.*"

"But they didn't."

"Because nothing has been called in from Despair. Which just doesn't add up. What the hell are they doing with the corpse? There's no morgue over there. Not even any cold storage, as far as I know. Not even a meat locker."

"So they're doing something else with him," Reacher said.

"Like what?"

"Burying him, probably."

"He wasn't road kill."

"Maybe they're covering something up."

"You claim he died of natural causes."

"He did," Reacher said. "From wandering through the scrub for days. Maybe because they ran him out of town. Which might embarrass them. Always assuming they're capable of embarrassment."

Vaughan shook her head again. "They didn't run him out of town. We didn't get a call. And they always call us. Always. Then they drive them to the line and dump them. This week there's been you and the girl. That's all."

"They never dump them to the west?"

"There's nothing there. It's unincorporated land."

"Maybe they're just slow. Maybe they'll call it in later."

"Doesn't compute," Vaughan said. "You find a dead one, you put one hand on your gun and the other on your radio. You call for backup, you call for the ambulance, you call the coroner. One, two, three. It's completely automatic. There and then."

"Maybe they aren't as professional as you."

"It's not about being unprofessional. It's about making a spur-of-the-moment decision to break procedure and not to call the coroner. Which would require some kind of real reason."

Reacher said nothing.

Vaughan said, "Maybe there were no cops involved. Maybe someone else found him."

"Civilians don't carry stretchers in their cars," Reacher said.

Vaughan nodded vaguely and got up. Said, "We should get out of here before the day guy gets in. And the watch commander."

"Embarrassed to be seen with me?"

"A little. And I'm a little embarrassed that I don't know what to do."

The breakfast rush at the diner was over. A degree of calm had been restored. Reacher ordered coffee.

Vaughan said she was happy with tap water. She sipped her way through half a glass and drummed her fingers on the table.

"Start over," she said. "Who was this guy?"

"Caucasian male," Reacher said.

"Not Hispanic? Not foreign?"

"I think Hispanics are Caucasians, technically. Plus Arabs and some Asians. All I'm going on is his hair. He wasn't black. That's all I know for sure. He could have been from anywhere in the world."

"Dark-skinned or pale?"

"I couldn't see anything."

"You should have taken a flashlight."

"I'm still glad I didn't."

"How did his skin feel?"

"Feel? It felt like skin."

"You should have been able to tell something. Olive skin feels different from pale skin. A little smoother and thicker."

"Really?"

"I think so. Don't you?"

Reacher touched the inside of his left wrist with his right forefinger. Then he tried his cheek, under his eye.

"Hard to tell," he said.

Vaughan stretched her arm across the table. "Now compare."

He touched the inside of her wrist, gently.

She said, "Now try my face."

"Really?"

"Purely for research purposes."

He paused a beat, then touched her cheek with

the ball of his thumb. He took his hand away and said, "Texture was thicker than either one of us. Smoothness was somewhere between the two of us."

"OK." She touched her own wrist where he had touched it, and then her face. Then she said, "Give me your wrist."

He slid his hand across the table. She touched his wrist, with two fingers, like she was taking his pulse. She rubbed an inch north and an inch south and then leaned over and touched his cheek with her other hand. Her fingertips were cold from her water glass and the touch startled him. He felt a tiny jolt of voltage in it.

She said, "So he wasn't necessarily white, but he was younger than you. Less lined and wrinkled and weather-beaten. Less of a mess."

"Thank you."

"You should use a good moisturizer."

"I'll bear that advice in mind."

"And sunscreen."

"Likewise."

"Do you smoke?"

"I used to."

"That's not good for your skin either."

Reacher said, "He might have been Asian, with the skimpy beard."

"Cheekbones?"

"Pronounced, but he was thin anyway."

"Wasted, in fact."

"Noticeably. But he was probably wiry to begin with."

"How long does it take for a wiry person to get wasted?"

"I don't know for sure. Maybe five or six days in a hospital bed or a cell, if you're sick or on a hunger strike. Less if you're moving about out-of-doors, keeping warm, burning energy. Maybe only two or three days."

Vaughan was quiet for a moment.

"That's a lot of wandering," she said. "We need to know why the good folks of Despair put in two or three days sustained effort to keep him out of there."

Reacher shook his head. "Might be more useful to know why he was trying so hard to stay. He must have had a damn good reason."

20

Vaughan finished her water and Reacher finished his coffee and asked, "Can I borrow your truck?"

"When?"

"Now. While you sleep."

Vaughan said, "No."

"Why not?"

"You'll use it to go back to Despair, you'll get arrested, and I'll be implicated."

"Suppose I don't go back to Despair?"

"Where else would you want to go?"

"I want to see what lies to the west. The dead guy must have come in that way. I'm guessing he didn't come through Hope. You would have seen him and remembered him. Likewise with the girl's missing husband."

"Good point. But there's not much west of Despair. A lot of not much, in fact."

"Got to be something."

Vaughan was quiet for a moment. Then she said, "It's a long loop around. You have to go back practically all the way to Kansas."

Reacher said, "I'll pay for the gas."

"Promise me you'll stay out of Despair."

"Where's the line?"

"Five miles west of the metal plant."

"Deal."

Vaughan sighed and slid her keys across the table.

"Go," she said. "I'll walk home. I don't want you to see where I live."

The old Chevy's seat didn't go very far back. The runners were short. Reacher ended up driving with his back straight and his knees splayed, like he was at the wheel of a farm tractor. The steering was vague and the brakes were soft. But it was better than walking. Much better, in fact. Reacher was done with walking, for a day or two at least.

His first stop was his motel in Hope. His room was at the end of the row, which put Lucy Anderson in a room closer to the office. She couldn't be anywhere else. He hadn't seen any other overnight accommodation in town. And she wasn't staying with friends, because they would have been with her in the diner the night before, in her hour of need.

The motel had its main windows all in back. The front of the row had a repeating sequence of doors and lawn chairs and head-high pebbled-glass slits that put daylight into the bathrooms. Reacher started with the room next to his own and walked down the row, looking for the white blur of underwear drying over a tub. In his experience women of Lucy Anderson's station and generation were very particular about personal hygiene.

The twelve rooms yielded two possibilities. One

had a larger blur than the other. Not necessarily more underwear. Just bigger underwear. An older or a larger woman. Reacher knocked at the other door and stepped back and waited. A long moment later Lucy Anderson opened up and stood in the inside shadows, warily, with one hand on the handle.

Reacher said, "Hello, Lucky."

"What do you want?"

"I want to know why your husband went to Despair, and how he got there."

She was wearing the same sneakers, and the same kind of abbreviated socks. Above them was a long expanse of leg, smooth and toned and tanned to perfection. Maybe she played soccer for UCLA. Maybe she was a varsity star. Above the expanse of leg was a pair of cut-off denims, frayed higher on the outside of her thighs than the inside, which was to say frayed very high indeed, because the effective remaining inseam had to have been less than three-quarters of an inch.

Above the shorts was another sweatshirt, mid-blue, with nothing written on it.

She said, "I don't want you looking for my husband."

"Why not?"

"Because I don't want you to find him."

"Why not?"

"It's obvious."

"Not to me," Reacher said.

She said, "I'd like you to leave me alone now."

"You were worried about him yesterday. Today you're not?"

She stepped forward into the light, just a pace, and

glanced left and right beyond Reacher's shoulders. The motel's lot was empty. Nothing there, except Vaughan's old truck parked at Reacher's door. Lucy Anderson's sweatshirt was the same color as her eyes, and her eyes were full of panic.

"Just leave us alone," she said, and stepped back into her room and closed the door.

Reacher sat a spell in Vaughan's truck, with a map from her door pocket. The sun was out again and the cab was warm. In Reacher's experience cars were always either warm or cold. Like a primitive calendar. Either it was summer or winter. Either the sun came through the glass and the metal, or it didn't.

The map confirmed what Vaughan had told him. He was going to have to drive a huge three-and-a-half-sided rectangle, first east almost all the way back to the Kansas line, then north to I-70, then west again, then south on the same highway spur the metal trucks used. Total distance, close to two hundred miles. Total time, close to four hours. Plus four hours and two hundred miles back, if he obeyed Vaughan's injunction to keep her truck off Despair's roads.

Which he planned to.

Probably.

He pulled out of the lot and headed east, retracing the route he had come in on with the old guy in the Grand Marquis. The mid-morning sun was low on his right. The old truck's battered exhaust was leaking fumes, so he kept the windows cracked. No electric winders. Just old-fashioned handles, which he preferred for the precision they permitted. He had the left window down less than an inch, and the right window half as much. At a steady sixty the wind whistled in and sounded a mellifluous high-pitched chord, underpinned by the bass growl of a bad bearing and the tenor burble of the tired old motor. The truck was a pleasant traveling companion on the state roads. On I-70 it was less pleasant. Passing semis blew it all over the place. The geometry was out and it had no stability. Reacher's wrists ached after the first ten highway miles, from holding it steady. He stopped once for gas and once for coffee and both times he was happy to get a break.

The spur came off I-70 west of Despair and petered out into a heavy-duty county two-lane within thirty miles. Reacher recognized it. It was the same piece of road he had observed leaving the plant at the other end. Same sturdy construction, same width, same coarse blacktop, same sand shoulders. Exactly four hours after leaving the motel he slowed and coasted and crossed the rumble strip and came to a stop with two wheels in the sand. Traffic was light, limited to trucks of all types heading in and out of the recycling plant twenty miles ahead. They were mostly flat-bed semis, but with some container trucks and box vans mixed in. Plates were mostly from Colorado and its adjacent states, but there were some from California and Washington and New Jersey and some from Canada. They blew past and their bow waves rocked the old truck on its suspension.

Despair itself was invisible in the far distance, except for the hint of a smudge on the horizon and a thin pall of smog hanging motionless in the air. Five miles closer but still fifteen miles away was the group of low gray buildings Reacher had seen before, now on his right, a tiny indistinct blur. A gas station, maybe. Or a motel. Or both. Maybe a full-blown truck stop, with a restaurant. Maybe it was the kind of place he could get a high-calorie meal.

Maybe it was the kind of place Lucy Anderson's husband and the unidentified dead guy might have gotten a high-calorie meal, on their way into Despair. In the case of the unidentified dead guy at least, maybe his last meal ever.

Maybe someone would remember them.

Maybe the place was outside Despair's city limit.

Maybe it wasn't.

Reacher checked his mirror and put the truck in gear and bumped his right-hand wheels back onto the road and headed for the horizon. Twelve minutes later he stopped again, just short of a pole that held a small green sign that said: *Entering Despair, Pop. 2691.* A hundred yards the wrong side of the line was the group of low buildings.

They weren't gray. That had been a trick of light and haze and distance.

They were olive green.

Not a gas station.

Not a motel.

No kind of a truck stop.

21

There were six low green buildings. They were identical metal prefabrications clustered together according to exact specifications and precise regulations. They were separated by roadways of uniform width graded from raw dirt and edged with white-painted boulders of small and consistent size. They were ringed by a razor-wire fence, tall, straight, and true. The fence continued west to enclose a parking lot. The lot was filled with six up-armored Humvees. Each one had a machine-gun mount on top. Next to the parking lot there was a slender radio mast protected by a fence all its own.

Not a motel.

Not a truck stop.

A military facility.

Specifically, an army facility. More specifically, a Military Police facility. More specifically still, a temporary advanced encampment for a combat MP unit. An FOB, a forward operating base. Reacher recognized the format and the equipment mix. Confirmation was right there on a board at the gate. The gate was a white counterbalanced pole with a guard shack next to it. The board was on stilts next to the shack and was painted glossy army green and had a formal unit ID stenciled on it in white.

Not a National Guard unit.

Not reservists.

A regular army unit, and a pretty good one, too. At least it always had been, back in Reacher's day, and there was no reason to believe it had gotten sloppy in the intervening years. No reason at all.

How sloppy it hadn't gotten was proved almost immediately.

The guard shack was a metal affair with tall wide windows on all four sides. Four guys in it. Two stayed where they were, and would forever, no matter what. The other two came out. They were dressed in desert BDUs and boots and armored vests and helmets and they were carrying M16 rifles. They ducked under the boom and formed up side by side and sloped arms and stepped out to the roadway. They executed a perfect left turn and jogged toward Reacher's truck, exactly in step, at exactly seven miles an hour, like they had been trained to. When they were thirty yards away they separated to split the target they were presenting. One guy headed for the sand and came up on Reacher's right and stood off ten yards distant and swapped his rifle into the ready position. The other guy stayed on the blacktop and looped around and checked the truck's load bed and then came back and stood off six feet from Reacher's door and called out in a loud clear voice.

He said, "Sir, please lower your window."

And keep your hands where I can see them, Reacher

thought. *For your own safety.* He wound the window all the way down and glanced left.

"Sir, please keep your hands where I can see them," the guy said. "For your own safety."

Reacher put his hands high on the wheel and kept on staring left. The guy he was looking at was a specialist, young but with some years in, with pronounced squint lines either side of his eyes. He was wearing glasses with thin black frames. The name tape on the right side of his vest said *Morgan.* In the distance a truck's air horn sounded and the soldier stepped closer to the curb and a semi blasted past from behind in a howl of sound and wind and grit. There was a long whine of stressed tires and Reacher's truck rocked on its springs and then silence came down again. The soldier stepped back to where he had been before and took up the same stance, wary but challenging, in control but cautious, his M16 held barrel-down but ready.

"At ease, Corporal," Reacher said. "Nothing to see here."

The guy called Morgan said, "Sir, that's a determination I'll need to make for myself."

Reacher glanced ahead. Morgan's partner was still as a statue, the stock of his M16 tucked tight into his shoulder. He was a private first class. He was sighting with his right eye, aiming low at Reacher's front right-hand tire.

Morgan asked, "Sir, why are you stopped here?"

Reacher said, "Do I need a reason?"

"Sir, you appear to me to be surveilling a restricted military installation."

"Well, you're wrong. I'm not."

"Sir, why are you stopped?"

"Stop calling me *sir,* will you?"

"Sir?"

Reacher smiled to himself. An MP with Morgan's years in had probably read a whole foot-thick stack of orders titled *Members of the Public, Domestic, Required Forms of Address,* endlessly revised, revisited, and updated.

"Maybe I'm lost," Reacher said.

"You're not local?"

"No."

"Your vehicle has Colorado plates."

"Colorado is a big state," Reacher said. "More than a hundred thousand square miles, soldier, the eighth largest in the Union. By land area, that is. Only the twenty-second largest by population. Maybe I come from a remote and distant corner."

Morgan went blank for a second. Then he asked, "Sir, where are you headed?"

The question gave Reacher a problem. The spur off I-70 had been small and hard to find. No way could a driver headed for Colorado Springs or Denver or Boulder have taken it by mistake. To claim a navigation error would raise suspicion. To raise suspicion would lead to a radio check against Vaughan's plates, which would drag her into something she was better left out of.

So Reacher said, "I'm headed for Hope."

Morgan took his left hand off his rifle and pointed straight ahead.

"That way, sir," he said. "You're on track. Twenty-two miles to downtown Hope."

Reacher nodded. Morgan was pointing south but hadn't taken his eyes off Reacher's hands. He was a good soldier. Experienced. Well turned out. His BDUs were old but in good order. His boots were worn and scratched but well cared for and immaculately brushed. The top of his eyeglass frame ran exactly parallel with the lip of his helmet. Reacher liked soldiers in eyeglasses. Eyeglasses added a vulnerable human detail that balanced the alien appearance of the weapons and the armor.

The face of the modern army.

Morgan stepped in close to Reacher's fender again and another truck blew by. This one was a New Jersey semi loaded with a closed forty-foot shipping container. Like a giant brick, doing sixty miles an hour. Noise, wind, a long tail of swirling dust. Morgan's BDU pants flattened against his legs and skittering miniature tornadoes of dust danced all around his feet. But he didn't blink behind his glasses.

He asked, "Sir, does this vehicle belong to you?"

Reacher said, "I'm not sure you're entitled to information like that."

"In the vicinity of a restricted military installation I would say I'm entitled to pretty much any information I want."

Reacher didn't answer that.

Morgan said, "Do you have registration and insurance?"

"Glove box," Reacher said, which was a pretty safe

guess. Vaughan was a cop. Most cops kept their paperwork straight. Too embarrassing, if they didn't.

Morgan asked, "Sir, may I see those documents?"

Reacher said, "No."

"Sir, now it seems to me that you're approaching a restricted military installation in a stolen load-bearing vehicle."

"You already checked the back. It's empty."

Morgan said nothing.

"Relax, Corporal," Reacher said. "This is Colorado, not Iraq. I'm not looking to blow anything up."

"Sir, I wish you hadn't used those words."

"At ease, Morgan. I was speaking negatively. I was telling you what I wasn't going to do."

"No laughing matter."

"I'm not laughing."

"I need to see those vehicle documents, sir."

"You're overstepping your authority."

"Sir, I need to see them real quick."

"You got a JAG lawyer on post?"

"Negative, sir."

"You happy to make this decision on your own?"

Morgan didn't answer. He stepped close to the fender again and a tanker truck blew by. It had an orange hazardous chemicals diamond on the back and a stainless-steel body polished so bright that Reacher saw himself reflected in it like a funhouse mirror. Then its slipstream died away and Morgan stepped back into position and said, "Sir, I need you to show me those documents. Just wave them at me, if you like. To prove to me you can put your hands on them."

Reacher shrugged and leaned over and opened the

glove box lid. Dug through ballpoint pens and envelopes of facial tissues and other miscellaneous junk and found a small plastic wallet. The wallet was black and was printed with a silver shape resembling a steering wheel. It was the kind of cheap thing found for sale at gas stations and car washes, alongside air fresheners shaped like conifer trees and ball compasses that attached to windshields with suction cups. The plastic was stiff and brittle with age and the black color had leached to a dusty gray.

Reacher opened the wallet, out of Morgan's sight. On the left behind a plastic window was a current insurance certificate. On the right, a current registration.

Both were made out to David Robert Vaughan, of Hope, Colorado.

Reacher kept the wallet open with his thumb and waved it in Morgan's direction, long enough for the documents to register, short enough for neither of them to be read.

Morgan said, "Sir, thank you."

Reacher put the wallet back in the glove box and slammed the lid.

Morgan said, "Sir, now it's time to be moving along."

Which gave Reacher another problem. If he moved forward, he would be in Despair township. If he U-turned, Morgan would wonder why he had suddenly gotten cold feet and abandoned Hope as a destination, and would be tempted to call in the plate.

Which was the greater danger?

Morgan, easily. A contest between the Despair PD

and a combat MP unit was no kind of a contest at all. So Reacher put the truck in gear and turned the wheel.

"Have a great day, Corporal," he said, and hit the gas. A yard later he passed the little green sign and temporarily increased Despair's population by one, all the way up to 2692.

22

The sturdy two-lane continued basically straight for five miles to the recycling plant's vehicle gate. An unsignposted left fork speared off into the brush and formed the western end of Despair's only through road. Reacher paused for an approaching semi loaded with bright steel bars and then waited again for a container truck heading for Canada. Then he made the left and bounced up onto the uneven surface and drove on and saw all the same stuff he had seen the day before, but in reverse order. The plant's long end wall, welded metal, bright white paint, the sparks and the smoke coming from the activity inside, the moving cranes. He stretched a long arm across the cab and dropped the passenger window and heard the noise of clanging hammers and smelled the acrid odors of chemical compounds.

He got to the acres of parking near the personnel gate and saw the clockwise security Tahoe bouncing across the scrub in the distance far to his right. Its counterclockwise partner was right there in the lot, black tinted windows, coming on slow, looking to cross the road at a right angle. Reacher sped up and the Tahoe slowed down and crossed right behind him.

Reacher saw it slide past, huge in his mirror. He drove on and then the plant was behind him and downtown Despair was looming up three miles ahead on the right. The low brick cubes, sullen in the afternoon light. The road was clear. It rose and fell and meandered gently left and right, avoiding any geological formation larger than a refrigerator. Cheap engineering, never graded or straightened since its origin as a cart track.

A mile ahead, a cop car pulled out of a side street.

It was unmistakable. A Crown Vic, white and gold, black push bars on the front, a light bar on the roof, antennas on the trunk lid. It nosed out and paused a beat and turned left.

West.

Straight toward Reacher.

Reacher checked his speed. He was doing fifty, which was all that was comfortable. He had no idea of the local limit. He dropped to forty-five, and cruised on. The cop was less than a mile away, coming on fast. Closing speed, more than a hundred miles an hour. Time to contact, approximately thirty-five seconds.

Reacher cruised on.

The sun was behind him, and therefore in the cop's eyes, which was a good thing. The old Chevy truck had a plain untinted windshield, which was a bad thing. Ten seconds before contact Reacher took his left hand off the wheel and put it against his forehead, like he was massaging his temple against a headache. He kept his speed steady and stared straight ahead.

The cop car blew past.

Reacher put his hand back on the wheel and checked his mirror.

The cop was braking hard.

Reacher kept one eye on the mirror and ran a fast calculation. He had maybe fifteen miles to go before the Hope town line and the arthritic old Chevy would top out at about seventy, max, which gave him a thirteen-minute trip. The Crown Vic was not a fantastically powerful car but the Police Interceptor option pack gave it a low axle ratio for fast acceleration and twin exhausts for better breathing. It would do ninety, comfortably. Therefore it would overhaul him within three minutes, just about level with the abandoned motor court, at the start of twelve whole miles of empty road.

Not good.

Behind him the Crown Vic was pulling through a fast U-turn.

Why?

Despair was a company town but its road had to be a public thoroughfare. Any Hope resident would use it to head home off the Interstate. Some Kansas residents would do the same. Unfamiliar vehicles in Despair could not possibly be rarities.

Reacher checked the mirror again. The Crown Vic was accelerating after him. Nose high, tail squatting low.

Maybe the security guy in the counterclockwise Tahoe had called it in. Maybe he had seen Reacher's face and recognized it. Maybe the deputies from the family restaurant took turns as the security drivers.

Reacher drove on. He hit the first downtown block.

Ten blocks ahead, a second Crown Vic pulled out.

And stopped, dead across the road.

Reacher braked hard and hauled on the wheel and pulled a fast right into the checkerboard of downtown streets. A desperation move. He was the worst guy in the world to win a car chase. He wasn't a great driver. He had taken the evasive-driving course at Fort Rucker during the MP Officers' Basic School and had impressed nobody. He had scraped a passing grade, mostly out of charity. A year later the school had moved to Fort Leonard Wood and the obstacle course had gotten harder and he knew he would have failed it. Time and chance. Sometimes it helps a person.

Sometimes it leaves a person unprepared.

He hit three four-way stops in succession and turned left, right, left without pausing or thinking. The streets were boxed in tight by dour brick buildings but his sense of direction was better than his driving and he knew he was heading east again. Downtown traffic was light. He got held up by a woman driving slow in an old Pontiac but the blocks were short and he solved his problem by turning right and left again and bypassing her one block over.

The chase car didn't show behind him. Statistics were on his side. He figured the downtown area was about twelve blocks square, which meant there were about 288 distinct lengths of road between opportunities to turn off, which meant that if he kept moving, the chances of direct confrontation were pretty low.

But the chances of ever getting out of the maze

were pretty low, too. As long as the second cop was blocking Main Street at its eastern end, then Hope was unavailable as a destination. And presumably the metal plant Tahoes were on duty to the west. And presumably Despair was full of helpful citizens with four-wheel-drive SUVs that would be a lot quicker over open ground than Vaughan's ancient Chevy. They could get up a regular posse.

Reacher turned a random left, just to keep moving. The chase car flashed through the intersection, dead ahead. It moved left to right and disappeared. Reacher turned left on the same street and saw it in his mirror, moving away from him. Now he was heading west. His gas tank was more than a quarter full. He turned right at the next four-way and headed north two blocks to Main Street. He turned east there and took a look ahead.

The second Crown Vic was still parked across the road, blocking both lanes just beyond the dry goods store. Its light bar was flashing red, as a warning to oncoming traffic. It was nearly eighteen feet long. One of the last of America's full-sized sedans. A big car, but at one end it was leaving a gap of about four feet between the front of its hood and the curb, and about three feet between its trunk and the curb at the other.

No good. Vaughan's Chevy was close to six feet wide.

Back at Fort Rucker the evasive driving aces had a mantra: *Keep death off the road: Drive on the sidewalk.* Which Reacher could do. He could get past the cop with two wheels up on the curb. But then what? He would be faced with a twelve-mile high-speed chase, in a low-speed vehicle.

No good.

He turned right again and headed back to the downtown maze. Saw the first Crown Vic flash past again, this time hunting east to west, three blocks away. He turned left and headed away from it. He slowed and started looking for used-car lots. In the movies, you parked at the end of a line of similar vehicles and the cops blew past without noticing.

He found no used-car lots.

In fact he found nothing much at all. Certainly nothing useful. He saw the police station twice, and the grocery store and the barber shop and the bar and the rooming house and the faded old hotel that he had seen before, on his walk down to the restaurant he had been thrown out of. He saw a storefront church. Some kind of a strange fringe denomination, something about the end times. The only church in town, Vaughan had said, where the town's feudal boss was the lay preacher. It was an ugly one-story building, built from brick, with a squat steeple piled on top to make it taller than the neighboring buildings. The steeple had a copper lightning rod on it and the grounding strap that ran down to the street had weathered to a bright verdigris green. It was the most colorful thing on display in Despair, a vivid vertical slash among the dullness.

He drove on. He looked, but he saw nothing else of significance. He would have liked a tire bay, maybe, where he could get the old Chevy up on a hoist and out of sight. He could have hidden out and gotten Vaughan's bad geometry fixed, all at the same time.

He found no tire bays.

He drove on, making random turns left and right. He saw the first Crown Vic three more times in the next three minutes, twice ahead of him and once behind him in his mirrors. The fourth time he saw it was a minute later. He paused at a four-way and it came up at the exact same moment and paused in the mouth of the road directly to his right. Reacher and the cop were at right angles to each other, nose to nose, ten feet apart, immobile. The cop was the same guy who had arrested him. Big, dark, wide. Tan jacket. He looked over and smiled. Gestured *Go ahead* like he was yielding, as if he had been second to the line.

Reacher was a lousy driver, but he wasn't stupid. No way was he going to let the cop get behind him, heading in the same direction. He jammed the old Chevy into reverse and backed away. The cop darted forward, turning, aiming to follow. Reacher waited until the guy was halfway through the maneuver and jammed the stick back into Drive and snaked past him, close, flank to flank. Then he hung a left and a right and a left again until he was sure he was clear.

Then he drove on, endlessly. He concluded that his random turns weren't helping him. He was as likely to turn into trouble as away from it. So mostly he stayed straight, until he ran out of street. Then he would turn. He ended up driving in wide concentric circles, slow enough to be safe, fast enough that he could kick the speed up if necessary without the weak old motor bogging down.

He passed the church and the bar and the grocery and the faded old hotel for the third time each. Then the rooming house. Its door slid behind his shoulder and opened. In the corner of his eye he saw a guy step out.

A young guy.

A big guy.

Tall, and blond, and heavy. An athlete. Blue eyes and a buzz cut and a dark tan. Jeans and a white T-shirt under a gray V-neck sweater.

Reacher stamped on the brake and turned his head. But the guy was gone, moving fast, around the corner. Reacher shoved the stick into Reverse and backed up. A horn blared and an old SUV swerved. Reacher didn't stop. He entered the four-way going backward and stared down the side street.

No guy. Just empty sidewalk. In his mirror Reacher saw the chase car three blocks west. He shoved the stick back into Drive and took off forward. Turned left, turned right, drove more wide aimless circles.

He didn't see the young man again.

But he saw the cop twice more. The guy was nosing around through distant intersections like he had all the time in the world. Which he did. Two-thirty in the afternoon, half the population hard at work at the plant, the other half baking pies or slumped in armchairs watching daytime TV, the lone road bottlenecked at both ends of town. The cop was just amusing himself. He had Reacher trapped, and he knew it.

And Reacher knew it, too.

No way out.

Time to stand and fight.

23

Some jerk instructor at the Fort Rucker MP School had once trotted out the tired old cliché *to assume makes an ass out of you and me.* He had demonstrated at the classroom chalkboard, dividing the word into *ass, u,* and *me.* On the whole Reacher had agreed with him, even if the guy was a jerk. But sometimes assumptions just had to be made, and right then Reacher chose to assume that however half-baked the Despair cops might be, they wouldn't risk shooting with bystanders in the line of fire. So he pulled to the curb outside the family restaurant and got out of Vaughan's truck and took up a position leaning on one of the restaurant's floor-to-ceiling plate glass windows.

Behind him, the same waitress was on duty. She had nine customers eating late lunches. A trio, a couple, four singletons, equally distributed around the room.

Collateral damage, just waiting to happen.

The window glass was cold on Reacher's shoulders. He could feel it through his shirt. The sun was still out but it was low in the sky and the streets were in shadow. There was a breeze. Small eddies of grit blew here and there on the sidewalk. Reacher unbuttoned his cuffs and folded them up on his forearms. He arched his back against the cramp he had gotten from sitting in the Chevy's undersized cab for so long. He flexed his hands and rolled his head in small circles to loosen his neck.

Then he waited.

The cop showed up two minutes and forty seconds later. The Crown Vic came in from the west and stopped two intersections away and paused, like the guy was having trouble processing the information visible right in front of him. *The truck, parked. The suspect, just standing there.* Then the car leapt forward and came through the four-ways and pulled in tight behind the Chevy, its front fender eight feet from where Reacher was waiting. The cop left the engine running and opened his door and slid out into the roadway. Déjà vu all over again. Big guy, white, maybe forty, black hair, wide neck. Tan jacket, brown pants, the groove in his forehead from his hat. He took his Glock off his belt and held it straight out two-handed and put his spread thighs against the opposite fender and stared at Reacher across the width of the hood.

Sound tactics, except for the innocents behind the glass.

The cop called out, "Freeze."

"I'm not going anywhere," Reacher said. "Yet."

"Get in the car."

"Make me."

"I'll shoot."

"You won't."

The guy went blank for a beat and then shifted his focus beyond Reacher's face to the scene inside the restaurant. Reacher was absolutely certain that the Despair PD had no Officer Involved Shooting investigative team, or even any kind of Officer Involved Shooting protocol, so the guy's hesitation was down to pure common sense. Or maybe the guy had relatives who liked to lunch late.

"Get in the car," the guy said again.

Reacher said, "I'll take a pass on that." He stayed relaxed, leaning back, unthreatening.

"I'll shoot," the cop said again.

"You can't. You're going to need backup."

The cop paused again. Then he shuffled to the left, back toward the driver's door. He kept his eyes and the gun tight on Reacher and fumbled one-handed through the car window and grabbed up his Motorola microphone and pulled it all the way out until its cord went tight. He brought it to his mouth and clicked the button. Said, "Bro, the restaurant, right now." He clicked off again and tossed the microphone back on the seat and put both hands back on the gun and shuffled back to the fender.

And the clock started ticking.

One guy would be easy.

Two might be harder.

The second guy had to move, but Reacher couldn't afford for him to arrive.

No sound, except the idling cruiser and the distant clash of plates inside the restaurant kitchen.

"Pussy," Reacher called. "A thing like this, you should have been able to handle it on your own."

The cop's lips went tight and he shuffled toward the front of the car, tracking with his gun, adjusting his aim. He reached the front bumper and felt for the push bars with his knees. Came on around, getting nearer.

He stepped up out of the gutter onto the sidewalk.

Reacher waited. The cop was now on his right, so Reacher shuffled one step left, to keep the line of fire straight and dangerous and inhibiting. The Glock tracked his move, locked in a steady two-handed grip.

The cop said, "Get in the car."

The cop took one step forward.

Now he was five feet away, one cast square of concrete sidewalk.

Reacher kept his back against the glass and moved his right heel against the base of the wall.

The cop stepped closer.

Now the Glock's muzzle was within a foot of Reacher's throat. The cop was a big guy, with long arms fully extended, and both feet planted apart in a useful combat stance.

Useful if he was prepared to fire.

Which he wasn't.

Taking a gun from a man ready to use it was not always difficult. Taking one from a man who had already decided not to use it verged on the easy. The cop took his left hand off the gun and braced to grab Reacher by the collar. Reacher slid right, his back hard on the window, washed cotton on clean glass, no friction at all, and moved inside the cop's aim. He brought his left forearm up and over, fast, *one two,* and clamped his hand right over the Glock and the cop's hand together. The cop was a big guy with big hands, but Reacher's were bigger. He clamped down and squeezed hard and forced the gun down and away in one easy movement. He got it pointing at the ground and increased the squeeze to paralyze the cop's trigger finger and then he looked him in the eye and smiled briefly and jerked forward off his planted heel and delivered a colossal head butt direct to the bridge of the cop's nose.

The cop sagged back on rubber legs.

Reacher kept tight hold of the guy's gun hand and kneed him in the groin. The cop went down more or less vertically but Reacher kept his hand twisted up and back so that the cop's own weight dislocated his elbow as he fell. The guy screamed and the Glock came free pretty easily after that.

Then it was all about getting ready in a hurry.

Reacher scrambled around the Crown Vic's hood and hauled the door open. He tossed the Glock inside and slid in the seat and buckled the seat belt and pulled it snug and tight. The seat was still warm from the cop's body and the car smelled of sweat. Reacher put the transmission in reverse and backed away from the Chevy and spun the wheel and came back level with it, in the wrong lane, facing east, just waiting.

24

The second cop showed up within thirty seconds, right on cue. Reacher saw the flare of flashing red lights a second before the Crown Vic burst around a distant corner. It fishtailed a little, then accelerated down the narrow street toward the restaurant, hard and fast and smooth.

Reacher let it get through one four-way, and another, and when it was thirty yards away he stamped on the gas and took off straight at it and smashed into it head-on. The two Crown Vics met nose to nose and their rear ends lifted off the ground and sheet metal crumpled and hoods flew open and glass burst and airbags exploded and steam jetted everywhere. Reacher was smashed forward against his seat belt. He had his hands off the wheel and his elbows up to fend off the punch of his airbag. Then the airbag collapsed again and Reacher was tossed back against the headrest. The rear of his car thumped back to earth and bounced once and came to rest at an angle. He pulled the Mossberg pump out of its between-the-seats holster and forced the door open against the crumpled fender and climbed out of the car.

The other guy hadn't been wearing his seat belt.

He had taken the impact of his airbag full in the face and was lying sideways across the front bench with blood coming out of his nose and his ears. Both cars were wrecked as far back as the windshield pillars. The passenger compartments were basically OK. Full-sized sedans, five-star crash ratings. Reacher was pretty sure both cars were undrivable but he was no kind of an automotive expert and so he made sure by racking the Mossberg twice and firing two booming shots into the rear wheel wells, shredding the tires and ripping up all kinds of other small essential components. Then he tossed the pump back through the first Crown Vic's window and walked over and climbed into Vaughan's Chevy and backed away from all the wreckage. The waitress and the nine customers inside the restaurant were all staring out through the windows, mouths wide open in shock. Two of the customers were fumbling for their cell phones.

Reacher smiled. *Who are you going to call?*

He K-turned the Chevy and made a right and headed north for Main Street and made another right and cruised east at a steady fifty. When he hit the lonely road after the gas station he kicked it up to sixty and kept one eye on the mirror. Nobody came after him. He felt the roughness under his tires but the roar was quieter than before. He was a little deaf from the airbags and the twin Mossberg blasts.

Twelve minutes later he bumped over the expansion joint and cruised into Hope, at exactly three o'clock in the afternoon.

He didn't know how long Vaughan would sleep. He guessed she had gotten her head on the pillow a little after nine that morning, which was six hours ago. Eight hours' rest would take her to five o'clock, which was reasonable for an on-deck time of seven in the evening. Or maybe she was already up and about. Some people slept worse in the daytime than the night. Habit, degree of acclimatization, circadian rhythms. He decided to head for the diner. Either she would be there already or he could leave her keys with the cashier.

She was there already.

He pulled to the curb and saw her alone in the booth they had used before. She was dressed in her cop uniform, four hours before her watch. She had an empty plate and a full coffee cup in front of her.

He locked the truck and went in and sat down opposite her. Up close, she looked tired.

"Didn't sleep?" he asked.

"Is it that obvious?"

"I have a confession to make."

"You went to Despair. In my truck. I knew you would."

"I had to."

"Sure."

"When was the last time you drove out to the west?"

"I try to stay out of Despair."

"There's a military base just inside the line. Fairly new. Why would that be?"

Vaughan said, "There are military bases all over."

"This was a combat MP unit."

"They have to put them somewhere."

"Overseas is where they need to put them. The army is hurting for numbers right now. They can't afford to waste good units in the back of beyond."

"Maybe it wasn't a good unit."

"It was."

"So maybe it's about to ship out."

"It just shipped back in. It just spent a year under the sun. The guy I spoke to had squint lines like you wouldn't believe. His gear was worn from the sand."

"We have sand here."

"Not like that."

"So what are you saying?"

The waitress came by and Reacher ordered coffee. Vaughan's cup was still full. Reacher said, "I'm asking why they pulled a good unit out of the Middle East and sent it here."

Vaughan said, "I don't know why. The Pentagon doesn't explain itself to neighboring police departments."

The waitress brought a cup for Reacher and filled it from a Bunn flask. Vaughan asked, "What does a combat MP unit do exactly?"

Reacher took a sip of coffee and said, "It guards things. Convoys or installations. It maintains security and repels attacks."

"Actual fighting?"

"When necessary."

"Did you do that?"

"Some of the time."

Vaughan opened her mouth and then closed it

again as her mind supplied the answer to the question she was about to ask.

"Exactly," Reacher said. "What's to defend in Despair?"

"And you're saying these MPs made you drive on through?"

"It was safer. They would have checked your plate if I hadn't."

"Did you get through OK?"

"Your truck is fine. Although it's not exactly yours, is it?"

"What do you mean?"

"Who is David Robert Vaughan?"

She looked blank for a second. Then she said, "You looked in the glove box. The registration."

"A man with a gun wanted to see it."

"Good reason."

"So who is David Robert?"

Vaughan said, "My husband."

25

Reacher said, "I didn't know you were married." Vaughan turned her attention to her lukewarm coffee and took a long time to answer.

"That's because I didn't tell you," she said. "Would you expect me to?"

"Not really, I suppose."

"Don't I look married?"

"Not one little bit."

"You can tell just by looking?"

"Usually."

"How?"

"Fourth finger, left hand, for a start."

"Lucy Anderson doesn't wear a ring either."

Reacher nodded. "I think I saw her husband today."

"In Despair?"

"Coming out of the rooming house."

"That's way off Main Street."

"I was dodging roadblocks."

"Terrific."

"Not one of my main talents."

"So how did they not catch you? They've got one road in and one road out."

"Long story," Reacher said.

"But?"

"The Despair PD is temporarily understaffed."

"You took one of them out?"

"Both of them. And their cars."

"You're completely unbelievable."

"No, I'm a man with a rule. People leave me alone, I leave them alone. If they don't, I don't."

"They'll come looking for you here."

"No question. But not soon."

"How long?"

"They'll be hurting for a couple of days. Then they'll saddle up."

Reacher left her alone with her truck keys on the table in front of her and walked down to Third Street and bought socks and underwear and a dollar T-shirt in an old-fashioned outfitters next to a supermarket. He stopped in at a pharmacy and bought shaving gear and then headed up to the hardware store at the western end of First Street. He picked his way past ladders and wheelbarrows and wound through aisles filled with racks of tools and found a rail of canvas work pants and flannel shirts. Traditional American garments, made in China and Cambodia, respectively. He chose dark olive pants and a mud-colored check shirt. Not as cheap as he would have liked, but not outrageous. The clerk folded them up into a brown paper bag and he carried it back to the motel and shaved and took a long shower and dried off and dressed in the new stuff. He crammed his old gray janitor uniform in the trash receptacle.

Better than doing laundry.

The new clothes were as stiff as boards, to the point where walking around was difficult. Clearly the Far Eastern garment industry took durability very seriously. He did squats and bicep curls until the starch cracked and then he stepped out and walked down the row to Lucy Anderson's door. He knocked and waited. A minute later she opened up. She looked just the same. Long legs, short shorts, plain blue sweatshirt. Young, and vulnerable. And wary, and hostile. She said, "I asked you to leave me alone."

He said, "I'm pretty sure I saw your husband today."

Her face softened, just for a second.

"Where?" she asked.

"In Despair. Looks like he's got a room there."

"Was he OK?"

"He looked fine to me."

"What are you going to do about him?"

"What would you like me to do about him?"

Her face closed up again. "You should leave him alone."

"I am leaving him alone. I told you, I'm not a cop anymore. I'm a vagrant, just like you."

"So why would you go back to Despair?"

"Long story. I had to."

"I don't believe you. You're a cop."

"You saw what was in my pockets."

"You left your badge in your room."

"I didn't. You want to check? My room is right here."

She stared at him in panic and put both hands on the door jambs like he was about to seize her around her waist and drag her away to his quarters. The motel clerk stepped out of the office, forty feet to Reacher's left. She was a stout woman of about fifty. She saw Reacher and saw the girl and stopped walking and watched. Then she moved again but changed direction and started heading toward them. In Reacher's experience motel clerks were either nosy about or else completely uninterested in their guests. He figured this one was the nosy kind. He stepped back a pace and gave Lucy Anderson some air and held up his hands, palms out, friendly and reassuring.

"Relax," he said. "If I was here to hurt you, you'd already be hurt by now, don't you think? You and your husband."

She didn't answer. Just turned her head and saw the clerk's approach and then ducked back to the inside shadows and slammed her door, all in one neat move. Reacher turned away but knew he wasn't going to make it in time. The clerk was already within calling distance.

"Excuse me," she said.

Reacher stopped. Turned back. Said nothing.

The woman said, "You should leave that girl alone."

"Should I?"

"If you want to stay here."

"Is that a threat?"

"I try to maintain standards."

"I'm trying to help her."

"She thinks the exact opposite."

"You've talked?"

"I hear things."

"I'm not a cop."

"You look like a cop."

"I can't help that."

"You should investigate some real crimes."

Reacher said, "I'm not investigating any kind of crimes. I told you, I'm not a cop."

The woman didn't answer.

Reacher asked, "What real crimes?"

"Violations."

"Where?"

"At the metal plant in Despair."

"What kind of violations?"

"All kinds."

"I don't care about violations. I'm not an EPA inspector. I'm not any kind of an inspector."

The woman said, "Then you should ask yourself why that plane flies every night."

26

Reacher got halfway back to his room and saw Vaughan's old pick-up turn in off the street. It was moving fast. It bounced up over the curb and headed through the lot straight at him. Vaughan was at the wheel in her cop uniform. Incongruous. And urgent. She hadn't taken time to go fetch her official cruiser. She braked hard and stopped with her radiator grille an inch away from him. She leaned out the window and said, "Get in, now."

Reacher asked, "Why?"

"Just do it."

"Do I have a choice?"

"None at all."

"Really?"

"I'm not kidding."

"Are you arresting me?"

"I'm prepared to. I'll use my gun and my cuffs if that's what it takes. Just get in the car."

Reacher studied her face through the windshield glass. She was serious about something. And determined. That was for sure. The evidence was right there in the set of her jaw. So he climbed in. Vaughan waited until he closed his door behind him and asked,

"You ever done a ride-along with a cop before? All night? A whole watch?"

"Why would I? I *was* a cop."

"Well, whatever, you're doing one tonight."

"Why?"

"We got a courtesy call. From Despair. You're a wanted man. They're coming for you. So tonight you stay where I can see you."

"They can't be coming for me. They can't even have woken up yet."

"Their deputies are coming. All four of them."

"Really?"

"That's what deputies do. They deputize."

"So I hide in your car? All night?"

"Damn straight."

"You think I need protection?"

"My town needs protection. I don't want trouble here."

"Those four won't be any trouble. One of them is already busted up and one was throwing his guts up the last time I saw him."

"So you could take them?"

"With one hand behind my back and my head in a bag."

"Exactly. I'm a cop. I have a responsibility. No fighting in my streets. It's unseemly." She pulled a tight U-turn in the motel lot and headed back the way she had come. Reacher asked, "When will they get here?"

"The plant shuts down at six. I imagine they'll head right over."

"How long will they stay?"

"The plant opens up again at six tomorrow morning."

Reacher said, "You don't want me in your car all night."

"I'll do what it takes. Like I said. This is a decent place. I'm not going to let it get trashed, either literally or metaphorically."

Reacher paused and said, "I could leave town."

"Permanently?" Vaughan asked.

"Temporarily."

"And go where?"

"Despair, obviously. I can't get in trouble there, can I? Their cops are in the hospital and their deputies will be here all night."

Vaughan made a right and a left and headed down Second Street toward the diner. She stayed quiet for a moment and then she said, "There's another one in town today."

"Another what?"

"Another girl. Just like Lucy Anderson. But dark, not blonde. She blew in this afternoon and now she's sitting around and staring west like she's waiting for word from Despair."

"From a boyfriend or a husband?"

"Possibly."

"Possibly a dead boyfriend or husband, Caucasian, about twenty years old, five-eight and one-forty."

"Possibly."

"I should go there."

Vaughan drove past the diner and kept on driving. She drove two blocks south and came back east on Fourth Street. No real reason. Just motion, for the sake of it. Fourth Street had trees and retail establishments behind the north sidewalk and trees and a long line of neat homes behind the south. Small yards, picket fences, foundation plantings, mailboxes on poles that had settled to every angle except the truly vertical.

"I should go there," Reacher said again.

"Wait until the deputies get here. You don't want to pass them on the road."

"OK."

"And don't let them see you leave."

"OK."

"And don't make trouble over there."

"I'm not sure there's anybody left to make trouble with. Unless I meet the judge."

27

For the second time that day Vaughan gave up her pick-up truck and walked home to get her cruiser. Reacher drove the truck to a quiet side street and parked facing north in the shadow of a tree and watched the traffic on First Street directly ahead of him. He had a limited field of view. But there wasn't much to see, anyway. Whole ten-minute periods passed without visible activity. Not surprising. Residents returning from the Kansas direction would have peeled off into town down earlier streets. And no one in their right mind was returning from Despair, or heading there. The daylight was fading fast. The world was going gray and still. The clock in Reacher's head was ticking around, relentlessly.

When it hit six-thirty-two he saw an old crew-cab pick-up truck flash through his field of vision. Moving smartly, from the Despair direction. A driver, and three passengers inside. Big men, close together. They filled the cramped quarters, shoulder to shoulder.

Reacher recognized the truck.

He recognized the driver.

He recognized the passengers.

The Despair deputies, right on time.

He paused a beat and started the old Chevy's engine and moved off the curb. He eased north to First Street and turned left. Checked his mirror. The old crew-cab was already a hundred yards behind him, moving away in the opposite direction, slowing down and getting ready to turn. The road ahead was empty. He passed the hardware store and hit the gas and forced the old truck up to sixty miles an hour. Five minutes later he thumped over the expansion joint and settled in to a noisy cruise west.

Twelve miles later he coasted past the vacant lot and the shuttered motor court and the gas station and the household goods store and then he turned left into Despair's downtown maze. First port of call was the police station. He wanted to be sure that no miraculous recoveries had been made, and that no replacement personnel had been provided.

They hadn't, and they hadn't.

The place was dark inside and quiet outside. No lights, no activity. There were no cars at the curb. No stand-in State Police cruisers, no newly-deputized pick-up trucks, no plain sedans with temporary *Police* signs stickered on their doors.

Nothing.

Just silence.

Reacher smiled. Open season and lawless, he thought, like a bleak view of the future in a movie. The way he liked it. He U-turned through the empty diagonal parking slots and headed back toward the rooming house. He parked on the curb out front and killed the motor and wound the window down. Heard a single aero engine in the far distance, climbing hard. Seven o'clock in the evening. The Cessna or the Beech or the Piper, taking off again. *You should ask yourself why that plane flies every night,* the motel clerk had said.

Maybe I will, Reacher thought. *One day.*

He climbed out of the truck. The rooming house was built of dull brick, on a corner lot. Three stories high, narrow windows, flat roof, four stone steps up to a doorway set off center in the façade. There was a wooden board on the wall next to the door, under a swan-neck lamp with a dim bulb. The board had been painted maroon way back in its history, and the words *Rooms to Rent* had been lettered in white over the maroon by a careful amateur. A plain and to-the-point announcement. Not the kind of place Reacher favored. Such establishments implied residency for longer periods than he was interested in. Generally they rented by the week, and had electric cooking rings in the rooms. Practically the same thing as setting up housekeeping.

He went up the stone steps and pushed the front door. It was open. Behind it was a square hallway with a brown linoleum floor and a steep staircase on the right. The walls were painted brown with some kind of a trick effect that matched the swirls in the linoleum. A bare bulb was burning dimly a foot below the ceiling. The air smelled of dust and cabbage. There were four interior doors, all dull green, all closed. Two were in back and two were in front, one at the foot of the staircase and the other directly opposite it across the hallway. Two front rooms, one of which would house the owner or the super. In Reacher's experience the owner or the super always chose a ground-floor room at the front, to monitor entrances and exits. Entrances and exits were very important to owners and supers. Unauthorized guests and multiple occupancies were to be discouraged, and tenants had been known to try to sneak out quietly just before final payment of long-overdue rent had been promised.

He opted to start with the door at the foot of the staircase. Better surveillance potential. He knocked and waited. A long moment later the door opened and revealed a thin man in a white shirt and a black tie. The guy was close to seventy years old, and his hair was the same color as his shirt. The shirt wasn't clean. Neither was the tie, but it had been carefully knotted.

"Help you?" the old guy said.

"Is this your place?" Reacher asked.

The old guy nodded. "And my mother's before me. In the family for close to fifty years."

"I'm looking for a friend of mine," Reacher said. "From California. I heard he was staying here."

No reply from the old man.

"Young guy," Reacher said. "Maybe twenty. Very big. Tan, with short hair."

"Nobody like that here."

"You sure?"

"Nobody here at all."

"He was seen stepping out your door this afternoon."

"Maybe he was visiting."

"Visiting who, if there's nobody here at all?"

"Visiting me," the old man said.

"Did he visit you?"

"I don't know. I was out. Maybe he knocked on my door and got no reply and left again."

"Why would he have been knocking on your door?"

The old guy thought for a moment and said, "Maybe he was at the hotel and wanted to economize. Maybe he had heard the rates were cheaper here."

"What about another guy, shorter, wiry, about the same age?"

"No guys here at all, big or small."

"You sure?"

"It's my house. I know who's in it."

"How long has it been empty?"

"It's not empty. I live here."

"How long since you had tenants?"

The old guy thought for another moment and said, "A long time."

"How long?"

"Years."

"So how do you make a living?"

"I don't."

"You own this place?"

"I rent it. Like my mother did. Close to fifty years."

Reacher said, "Can I see the rooms?"

"Which rooms?"

"All of them."

"Why?"

"Because I don't believe you. I think there are people here."

"You think I'm lying?"

"I'm a suspicious person."

"I should call the police."

"Go right ahead."

The old guy stepped away into the gloom and picked up a phone. Reacher crossed the hallway and tried the opposite door. It was locked. He walked back and the old guy said, "There was no answer at the police station."

"So it's just you and me," Reacher said. "Better that you lend me your passkey. Save yourself some repair work later, with the door locks."

The old guy bowed to the inevitable. He took a key from his pocket and handed it over. It was a worn brass item with a length of furred string tied through the hole. The string had an old metal eyelet on it, as if the eyelet was all that was left of a paper label.

There were three guest rooms on the ground floor, four on the second, and four on the third. All eleven were identical. All eleven were empty. Each room had a narrow iron cot against one wall. The cots were like something from an old-fashioned fever hospital or an army barracks. The sheets had been washed so many times they were almost transparent. The blankets had started out thick and rough and had worn thin and smooth. Opposite the beds were chests of drawers and freestanding towel racks. The towels were as thin as the sheets. Near the ends of the beds were pine kitchen tables with two-ring electric burners plugged into outlets with frayed old cords. At the ends of the hallways on each of the floors were shared bathrooms, tiled black and white, with iron claw-foot tubs and toilets with cisterns mounted high on the walls.

Basic accommodations, for sure, but they were in good order and beautifully kept. The bathroom fitments were stained with age, but not with dirt. The floors were swept shiny. The beds were made tight. A dropped quarter would have bounced two feet off the blankets. The towels on the racks were folded precisely and perfectly aligned. The electric burners were immaculately clean. No crumbs, no spills, no dried splashes of bottled sauce.

Reacher checked everywhere and then stood in the doorway of each room before leaving it, smelling the air and listening for echoes of recent hasty departures. He found nothing and sensed nothing, eleven times over. So he headed back downstairs and returned the key and apologized to the old guy. Then he asked, "Is there an ambulance service in town?"

The old guy asked, "Are you injured?"

"Suppose I was. Who would come for me?"

"How bad?"

"Suppose I couldn't walk. Suppose I needed a stretcher."

The old man said, "There's a first-aid station up at the plant. And an infirmary. In case a guy gets hurt on the job. They have a vehicle. They have a stretcher."

"Thanks," Reacher said.

He drove Vaughan's old Chevy on down the street. Paused for a moment in front of the storefront church. It had a painted sign running the whole width of the building: *Congregation of the End Times.* In one window it had a poster written in the same way that a supermarket would advertise brisket for three bucks a pound: *The Time Is at Hand.* A quotation from the Book of Revelation. Chapter one, verse three. Reacher recognized it. The other window had a similar poster: *The End Is Near.* Inside, the place was as dark and gloomy as its exterior messages. Rows of metal chairs, a wood floor, a low stage, a podium. More posters, each one predicting with confident aplomb that the clock was ticking. Reacher read them all and then drove on, to the hotel. It was dark when he got there. He remembered the place from earlier daytime sightings as looking dowdy and faded, and by night it looked worse. It could have been an old city prison, in Prague, maybe, or Warsaw, or Leningrad. The walls were featureless and the windows were blank and unlit. Inside it had an empty and unappealing dining room on the left and a deserted bar on the right. Dead ahead in the lobby was a deserted reception desk. Behind the reception desk was a small swaybacked version of a grand staircase. It was covered with matted carpet. There was no elevator.

Hotels were required by state and federal laws and private insurance to maintain accurate guest records. In case of a fire or an earthquake or a tornado, it was in everyone's interest to know who was resident in the building, and who wasn't. Therefore Reacher had learned a long time ago that when searching a hotel the place to start was with the register. Which over the years had become increasingly difficult, with computers. There were all kinds of function keys to hit and passwords to discover. But Despair as a whole was behind the times, and its hotel was no exception. The register was a large square book bound in old red leather. Easy to grab, easy to swivel around, easy to open, easy to read.

The hotel had no guests.

According to the handwritten records the last room had rented seven months previously, to a couple from California, who had arrived in a private car and stayed two nights. Since then, nothing. No names that might have corresponded to single twenty-year-old men, either large or small. No names at all.

Reacher left the hotel without a single soul having seen him and got back in the Chevy. Next stop was two blocks over, in the town bar, which meant mixing with the locals.

28

The bar was on the ground floor of yet another dull brick cube. One long narrow room. It ran the full depth of the building and had a short corridor with restrooms and a fire door way in back. The bar itself was on the left and there were tables and chairs on the right. Low light. No music. No television. No pool table, no video games. Maybe a third of the bar stools and a quarter of the chairs were occupied. The after-work crowd. But not exactly happy hour. All the customers were men. They were all tired, all grimy, all dressed in work shirts, all sipping beer from tall glasses or long-neck bottles. Reacher had seen none of them before.

He stepped into the gloom, quietly. Every head turned and every pair of eyes came to rest on him. Some kind of universal barroom radar. *Stranger in the house.* Reacher stood still and let them take a good look. *A stranger for sure, but not the kind you want to mess with.* Then he sat down on a stool and put his elbows on the bar. He was two gaps away from the nearest guy on his left and one away from the nearest guy on his right. The stools had iron bases and iron pillars and shaped mahogany seats that turned on rough bearings. The bar itself was made from scarred mahogany that didn't match the walls, which were paneled with pine. There were mirrors all over the walls, made of plain reflective glass screen-printed with beer company advertisements. They were framed with rustic wood and were fogged with years of alcohol fumes and cigarette smoke.

The bartender was a heavy pale man of about forty. He didn't look smart and he didn't look pleasant. He was ten feet away, leaning back with his fat ass against his cash register drawer. Not moving. Not about to move, either. That was clear. Reacher raised his eyebrows and put a beckoning expression on his face and got no response at all.

A company town.

He swiveled his stool and faced the room.

"Listen up, guys," he called. "I'm not a metalworker and I'm not looking for a job."

No response.

"You couldn't pay me enough to work here. I'm not interested. I'm just a guy passing through, looking for a beer."

No response. Just sullen and hostile stares, with bottles and glasses frozen halfway between tables and mouths.

Reacher said, "First guy to talk to me, I'll pay his tab."

No response.

"For a week."

No response.

Reacher turned back and faced the bar again. The bartender hadn't moved. Reacher looked him in the eye and said, "Sell me a beer or I'll start busting this place up."

The bartender moved. But not toward his refrigerator cabinets or his draft pumps. Toward his telephone instead. It was an old-fashioned instrument next to the register. The guy picked it up and dialed a long number. Reacher waited. The guy listened to a lot of ring tone and then started to say something but then stopped and put the phone down again.

"Voice mail," he said.

"Nobody home," Reacher said. "So it's just you and me. I'll take a Budweiser, no glass."

The guy glanced beyond Reacher's shoulder, out into the room, to see if any ad hoc coalitions were forming to help him out. They weren't. Reacher was already monitoring the situation in a dull mirror directly in front of him. The bartender decided not to be a hero. He shrugged and his attitude changed and his face sagged a little and he bent down and pulled a cold bottle out from under the bar. Opened it up and set it down on a napkin. Foam swelled out of the neck and ran down the side of the bottle and soaked into the paper. Reacher took a ten from his pocket and folded it lengthways so it wouldn't curl and squared it in front of him.

"I'm looking for a guy," he said.

The bartender said, "What guy?"

"A young guy. Maybe twenty. Suntan, short hair, as big as me."

"Nobody like that here."

"I saw him this afternoon. In town. Coming out of the rooming house."

"So ask there."

"I did."

"I can't help you."

"This guy looked like a college athlete. College athletes drink beer from time to time. He was probably in here once or twice."

"He wasn't."

"What about another guy? Same age, much smaller. Wiry, maybe five-eight, one-forty."

"Didn't see him."

"You sure?"

"I'm sure."

"You ever work up at the plant?"

"Couple of years, way back."

"And then?"

"He moved me here."

"Who did?"

"Mr. Thurman. He owns the plant."

"And this bar, too?"

"He owns everything."

"And he moved you? He sounds like a hands-on manager."

"He figured I'd be better working here than there."

"And are you?"

"Not for me to say."

Reacher took a long pull on his bottle. Asked, "Does Mr. Thurman pay you well?"

"I don't complain."

"Is that Mr. Thurman's plane that flies every night?"

"Nobody else here owns a plane."

"Where does he go?"

"I don't ask."

"Any rumors?"

"No."

"You sure you never saw any young guys around here?"

"I'm sure."

"Suppose I gave you a hundred bucks?"

The guy paused a beat and looked a little wistful, as if a hundred bucks would make a welcome change in his life. But in the end he just shrugged again and said, "I'd still be sure."

Reacher drank a little more of his beer. It was warming up a little and tasted metallic and soapy. The bartender stayed close. Reacher glanced at the mirrors. Checked reflections of reflections. Nobody in the room was moving. He asked, "What happens to dead people here?"

"What do you mean?"

"You got undertakers in town?"

The bartender shook his head. "Forty miles west. There's a morgue and a funeral home and a burial ground. No consecrated land in Despair."

"The smaller guy died," Reacher said.

"What smaller guy?"

"The one I was asking you about."

"I didn't see any small guys, alive or dead."

Reacher went quiet again and the bartender said, "So, you're just passing through?" A meaningless, for-the-sake-of-it conversational gambit, which confirmed what Reacher already knew. *Bring it on,* he thought. He glanced at the fire exit in back and checked the front door in the mirrors. He said, "Yes, I'm just passing through."

"Not much to see here."

"Actually I think this is a pretty interesting place."

"You do?"

"Who hires the cops here?"

"The mayor."

"Who's the mayor?"

"Mr. Thurman."

"There's a big surprise."

"It's his town."

Reacher said, "I'd like to meet him."

The bartender said, "He's a very private man."

"I'm just saying. I'm not asking for an appointment."

Six minutes, Reacher thought. *I've been working on this beer for six minutes. Maybe ten more to go.* He asked, "Do you know the judge?"

"He doesn't come in here."

"I didn't ask where he goes."

"He's Mr. Thurman's lawyer, up at the plant."

"I thought it was an elected position."

"It is. We all voted for him."

"How many candidates were on the ballot?"

"He was unopposed."

Reacher said, "Does this judge have a name?"

The bartender said, "His name is Judge Gardner."

"Does Judge Gardner live here in town?"

"Sure. You work for Mr. Thurman, you have to live in town."

"You know Judge Gardner's address?"

"The big house on Nickel."

"Nickel?"

"All the residential streets here are named for metals."

Reacher nodded. Not so very different from the way streets on army bases were named for generals or Medal of Honor winners. He went quiet again and waited for the bartender to fill the silence, like he had to. Like he had been told to. The guy said, "A hundred and some years ago there were only five miles of paved road in the United States."

Reacher said nothing.

The guy said, "Apart from city centers, of course, which were cobbled anyway, not really paved. Not with blacktop, like now. Then county roads got built, then state, then the Interstates. Towns got passed by. We were on the main road to Denver, once. Not so much anymore. People use I-70 now."

Reacher said, "Hence the closed-down motel."

"Exactly."

"And the general feeling of isolation."

"I guess."

Reacher said, "I know those two young guys were here. It's only a matter of time before I find out who they were and why they came."

"I can't help you with that."

"One of them died."

"You told me that already. And I still don't know anything about it."

Eleven minutes, Reacher thought. *Five to go.* He asked, "Is this the only bar in town?"

The guy said, "One is all we need."

"Movies?"

"No."

"So what do people do for entertainment?"

"They watch satellite television."

"I heard there's a first-aid station at the plant."

"That's right."

"With an ambulance."

"An old one. It's a big plant. It covers a big area."

"Are there a lot of accidents?"

"It's an industrial operation. Shit happens."

"Does the plant pay disability?"

"Mr. Thurman looks after people if they get hurt on the job."

Reacher nodded and sipped his beer. Watched the other customers sipping theirs, directly and in the mirrors. *Three minutes,* he thought.

Unless they're early.

Which they were.

Reacher looked to his right and saw two deputies step in through the fire door. He glanced in a mirror and saw the other two walk in the front.

29

The telephone. A useful invention, and instructive in the way it was used. Or not used. Four deputies heading east to make a surprise arrest would not tip their hand with a courtesy telephone call. Not in the real world. They would swoop down unannounced. They would aim to grab up their prey unawares. Therefore their courtesy call was a decoy. It was a move in a game. A move designed to flush Reacher westward into safer territory. It was an invitation.

Which Reacher had interpreted correctly.

And accepted.

And the bartender had not called the station house. Had not gotten voice mail. Had not made a local call at all. He had dialed too many digits. He had called a deputy's cell, and spoken just long enough to let the deputy know who he was, and therefore where Reacher was. Whereupon he had changed his attitude and turned talkative and friendly, to keep Reacher sitting tight. Like he had been told to, beforehand, should the opportunity arise.

Which is why Reacher had not left the bar. If the guy wanted to participate, he was welcome to. He could participate by cleaning up the mess.

And there was going to be a mess.

That was for damn sure.

The deputies who had come in the back walked through the short corridor past the restrooms and stopped where the main room widened out. Reacher kept his eyes on them. Didn't turn his head. A two-front attack was fairly pointless in a room full of mirrors. He could see the other guys quite clearly, smaller than life and reversed. They had stopped a yard inside the front door and were standing shoulder to shoulder, waiting.

The big guy who had thrown up the night before was one of the pair that had come in the front. With him was the guy Reacher had smacked outside the family restaurant. Neither one of them looked in great shape. The two who had come in the back looked large and healthy enough, but manageable. Four against one, but no real cause for concern. Reacher had first fought four-on-one when he was five years old, against seven-year-olds, on his father's base in the Philippines. He had won then, easily, and he expected to win now.

But then the situation changed.

Two guys stood up from the body of the room. They put their glasses down and dabbed their lips with napkins and scraped their chairs back and stepped forward and separated. One went left, and one went right. One lined up with the guys in back, and one lined up with the guys in front. The newcomers were not the biggest people Reacher had ever seen, but they weren't the smallest, either. They could have been the deputies' brothers or cousins. They probably were. They were dressed the same and looked the same and were built the same.

So, thirteen minutes previously the bartender had not been glancing into the room in hopes of immediate short-term assistance. He had been catching the ringers' eyes and tipping them off: *Stand by, the others are on their way.* Reacher clamped his jaw and the beer in his stomach went sour. *Mistake.* A bad one. He had been smart, but not smart enough.

And now he was going to pay, big time.

Six against one.

Twelve hundred pounds against two-fifty.

No kind of excellent odds.

He realized he was holding his breath. He exhaled, long and slow. Because: *Dum spero speri.* Where there's breath, there's hope. Not an aphorism Zeno of Cittium would have understood or approved of. Zeno spoke Greek, not Latin, and preferred passive resignation to reckless optimism. But the saying worked well enough for Reacher, when all else failed. He took a last sip of Bud and set the bottle back on his napkin. Swiveled his stool and faced the room. Behind him he sensed the bartender moving away to a safe place by the register. In front of him he saw the other customers sidling backward toward the far wall, cradling their glasses and bottles, huddling together, hunkering down. Beside him guys slipped off their stools and melted across the room into the safety of the crowd.

There was movement at both ends of the bar.

Both sets of three men took long paces forward.

Now they defined the ends of an empty rectangle

of space. Nothing in it, except Reacher alone on his stool, and the bare wooden floor.

The six guys weren't armed. Reacher was pretty sure about that. Vaughan had said that in Colorado police deputies were limited to civilian status. And the other two guys were just members of the public. Plenty of members of the public in Colorado had private weapons, of course, but generally people pulled weapons at the start of a fight, not later on. They wanted to display them. Show them off. Intimidate, from the get-go. Nobody in Reacher's experience had ever waited to pull a gun.

So, unarmed combat, six-on-one.

The big guy spoke, from six feet inside the front door. He said, "You're in so much trouble you couldn't dig your way out with a steam shovel."

Reacher said, "You talking to me?"

"Damn straight I am."

"Well, don't."

"You showed up one too many times, pal."

"Save your breath. Go outside and throw up. That's what you're good at."

"We're not leaving. And neither are you."

"Free country."

"Not for you. Not anymore."

Reacher stayed on his stool, tensed up and ready, but not visibly. Outwardly he was still calm and relaxed. His brother Joe had been two years older, physically very similar, but temperamentally very different. Joe had eased into fights. He had met escalation with escalation, reluctantly, slowly, rationally, patiently, a little sadly. Therefore he had been a frustrating opponent. Therefore according to the peculiar little-boy dynamics of the era, Joe's enemies had turned on Reacher himself, the younger brother. The first time, confronted with four baiting seven-year-olds, the five-year-old Reacher had felt a jolt of real fear. The jolt of fear had sparked wildly and jumped tracks in his brain and emerged as intense aggression. He had exploded into action and the fight was over before his four assailants had really intended it to begin. When they got out of the pediatric ward they had stayed well away from him, and his brother, forever. And in his earnest childhood manner Reacher had pondered the experience and felt he had learned a valuable lesson. Years later during advanced army training that lesson had been reinforced. At the grand strategic level it even had a title: *Overwhelming Force.* At the individual level in sweaty gyms the thugs doing the training had pointed out that gentlemen who behaved decently weren't around to train anyone. They were already dead. Therefore: *Hit early, hit hard.*

Overwhelming force.

Hit early, hit hard.

Reacher called it: *Get your retaliation in first.*

He slipped forward off his stool, turned, bent, grasped the iron pillar, spun, and hurled the stool head-high as hard as he could at the three men at the back of the room. Before it hit he launched the other way and charged the new guy next to the guy with the damaged jaw. He led with his elbow and smashed it flat against the bridge of the guy's nose. The guy went down like a tree and before he hit the boards Reacher jerked sideways from the waist and put the same elbow into the big guy's ear. Then he bounced away from the impact and backed into the guy with the bad jaw and buried the elbow deep in his gut. The guy folded forward and Reacher put his hand flat on the back of the guy's head and powered it downward into his raised knee and then shoved the guy away and turned around fast.

The stool had hit one of the deputies and the other new guy neck-high. Wood and iron, thrown hard, spinning horizontally. Maybe they had raised their hands instinctively and broken their wrists, or maybe they hadn't been fast enough and the stool had connected. Reacher wasn't sure. But either way the two guys were sidelined for the moment. They were turned away, bent over, crouched, with the stool still rolling noisily at their feet.

The other deputy was untouched. He was launching forward with a wild grimace on his face. Reacher danced two steps and took a left hook on the shoulder and put a straight right into the center of the grimace. The guy stumbled back and shook his head and Reacher's arms were clamped from behind in a bear hug. The big guy, presumably. Reacher forced him backward and dropped his chin to his chest and snapped a reverse head butt that made solid contact. Not as good as a forward-going blow, but useful. Then Reacher accelerated all the way backward and crushed the breath out of the guy against the wall. A mirror smashed and the arms loosened and Reacher pulled away and met the other deputy in the center of the room and dodged an incoming right and snapped a right of his own to the guy's jaw. Not a powerful blow, but it rocked the guy enough to open him up for a colossal left to the throat that put him down in a heap.

Eight blows delivered, one taken, one guy down for maybe a seven count, four down for maybe an eight count, the big guy still basically functional.

Not efficient.

Time to get serious.

The bartender had said: *Mr. Thurman looks after people if they get hurt on the job.* Reacher thought: *So let him. Because these guys are following Thurman's orders. Clearly nothing happens here except what Thurman wants.*

The deputy in the back of the room was rolling around and clutching his throat. Reacher kicked him in the ribs hard enough to break a couple and then forced the guy's forearm to the floor with one foot and stamped on it with the other. Then he moved on to the two guys he had hit with the stool. The second deputy, and the new guy. One was crouched down, clutching his forearm, whimpering. Reacher put the flat of his foot on the guy's backside and drove him headfirst into the wall. The other guy had maybe taken the edge of the seat in the chest, like a dull blade. He was having trouble breathing. Reacher kicked his feet out from under him and then kicked him in the head. Then he turned in time to dodge a right hook from the big guy. He took it in the shoulder. Looked for a response. But his balance wasn't good. Floor space was limited by inert assailants. The big guy threw a straight left and Reacher swatted it away and bulldozed a path back to the center of the room.

The big guy followed, fast. Threw a straight right.

Reacher jerked his head to the side and took the blow on the collarbone. It was a weak punch. The guy was pale in the face. He threw a wild breathless haymaker and Reacher stepped back out of range and glanced around.

One stool damaged, one mirror broken, five guys down, twenty spectators still passive. *So far so good.* The big guy stepped back and straightened like they were in a timeout and called, "Like you said, one of us would stay on his feet long enough to get to you."

Reacher said, "You're not getting to me. Not even a little bit." Which puzzled him, deep down. He was close to winning a six-on-one bar brawl and he had nothing to show for it except two bruised shoulders and an ache in his knuckles. It had gone way better than he could have hoped.

Then it started to go way worse.

The big guy said, "Think again." He put his hands in his pants pockets and came out with two switch-blades. Neat wooden handles, plated bindings, plated buttons. He stood in the dusty panting silence and popped the first blade with a precision *click* and then paused and popped the second.

30

The two small clicks the blades made were not attractive sounds. Reacher's stomach clenched. He hated knives. He would have preferred it if the guy had pulled a pair of six-shooters. Guns can miss. In fact they usually did, given stress and pressure and trembling and confusion. After-action reports proved it. The papers were always full of DOAs gunned down with seven bullets to the body, which sounded lethal until you read down into the third paragraph and learned that a hundred and fifty shots had been fired in the first place.

Knives didn't miss. If they touched you, they cut you. The only opponents Reacher truly feared were small whippy guys with fast hands and sharp blades. The big deputy was not fast or nimble, but with knives in his hands dodged blows would not mean dull impacts to the shoulders. They would mean open wounds, pouring blood, severed ligaments and arteries.

Not good.

Reacher clubbed a spectator out of his seat and grabbed the empty chair and held it out in front of him like a lion tamer. The best defense against knives was distance. The best countermove was entanglement. A swung net or coat or blanket was often effective. The blade would hang up in the fabric. But Reacher didn't have a net or a coat or a blanket. A horizontal forest of four chair legs was all he had. He jabbed forward like a fencer and then fell back and shoved another guy out of his seat. Picked up the second empty chair and threw it overhand at the big guy's head. The big guy turned away reflexively and brought his right hand up to shield his face and took the chair on the forearm. Reacher stepped back in and jabbed hard. Got one chair leg in the guy's solar plexus and another in his gut. The guy fell back and took a breath and then came on hard, arms swinging, the blades hissing through the air and winking in the lights.

Reacher danced backward and jabbed with his chair. Made solid contact with the guy's upper arm. The guy spun one way and then the other. Reacher moved left and jabbed again. Got a chair leg into the back of the guy's head. The guy staggered one short step and then came back hard, hands low and apart, the blades moving through tiny dangerous arcs.

Reacher backed off. Shoved a third spectator out of his seat and threw the empty chair high and hard. The big guy flinched away and jerked his arms up and the chair bounced off his elbows. Reacher was ready. He stepped in and jabbed hard and caught the guy low down in the side, below the ribs, above the waist, two hundred and fifty pounds of weight punched through the blunt end of a chair leg into nothing but soft tissue.

The big guy stopped fighting.

His body froze and went rigid and his face crumpled. He dropped both knives and clamped both hands low down on his stomach. For a long moment he stood like a statue and then he jerked forward from the waist and bent down and puked a long stream of blood and mucus on the floor. He staggered away in a crouch and fell to his knees. His shoulders sagged and his face went waxy and bloodless. His stomach heaved and he puked again. More blood, more mucus. He braced his spread fingertips either side of the spreading pool and tried to push himself upward. But he didn't make it. He collapsed sideways in a heap. His eyes rolled up in his head and he rolled on his back and he started breathing fast and shallow. One hand moved back to his stomach and the other beat on the floor. He threw up again, projectile, a fountain of blood vertically into the air. Then he rolled away and curled into a fetal ball.

Game over.

The bar went silent. No sound, except ragged breathing. The air was full of dust and the stink of blood and vomit. Reacher was shaky with excess adrenaline. He forced himself back under control and put his chair down quietly and bent and picked up the fallen knives. Pressed the blades back into the handles against the wood of the bar and slipped both knives into one pocket. Then he stepped around in the silence and checked his results. The first guy he had hit was unconscious on his back. The elbow to the bridge of the nose was always an effective blow.

Too hard, and it can slide shards of bone into the frontal lobes. Badly aimed, it can put splinters of cheekbone into the eye sockets. But this one had been perfectly judged. The guy would be sick and groggy for a week, but he would recover.

The guy who had started the evening with a busted jaw had added a rebroken nose and a bad headache. The new guy at the back of the room had a broken arm from the stool and maybe a concussion from being driven headfirst into the wall. The guy next to him was unconscious from the kick in the head. The deputy who the stool had missed had busted ribs and a broken wrist and a cracked larynx.

Major damage all around, but the whole enterprise had been voluntary from the start.

So, five for five, plus some kind of a medical explanation for the sixth. The big guy had stayed in the fetal position and looked very weak and pale. Like he was hollowed out with sickness. Reacher bent down and checked the pulse in his neck and found it weak and thready. He went through the guy's pockets and found a five-pointed star in the front of the shirt. The badge was made of pewter and two lines were engraved in its center: *Township of Despair, Police Deputy.* Reacher put it in his own shirt pocket. He found a bunch of keys and a thin wad of money in a brass clip. He kept the keys and left the cash. Then he looked around until he found the bartender. The guy was where he had started, leaning back with his fat ass against his register drawer.

"Call the plant," Reacher said. "Get the ambulance down here. Take care with the big guy. He doesn't look good."

His beer was where he had left it, still upright on its napkin. He drained the last of it and set the bottle back down again and walked out the front door into the night.

31

It took ten minutes of aimless driving south of the main drag before he found Nickel Street. The road signs were small and faded and the headlights on Vaughan's old truck were weak and set low. He deciphered Iron and Chromium and Vanadium and Molybdenum and then lost metals altogether and ran through a sequence of numbered avenues before he hit Steel and Platinum and then Gold. Nickel was a dead end off Gold. It had sixteen houses, eight facing eight, fifteen of them small and one of them bigger.

Thurman's pet judge Gardner lived in the big house on Nickel, the bartender had said. Reacher paused at the curb and checked the name on the big house's mailbox and then pulled the truck into the driveway and shut it down. Climbed out and walked to the porch. The place was a medium-sized farmhouse-style structure and looked pretty good relative to its neighbors, but there was no doubt that Gardner would have done better for himself if he had gotten out of town and made it to the Supreme Court in D.C. Or to whatever Circuit included Colorado, or even to night traffic court in Denver. The porch sagged against rotted underpinnings and the paint on the clapboards had aged to dust. Millwork had dried and split. There were twin newel posts at the top of the porch steps. Both had decorative ball shapes carved into their tops and both balls had split along the grain, like they had been attacked with cleavers.

Reacher found a bell push and tapped it twice with his knuckle. An old habit, about not leaving fingerprints if not strictly necessary. Then he waited. In Reacher's experience the average delay when knocking at a suburban door in the middle of the evening was about twenty seconds. Couples looked up from the television and looked at each other and asked, *Who could that be? At this time of night?* Then they mimed their way through offer and counteroffer and finally decided which one of them should make the trip down the hall. Before nine o'clock it was usually the wife. After nine, it was usually the husband.

It was Mrs. Gardner who opened up. The wife, after a twenty-three-second delay. She looked similar to her husband, bulky and somewhere over sixty, with a full head of white hair. Only the amount of the hair and the style of her clothing distinguished her gender. She had the kind of large firm curls that women get from big heated rollers and she was wearing a shapeless gray dress that reached her ankles. She stood there, patterned and indistinct behind a screen door. She said, "May I help you?"

Reacher said, "I need to see the judge."

"It's awful late," Mrs. Gardner said, which it wasn't. According to an old longcase clock in the hallway behind her it was eight twenty-nine, and according to the clock in Reacher's head it was eight thirty-one, but what the woman meant was: *You're a big ugly customer.* Reacher smiled. *Look at yourself,* Vaughan had said. *What do you see?* Reacher knew he was no kind of an ideal nighttime visitor. Nine times out of ten only Mormon missionaries were less welcome than him.

"It's urgent," he said.

The woman stood still and said nothing. In Reacher's experience the husband would show up if the doorstep interview lasted any longer than thirty seconds. He would crane his neck out of the living room and call, *Who is it, dear?* And Reacher wanted the screen door open long before that happened. He wanted to be able to stop the front door from closing, if necessary.

"It's urgent," he said again, and pulled the screen door. It screeched on worn hinges. The woman stepped back, but didn't try to slam the front door. Reacher stepped inside and let the screen slap shut behind him. The hallway smelled of still air and cooking. Reacher turned and closed the front door gently and clicked it against the latch. At that point the thirty seconds he had been counting in his head elapsed and the judge stepped out to the hallway.

The old guy was dressed in the same gray suit pants Reacher had seen before, but his suit coat was off and his tie was loose. He stood still for a moment, evidently searching his memory, because after ten long seconds puzzlement left his face and was replaced by an altogether different emotion, and he said, "You?"

Reacher nodded.

"Yes, me," he said.

"What do you want? What do you mean by coming here?"

"I came here to talk to you."

"I meant, what are you doing in Despair at all? You were excluded."

"Didn't take," Reacher said. "So sue me."

"I'm going to call the police."

"Please do. But they won't answer, as I'm sure you know. Neither will the deputies."

"Where are the deputies?"

"On their way up to the first-aid station."

"What happened to them?"

"I did."

The judge said nothing.

Reacher said, "And Mr. Thurman is up in his little airplane right now. Out of touch for another five and a half hours. So you're on your own. It's initiative time for Judge Gardner."

"What do you want?"

"I want you to invite me into your living room. I want you to ask me to sit down and whether I take cream and sugar in my coffee, which I don't, by the way. Because so far I'm here with your implied permission, and therefore I'm not trespassing. I'd like to keep it that way."

"You're not only trespassing, you're in violation of a town ordinance."

"That's what I'd like to talk about. I'd like you to reconsider. Consider it an appeals process."

"Are you nuts?"

"A little unconventional, maybe. But I'm not armed and I'm not making threats. I just want to talk."

"Get lost."

"On the other hand I am a large stranger with nothing to lose. In a town where there is no functioning law enforcement."

"I have a gun."

"I'm sure you do. In fact I'm sure you have several. But you won't use any of them."

"You think not?"

"You're a man of the law. You know what kind of hassle comes afterward. I don't think you want to face that kind of thing."

"You're taking a risk."

"Getting out of bed in the morning is a risk."

The judge said nothing to that. Didn't yield, didn't accede. Impasse. Reacher turned to the wife and took all the amiability out of his face and replaced it with the kind of thousand-yard stare he had used years ago on recalcitrant witnesses.

He asked, "What do you think, Mrs. Gardner?"

She started to speak a couple of times but couldn't get any words past a dry throat. Finally she said, "I think we should all sit down and talk." But the way she said it showed she wasn't all the way scared. She was a tough old bird. Probably had to be, to have survived sixty-some years in Despair, and marriage to the boss man's flunky.

Her husband huffed once and turned around and led the way into the living room. A sofa, an armchair, another armchair, with a lever on the side that meant it was a recliner. There was a coffee table and a large television set wired to a satellite box. The furniture was covered in a floral pattern that was duplicated in the drapes. The drapes were closed and had a ruffled pelmet made from the same fabric. Reacher suspected that Mrs. Gardner had sewed them herself.

The judge said, "Take a seat, I guess."

Mrs. Gardner said, "I'm not going to make coffee. I think under the circumstances that would be a step too far."

"Your choice," Reacher said. "But I have to tell you I'd truly appreciate some." He paused a moment and then sat down in the armchair. Gardner sat in the recliner. His wife stood for a moment longer and then sighed once and headed out of the room. A minute later Reacher heard water running and the quiet metallic sound of an aluminum percolator basket being rinsed.

Gardner said, "There is no appeal."

"There has to be," Reacher said. "It's a constitutional issue. The Fifth and the Fourteenth Amendments guarantee due process. At the very least there must be the possibility of judicial review."

"Are you serious?"

"Completely."

"You want to go to federal court over a local vagrancy ordinance?"

"I'd prefer you to concede that a mistake has been made, and then go ahead and tear up whatever paperwork was generated."

"There was no mistake. You are a vagrant, as defined by law."

"I'd like you to reconsider that."

"Why?"

"Why not?"

"I'd like to understand why it's so important to you to have free rein in our town."

"And I'd like to understand why it's so important to you to keep me out."

"Where's your loss? It's not much of a place."

"It's a matter of principle."

Gardner said nothing. A moment later his wife came in, with a single mug of coffee in her hand. She placed it carefully on the table in front of Reacher's chair and then backed away and sat down on the sofa. Reacher picked up the mug and took a sip. The coffee was hot, strong, and smooth. The mug was cylindrical, narrow in relation to its height, made of delicate bone china, and it had a thin lip.

"Excellent," Reacher said. "Thank you very much. I'm really very grateful."

Mrs. Gardner paused a beat and said, "You're really very welcome."

Reacher said, "You did a great job with the drapes, too."

Mrs. Gardner didn't reply to that. The judge said, "There's nothing I can do. There's no provision for an appeal. Sue the town, if you must."

Reacher said, "You told me you'd welcome me with open arms if I got a job."

The judge nodded. "Because that would remove the presumption of vagrancy."

"There you go."

"Have you gotten a job?"

"I have prospects. That's the other thing we need

to talk about. It's not healthy that this town has no functioning law enforcement. So I want you to swear me in as a deputy."

There was silence for a moment. Reacher took the pewter star from his shirt pocket. He said, "I already have the badge. And I have a lot of relevant experience."

"You're crazy."

"Just trying to fill a hole."

"You're completely insane."

"I'm offering my services."

"Finish your coffee and get out of my home."

"The coffee is hot and it's good. I can't just gulp it down."

"Then leave it. Get the hell out. Now."

"So you won't swear me in?"

The judge stood up and planted his feet wide and made himself as tall as he could get, which was about five feet nine inches. His eyes narrowed as his brain ran calculations about present dangers versus future contingencies. He was silent with preoccupation for a long moment and then he said, "I'd rather deputize the entire damn population. Every last man, woman, and child in Despair. In fact, I think I will. Twenty-six hundred people. You think you can get past them all? Because I don't. We aim to keep you out, mister, and we're going to. You better believe it. You can take that to the bank."

32

Reacher thumped back over the expansion joint at nine-thirty in the evening and was outside the diner before nine-thirty-five. He figured Vaughan might swing by there a couple of times during the night. He figured that if he left her truck on the curb she would see it and be reassured that he was OK. Or at least that her truck was OK.

He went inside to leave her keys at the register and saw Lucy Anderson sitting alone in a booth. Short shorts, blue sweatshirt, tiny socks, big sneakers. A lot of bare leg. She was gazing into space and smiling. The first time he had seen her he had characterized her as not quite a hundred percent pretty. Now she looked pretty damn good. She looked radiant, and taller, and straighter. She looked like a completely different person.

She had changed.

Before, she had been hobbled by worry.

Now she was happy.

He paused at the register and she noticed him and looked over and smiled. It was a curious smile. There was a lot of straightforward contentment in it, but a little triumph, too. A little superiority. Like she had won a significant victory, at his expense.

He handed Vaughan's keys to the cashier and the woman asked, "Are you eating with us tonight?" He thought about it. His stomach had settled. The adrenaline had drained away. He realized he was hungry. No sustenance since breakfast, except for coffee and some empty calories from the bottle of Bud in the bar. And he had burned plenty of calories in the bar. That was for sure. He was facing an energy deficit. So he said, "Yes, I guess I'm ready for dinner."

He walked over and slid into Lucy Anderson's booth. She looked across the table at him and smiled the same smile all over again. Contentment, triumph, superiority, victory. Up close the smile looked a lot bigger and it had a bigger effect. It was a real megawatt grin. She had great teeth. Her eyes were bright and clear and blue. He said, "This afternoon you looked like Lucy. Now you look like Lucky."

She said, "Now I feel like Lucky."

"What changed?"

"What do you think?"

"You heard from your husband."

She smiled again, a hundred percent happiness.

"I sure did," she said.

"He left Despair."

"He sure did. Now you'll never get him."

"I never wanted him. I never heard of him before I met you."

"Really," she said, in the exaggerated and sarcastic way he had heard young people use the word. As far as he understood it, the effect was intended to convey: *How big of an idiot do you think I am?*

He said, "You're confusing me with someone else."

"Really."

Look at yourself, Vaughan had said. *What do you see?*

"I'm not a cop," Reacher said. "I was one oncc, and maybe I still look like one to you, but I'm not one anymore."

She didn't answer. But he knew she wasn't convinced. He said, "Your husband must have left late this afternoon. He was there at three and gone before seven."

"You went back?"

"I've been there twice today."

"Which proves you were looking for him."

"I guess I was. But only on your behalf."

"Really."

"What did he do?"

"You already know."

"If I already know, it can't hurt to tell me again, can it?"

"I'm not stupid. My position is I don't know about anything he's done. Otherwise you'll call me an accessory. We have lawyers, you know."

"We?"

"People in our position. Which you know all about."

"I'm not a cop, Lucky. I'm just a passing stranger. I don't know all about anything."

She smiled again. Happiness, triumph, victory.

Reacher asked, "Where has he gone?"

"Like I'd tell you *that.*"

"When are you joining him, wherever he is?"

"In a couple of days."

"I could follow you."

She smiled again, impregnable. "Wouldn't do you any good."

The waitress came by and Reacher asked her for coffee and steak. When she had gone away again he looked across at Lucy Anderson and said, "There are others in the position you were in yesterday. There's a girl in town right now, just waiting."

"I hope there are plenty of us."

"I think maybe she's waiting in vain. I know that a boy died out there a day or two ago."

Lucy Anderson shook her head.

"Not possible," she said. "I know that none of us died. I would have heard."

"Us?"

"People in our position."

"Somebody died."

"People die all the time."

"Young people? For no apparent reason?"

She didn't answer that, and he knew she never would. The waitress brought his coffee. He took a sip. It was not as good as Mrs. Gardner's, either in terms of brew or receptacle. He put the mug down and looked at the girl again and said, "Whatever, Lucy. I wish you nothing but good luck, whatever the hell you're doing and wherever the hell you're going."

"That's it? No more questions?"

"I'm just here to eat."

He ate alone, because Lucy Anderson left before his steak arrived. She smiled and slid out of the booth and walked away. More accurately, she skipped away. Light on her feet, happy, full of energy. She pushed out through the door and instead of huddling into her shirt against the chill she squared her shoulders and turned her face upward and breathed the night air like she was in an enchanted forest. Reacher watched her until she was lost to sight and then gazed into space until his food showed up.

He was through eating by ten-thirty and headed back to the motel. He dropped by the office, to pay for another night's stay. He always rented rooms one night at a time, even when he knew he was going to hang out in a place longer. It was a reassuring habit. A comforting ritual, intended to confirm his absolute freedom to move on. The day clerk was still on duty. The stout woman. The nosy woman. He assembled a collection of small bills and waited for his change and said, "Go over what you were telling me about the metal plant."

"What was I telling you?"

"Violations. Real crimes. You were interested in why the plane flies every night."

The woman said, "So you *are* a cop."

"I used to be. Maybe I still have the old habits."

The woman shrugged and looked a little sheepish. Maybe even blushed a little.

"It's just silly amateur stuff," she said. "That's what you'll think."

"Amateur?"

"I'm a day trader. I do research on my computer. I was thinking about that operation."

"What about it?"

"It seems to make way too much money. But what do I know? I'm not an expert. I'm not a broker or a forensic accountant or anything."

"Talk me through it."

"Business sectors go up and down. There are cycles, to do with commodity prices and supply and demand and market conditions. Right now metal recycling as a whole is in a down cycle. But that place is raking it in."

"How do you know?"

"Employment seems to be way up."

"That's pretty vague."

"It files taxes, federal and state. I looked at the figures, to pass the time."

And because you're a nosy neighbor, Reacher thought.

"And?" he asked.

"It's reporting great profits. If it was a public company, I'd be buying stock, big time. If I had any money, that is. If I wasn't a motel clerk."

"OK."

"But it's not a public company. It's private. So it's probably making more than it's reporting."

"So you think they're cutting corners out there? With environmental violations?"

"I wouldn't be surprised."

"Would that make much difference? I thought rules were pretty slack now anyway."

"Maybe."

"What about the plane?"

The woman glanced away. "Just silly thoughts."

"Try me."

"Well, I was just thinking, if the fundamentals don't support the profits, and it's not about violations, then maybe there's something else going on."

"Like what?"

"Maybe that plane is bringing stuff in every night. To sell. Like smuggling."

"What kind of stuff?"

"Stuff that isn't metal."

"From where?"

"I'm not sure."

Reacher said nothing.

The woman said, "See? What do I know? I have too much time on my hands, that's all. Way too much. And broadband. That can really do a person's head in."

She turned away and busied herself with an entry in a book and Reacher put his change in his pocket. Before he left he glanced at the row of hooks behind the clerk's shoulder and saw that four keys were missing. Therefore four rooms were occupied. His own, Lucy Anderson's, one for the woman with the large underwear, and one for the new girl in town, he guessed. The dark girl, who he hadn't met yet, but who he might meet soon. He suspected that she was going to be in town longer than Lucy Anderson, and he suspected that at the end of her stay she wasn't going to be skipping away with a smile on her face.

He went back to his room and showered, but he was too restless to sleep. So as soon as the stink of the bar fight was off him he dressed again and went out and walked. On a whim he stopped at a phone booth under a streetlight and pulled the directory and looked up David Robert Vaughan. He was right there in the book. Vaughan, D. R., with an address on Fifth Street, Hope, Colorado.

Two blocks south.

He had seen Fourth Street. Perhaps he should take a look at Fifth Street, too. Just for the sake of idle curiosity.

33

Fifth Street was more or less a replica of Fourth Street, except that it was residential on both sides. Trees, yards, picket fences, mailboxes, small neat houses resting quietly in the moonlight. A nice place to live, probably. Vaughan's house was close to the eastern limit. Nearer Kansas than Despair. It had a plain aluminum mailbox out front, mounted on a store-bought wooden post. The post had been treated against decay. The box had *Vaughan* written on both sides with stick-on italic letters. They had been carefully applied and were perfectly aligned. Rare, in Reacher's experience. Most people seemed to have trouble with stick-on letters. He imagined that the glue was too aggressive to allow the correction of mistakes. To get seven letters each side level and true spoke of meticulous planning. Maybe a straightedge had been taped in position first, and then removed.

The house and the yard had been maintained to a high standard, too. Reacher was no expert, but he could tell the difference between care and neglect. The yard had no lawn. It was covered with golden gravel, with shrubs and bushes pushing up through the stones. The driveway was paved with small riven slabs that seemed to be the same color as the gravel. The same slabs made a narrower winding walkway to the door. More slabs were set here and there in the gravel, like stepping-stones. The bushes and the shrubs were neatly pruned. Some of them had small flowers on their branches, all closed up for the night against the chill.

The house itself was a low one-story ranch maybe fifty years old. At the right-hand end was a single attached garage and at the left was a T-shaped bump-out that maybe housed the bedrooms, one front, one back. Reacher guessed the kitchen would be next to the garage and the living room would be between the kitchen and the bedrooms. There was a chimney. The siding and the roof tiles were not new, but they had been replaced within living memory and had settled and weathered into pleasant maturity.

A nice house.

An empty house.

It was dark and silent. Some drapes were halfway open, and some were all the way open. No light inside, except a tiny green glow in one window. Probably the kitchen, probably a microwave clock. Apart from that, no sign of life. Nothing. No sound, no subliminal hum, no vibe. Once upon a time Reacher had made his living storming darkened buildings, and more than once it had been a matter of life or death to decide whether they were occupied or not. He had developed a sense, and his sense right then was that Vaughan's house was empty.

So where was David Robert?

At work, possibly. Maybe they both worked nights.

Some couples chose to coordinate their schedules that way. Maybe David Robert was a nurse or a doctor or worked night construction on the Interstates. Maybe he was a journalist or a print worker, involved with newspapers. Maybe he was in the food trade, getting stuff ready for morning markets. Maybe he was a radio DJ, broadcasting through the night on a powerful AM station. Or maybe he was a long-haul trucker or an actor or a musician and was on the road for lengthy spells. Maybe for months at a time. Maybe he was a sailor or an airline pilot.

Maybe he was a state policeman.

Vaughan had asked: *Don't I look married?*

No, Reacher thought. *You really don't. Not like some people do.*

He found a leafy cross-street and walked back north to Second Street. Vaughan's truck was still parked where he had left it. The diner's lights were spilling out all over it. He walked another block and came out on First Street. There was no cloud in the sky. Plenty of moon. To his right there was silvery flatness all the way to Kansas. To his left the Rockies were faintly visible, dim and blue and bulky, with their north-facing snow channels lit up like ghostly blades, impossibly high. The town was still and silent and lonely. Not quite eleven-thirty in the evening, and no one was out and about. No traffic. No activity at all.

Reacher was no kind of an insomniac, but he didn't feel like sleep. Too early. Too many questions. He walked a block on First Street and then headed south again, toward the diner. He was no kind of a social animal either, but right then he wanted to see people, and he figured the diner was the only place he was going to find any.

He found four. The college-girl waitress, an old guy in a seed cap eating alone at the counter, a middle-aged guy alone in a booth with a spread of tractor catalogs in front of him, and a frightened Hispanic girl alone in a booth with nothing.

Dark, not blonde, Vaughan had said. *Sitting around and staring west like she's waiting for word from Despair.*

She was tiny. She was about eighteen or nineteen years old. She had long center-parted jet-black hair that framed a face that had a high forehead and enormous eyes. The eyes were brown and looked like twin pools of terror and tragedy. Under them were a small nose and a small mouth. Reacher guessed she had a pretty smile but didn't use it often and certainly hadn't used it for weeks. Her skin was mid-brown and her pose was absolutely still. Her hands were out of sight under the table but Reacher was sure they were clasped together in her lap. She was wearing a blue San Diego Padres warm-up jacket with a blue scoop-neck T-shirt under it. There was nothing on the table in front of her. No plate, no cup. But she hadn't just arrived. The way she was settled meant she must have been sitting there for ten or fifteen minutes at least. Nobody could have gotten so still any faster.

Reacher stepped to the far side of the register and the college-girl waitress joined him there. Reacher bent his head, at an angle, universal body language for: *I want to talk to you quietly.* The waitress moved a little closer and bent her own head at a parallel angle, like a co-conspirator.

"That girl," Reacher said. "Didn't she order?"

The waitress whispered, "She has no money."

"Ask her what she wants. I'll pay for it." He moved away to a different booth, where he could watch the girl without being obvious about it. He saw the waitress approach her, saw incomprehension on the girl's face, then doubt, then refusal. The waitress stepped over to Reacher's booth and whispered, "She says she can't possibly accept."

Reacher said, "Go back and tell her there are no strings attached. Tell her I'm not hitting on her. Tell her I don't even want to talk to her. Tell her I've been broke and hungry, too."

The waitress went back. This time the girl relented. She pointed to a couple of items on the menu. Reacher was sure they were the cheapest choices. The waitress went away to place the order and the girl turned a little in her seat and inclined her head in a courteous little nod, full of dignity, and the corners of her mouth softened like the beginnings of a smile. Then she turned back and went still again.

The waitress came straight back to Reacher and he asked for coffee. The waitress whispered, "Her check is going to be nine-fifty. Yours will be a dollar and a half." Reacher peeled a ten and three ones off the roll in his pocket and slid them across the table. The waitress picked them up and thanked him for the tip and asked, "So when were you broke and hungry?"

"Never," Reacher said. "My whole life I got three

squares a day from the army and since then I've always had money in my pocket."

"So you made that up just to make her feel better?"

"Sometimes people need convincing."

"You're a nice guy," the waitress said.

"Not everyone agrees with that."

"But some do."

"Do they?"

"I hear things."

"What things?"

But the girl just smiled at him and walked away.

From a safe distance Reacher watched the Hispanic girl eat a tuna melt sandwich and drink a chocolate milk shake. Good choices, nutritionally. Excellent value for his money. Protein, fats, carbs, some sugar. If she ate like that every day she would weigh two hundred pounds before she was thirty, but in dire need on the road it was wise to load up. After she was finished she dabbed her lips with her napkin and pushed her plate and her glass away and then sat there, just as quiet and still as before. The clock in Reacher's head hit midnight and the clock on the diner's wall followed it a minute later. The old guy in the seed cap crept out with a creaking arthritic gait and the tractor salesman gathered his paperwork together and called for another cup of coffee.

The Hispanic girl stayed put. Reacher had seen plenty of people doing what she was doing, in cafés and diners near bus depots and railroad stations. She was staying warm, saving energy, passing time. She was enduring. He watched her profile and figured she was a lot closer to Zeno's ideal than he was. *The unquestioning acceptance of destinies.* She looked infinitely composed and patient.

The tractor salesman drained his final cup and gathered his stuff and left. The waitress backed away to a corner and picked up a paperback book. Reacher curled his fist around his mug to keep it warm.

The Hispanic girl stayed put.

Then she moved. She shifted sideways on her vinyl bench and stood up all in one smooth, delicate motion. She was extremely petite. Not more than five-nothing, not more than ninety-some pounds. Below the T-shirt she was wearing jeans and cheap shoes. She stood still and faced the door and then she turned toward Reacher's booth. There was nothing in her face. Just fear and shyness and loneliness. She came to some kind of a decision and stepped forward and stood off about a yard and said, "You can talk to me if you really want to."

Reacher shook his head. "I meant what I said."

"Thank you for my dinner." Her voice matched her physique. It was small and delicate. It was lightly accented, but English was probably her primary language. She was from southern California for sure. The Padres were probably her home team.

Reacher asked, "You OK for breakfast tomorrow?"

She was still for a moment while she fought her pride and then she shook her head.

Reacher asked, "Lunch? Dinner tomorrow?"

She shook her head.

"You OK at the motel?"

"That's why. I paid for three nights. It took all my money."

"You have to eat."

The girl said nothing. Reacher thought, *Ten bucks a meal is thirty bucks a day, three days makes ninety, plus ten for contingencies or phone calls makes a hundred.* He peeled five ATM-fresh twenties off his roll and fanned them on the table. The girl said, "I can't take your money. I couldn't pay it back."

"Pay it forward instead."

The girl said nothing.

"You know what pay it forward means?"

"I'm not sure."

"It means years from now you'll be in a diner somewhere and you'll see someone who needs a break. So you'll help them out."

The girl nodded.

"I could do that," she said.

"So take the money."

She stepped closer and picked up the bills.

"Thank you," she said.

"Don't thank me. Thank whoever helped me way back. And whoever helped him before that. And so on."

"Have you ever been to Despair?"

"Four times in the last two days."

"Did you see anyone there?"

"I saw lots of people."

She moved closer still and put her slim hips against the end of his table. She hoisted a cheap vinyl purse and propped it on the laminate against her belly and unsnapped the clasp. She dipped her head and her hair fell forward. Her hands were small and brown and had no rings on the fingers or polish on the nails. She rooted around in her bag for a moment and came out with an envelope. It was stiff and nearly square. From a greeting card, probably. She opened the flap and pulled out a photograph. She held it neatly between her thumb and her forefinger and put her little fist on the table and adjusted its position until Reacher could see the picture at a comfortable angle.

"Did you see this man?" she asked.

It was another standard one-hour six-by-four color print. Glossy paper, no border. Shot on Fuji film, Reacher guessed. Back when it had mattered for forensic purposes he had gotten pretty good at recognizing film stock by its color biases. This print had strong greens, which was a Fuji characteristic. Kodak products favored the reds and the warmer tones. The camera had been a decent unit with a proper glass lens. There was plenty of detail. Focus was not quite perfect. The choice of aperture was not inspired. The depth of field was neither shallow nor deep. An old SLR, Reacher thought, therefore bought secondhand or borrowed from an older person. There was no retail market for decent film cameras anymore. Everyone had moved into digital technology. The print in the girl's hand was clearly recent, but it looked like a much older product. It was a pleasant but unexceptional picture from an old SLR loaded with Fujicolor and wielded by an amateur.

He took the print from the girl and held it between his own thumb and forefinger. The bright greens in the photograph were in a background expanse of grass and a foreground expanse of T-shirt. The grass looked watered and forced and manicured and was probably in a city park somewhere. The T-shirt was a cheap cotton product being worn by a thin guy of about nineteen or twenty. The camera was looking up at him, as if the photograph was being taken by a much shorter person. The guy was posing quite formally and awkwardly. There was no spontaneity in his stance. Maybe repeated fumbles with the camera's controls had required him to hold his position a little too long. His smile was genuine but a little frozen. He had white teeth in a brown face. He looked young, and friendly, and amiable, and fun to be around, and completely harmless.

Not thin, exactly.

He looked lean and wiry.

Not short, not tall. About average, in terms of height.

He looked to be about five feet eight.

He looked to weigh about a hundred and forty pounds.

He was Hispanic, but as much Mayan or Aztec as Spanish. There was plenty of pure Indian blood in him. That was for sure. He had shiny black hair, not brushed, a little tousled, neither long nor short. Maybe an inch and a half or two inches, with a clear tendency to wave.

He had prominent cheekbones.

He was casually dressed, and casually turned out.

He hadn't shaved.

His chin and his upper lip were rough with black stubble.

His cheeks and his throat, not so much.

Young.

Not much more than a boy.

The girl asked, "Did you see him?"

Reacher asked, "What's your name?"

"*My* name?"

"Yes."

"Maria."

"What's his name?"

"Raphael Ramirez."

"Is he your boyfriend?"

"Yes."

"How old is he?"

"Twenty."

"Did you take this picture?"

"Yes."

"In a park in San Diego?"

"Yes."

"With your dad's camera?"

"My uncle's," the girl said. "How did you know?"

Reacher didn't answer. He looked again at Raphael Ramirez in the photograph. Maria's boyfriend. Twenty years old. Five-eight, one-forty. The build. The hair, the cheekbones, the stubble.

The girl asked, "Did you see him?"

Reacher shook his head.

"No," he said. "I didn't see him."

34

The girl left the diner. Reacher watched her go. He thought that an offer to walk her back to the motel might be misinterpreted, as if he was after something more for his hundred bucks than a feel-good glow. And she was in no kind of danger, anyway. Hope seemed to be a safe enough place. Unlikely to be packs of malefactors roaming the streets, mainly because nobody was roaming the streets. It was the middle of the night in a quiet, decent place in the middle of nowhere. So Reacher let her walk away and sat alone in his booth and roused the college girl from her book and had her bring him more coffee.

"You'll never sleep," she said.

"How often does Officer Vaughan swing by during the night?" he asked.

The girl smiled the same smile she had used before, right after she said *I hear things*.

"At least once," she said, and smiled again.

He said, "She's married."

She said, "I know." She took the flask away and headed back to her book and left him with a steaming mug. He dipped his head and inhaled the smell. When he looked up again he saw Vaughan's cruiser glide by outside. She slowed, as if she was noting that her truck was back. But she didn't stop. She slid right by the diner's window and drove on down Second Street.

Reacher left the diner at one o'clock in the morning and walked back to the motel. The moon was still out. The town was still quiet. The motel office had a low light burning. The rooms were all dark. He sat down in the plastic lawn chair outside his door and stretched his legs straight out and put his hands behind his head and listened to the silence, eyes wide open, staring into the moonlight.

It didn't work. He didn't relax.

You'll never sleep, the waitress had said.

But not because of the coffee, he thought.

He got up again and walked away. Straight back to the diner. There were no customers. The waitress was reading her book. Reacher stepped straight to the register and took Vaughan's truck keys off the counter. The waitress looked up but didn't speak. Reacher stepped back to the door and caught it before it closed. Headed out across the sidewalk to the truck. Unlocked it, got in, started it up. Five minutes later he thumped over the line and was back in Despair.

The first twelve miles of empty road were predictably quiet. The town was quiet, too. Reacher slowed at the gas station and coasted down to twenty miles an hour and took a good look around. Main Street was deserted and silent. No cars on the streets, nobody on the sidewalks. The police station was dark. The rooming house was dark. The bar was closed up and shuttered. The hotel was just a blank façade, with a closed street door and a dozen dark windows. The church was empty and silent. The green grounding strap from the lightning rod was stained gray by the moonlight.

He drove on until the street petered out into half-colonized scrubland. He pulled a wide circle on the packed sand and stopped and idled with the whole town laid out north of him. It was lit up silver by the moon. It was just crouching there, silent and deserted and insignificant in the vastness.

He threaded his way back to Main Street. Turned left and headed onward, west, toward the metal plant.

The plant was shut down and dark. The wall around it glowed ghostly white in the moonlight. The personnel gate was closed. The acres of parking were deserted. Reacher followed the wall and steered the truck left and right until its weak low beams picked up the Tahoes' tracks. He followed their giant figure 8, all the way around the plant and the residential compound. The plantings were black and massive. The windsocks hung limp in the air. The plant's vehicle gate was shut. Reacher drove slowly past it and then bumped up across the truck road and drove another quarter-turn through the dirt and stopped where the figure 8's two loops met, in the throat between the plant's metal wall and the residential compound's fieldstone wall. He shut off his lights and shut down the engine and rolled down the windows and waited.

He heard the plane at five past two in the morning. A single engine, far in the distance, feathering and blipping. He craned his neck and saw a light in the sky, way to the south. A landing light. It looked motionless, like it would be suspended up there forever. Then it grew imperceptibly bigger and started hopping slightly, side to side, up and down, but mostly down. A small plane, on approach, buffeted by nighttime thermals and rocked by a firm hand on nervous controls. Its sound grew closer, but quieter, as the pilot shed power and looked for a glide path.

Lights came on beyond the fieldstone wall. A dull reflected glow. Runway markers, Reacher guessed, one at each end of the strip. He saw the plane move in the air, jumping left, correcting right, lining up with the lights. It was coming in from Reacher's left. When it was three hundred yards out he saw that it was a smallish low-wing monoplane. It was white. When it was two hundred yards out he saw that it had a fixed undercarriage, with fairings over all three wheels, called *pants* by airplane people. When it was a hundred yards out he identified it as a Piper, probably some kind of a Cherokee variant, a four-seater, durable, reliable, common, and popular. Beyond that, he had no information. He knew a little about small planes, but not a lot.

It came in low left-to-right across his windshield in a high-speed rush of light and air and sound. It cleared the fieldstone wall by six feet and dropped out of sight. The engine blipped and feathered and then a minute later changed its note to a loud angry buzzing. Reacher imagined the plane taxiing like a fat self-important insect, white in the moonlight, bumping sharply over rough ground, turning abruptly on its short wheelbase, heading for its barn. Then he heard it shut down and stunned silence flooded in his windows, even more intense than before.

The runway lights went off.

He saw and heard nothing more.

He waited ten minutes for safety's sake and then started the truck and backed up and turned and drove away on the blind side, with the bulk of the plant between him and the house. He bumped through the acres of empty parking, skirted the short end of the plant, and joined the truck route. He put his headlights on and got comfortable in his seat and settled to a fast cruise on the firm wide surface, heading out of town westward, toward the MPs and whatever lay forty miles beyond them.

35

The MPs were all asleep, except for two on sentry duty inside the guard shack. Reacher saw them as he drove past, bulky figures in the gloom, dressed in desert camos and vests, MP brassards, no helmets. They had an orange nightlight burning near the floor, to preserve their night vision. They were standing back to back, one watching the southern approach, one the northern. Reacher slowed and waved, and then hit the gas again and kept on going.

Thirty miles later the solid truck road swung sharply to the right and speared north through the darkness toward the distant Interstate. But the old route it must have been built over meandered on straight ahead, unsignposted and apparently aimless. Reacher followed it. He bumped down off the flat coarse blacktop onto a surface as bad as Despair's own road. Lumpy, uneven, cheaply top-dressed with gravel on tar. He followed it between two ruined farms and entered an empty spectral world with nothing on his left and nothing on his right and nothing ahead of him except the wandering gray ribbon of road and the silver moonlit mountains remote in the distance. Nothing happened for four more miles. He seemed to make no progress at all through the landscape. Then he passed a lone roadside sign that said: *Halfway County Route 37*. A mile later he saw a glow in the air. He came up a long rise and the road peaked and fell away into the middle distance and suddenly laid out right in front of him was a neat checkerboard of lit streets and pale buildings. Another mile later he passed a sign that said: *Halfway Township*. He slowed and checked his mirrors and pulled to the shoulder and stopped.

The town in front of him was aptly named. Another trick of topography put the moonlit Rockies closer again. The hardy souls who had struggled onward from Despair had been rewarded for forty miles of actual travel with an apparent hundred miles of progress. But by then they would have been wise enough and bitter enough not to get carried away with enthusiasm, so they had given their next resting place the suitably cautious name of Halfway, perhaps secretly hoping that their unassuming modesty would be further rewarded by finding out that they were in fact more than halfway there. *Which they weren't,* Reacher thought. Forty miles was forty miles, optical illusions notwithstanding. They were only a fifth of the way there. But the wagons had rolled out of Despair with only the optimists aboard, and the town of Halfway reflected their founding spirit. The place looked crisp and bright and livelier in the dead of night than Despair had in the middle of the day. It had been rebuilt, perhaps several times. There was nothing ancient visible. The structures Reacher could make out seemed to be seventies' stucco and eighties' glass, not nineteenth-century brick. In the age of fast transportation there was no real reason why one nearby town rather than another should be chosen for investment and development, except for inherited traits of vibrancy and vigor. Despair had suffered and Halfway had prospered, and the optimists had won, like they sometimes deserved to.

Reacher coasted down the rise into town. It was a quarter past three in the morning. Plenty of places were lit up but not many were actually open. A gas station and a coffee shop was about all, at first sight. But the town and the county shared the same name, which in Reacher's experience implied that certain services would be available around the clock. County police, for instance. They would have a station somewhere, manned all night. There would be a hospital, too, with a 24-7 emergency room. And to serve the gray area in between, where perhaps the county police were interested and the emergency room had failed, there would be a morgue. And it would be open for business night and day. A county town with a cluster of dependent municipalities all around it had to provide essential services. There was no morgue in Hope or Despair. *Not even a meat locker,* Vaughan had said, and presumably other local towns were in the same situation. And shit happened, and ambulances had to go somewhere. Dead folks couldn't be left out in the street until the next business day. Usually.

Morgues were normally close to hospitals, and a redeveloped county seat would normally have a new hospital, and new hospitals were normally built on the outskirts of towns, where land was empty and available and cheap. Halfway had one road in from the east, and a spider web of four roads out north and west, and Reacher found the hospital a half mile out on the second exit road he tried. It was a place the size of a university campus, long, low, and deep, with buildings like elongated ski chalets. It looked calm and friendly, like sickness and death were really no big deal. It had a vast parking lot, empty except for a cluster of battered cars near a staff entrance and a lone shiny sedan in a section marked off with ferocious warning signs: *MD Parking Only.* Steam drifted from vents from a building in back. The laundry, Reacher guessed, where sheets and towels were being washed overnight by the drivers of the battered cars, while the guy from the shiny sedan tried to keep people alive long enough to use them in the morning.

He avoided the front entrances. He wanted dead people, not sick people, and he knew how to find them. He had visited more morgues than wards in his life, by an order of magnitude. Morgues were usually well hidden from the public. A sensitivity issue. They were often not signposted at all, or else labeled something anodyne like *Special Services.* But they were always accessible. Meat wagons had to be able to roll in and out unobstructed.

He found Halfway's county morgue in back, next to the hospital laundry, which he thought was a smart design. The laundry's drifting steam would camouflage the output of the morgue's crematorium chimney. The place was another low, wide, chalet-style building. It had a high steel fence, and a sliding gate, and a guard shack.

The fence was solid, and the gate was closed, and there was a guard in the shack.

Reacher parked off to one side and climbed out of the truck and stretched. The guard watched him do it. Reacher finished stretching and glanced around like he was getting his bearings and then headed straight for the shack. The guard slid back the bottom part of his window and ducked his head down, like he needed to line up his ears with the empty space to hear properly. He was a middle-aged guy, lean, probably competent but not ambitious. He was a rent-a-cop. He was wearing a dark generic uniform with a molded plastic shield like something from a toy store. It said *Security* on it. Nothing more. It could have done double duty at an outlet mall. Maybe it did. Maybe the guy worked two jobs, to make ends meet.

Reacher ducked his own head toward the open section of window and said, "I need to check some details on the guy Despair brought in yesterday morning."

The guard said, "The attendants are inside."

Reacher nodded as if he had received new and valuable information and waited for the guy to hit the button that would slide the gate.

The guy didn't move.

Reacher asked, "Were you here yesterday morning?"

The guard said, "Everything after midnight is morning."

"This would have been daylight hours."

The guard said, "Not me, then. I get off at six."

Reacher said, "So can you let me through? To ask the attendants?"

"They change at six, too."

"They'll have paperwork in there."

The guard said, "I can't."

"Can't what?"

"Can't let you through. Law enforcement personnel only. Or paramedics with a fresh one."

Reacher said, "I am law enforcement. I'm with the Despair PD. We need to check something."

"I'd need to see some credentials."

"They don't give us much in the way of credentials. I'm only a deputy."

"I'd have to see something."

Reacher nodded and took the big guy's pewter star out of his shirt pocket. Held it face out, with the pin between his thumb and forefinger. The guard looked at it carefully. *Township of Despair, Police Deputy.*

"All they give us," Reacher said.

"Good enough for me," the guy said, and hit the button. A motor spun up and a gear engaged and drove the gate along a greased track. As soon as it was three feet open Reacher stepped through and headed across a yard through a pool of yellow sulfur light to a personnel door labeled *Receiving.* He went straight in and found a standby room like a million others he had seen. Desk, computer, clipboards, drifts of paper, bulletin boards, low wood-and-tweed armchairs. Everything was reasonably new but already battered. There were heaters going but the air was cold. There was an internal door, closed, but Reacher could smell sharp cold chemicals through it. Two of the low armchairs were occupied by two guys. They were white, young, and lean. They looked equally equipped for either manual or clerical labor. They looked bored and a little irreverent, which is exactly what Reacher expected from people working night shifts around a cold store full of stiffs. They glanced up at him, a little put out by the intrusion into their sealed world, a little happy about the break in their routine.

"Help you?" one of them said.

Reacher held up his pewter star again and said, "I need to check something about the guy we brought in yesterday."

The attendant who had spoken squinted at the star. "Despair?"

Reacher nodded and said, "Male DOA, young, not huge."

One guy heaved himself out of his chair and dumped himself down in front of the desk and tapped the keyboard to wake the computer screen. The other guy swiveled in his seat and grabbed a clipboard and licked his thumb and leafed through sheets of paper. They both reached the same conclusion at the same time. They glanced at each other and the one who had spoken before said, "We didn't get anything from Despair yesterday."

"You sure about that?"

"Did you bring him in yourself?"

"No."

"You sure he was DOA? Maybe he went to the ICU."

"He was DOA. No doubt about it."

"Well, we don't have him."

"No possibility of a mistake?"

"Couldn't happen."

"Your paperwork is always a hundred percent?"

"Has to be. Start of the shift, we eyeball the toe tags and match them against the list. Procedure. Because people get sensitive about shit like dead relatives going missing."

"Understandable, I guess."

"So tonight we've got five on the list and five in the freezer. Two female, three male. Not a one of them young. And not a one of them from Despair."

"Anywhere else they could have taken him?"

"Not in this county. And no other county would have accepted him." The guy tapped some more keys. "As of this exact minute the last Despair stiff we had was over a year ago. Accident at their metal plant. Adult male all chewed up, as I recall, by a machine. Not pretty. He was so spread out we had to put him in two drawers."

Reacher nodded and the guy spun his chair and put himself back-to against the desk with his feet straight out and his elbows propped behind him.

"Sorry," he said.

Reacher nodded again and stepped back outside to the pool of sulfur light. The door sucked shut behind him, on a spring closer. *To assume makes an ass out of you and me. Ass, u, me.* The classroom jerks at Rucker had added: *You absolutely have to verify.*

Reacher walked back across the concrete and waited for the gate to grind open a yard and stepped through and climbed into Vaughan's truck.

He had verified.

Absolutely.

36

Reacher drove a mile and stopped at Halfway's all-night coffee shop and ate a cheeseburger and drank three mugs of coffee. The burger was rare and damp and the coffee was about as good as the Hope diner's. The mug was a little worse, but acceptable. He read a ragged copy of the previous morning's newspaper all the way through and then jammed himself into the corner of his booth and dozed upright for an hour. He left the place at five in the morning, when the first of the breakfast customers came in and disturbed him with bright chatter and the smell of recent showers. He filled Vaughan's truck at the all-night gas station and then drove back out of town, heading east on the same rough road he had come in on, the mountains far behind him and the dawn waiting to happen up ahead.

He kept the speedometer needle fixed on forty and passed the MP post again fifty-two minutes later. The place was still quiet. Two guys were in the guard shack, one facing north and one facing south. Their nightlight was still burning. He figured reveille would be at six-thirty and chow at seven. The night watch would eat dinner and the day watch would eat breakfast all in the same hour. Same food, probably. Combat FOBs were light on amenities. He waved and kept on going at a steady forty miles an hour, which put him next to the metal plant at exactly six o'clock in the morning.

The start of the workday.

The arena lights were already on and the place was lit up bright and blue, like day. The parking lot was filling up fast. Headlights were streaming west out of town, dipping, turning, raking the rough ground, stopping, clicking off. Reacher parked neatly between a sagging Chrysler sedan and a battered Ford pick-up. He slid out and locked up and put the keys in his pocket and joined a converging crowd of men shuffling their way toward the personnel gate. An uneasy feeling. Same sensation as entering a baseball stadium wearing the colors of the visiting team. *Stranger in the house.* All around him guys glanced at him curiously and gave him a little more space than they were giving each other. But nothing was said. There was no overt hostility. Just wariness and covert inspection, as the crowd shuffled along through the predawn twilight, a yard at a time.

The personnel gate was a double section of the metal wall, folded back on hinges complex enough to accommodate the quilted curves of the wall's construction. The dirt path through it was beaten dusty by a million footsteps. Close to the gate there was no jostling. No impatience. Men lined up neatly like automatons, not fast, not slow, but resigned. They all needed to clock in, but clearly none of them wanted to.

The line shuffled slowly forward, a yard, two, three.

The guy in front of Reacher stepped through the gate.

Reacher stepped through the gate.

Immediately inside there were more metal walls, head-high, like cattle chutes, dividing the crowd left and right. The right-hand chute led to a holding pen where Reacher guessed the part-time workers would wait for the call. It was already a quarter full with men standing quiet and patient. The guys going left didn't look at them.

Reacher went left.

The left-hand chute dog-legged immediately and narrowed down to four feet in width. It carried the line of shuffling men past an old-fashioned punch-clock centered in a giant slotted array of time cards. Each man pulled his card and offered it up to the machine and waited for the dull thump of the stamp and then put the card back again. The rhythm was slow and relentless. The whisk of stiff paper against metal, the thump of the stamp, the click as the card was bottomed back in its slot. The clock was showing six-fourteen, which was exactly right according to the time in Reacher's head.

Reacher walked straight past the machine. The chute turned again and he followed the guy in front for thirty feet and then stepped out into the northeast corner of the arena. The arena was vast. Just staggeringly huge. The line of lights on the far wall ran close to a mile into the distance and dimmed and shrank and blended into a tiny vanishing point in the southwest corner. The far wall itself was at least a half-mile away. The total enclosed area must have been three hundred acres. Three *hundred* football fields.

Unbelievable.

Reacher stepped aside to let the line of men get past him. Here and there in the vastness small swarms of guys were already busy. Trucks and cranes were moving. They threw harsh shadows in the stadium lights. Some of the cranes were bigger than anything Reacher had seen in a dockyard. Some of the trucks were as big as earth-moving machines. There were gigantic crushers set on enormous concrete plinths. The crushers had bright oily hydraulic rams thicker than redwood trunks. There were crucibles as big as sailboats and retorts as big as houses. There were piles of wrecked cars ten stories high. The ground was soaked with oil and rainbow puddles of diesel and littered with curled metal swarf and where it was dry it glittered with shiny dust. Steam and smoke and fumes and sharp chemical smells were drifting everywhere. There was roaring and hammering rolling outward in waves and beating against the metal perimeter and bouncing straight back in again. Bright flames danced behind open furnace doors.

Like a vision of hell.

Some guys seemed to be heading for preassigned jobs and others were milling in groups as if waiting for direction. Reacher skirted around behind them and followed the north wall, tiny and insignificant in the chaos. Way ahead of him the vehicle gate was opening. Five semi trailers were parked in a line, waiting to move out. On the road they would look huge and lumbering. Inside the plant they looked like toys. The two security Tahoes were parked side by side, tiny white dots in the vastness. Next to them was a stack of forty-foot shipping containers. They were piled five high. Each one looked tiny.

South of the vehicle gate was a long line of prefabricated metal offices. They were jacked up on short legs to make them level. They had lights on inside. At the left-hand end of the line two offices were painted white and had red crosses on their doors. The first-aid station. Next to it a white vehicle was parked. The ambulance. Next to the ambulance was a long line of fuel and chemical tanks. Beyond them a sinister platoon of men in thick aprons and black welding masks used cutting torches on a pile of twisted scrap. Blue flames threw hideous shadows. Reacher hugged the north wall and kept on moving. Men looked at him and looked away, unsure. A quarter of the way along the wall his path was blocked by a giant pyramid of old oil drums. They were painted faded red and stacked ten high, stepped like a staircase. Reacher paused and glanced around and levered himself up to the base of the tier. Glanced around again and climbed halfway up the stack and then turned and stood precariously and held on tight and used the elevation to get an overview of the whole place.

He hadn't seen the whole place.

Not yet.

There was more.

Much more.

What had looked like the south boundary was in fact an interior partition. Same height as the perimeter walls, same material, same color, same construction, with the sheer face and the horizontal cylinder. Same purpose, as an impregnable barrier. But it was only an internal division, with a closed gate. Beyond it the outer perimeter enclosed at least another hundred acres. Another hundred football fields. The gate was wide enough for large trucks. There were deep ruts in the ground leading to it. Beyond it there were heavy cranes and high stacks of shipping containers piled in chevron shapes. The containers looked dumped, as if casually, but they were placed and combined carefully enough to block a direct view of ground-level activity from any particular direction.

The internal gate had some kind of a control point in front of it. Reacher could make out two tiny figures stumping around in small circles, bored, their hands in their pockets. He watched them for a minute and then lifted his gaze again beyond the partition. Cranes, and screens. Some smoke, some distant sparks. Some kind of activity. Other than that, nothing to see. Plenty to hear, but none of it was useful. It was impossible to determine which noises were coming from where. He waited another minute and watched the plant's internal traffic. Plenty of things were moving, but nothing was heading for the internal gate. It was going to stay closed. He turned east and looked at the sky. Dawn was coming.

He turned back and got his balance and climbed down the oil drum staircase. Stepped off to the rough ground and a voice behind him said, "Who the hell are you?"

37

Reacher turned slowly and saw two men. One was big and the other was a giant. The big guy was carrying a two-way radio and the giant was carrying a two-headed wrench as long as a baseball bat and probably heavier than ten of them. The guy was easily six-six and three hundred and fifty pounds. He looked like he wouldn't need a wrench to take a wrecked car apart.

The guy with the radio asked again, "Who the hell are you?"

"EPA inspector," Reacher said.

No reply.

"Just kidding," Reacher said.

"You better be."

"I am."

"So who are you?"

Reacher said, "You first. Who are you?"

"I'm the plant foreman. Now, who are you?"

Reacher pulled the pewter star from his pocket and said, "I'm with the PD. The new deputy. I'm familiarizing myself with the community."

"We didn't hear about any new deputies."

"It was sudden."

The guy raised his radio to his face and clicked a

button and spoke low and fast. Names, codes, commands. Reacher didn't understand them, and didn't expect to. Every organization had its own jargon. But he recognized the tone and he guessed the general drift. He glanced west and saw the Tahoes backing up and turning and getting set to head over. He glanced south and saw groups of men stopping work, standing straight, preparing to move.

The foreman said, "Let's go visit the security office."

Reacher stood still.

The foreman said, "A new deputy should want to visit the security office. Meet useful folks. Establish liaison. If that's what you really are."

Reacher didn't move. He glanced west again and saw the Tahoes halfway through their half-mile of approach. He glanced south again and saw knots of men walking his way. The crew in the aprons and the welders' masks was among them. Ten guys, clumping along awkwardly in heavy spark-proof boots. Plenty of others were coming in from other directions. Altogether maybe two hundred men were converging. Five minutes into the future there was going to be a big crowd by the oil drums. The giant with the wrench took a step forward. Reacher stood his ground and looked straight at him, and then checked west again, and south. The Tahoes were already close and slowing. The workers were forming up shoulder to shoulder. They were close enough that Reacher could see tools in their hands. Hammers, pry bars, cutting torches, foot-long cold chisels.

The foreman said, "You can't fight them all."

Reacher nodded. The giant on his own would be hard, but maybe feasible, if he missed with the first swing of the wrench. Then four-on-one or even six-on-one might be survivable. But not two-hundred-on-one. No way. Not two hundred and fifty pounds against twenty tons of muscle. He had two captured switchblades in his pocket, but they would be of limited use against maybe a couple of tons of improvised weaponry.

Not good.

Reacher said, "So let's go. I can give you five minutes."

The foreman said, "You'll give us whatever we want." He waved to the nearer Tahoe and it turned in close. Reacher heard oily stones and curly fragments of metal crushing under its tires. The giant opened its rear door and used his wrench to make a sweeping *Get in* gesture. Reacher climbed up into the back seat. The vehicle had a plain utilitarian interior. Plastic and cloth. No wood or leather, no bells or whistles. The giant climbed in after him and crowded him against the far door panel. The foreman climbed in the front next to the driver and slammed his door and the vehicle took off again and turned and headed for the line of office buildings south of the vehicle gate. It drove through the middle of the approaching crowd, slowly, and Reacher saw faces staring in at him through the windows, gray skin smeared with grease, bad teeth, white eyes wide with fascination.

The security office was at the north end of the array, closest to the vehicle gate. The Tahoe stopped directly outside of it next to a tangled pile of webbing straps, presumably once used to tie down junk on flat-bed trailers. Reacher spilled out of the car ahead of the giant and found himself at the bottom of a short set of wooden steps that led up to the office door. He pushed through the door and found himself inside a plain metal prefabricated box that had probably been designed for use on construction sites. There were five small windows fitted with thick plastic glass and covered from the outside with heavy steel mesh. Other than that it looked a lot like the ready room he had seen at the Halfway county morgue. Desk, paper, bulletin boards, armchairs, all of it showing the signs of casual abuse a place gets when its users are not its owners.

The foreman pointed Reacher toward a chair and then left again. The giant dragged a chair of his own out of position and turned it around and dumped himself down in it so that he was blocking the door. He laid the wrench on the floor. The floor was warped plywood and the wrench made an iron clatter as it dropped. Reacher sat in a chair in a corner. Wooden arms, tweed seat and back. It was reasonably comfortable.

"Got coffee?" he asked.

The giant paused a second and said, "No." A short word and a negative answer, but at least it was a response. In Reacher's experience the hardest part of any adversarial conversation was the beginning. An early answer was a good sign. Answering became a habit.

He asked, "What's your job?"

The giant said, "I help out where I'm needed." His voice was like a normal guy's, but muffled by having to come out of such a huge chest cavity.

"What happens here?" Reacher asked.

"Metal gets recycled."

"What happens in the secret section?"

"What secret section?"

"To the south. Behind the partition."

"That's just a junkyard. For stuff that's too far gone to use. Nothing secret about it."

"So why is it locked and guarded?"

"To stop people getting lazy. Someone gets tired of working, dumps good stuff in there, we lose money."

"You part of management?"

"I'm a supervisor."

"You want to supervise my way out of here?"

"You can't leave."

Reacher glanced out the window. The sun was over the horizon. In five minutes it would be over the east wall. *I could leave,* he thought. The vehicle gate was open and trucks were moving out. Time it right, get past the big guy, run for the gate, hop aboard a flatbed, game over. With the wrench on the floor the big guy was less of a problem than he had been before. He was unarmed, and down in a low chair. He was heavy, and gravity was gravity. And big guys were slow. And Reacher had knives.

"I played pro football," the big guy said.

"But not very well," Reacher said.

The big guy said nothing.

"Or you'd be doing color commentary on Fox, or living in a mansion in Miami, not slaving away here."

The big guy said nothing.

"I bet you're just as bad at this job."

The big guy said nothing.

I could leave, Reacher thought again.

But I won't.

I'll wait and see what happens.

He waited twenty more minutes before anything happened. The giant sat still and quiet by the door and Reacher whiled the time away in the corner. He wasn't unhappy. He could kill time better than anyone. The morning sun rose higher and came streaming in through the plastic window. The rays cast a clouded beam over the desk. All the colors of the rainbow were in it.

Then the door opened and the giant sat up straight and scooted his chair out of the way and the foreman walked in again. He still had his two-way radio in his hand. Behind him in the bright rectangle of daylight Reacher could see the plant working. Trucks were moving, cranes were moving, swarms of men were beavering away, sparks were showering, loud noises were being made. The foreman stopped halfway between the door and Reacher's chair and said, "Mr. Thurman wants to see you."

Seven o'clock, Reacher thought. Vaughan was ending her watch. She was heading to the diner in Hope, looking for breakfast, looking for her truck, maybe looking for him. Or maybe not.

He said, "I can give Mr. Thurman five minutes."

"You'll give Mr. Thurman however long he wants."

"He might own you, but he doesn't own me."

"Get up," the foreman said. "Follow me."

38

The trailer next door was an identical metal box, but better appointed inside. There was carpet, the armchairs were leather, and the desk was mahogany. There were pictures on the walls, all of them dimestore prints of Jesus. In all of them Jesus had blue eyes and wore pale blue robes and had long blond hair and a neat blond beard. He looked more like a Malibu surfer than a Jew from two thousand years ago.

On the corner of the desk was a Bible.

Behind the desk was a man Reacher assumed was Mr. Thurman. He was wearing a three-piece suit made of wool. He looked to be close to seventy years old. He looked pink and plump and prosperous. He had white hair, worn moderately long and combed and teased into waves. He had a big patient smile on his face. He looked like he had just stepped out of a television studio. He could have been a game show host, or a televangelist. Reacher could picture him, clutching his chest and promising God would fell him with a heart attack unless the audience sent him money.

And the audience would, Reacher thought. With a face like that, the idiots would bury him under fives and tens.

The foreman waited for a nod, then left again. Reacher sat down in a leather armchair and said, "I'm Jack Reacher. You've got five minutes."

The guy behind the desk said, "I'm Jerry Thurman. I'm very pleased to meet you."

Reacher said, "Now you've got four minutes and fifty-six seconds."

"Actually, sir, I've got as long as it takes." Thurman's voice was soft and mellifluous. His cheeks quivered as he spoke. Too much fat, not enough muscle tone. Not an attractive sight. "You've been making trouble in my town and now you're trespassing on my business premises."

"Your fault," Reacher said. "If you hadn't sent those goons to the restaurant I would have eaten a quick lunch and moved on days ago. No reason to stay. You're not exactly running the Magic Kingdom here."

"I don't aim to. This is an industrial enterprise."

"So I noticed."

"But you knew that days ago. I'm sure the people in Hope were quick to tell you all about us. Why poke around?"

"I'm an inquisitive person."

"Evidently," Thurman said. "Which raised our suspicions a little. We have proprietary processes here, and methodologies of our own invention, which might all be called industrial secrets. Espionage could hurt our bottom line."

"I'm not interested in metal recycling."

"We know that now."

"You checked me out?"

Thurman nodded.

"We made inquiries," he said. "Last night, and this morning. You are exactly what you claimed to be, in Judge Gardner's vagrancy hearing. A passerby. A nobody who used to be in the army ten years ago."

"That's me."

"But you're a very persistent nobody. You made a ludicrous request to be sworn in as a deputy. After taking a badge from a man in a fight."

"Which he started. On your orders."

"So we ask ourselves, why are you so keen to know what happens here?"

"And I ask myself, why are you so keen to hide it?"

Thurman shook his great white head.

"We're not hiding anything," he said. "And you're no danger to me commercially, so I'll prove it to you. You've seen the town, you've met some of the folks who live here, and now I'm going to give you a tour of the plant. I'll be your personal guide and escort. You can see everything and ask me anything."

They went in Thurman's personal vehicle, which was a Chevy Tahoe the same style and vintage as the security vehicles, but painted black, not white. Same modest interior. A working truck. The keys were already in the ignition. Habit, probably. And safe enough. Nobody would use the boss's car without permission. Thurman drove himself and Reacher sat next to him in the front. They were alone in the vehicle. They headed to the west wall, away from the vehicle gate, moving slow. Thurman started talking immediately. He described the various office functions, which in order of appearance were operations management, and invoicing, and purchasing, and he pointed out the first-aid station, and described its facilities and capabilities, and made a mildly pointed comment about the people Reacher had put in there. Then they moved on to the line of storage tanks, and he described their capacities, which were five thousand gallons each, and their contents, which were gasoline for the Tahoes and some of the other trucks, and diesel for the cranes and the crushers and the heavier equipment, and a liquid chemical called trichloroethylene, which was an essential metal degreaser, and oxygen and acetylene for the cutting torches, and kerosene, which fueled the furnaces.

Reacher was bored rigid after sixty seconds.

He tuned Thurman out and looked at things for himself. Didn't see much. Just metal, and people working with it. He got the general idea. Old stuff was broken up and melted down, and ingots were sold to factories, where new stuff was made, and eventually the new stuff became old stuff and showed up again to get broken up and melted down once more.

Not rocket science.

Close to a mile later they arrived at the internal partition and Reacher saw that a truck had been parked across the gate, as if to hide it. Beyond the wall no more sparks were flying and no more smoke was rising. Activity seemed to have been abandoned for the day. He asked, "What happens back there?"

Thurman said, "That's our junkyard. Stuff that's too far gone to work with goes in there."

"How do you get it in, with that truck in the way?"

"We can move the truck if we need to. But we don't need to often. Our processes have gotten very developed. Not much defeats us anymore."

"Are you a chemist or a metallurgist or what?"

Thurman said, "I'm a born-again-Christian American and a businessman. That's how I would describe myself, in that order of importance. But I hire the best talent I can find, at the executive level. Our research and development is excellent."

Reacher nodded and said nothing. Thurman turned the wheel and steered a slow curve and headed back north, close to the east wall. The jaws of a giant crusher were closing on about ten wrecked cars at once. Beyond it a furnace door swung open and men ducked away from the blast of heat. A crucible moved slowly on an overhead track, full of liquid metal, all bubbling and crusting.

Thurman asked, "Are you born again?"

Reacher said, "Once was enough for me."

"I'm serious."

"So am I."

"You should think about it."

"My father used to say, why be born again, when you can just grow up?"

"Is he no longer with us?"

"He died a long time ago."

"He's in the other place, then, with an attitude like that."

"He's in a hole in the ground in Arlington Cemetery."

"Another veteran?"

"A Marine."

"Thank you for his service."

"Don't thank me. I had nothing to do with it."

Thurman said, "You should think about getting your life in order, you know, before it's too late. Something might happen. The Book of Revelation says, the time is at hand."

"As it has every day since it was written, nearly two thousand years ago. Why would it be true now, when it wasn't before?"

"There are signs," Thurman said. "And the possibility of precipitating events." He said it primly, and smugly, and with a degree of certainty, as if he had regular access to privileged insider information.

Reacher said nothing in reply.

They drove on, past a small group of tired men wrestling with a mountain of tangled steel. Their backs were bent and their shoulders were slumped. *Not yet eight o'clock in the morning,* Reacher thought. More than ten hours still to go.

"God watches over them," Thurman said.

"You sure?"

"He tells me so."

"Does he watch over you, too?"

"He knows what I do."

"Does he approve?"

"He tells me so."

"Then why is there a lightning rod on your church?"

Thurman didn't answer that. He just clamped his mouth shut and his cheeks drooped lower than his jawbone. They arrived at the mouth of the cattle chute leading to the personnel gate. He stopped the truck and jiggled the stick into Park and sat back in his seat.

"Seen enough?" he asked.

"More than enough," Reacher said.

"Then I'll bid you goodbye," Thurman said. "I imagine our paths won't cross again." He tucked his elbow in and offered his hand, sideways and awkwardly. Reacher shook it. It felt soft and warm and boneless, like a child's balloon filled with water. Then Reacher opened his door and slid out and walked through the doglegged chute and back to the acres of parking.

Every window in Vaughan's truck was smashed.

39

Reacher stood for a long moment and ran through his options and then unlocked the truck and swept pebbles of broken glass off the seats and the dash. He raked them out of the driver's footwell. He didn't want the brake pedal to jam halfway through its travel. Or the gas pedal. The truck was slow enough already.

Three miles back to town, twelve to the line, and then five to the center of Hope. A twenty-mile drive, cold and slow and very windy. Like riding a motorcycle without eye protection. Reacher's face was numb and his eyes were watering by the end of the trip. He parked outside the diner a little before nine o'clock in the morning. Vaughan's cruiser wasn't there. She wasn't inside. The place was three-quarters empty. The breakfast rush was over.

Reacher took the back booth and ordered coffee and breakfast from the day-shift waitress. The college girl was gone. The woman brought him a mug and filled it from a flask and he asked her, "Did Officer Vaughan stop by this morning?"

The woman said, "She left about a half-hour ago."

"Was she OK?"

"She seemed quiet."

"What about Maria? The girl from San Diego?"

"She was in before seven."

"Did she eat?"

"Plenty."

"What about Lucy? The blonde from LA?"

"Didn't see her. I think she left town."

"What does Officer Vaughan's husband do?"

The waitress said, "Well, not much anymore," as if it was a dumb question to ask. As if that particular situation should have been plain to everybody.

That particular situation wasn't plain to Reacher.

He said, "What, he's unemployed?"

The woman started to answer him, and then she stopped, as if she suddenly remembered that the situation wasn't necessarily plain to everybody, and it wasn't her place to make it plain. As if she was on the point of revealing something that shouldn't be revealed, like private neighborhood business. She just shook her head with embarrassment and bustled away with her flask. She didn't speak at all when she came back five minutes later with his food.

Twenty minutes later Reacher got back in the damaged truck and drove south and crossed Third Street, and Fourth, and turned left on Fifth. Way ahead of him he could make out Vaughan's cruiser parked at the curb. He drove on and pulled up behind it, level with the mailbox with the perfectly aligned letters. He idled in the middle of the traffic lane for a moment. Then he got out and walked ahead and put a palm on the Crown Vic's hood. It was still very warm. She had left the diner nearly an hour ago, but clearly she had driven around a little afterward. Maybe looking for her Chevy, or looking for him. Or neither, or both. He got back in the truck and backed up and swung the wheel and bumped up onto her driveway. He parked with the grille an inch from her garage door and slid out. Didn't lock up. There didn't seem to be much point.

He found the winding path and followed it through the bushes to her door. He hooked her keyring on his finger and tapped the bell, briefly, just once. If she was awake, she would hear it. If she was asleep, it wouldn't disturb her.

She was awake.

The door opened and she looked out of the gloom straight at him. Her hair was wet from the shower and combed back. She was wearing an oversized white T-shirt. Possibly nothing else. Her legs were bare. Her feet were bare. She looked younger and smaller than before.

She said, "How did you find me?"

He said, "Phone book."

"You were here last night. Looking. A neighbor told me."

"It's a nice house."

She said, "I like it."

She saw the truck keys on his finger. He said, "I have a confession to make."

"What now?"

"Someone broke all the windows."

She pushed past him and stepped out to the path. Turned to face the driveway and studied the damage and said, "Shit." Then it seemed to dawn on her that she was out in the yard barefoot in her nightwear and she pushed back inside.

"Who?" she asked.

"One of a thousand suspects."

"When?"

"This morning."

"Where?"

"I stopped by the metal plant."

"You're an idiot."

"I know. I'm sorry. I'll pay for the glass." He slipped the keys off his finger and held them out. She didn't take them. Instead she said, "You better come in."

The house was laid out the way he had guessed. Right to left it went garage, mudroom, kitchen, living room, bedrooms. The kitchen seemed to be the heart of the home. It was a pretty space with painted cabinets and a wallpaper border at the top of the walls. The dishwasher was running and the sink was empty and the counters were tidy but there was enough disarray to make the room feel lived in. There was a four-place table with only three chairs. There were what Reacher's mother had called "touches." Dried flowers, bottles of virgin olive oil that would never be used, antique spoons. Reacher's mother had said such things gave a room personality. Reacher himself had been unsure how anything except a person could have personality. He had been a painfully literal child. But over the years he had come to see what his mother had meant. And Vaughan's kitchen had personality.

Her personality, he guessed.

It seemed to him that one mind had chosen everything and one pair of hands had done everything. There was no evidence of compromise or dueling tastes. He knew that way back a kitchen was considered a woman's domain. Certainly it had been that way in his mother's day, but she had been French, which had made a difference. And since then he had been led to believe that things had changed. Guys cooked now, or at least left six-packs lying around, or put oil stains on the linoleum from fixing motorcycle engines.

There was no evidence of a second person in the house. None at all. Not a trace. From his position by the sink Reacher could see into the living room through an arch that was really just a doorway with the door taken out. There was a single armchair in there, and a TV set, and a bunch of moving boxes still taped shut.

Vaughan said, "Want coffee?"

"Always."

"Did you sleep last night?"

"No."

"Don't have coffee, then."

"It keeps me awake until bedtime."

"What's the longest you ever stayed awake?"

"Seventy-two hours, maybe."

"Working?"

He nodded. "Some big deal, twenty years ago."

"A big MP deal?"

He nodded again. "Somebody was doing something to somebody. I don't recall the details."

Vaughan rinsed her coffee pot and filled her

machine with water. The machine was a big steel thing with *Cuisinart* embossed on it in large letters. It looked reliable. She spooned coffee into a gold basket and hit a switch. She said, "Last night the deputies from Despair headed home after an hour."

"They found me in the bar," Reacher said. "They flushed me west with the phone call and then came after me. It was a trap."

"And you fell for it."

"*They* fell for it. I knew what they were doing."

"How?"

"Because twenty years ago I used to stay up for seventy-two hours at a time dealing with worse folks than you'll ever find in Despair."

"What happened to the deputies?"

"They joined their full-time buddies in the infirmary."

"All four of them?"

"All six of them. They added some on-site moral support."

"You're a one-man crime wave."

"No, I'm Alice in Wonderland."

Now Vaughan nodded.

"I know," she said. "Why aren't they doing anything about it? You've committed assault and battery on eight individuals, six of them peace officers, and you've wrecked two police cars. And yet you're still walking around."

"That's the point," Reacher said. "I'm still walking around, but in Hope, not in Despair. That's weirdness number one. All they ever want to do is keep people out of there. They're not interested in the law or justice or punishment."

"What's weirdness number two?"

"They came at me six against one and I walked away with two bruises and sore knuckles from pounding on them. They're all weak and sick. One of them even had to call it quits so he could find time to throw up."

"So what's that about?"

"The clerk at my motel figures they're breaking environmental laws. Maybe there's all kinds of poisons and pollution out there."

"Is that what they're hiding?"

"Possibly," Reacher said. "But it's kind of odd that the victims would help to hide the problem."

"People worry about their jobs," Vaughan said. "Especially in a company town, because they don't have any alternatives." She opened a cabinet and took out a mug. It was white, perfectly cylindrical, four inches high, and two and a half inches wide. It was made of fine bone china as thin as paper. She filled it from the pot and immediately from the aroma Reacher knew it was going to be a great one. She glanced at the living room but carried the mug to the kitchen table instead, and placed it down in front of one of the three chairs. Reacher glanced at the boxes and the lone armchair in the living room and said, "Just moved in?"

"A year and a half ago," Vaughan said. "I guess I'm a little slow unpacking."

"From where?"

"Third Street. We had a little cottage with an upstairs, but we decided we wanted a ranch."

"We?"

"David and I."

Reacher asked, "So where is he?"

"He's not here right now."

"Should I be sorry about that?"

"A little."

"What does he do?"

"Not so much anymore." She sat in one of the chairs without the mug in front of it and tugged the hem of her T-shirt down. Her hair was drying and going wavy again. She was naked under the shirt, and confident about it. Reacher was sure of that. She was looking straight at him, like she knew he knew.

He sat down opposite her.

She asked, "What else?"

"My motel clerk figures the plant makes way too much money."

"That's common knowledge. Thurman owns the bank, and bank auditors gossip. He's a very rich man."

"My motel clerk figures he's smuggling dope or something with his little airplane."

"Do you think he is?"

"I don't know."

"That's your conclusion?"

"Not entirely."

"So what else?"

"A quarter of the plant is screened off. There's a secret area. I think he's got a contract to recycle military scrap. Hence the wealth. A Pentagon contract is the fastest way on earth to get rich these days. And hence the MP unit down the road. Thurman is breaking up classified stuff back there, and people would be interested in it. Armor thickness, materials, construction techniques, circuit boards, all that kind of stuff."

"So that's all? Legitimate government business?"

"No," Reacher said. "That's not all."

40

Reacher took the first sip of his coffee. It was perfect. Hot, strong, smooth, and a great mug. He looked across the table at Vaughan and said, "Thank you very much."

She said, "What else is going on there?"

"I don't know. But there's a hell of a vigilante effort going on about something. After the PD ended up depopulated I went to see the local judge about getting sworn in as a deputy."

"You weren't serious."

"Of course not. But I pretended I was. I wanted to see the reaction. The guy panicked. He went crazy. He said he'd deputize the whole population first. They're totally serious about keeping strangers out."

"Because of the military stuff."

"No," Reacher said. "That's the MPs' job. Any hint of espionage, Thurman's people would get on the radio and the MPs would lock and load and about a minute later the whole town would be swarming with Humvees. The townspeople wouldn't be involved."

"So what's going on?"

"At least two other things."

"Why two?"

"Because their responses are completely incoherent. Which means there are at least two other factions in play, separate and probably unaware of each other. Like this morning, Thurman had me checked out. He saw that my paper trail went cold ten years ago, and therefore I was no obvious danger to him, and then he ran your plate and saw that I was in some way associated with a cop from the next town, and therefore in some way untouchable, so he played nice and gave me a guided tour. But meanwhile without all that information someone else was busy busting your windows. And nobody busts a cop's windows for the fun of it. Therefore the left hand doesn't know what the right hand is doing."

"Thurman gave you a tour?"

"He said he'd show me everything."

"And did he?"

"No. He stayed away from the secret area. He said it was just a junkyard."

"Are you sure it isn't?"

"I saw activity in there earlier. Smoke and sparks. Plus it's carefully screened off. Who does that, for a junkyard?"

"What are the two other factions?"

"I have no idea. But these young guys are involved somehow. Lucy Anderson's husband and the dead guy. And Lucy Anderson's husband is another example of the left hand not knowing what the right hand is doing. They sheltered him and moved him on but threw his wife out of town like a pariah. How much sense does that make?"

"He moved on?"

"I saw him at the rooming house at three o'clock and he was gone by seven. No trace of him, and nobody would admit he had ever been there."

"The plane flies at seven," Vaughan said. "Is that connected?"

"I don't know."

"No trace at all?"

"No physical sign, and a lot of zipped lips."

"So what's going on?"

"When was the last time any normal person entered Despair and stayed as long as he wanted and left of his own accord? To your certain knowledge?"

"I don't know," Vaughan said. "Months, certainly."

"There was an entry in the hotel register from seven months ago."

"That sounds about right."

"I met the new girl last night," Reacher said. "Sweet kid. Her name is Maria. I'm pretty sure the dead guy was her boyfriend. She showed me his picture. His name was Raphael Ramirez."

"Did you tell her?"

"No."

"Why not?"

"She asked me if I'd seen him. Truth is, I didn't actually see him. It was dark. And I can't give her news like that without being completely sure."

"So she's still swinging in the wind."

"I think she knows, deep down."

"What happened to the body?"

"It didn't go to the county morgue. I checked on that."

"We knew that already."

"No, we knew it didn't go straight to the morgue. That was all. So I wondered if it had been dumped somewhere out of town and found later by someone else. But it wasn't. Therefore it never left Despair. And the only meat wagon and the only stretcher in Despair belong to the metal plant. And the metal plant has furnaces that could vaporize a corpse in five minutes flat."

Vaughan got up and poured herself a glass of water, from a bottle in the refrigerator. She stood with her hips against the counter and stared out the window. Her heels were on the floor but most of her weight was on her toes. Her T-shirt had one lateral wrinkle where the base of her spine met her butt. The cotton material was very slightly translucent. The light was all behind her. Her hair was dry and there was fine golden down on her neck.

She looked spectacular.

She asked, "What else did Maria say?"

Reacher said, "Nothing. I didn't ask her anything else."

"Why ever not?"

"No point. The wives and the girlfriends aren't going to tell us anything. And what they do say will be misleading."

"Why?"

"Because they've got a vested interest. Their husbands and their boyfriends aren't just hiding out in Despair on their own account. They're aiming to get help there. They're aiming to ride some kind of an underground railroad for fugitives. Despair is a way station, in and out. The women want to keep it all secret.

Lucy Anderson was OK with me until I mentioned I used to be a cop. Then she started hating me. She thought I was still a cop. She thought I was here to bust her husband."

"What kind of fugitives?"

"I don't know what kind. But the Anderson guy was the right kind and Raphael Ramirez was the wrong kind."

Vaughan took Reacher's mug from him and refilled it from the machine. Then she refilled her glass from the refrigerator and sat down and said, "May I ask you a personal question?"

Reacher said, "Feel free."

"Why are you doing this?"

"Doing what?"

"Caring, I suppose. Caring about what's happening in Despair. Bad stuff happens everywhere, all the time. Why does this matter to you so much?"

"I'm curious, that's all."

"That's no answer."

"I have to be somewhere, doing something."

"That's still no answer."

"Maria," Reacher said. "She's the answer. She's a sweet kid, and she's hurting."

"Her boyfriend is a fugitive from the law. You said so yourself. Maybe she deserves to be hurting. Maybe Ramirez is a dope dealer or something. Or a gang member or a murderer."

"Ramirez looked like a harmless guy to me."

"You can tell by looking?"

"Sometimes. Would Maria hang out with a bad guy?"

"I haven't met her."

"Would Lucy Anderson?"

Vaughan said nothing.

"I don't like company towns," Reacher said. "I don't like feudal systems. I don't like smug fat bosses lording it over people. And I don't like people so broken down that they put up with it."

"You see something you don't like, you feel you have to tear it down?"

"Damn right I do. You got a problem with that?"

"No."

They sat in the kitchen and drank coffee and water in silence. Vaughan took her free hand out of her lap and laid it on the table, her fingers spread and extended. They were the closest part of her to Reacher. He wondered whether it was a gesture, either conscious or subconscious. An approach, or an appeal for a connection.

No wedding band.

He's not here right now.

He put his own free hand on the table.

She asked, "How do we know they were fugitives at all? Maybe they were undercover environmental activists, checking on the pollution. Maybe the Anderson guy fooled them and Ramirez didn't."

"Fooled them how?"

"I don't know. But it worries me, if they're using poisons over there. We share the same water table."

"Thurman mentioned something called trichloroethylene. It's a metal degreaser. I don't know whether it's dangerous or not."

"I'm going to check it out."

"Why would the wife of an environmental activist be scared of cops?"

"I don't know."

"The Anderson guy wasn't fooling anyone. He was a guest there. They gave him a place to stay and protection. He was *helped.*"

"But Lucy Anderson wasn't. She was thrown out."

"Like I said, the left hand doesn't know what the right is doing."

"And Ramirez was killed."

"Not killed. Left to die."

"So why help one and shun the other?"

"Why shun him at all? Why not just round him up and dump him at the line, like they did with me and Lucy?"

Vaughan sipped her water.

"Because Ramirez was different in some way," she said. "More specifically dangerous to them."

"Then why not just take him out immediately? Disappear him? The end result would have been the same."

"I don't understand it."

"Maybe I'm wrong," Reacher said. "Maybe they didn't shun him or keep him out. Maybe they never even knew he was there. Maybe he was sniffing around on the periphery, staying out of sight, trying to find a way in. Desperate enough to keep trying, not good enough to succeed."

Vaughan took her hand off the table.

"We need to know exactly who he was," she said. "We need to talk to Maria."

"She won't tell us anything."

"We can try. We'll find her in the diner. Meet me there, later."

"Later than what?"

"We both need to sleep."

Reacher said, "May I ask you a personal question?"

"Go ahead."

"Is your husband in prison?"

Vaughan paused a beat, and then smiled, a little surprised, a little sad.

"No," she said. "He isn't."

41

Reacher walked back to the motel, alone. Lucy Anderson's door was open. A maid's cart was parked outside. The bed was stripped and all the towels were on the floor. The closet was empty. *I think she left town,* the waitress had said, in the diner. Reacher watched for a moment and then he moved on. *Good luck, Lucky,* he thought, *whatever the hell you're doing and wherever the hell you're going.* He unlocked his own door and took a long hot shower and climbed into bed. He was asleep within a minute. The coffee didn't fight him at all.

He woke up in the middle of the afternoon with the MPs on his mind. The forward operating base. Its location. Its equipment mix. The place came at him like an analysis problem from the classrooms at Fort Rucker.

What was it for?

Why was it there?

The old County Route 37 wandered east to west through Hope, through Despair, through Halfway, and presumably onward. First he saw it laid out like a ribbon, like a line on a map, and then he pictured it in his head like a rotating three-dimensional diagram, like something on a computer screen, all green webs of origins and layers. Way back in its history it had been a wagon trail. Beaten earth, crushed rock, ruts and weeds. Then it had been minimally upgraded, when Model Ts had rolled out of Dearborn and flooded the country. Then Hope Township had upgraded ten miles of it again, for the sake of civic pride. They had done a conscientious job. Maybe foundation reinforcement had been involved. Certainly there had been grading and leveling. Maybe a little straightening. Possibly a little widening. Thick blacktop had been poured and rolled.

Despair Township had done none of that. Thurman and his father and his grandfather or whoever had owned the town before had ignored the road. Maybe they had grudgingly dumped tar and pebbles on it every decade or so, but fundamentally it was still the same road it had been back when Henry Ford ruled the world. It was narrow, weak, lumpy, and meandering.

Unfit for heavy traffic.

Except west of the metal plant. There, a thirty-five-mile stretch had been co-opted and rebuilt. Probably from the ground up. Reacher pictured a yard-deep excavation, drainage, a rock foundation, a thick concrete roadbed, rebar, a four-inch asphalt layer rolled smooth and true by heavy equipment. The shoulders were straight and the camber was good. Then after thirty-five miles the new road had been driven through virgin territory to meet the Interstate, and the old Route 37 had wound onward as before, once again in its native state, narrow, weak, and lumpy.

Weak, strong, weak.

There was no military presence east of Despair or west of the fork, across the weak parts of the road.

The MP base straddled the strong part.

The truck route.

Close to Despair, but not too close.

Not sealing the town like a trap, but guarding one direction only and leaving the other wide open.

The base was equipped with six up-armored Humvees, each one an eight-ton rhinoceros, each one reasonably fast and reasonably maneuverable, each one topped with a belt-fed 7.62-caliber M60 machine gun on a free-swinging mount.

Why all that?

Reacher lay in bed and closed his eyes and heard barking voices from the Rucker classrooms: *This is what you know. What's your conclusion?*

His conclusion was that nobody was worried about espionage.

He got out of bed at four o'clock and took another long hot shower. He knew he was out of step with the Western world in terms of how often he changed his clothes, but he tried to compensate by keeping his body scrupulously clean. The motel soap was white and came in a small thin paper-wrapped morsel, and he used the whole bar. The shampoo was a thick green liquid in a small plastic bottle. He used half of it. It smelled faintly of apples. He rinsed and stood under the water for a moment more and then shut it off and heard someone knocking at his door. He wrapped a towel around his waist and padded across the room and opened up.

Vaughan.

She was in uniform. Her HPD cruiser was parked neatly behind her. She was staring in at him, openly curious. Not an unusual reaction. *Look at yourself. What do you see?* He was a spectacular mesomorph, built of nothing except large quantities of bone and sinew and muscle. But with his shirt off most people saw only his scars. He had a dozen minor nicks and cuts, plus a dimpled .38 bullet hole in the left center of his chest, and a wicked spider web of white lacerations low down on the right side of his abdomen, all criss-crossed and puckered by seventy clumsy stitches done quick and dirty in a mobile army surgical hospital. Souvenirs, in the first instance of childhood mayhem, in the second of a psychopath with a small revolver, and in the third, shrapnel from a bomb blast. Survivable, because childhood mayhem was always survivable, and because the .38 that hit him had been packed with a weak load, and because the shrapnel had been someone else's bone, not white-hot metal. He had been a lucky man, and his luck was written all over his body.

Ugly, but fascinating.

Vaughan's gaze traveled upward to his face.

"Bad news," she said. "I went to the library."

"You get bad news at libraries?"

"I looked at some books and used their computer."

"And?"

"Trichloroethylene is called TCE for short. It's a metal degreaser."

"I know that."

"It's very dangerous. It causes cancer. Breast cancer, prostate cancer, all kinds of cancers. Plus heart disease, problems with the nervous system, strokes, liver disease, kidney disease, even diabetes. The EPA says a concentration of five parts per billion is acceptable. Some places have been measured twenty or thirty times worse than that."

"Like where?"

"There was a case in Tennessee."

"That's a long way from here."

"This is serious, Reacher."

"People worry too much."

"This isn't a joke."

He nodded.

"I know," he said. "And Thurman uses five thousand gallons at a time."

"And we drink the groundwater."

"You drink bottled water."

"Lots of people use tap."

"The plant is twenty miles away. There's a lot of sand. A lot of natural filtration."

"It's still a concern."

Reacher nodded. "Tell me about it. I had two cups of coffee right there. One in the restaurant and one at the judge's house."

"You feel OK?"

"Fine. And people seem OK here."

"So far."

She went quiet.

He said, "What else?"

"Maria is missing. I can't find her anywhere. The new girl."

42

Vaughan hung around in the open doorway and Reacher grabbed his clothes and dressed in the bathroom. He called out, "Where did you look?"

"All over," Vaughan called back. "She's not here in the motel, she's not in the diner, she's not in the library, she's not out shopping, and there isn't anywhere else to go."

"Did you speak to the motel clerk?"

"Not yet."

"Then that's where we'll go first. She knows everything." He came out of the bathroom, buttoning his shirt. The shirt was almost due for the trash, and the buttonholes were still difficult. He ran his fingers through his hair and checked his pockets.

"Let's go," he said.

The clerk was in the motel office, sitting on a high stool behind the counter, doing something with a ledger and a calculator. But she had no useful information. Maria had left her room before seven o'clock that morning, dressed as before, on foot, carrying only her purse.

"She ate breakfast before seven," Reacher said. "The waitress in the diner told me."

The clerk said she hadn't come back. That was all she knew. Vaughan asked her to open Maria's room. The clerk handed over her passkey immediately. No hesitation, no fuss about warrants or legalities or due process. *Small towns,* Reacher thought. Police work was easy. About as easy as it had been in the army.

Maria's room was identical to Reacher's, with only very slightly more stuff in it. A spare pair of jeans hung in the closet. They were neatly folded over the bar of a hanger. Above them on the shelf were one spare pair of cotton underpants, one bra, and one clean cotton T-shirt, all folded together in a low pile. On the floor of the closet was an empty suitcase. It was a small, sad, battered item. Blue in color, made from fiberboard, with a crushed lid, as if it had been stored for years with something heavy on top of it.

On the shelf next to the bathroom sink was a vinyl wash bag, white, with improbable pink daisies on it. It was empty, but it had clearly been overstuffed during transit. Its contents were laid out next to it, in a long line. Soaps, shampoos, lotions and ointments and unguents of every possible kind.

No personal items. They would have been in her purse.

"Day trip," Vaughan said. "She's expecting to return."

"Obviously," Reacher said. "She paid for three nights."

"She went to Despair. To look for Ramirez."

"That would be my guess."

"But how? Did she walk?"

Reacher shook his head. "I would have seen her.

It's seventeen miles. Six hours, for her. If she left at seven she wouldn't have arrived before one in the afternoon. I was on the road between eight-thirty and nine. I didn't pass her along the way."

"There's no bus or anything. There's never any traffic."

"Maybe there was," Reacher said. "I came in with an old guy in a car. He was visiting family, and then he was moving on to Denver. He'd head straight west. No reason to loop around. And if he was dumb enough to give me a ride, he'd have given Maria a ride for sure."

"If he happened to leave this morning."

"Let's find out."

They returned the passkey and got into Vaughan's cruiser. She fired it up and they headed west to the hardware store. The sidewalk was piled high with an elaborate display. Ladders, buckets, barrows, gasoline-driven machines of various types. The owner was inside, wearing a brown coat. He confirmed that he had been building the display early that morning. He thought hard and memory dawned in his eyes and he confirmed that he had seen a small dark girl in a blue warm-up jacket. She had been standing on the far sidewalk, right at the edge of town, half-turned, looking east but clearly aiming to head west, gazing at the empty traffic lane with a mixture of optimism and hopelessness. A classic hitchhiker's pose. Then later the store owner had seen a large bottle-green car heading west, a little before eight o'clock. He described the car as looking basically similar to Vaughan's cruiser, but without all the police equipment.

"A Grand Marquis," Reacher said. "Same platform. Same car. Same guy."

The store owner had not seen the car stop or the girl get in. But the inference was clear. Vaughan and Reacher drove the five miles to the town line. No real reason. They saw nothing. Just the smooth blacktop behind and the ragged gritty ribbon ahead.

"Is she in danger?" Vaughan asked.

"I don't know," Reacher said. "But she's probably not having the best day of her life."

"How will she get back?"

"I suspect she decided to worry about that later."

"We can't go there in this car."

"So what else have you got?"

"Just the truck."

"Got sunglasses? It's breezy, without the windshield."

"Too late. I already had it towed. It's being fixed."

"And then you went to the library? Don't you ever sleep?"

"Not so much anymore."

"Since when? Since what?"

"I don't want to talk about it."

"Your husband?"

"I said I don't want to talk about it."

Reacher said, "We need to find Maria."

"I know."

"We could walk."

"It's twelve miles."

"And twelve miles back."

"Can't do it. I'm on duty in two hours."

Reacher said, "She's domiciled in Hope. At least

temporarily. Now she's missing. The HPD should be entitled to head over there in a car and make inquiries."

"She's from San Diego."

"Only technically."

"Technicalities matter, Reacher."

"She took up residency."

"With one change of underwear?"

"What's the worst thing that can happen?"

"Despair could ask us for reciprocity."

"They already grabbed it. Their deputies came by last night."

"Two wrongs don't make a right."

"Says who?"

"Are you bullying me?"

"You're the one with the gun."

Vaughan started to say something, then shook her head and sighed and said, "Shit." Then she jammed her foot on the gas and the Crown Vic shot forward. The tires had traction on Hope's blacktop but lost it on Despair's loose gravel. The rear wheels spun and howled and the car stumbled for a second and then accelerated west in a cloud of blue smoke.

They drove eleven miles into the setting sun with nothing to show for it except eyestrain. The twelfth mile was different. Way ahead in the glare Reacher saw the familiar distant sights, all in sharp silhouette and shortened perspective. Vague smudges, on the horizon. The vacant lot, on the left. The abandoned motor court, low and forlorn. The gas station, on the right. Farther on, the dry goods store in the first brick building.

Plus something else.

From a mile away it looked like a shadow. Like a lone cloud was blocking the sun and casting a random shape on the ground. He craned his neck and looked up at the sky. Nothing there. The sky was clear. Just the gray-blue of approaching evening.

Vaughan drove on.

Three-quarters of a mile out the shape grew width, and depth, and height. The sun blazed behind it and winked around its edges. It looked like a low wide pile of something dark. Like a gigantic truck had strewn earth or asphalt right across the road, shoulder to shoulder, and beyond.

The pile looked to be fifty feet wide, maybe twenty deep, maybe six high.

From a half-mile out, it looked to be moving.

From a quarter-mile out, it was identifiable.

It was a crowd of people.

Vaughan slowed, instinctively. The crowd was two or three hundred strong. Men, women, and children. They were formed up in a rough triangle, facing east. Maybe six people at the front. Behind the six, twenty more. Behind the twenty, sixty more. Behind the sixty, a vast milling pool of people. The whole width of the road was blocked. The shoulders were blocked. The rearguard spilled thirty feet out into the scrub on both sides.

Vaughan stopped, fifty yards out.

The crowd compressed. People pushed inward from the sides. They made a human wedge. A solid mass. Two or three hundred people. They held together, but they didn't link arms.

They didn't link arms because they had weapons in their hands.

Baseball bats, pool cues, ax handles, broom handles, split firewood, carpenters' hammers. Two or three hundred people, pressed tight together, and moving. Moving as one. They were rocking in place from foot to foot and jabbing their weapons up and down in the air. Nothing wild. Their movements were small and rhythmic and controlled.

They were chanting.

At first Reacher heard only a primitive guttural shout, repeated over and over. Then he dropped his window an inch and heard the words *Out! Out! Out!* He hit the switch again and the glass thumped back up.

Vaughan was pale.

"Unbelievable," she said.

"Is this some weird Colorado tradition?" Reacher asked.

"I never saw it before."

"So Judge Gardner went and did it. He deputized the whole population."

"They don't look drafted. They look like true believers. What are we going to do?"

Out! Out! Out!

Reacher watched for a moment and said, "Drive on and see what happens."

"Are you serious?"

"Try it."

Vaughan took her foot off the brake and the car crept forward.

The crowd surged forward to meet it, short steps, crouched, weapons moving.

Vaughan stopped again, forty yards out.

Out! Out! Out!

Reacher said, "Use your siren. Scare them."

"Scare *them*? They're doing a pretty good job scaring me."

The crowd had quit rocking from side to side. Now people were rocking back and forth instead, one foot to the other, jabbing their clubs and sticks forward, whipping them back, jabbing them forward again. They were dressed in work shirts and faded sundresses and jean jackets, but collectively in terms of their actions they looked entirely primitive. Like a weird Stone Age tribe, threatened and defensive.

"Siren," Reacher said.

Vaughan lit it up. It was a modern synthesized unit, shatteringly loud in the emptiness, sequencing randomly from a basic *whoop-whoop-whoop* to a manic *pock-pock-pock* to a hysterical digital cackling.

It had no effect.

No effect at all.

The crowd didn't flinch, didn't move, didn't miss a beat.

Reacher said, "Can you get around them?"

Vaughan shook her head. "This car is no good on the scrub. We'd bog down and they'd be all over us."

"So fake them out. Drift left, then sneak past on the right real fast."

"You think?"

"Try it."

She took her foot off the brake again and crept forward. She turned the wheel and headed for the wrong side of the road and the crowd in front of her tracked the move, slow and infinitely fluid. Two or three hundred people, moving as one, like a pool of gray mercury, changing shape like an ameba. Like a disciplined herd. Vaughan reached the left shoulder.

"Can't do it," she said. "There's too many of them."

She stopped again, ten feet from the front rank.

She killed the siren.

The chanting grew louder.

Out! Out! Out!

Then the note dropped lower and the rhythm changed down. As one, the people started banging their clubs and sticks on the ground and shouting only every other beat.

Out!

Crash!

Out!

Crash!

They were close enough now to see clearly. Their faces jerked forward with every shouted word, gray and pink and contorted with hate and rage and fear and anger. Reacher didn't like crowds. He enjoyed solitude and was a mild agoraphobic, which didn't mean he was afraid of wide-open spaces. That was a common misconception. He liked wide-open spaces. Instead he was mildly unsettled by the *agora,* which was an ancient Greek word for a crowded public marketplace. Random crowds were bad enough. He had seen footage of stampedes and stadium disasters.

Organized crowds were worse. He had seen footage of riots and revolutions. A crowd two hundred strong was the largest animal on the face of the earth. The heaviest, the hardest to control, the hardest to stop. The hardest to kill. Big targets, but after-action reports always showed that crowds took much less than one casualty per round fired.

Crowds had nine lives.

"What now?" Vaughan asked.

"I don't know," he said. He especially didn't care for angry organized crowds. He had been in Somalia and Bosnia and the Middle East, and he had seen what angry crowds could do. He had seen the herd instinct at work, the anonymity, the removal of inhibition, the implied permissions of collective action. He had seen that an angry crowd was the most dangerous animal on the face of the earth.

Out!

Crash!

Out!

Crash!

He said, quietly, "Put the shifter in Reverse."

Vaughan moved the lever. The car settled back on its haunches, like prey ready to flee.

He said, "Back up a little."

Vaughan backed up and steered and got straight on the center line and stopped again, thirty yards out. Ninety feet. The distance from home plate to first base.

"What now?" she asked.

The crowd had tracked the move. It had changed shape again, back to what it had been at the beginning. A dense triangle, with a blunt vanguard of six men, and a wide base that petered out thirty feet into the scrub on both sides of the thoroughfare.

Out!

Crash!

Out!

Crash!

Reacher stared ahead through the windshield. He dropped his window again. He felt a change coming. He sensed it. He wanted to be a split second ahead of it.

Vaughan asked, "What do we do?"

Reacher said, "I'd feel better in a Humvee."

"We're not in a Humvee."

"I'm just saying."

"What do we do in a Crown Vic?"

Reacher didn't have time to answer. The change came. The chanting stopped. There was silence for a second. Then the six men at the front of the crowd raised their weapons high, with clamped fists and straight arms.

They screamed a command.

And charged.

They bolted forward, weapons high, screaming. The crowd streamed after them. Two or three hundred people, full speed, yelling, falling, stumbling, stampeding, eyes wide, mouths open, faces contorted, weapons up, free arms pumping. They filled the windshield, a writhing mob, a frantic screaming mass of humanity coming straight at them.

They got within five feet. Then Vaughan stamped on the gas. The car shot backward, the engine screaming, the low gear whining loud, the rear tires howling and making smoke. She got up to thirty miles an hour going backward and then she flung the car into an emergency one-eighty and smashed the shifter into Drive. Then she stamped on the gas. She accelerated east and didn't stop for miles, top speed, engine roaring, her foot jammed down. Reacher had been wrong in his earlier assessment. Way too cautious. A Crown Vic with the Police Interceptor pack was a very fast car. Good for a hundred and twenty, easily.

43

They got airborne over the peak of the rise that put the distant Rockies close again and then Vaughan lifted off the gas and took most of the next mile to coast to a stop. She craned her neck and spent a long minute staring out the back window. They were still deep in Despair's territory. But all was quiet behind them. She slumped in her seat and dropped both hands to her lap.

"We need the State Police," she said. "We've got mob rule back there and a missing woman. And whatever exactly Ramirez was to those people, we can't assume they're going to treat his girlfriend kindly."

"We can't assume anything," Reacher said. "We don't know for sure she's there. We don't even know for sure that the dead guy was Ramirez."

"You got serious doubts?"

"The state cops will. It's a fairy tale, so far."

"So what do we do?"

"We verify."

"How?"

"We call Denver."

"What's in Denver?"

"The green car," Reacher said. "And the guy who

was driving it. Three hundred miles, six hours' drive time, call it seven with a stop for lunch. If he left around eight this morning, he'll be there by now. We'll call him up, ask him if he gave Maria a ride, and if so, where exactly he let her out."

"You know his name?"

"No."

"Number?"

"No."

"Great plan."

"He was visiting three grandchildren in Hope. You need to get back to town and check with families that have three kids. Ask them if Grandpa just came by in his green Mercury. One of them will say yes. Then you'll get a number for his next stop. It'll be a brother or a sister in Denver, with four more kids for the old guy to visit."

"What are you going to do?"

"I'm going back to Despair."

He got out of the car at five-thirty-five, a little more than eight miles west of Hope, a little more than eight miles east of Despair. Right in the heart of no-man's-land. He watched Vaughan drive away and then he turned and started walking. He stayed on the road itself, for speed. He ran calculations in his head. *This is what you know.* Twenty-six hundred inhabitants, possibly a quarter of them too old or too young to be useful. Which left more than eighteen hundred people, with maximum availability after six o'clock in the evening, when the plant closed for the day. Newly deputized, newly marshaled, unsure of themselves, inexperienced. Daytime visibility had enabled deployment in large masses. In the dark, they would have to spread out, like a human perimeter. But they would want to stick fairly close together, for morale and effectiveness and mutual support. Therefore no outliers, and no sentinels. Children would be held close in family groups. Each element of the perimeter would want visual contact with the next. Which meant that groups or individuals wouldn't want to be more than maybe ten feet apart. Some people would have flashlights. Some would have dogs. All in all, worst case, they could assemble a human chain eighteen thousand feet long, which was six thousand yards, which was the circumference of a circle a fraction more than a mile in diameter.

A circle a mile in diameter would barely enclose the town. It couldn't enclose the town and the plant together. And it would bunch up on the road in and the road out, especially the road in, from Hope. Cover would be thin elsewhere. Probably very thin. Possibly guys with trucks would be out in the scrub. Possibly the security Tahoes from the plant would be on the prowl. Teenage boys would be unpredictable. Excited by the adventure, and hungry for glory. But easily bored. In fact all of them would get bored. And tired, and low. Efficiency would peak during the first hour, would wane over the next two or three, would be poor before midnight, and would be nonexistent in the small hours of the night.

What's your conclusion?

Not a huge problem, Reacher thought. The sun

was down behind the distant mountains. There was a soft orange glow on the horizon. He walked on toward it.

At seven o'clock he pictured Vaughan starting her night watch, in Hope. At seven-fifteen he was a mile from where the crowd had gathered before, in Despair. It was getting dark. He couldn't see anybody in the distance, and therefore nobody could see him in the distance. He struck off the road into the scrub, south and west, at an angle, hustling, unwilling to slow down. The town ahead was dark and quiet. Very quiet. By seven-thirty he was six hundred yards out in the sand and he realized he hadn't heard the plane take off. No aero engine, no light in the sky.

Why not?

He paused in the stillness and put together a couple of possible scenarios. Then he moved on, holding a wide radius, quiet and stealthy and invisible in the darkness.

By eight o'clock he was making his first approach. He was expected out of the east, therefore he was coming in from the southwest. Not a guarantee of safety, but better than a poke in the eye. Competent individuals would be distributed all around, but not equally. He had already outflanked most of the people he needed to worry about. He had seen one truck, a battered pick-up with four lights on a bar on its roof. It had been bouncing slowly along, over rough ground, heading away from him.

He moved up through the scrub and paused behind a rock. He was fifty yards from the back of a long line of workers' housing. Low one-story dwellings, well separated laterally, because desert land was cheap and septic systems didn't work with too much density. The gaps between the houses were three times as wide as the houses themselves. The sky had a minimal gray glow, moon behind cloud. There were guards in the gaps between the houses. Left to right he could make out an individual, a small group, another individual, and another. They all had sticks or clubs or bats. Together they made a chain that went: armed guard, house, armed guard, house, armed guard, house, armed guard.

They thought the houses themselves were defensive elements.

They were wrong.

He could hear dogs barking here and there in the distance, excited and unsettled by the unfamiliar evening activity. Not a problem. Dogs that barked too much were no more use than dogs that didn't bark at all. The guy second from the right between the houses had a flashlight. He was clicking it on at predictable intervals, sweeping an arc of ground in front of him, and then clicking it off again to save the battery.

Reacher moved left.

He lined himself up behind a house that was entirely dark. He dropped to the ground and low-crawled straight for it. The army record for a fifty-yard low crawl was about twenty seconds. At the other extreme, snipers could spend all day crawling fifty yards into position. On this occasion Reacher budgeted five minutes. Fast enough to get the job done, slow enough to get it done safely. Generally the human brain noticed speed and discontinuity. A tortoise heading inward worried nobody. A cheetah bounding in got everyone's attention. He kept at it, slow and steady, knees and elbows, head down. No pauses. No stop-start. He made it through ten yards. Then twenty. And thirty. And forty.

After forty-five yards he knew he was no longer visible from the spaces between the houses. The angle was wrong. But he stayed low all the way, until he crawled right into the back stoop. He stood up and listened for reaction, either outside the house or inside.

Nothing.

The stoop was a simple wooden assembly three steps high. He went up, slowly, feet apart, shuffling, putting his weight where the treads were bolted to the side rails. If a stair squeaked, ninety-nine times in a hundred it squeaked in the center, where it was weakest. He put his hand on the door handle and lifted. If a door squeaked, ninety-nine times in a hundred it was because it had dropped on its hinges. Upward pressure helped.

He eased the door up and in and stepped through the opening and turned and closed it again. He was in a dark and silent kitchen. A worn linoleum floor, the smell of fried food. Counters and cabinets, ghostly in the gloom. A sink, and a faucet with a bad washer. It released a fat drip every twenty-three seconds. The drip spattered against a ceramic surface. He pictured the perfect teardrop exploding into a coronet shape, flinging tinier droplets outward in a perfect circle.

He moved through the kitchen to the hallway door. Smelled dirty carpet and worn furniture from a living room on his right. He moved through the hallway to the front of the house. The front door was a plain hollow slab, with a rectangle of painted beading on it. He turned the handle and lifted. Eased it open, silently.

There was a screen door beyond it.

He stood still. There was no way to open a screen door quietly. No way at all. Lightweight construction, tight plastic hinges, a crude spring mechanism. Guaranteed to raise a whole symphony of screeching and slapping sounds. The door had a horizontal bar in the center, designed to add strength and resist warping. The upper void was less than three feet square. The lower void, the same. Both were meshed with nylon screen. The screen had been doing its job for many years. That was clear. It was filthy with dust and insect corpses.

Reacher pulled out one of his captured switchblades. Turned back to the hallway to muffle the sound and popped the blade. He slit a large *X* in the lower screen, corner to corner. Pressed the blade back in the handle and put the knife back in his pocket and sat down on the floor. Leaned back and jacked himself off the ground, like a crab. Shuffled forward and went out through the *X* feetfirst. Headfirst would have been more intuitive. The desire to see what was out there was overwhelming. But if what was out there was an ax handle or a bullet, better that it hit him in the legs than the head. Much better.

There was nothing out there. No bullet, no ax handle. He ducked and squirmed and got his shoulders through the gap and stood up straight and alert, one swift movement. He was standing on a front stoop made of concrete. A plain slab, four-by-four, cracked, canted down in one corner on an inadequate foundation. Ahead of him was a short path and a dark street. More houses on the other side. No guards between them. The guards were all behind him now, by a distance equal to half a house's depth. And they were all facing the wrong way.

44

Reacher threaded between houses and stayed off the roads where possible. He saw nobody on foot. Once he saw a moving vehicle two streets away. An old sedan, lights on bright. A designated supervisor, possibly, on an inspection tour. He ducked low behind a wooden fence and waited until the car was well away from him. Then he moved on and pressed up behind the first of the brick-built downtown blocks. He stood with his back against a wall and planned his moves. He was reasonably familiar with Despair's geography. He decided to stay away from the street with the restaurant on it. The restaurant was almost certainly still open for business. Close to nine in the evening, maybe late for normal supper hours, but with mass community action going on all night it was probably committed to staying open and supplying refreshments for the troops. Maybe the moving car had been a volunteer ferrying coffee.

He stayed in the shadows and used a narrow cross-street and turned and walked past the storefront church. It was empty. Maybe Thurman had been inside earlier, praying for success. In which case he was going to be sadly disappointed. Reacher moved on without a sound and turned again and headed for the police station. The streets were all dark and deserted. The whole active population was on the perimeter, staring out into the gloom, unaware of what was happening behind its back.

The street with the police station on it had one streetlight burning. It cast a weak pool of yellow light. The police station itself was dark and still. The street door was locked. Old wood, a new five-lever deadbolt inexpertly fitted. Reacher took out the keys he had taken from the deputy in the bar. He looked at the lock and looked at the keys and selected a long brass item and tried it. The lock turned, with plenty of effort. Either the key was badly cut, or the lock's tongue was binding against the striker plate, or both. But the door opened. It swung back and a smell of institutional floor polish wafted out. Reacher stepped inside and closed the door behind him and walked through the gloom the same way he had walked before, to the booking desk. Like the town's hotel, the Despair PD was still in the pen-and-paper age. Arrest records were kept in a large black ledger with gold-painted edges. Reacher carried it to a window and tilted it so that it caught what little light was coming through. Then he opened it up and flipped forward through the pages until he found his own entry, dated three days previously and timed in the middle of the afternoon: *Reacher, J, male vagrant.* The entry had been made well in advance of the town court hearing. Reacher smiled. *So much for the presumption of innocence,* he thought.

The entry immediately before his own was three days older and said: *Anderson, L, female vagrant.*

He flipped backward, looking for Lucy Anderson's husband. He didn't expect to find him, and he didn't find him. Lucy Anderson's husband had been helped, not hindered. Then he went looking for Ramirez. No trace. Nowhere in the book. Never arrested. Therefore the guy hadn't escaped from custody. He had never been picked up at all. If he had ever been there at all. If the dead guy in the dark wasn't someone else.

He leafed backward, patiently, a random three-month sample. Saw six names, *Bridge, Churchill, White, King, Whitehouse, Andrews,* five male, one female, all vagrants, roughly one every two weeks.

He flipped ahead again, past his own entry, looking for Maria herself. She wasn't there. There was only one entry after his own. It was in new handwriting, because the desk cop had been driving Despair's second Crown Vic and was therefore currently out sick with whiplash. The new entry had been made just seven hours previously and said: *Rogers, G, male vagrant.*

Reacher closed the book and stacked it back on the desk and walked to the head of the basement stair. He felt his way down and opened the cell block door. It was very bright inside. All the bulkhead lights were burning. But all the cells were empty.

A circle a mile in diameter would barely enclose the town. Reacher's next stop was out of town, which meant passing through the perimeter again, this time heading in the other direction. Easy at first, hard later. Easy to sneak up to the line, relatively easy to penetrate it, hard to walk away with a thousand eyes on his back. He didn't want to be the only thing moving, in front of a static audience. Better that the line moved, and broke over him like a wave over a rock.

He sorted through the bunch of keys.

Found the one he wanted.

Then he put the keys in his pocket and moved back to the booking desk and started opening drawers. He found what he wanted in the third drawer he tried. It was full of miscellaneous junk. Rubber bands, paper clips, dry ballpoint pens, slips of paper with scratched-out notes, a plastic ruler.

And a tin ashtray, and a quarter-full pack of Camel cigarettes, and three books of matches.

He cleared a space on the floor under the booking desk and put the arrest ledger in its center, standing on its edge, open to ninety degrees, with the pages fanned out. He piled every scrap of paper he could find on it and around it. He balled up memos and posters and old newspapers and built a pyramid. He hid two matchbooks in it, with the covers bent back and the matches bent forward at varying angles.

Then he lit a cigarette, with a match from the third book. He inhaled, gratefully. Camels had been his brand, way back in history. He liked Turkish tobacco. He smoked a half-inch and folded the cigarette into the matchbook in a *T* shape and used a paper clip to keep it secure. Then he nestled the assembly into the base of his paper pyramid and walked away.

He left the street door open two inches, to set up a breeze.

He had seen the big deputy's house from the back, the first night, when the guy got home from work and threw up in the yard. It was a five-minute walk that took him ten, due to stealth and caution. The house was another swaybacked old ranch. No landscaping, no real yard. Just beaten earth, including a foot-wide path to the door and twin ruts leading to a parking place close to the kitchen.

The old crew-cab pick-up was right there on it.

The driver's door was unlocked. Reacher slid in behind the wheel. The seat was worn and sagging. The windows were dirty and the upholstery smelled of sweat and grease and oil. Reacher pulled the bunch of keys and found the car key. Plastic head, distinctive shape. He tried it, just to be sure. He put it in the ignition and turned two clicks. The wheel unlocked and the dials lit up. He turned it back again and climbed over the seats and lay down in the rear of the cab.

It took more than thirty minutes for the townspeople to realize their police station was on fire. By which time it was well ablaze. From his low position in the truck Reacher saw smoke and sparks and an orange glow and the tentative start of leaping flames well before anyone reacted. But eventually someone on the perimeter must have smelled something or gotten bored and shuffled a full circle in the dirt and paused long enough to study the horizon behind.

There was uncertainty and confused shouting for about a minute.

Then there was pandemonium.

Discipline broke down instantly. The perimeter collapsed inward like a leaking balloon. Reacher lay still and people streamed past him, few and hesitant at first, then many and fast. They were running, singly and in groups, yelling, shouting, fascinated, uncertain, looking at nothing except the bright glow ahead of them. Reacher craned his head and saw them coming from all directions. The cross-streets were suddenly crowded with dozens of people, then hundreds. The flow was all one way. The downtown maze swallowed them all. Reacher sat up and turned and watched the last of the backs disappear around corners and between buildings.

Newly deputized, newly marshaled, unsure of themselves, inexperienced.

He smiled.

Like moths to a flame, he thought. *Literally.*

Then he scrambled over the seat backs and turned the key all the way. The engine turned over once and fired. He drove away slowly, with the lights off, heading a little south of west, through the deserted scrubland. He saw headlights on the roadway to his right. Four moving vehicles. Almost certainly the security Tahoes were coming in from the plant, plus probably the ambulance, plus maybe some firefighting equipment. He kept on going, looping west through the empty land, slowly, bouncing over washboard undulations and jarring over rocks. The wheel squirmed in his hands. He peered ahead through the dirty windshield and averaged less than twenty miles an hour. Faster than running, but even so, it took more than seven minutes before he saw the white gleam of the plant's wall in the darkness.

45

Reacher kept on going until the residential compound's fieldstone wall loomed up at him. It was hard to see in the darkness. But it was easy to climb. Plenty of toeholds, in the unmortared joints. He drove halfway around its circumference and parked the truck opposite where he guessed the oversized barn would be. He killed the engine and got out quietly and was over the wall less than ten seconds later. The runway was right in front of him. Maybe sixty feet wide, maybe nine hundred yards long, beaten flat, carefully graded, well maintained. At each end was a low hump, a concrete emplacement for a floodlight set to wash horizontally along the runway's length. Across it and directly ahead was a wide expanse of scrub, dotted here and there with landscaped areas. The plants were all sharp-leaved things that looked silver under the night sky. Native, adapted to the desert. Xeric plants, or xerophilous, drought tolerant, from the Greek prefix *xero-*, meaning dry. Hence *Xerox,* for copying without wet chemicals. Zeno of Cittium would have been puzzled by Xeroxing, but he would have approved of xeriscaping. He believed in going with the flow. The unquestioning acceptance of destiny. He believed in basking in the sun and eating green figs, instead of spending time and effort trying to change nature with irrigation.

Reacher crossed the runway. Ahead of him and behind the last planted area was the big barn. He headed straight for it. It was a three-sided building, open at the front. It was entirely filled with a white airplane. A Piper Cherokee, parked nose-out, settled dead level on its tricycle undercarriage, dormant and still and dewed over with cold. Close to ten o'clock in the evening. Close to the halfway point of its normal nightly flight plan. But that night, it was still on the ground. It hadn't flown at all.

Why not?

Reacher walked right into the barn and skirted the right-hand wing tip. Came back to the fuselage and found the step and climbed on the wing and peered in through the window. He had spent time in small planes, when the army had wanted him to get somewhere faster than a jeep or a train could have gotten him. He had found them small and trivial and somehow unserious. They were like flying cars. He had told himself they were better built than cars, but he hadn't found much concrete evidence to convince himself with. Thin metal, bent and folded and riveted, flimsy clips and wires, coughing engines. Thurman's Cherokee was a plain four-seat workhorse, a little worn, a little stained. It had tinny doors and a divided windshield and a dash less complicated than most new sedans. One window had a small crack. The seats looked caved in and the harnesses looked tangled and frayed.

There was no paperwork in the cabin. No charts, no maps, no scribbled latitudes and longitudes. There was no real freight capacity. Just a couple of small holds in various nacelles and voids, and the three spare seats. *People don't joyride at night,* Lucy Anderson had said. *There's nothing to see.* Therefore Thurman was carrying something, somewhere, in or out. Or visiting a friend. Or a mistress. Maybe that was what *lay preacher* meant. You preached, and you got laid.

Reacher climbed down off the wing. He strolled through the gloom and took a look at the other outbuildings. There was a three-car garage, at the end of a straight quarter-mile driveway that led to an ornamental iron gate in the wall. There was another, smaller, barn. The house itself was magnificent. It was built of oiled boards that shone halfway between blond and dark. It had numerous peaked gables, like a mountain chalet. Some windows were two stories high. Paneling glowed dark inside. There were cathedral ceilings. There were fieldstone accents and rich rugs and clubby leather sofas and armchairs. It was the kind of gentleman's retreat that should always smell of cigar smoke. Reacher could still taste the part-smoked cigarette in his mouth. He walked all the way around the house, thinking about Camels, and camels, and the eyes of needles. He arrived back at the big barn, and took a last look at the airplane. Then he retraced his steps through the landscaping, across the runway, to the wall. Ten seconds later he was back in the stolen truck.

The fieldstone wall had been easy to climb, but the metal wall was going to be impossible. It was a sheer eight-foot-high vertical plane, topped with a continuous horizontal cylinder six feet in diameter. Like a toilet roll balanced on a thick hardcover book. It was a design derived from prison research. Reacher knew the theory. He had been professionally interested in prisons, back in the day. Stone walls or brick walls or wire fences could be climbed, however high they were. Broken glass set in the tops could be padded or cushioned. Rolls of barbed wire could be crushed or cut. But six-foot cylinders were unbeatable. Compared to the length of an arm or the span of a hand, their surfaces were slick and flat and offered no grip at all. Getting over one was like trying to crawl across a ceiling.

So he drove on, through the empty acres of parking, hoping against hope that the personnel gate would be open, and if it wasn't, that one of the deputy's keys would unlock it. But it wasn't open, and none of the keys fit. Because it didn't have a keyhole. It had a gray metal box instead, set into the wall well to the right, where the gate's arc of travel wouldn't obscure it. The box was the kind of thing that normally held an outdoor electrical outlet. It opened against a spring closure. Inside was a ten-digit keypad. A combination lock. One through nine, plus zero, laid out like a telephone. A possible 3,628,800 variants. It would take seven months to try them all. A fast typist might do it in six.

Reacher drove on, tracking the north wall in the

Tahoes' established ruts, hoping against hope that the vehicle gate would be open. He was slightly optimistic. The Tahoes had left in a hurry, and the ambulance. And people in a hurry didn't always clean up after themselves.

The vehicle gate was open.

It was built like a double door. Each half cantilevered outward and then swung through a hundred degrees on a wheeled track. And both halves were standing wide open. Together they made a mouth, a chute, a funnel, a V-shaped invitation leading directly to an empty forty-foot gap in the wall, and to the darkness beyond.

Reacher parked the deputy's truck nose-out, right across the wheeled track, blocking the gate's travel, and he took the keys with him. He figured maybe the gate was motorized, or on a time switch. And come what may, he wanted to keep it open. He didn't want it to close with him on the wrong side. Climbing out would be as impossible as climbing in.

He walked a hundred feet into the plant. Felt the familiar terrain underfoot, heavy and sticky with grease and oil, crunchy with shards of metal. He stood still, and sensed giant shapes ahead. The crushers, and the furnaces, and the cranes. He glanced right, and half-saw the line of offices and storage tanks. Beyond them, nearly a mile away and invisible in the night, the secret compound. He took half a step in its direction.

Then the lights came on.

There was an audible *whoomp* as electricity surged

through cables thicker than wrists and in a split second the whole place lit up blue and brighter than day. A shattering sensation. Physical in its intensity. Reacher screwed his eyes shut and clamped his arms over his head and tried hard not to fall to his knees.

46

Reacher opened his eyes in a desperate hooded squint and saw Thurman walking toward him. He turned and saw the plant foreman heading in from a different direction. He turned again and saw the giant with the three-foot wrench blocking his path to the gate.

He stood still and waited, blinking, squinting, the muscles around his eyes hurting from clamping so hard. Thurman stopped ten feet away from him and then walked on and came close and took up a position alongside him, nearly shoulder to shoulder, as if they were two old buddies standing together, surveying a happy scene.

Thurman said, "I thought our paths were not going to cross again."

Reacher said, "I can't be responsible for what you think."

"Did you set our police station on fire?"

"You've got a human wall all around the town. How could I have gotten through?"

"Why are you here again?"

Reacher paused a beat. Said, "I'm thinking about leaving the state." Which was permanently true. Then he said, "Before I go, I thought I'd drop by the infirmary and pay my respects to my former opponents. Tell them no hard feelings."

Thurman said, "I think the hard feelings are all on the other side."

"Then they can tell me no hard feelings. Clearing the air is always good for a person's mental well-being."

"I can't permit a visit to the infirmary. Not at this hour."

"You can't prevent one."

"I'm asking you to leave the premises."

"And I'm denying your request."

"There's only one patient here at the moment. The others are all home now, on bed rest."

"Which one is here?"

"Underwood."

"Which one is Underwood?"

"The senior deputy. You left him in a sorry state."

"He was sick already."

"You need to leave now."

Reacher smiled. "That should be your town motto. It's all I ever hear. Like New Hampshire, live free or die. It should be Despair, you need to leave now."

Thurman said, "I'm not joking."

"You are," Reacher said. "You're a fat old man, telling me to leave. That's pretty funny."

"I'm not alone here."

Reacher turned and checked the foreman. He was standing ten feet away, empty hands by his sides, tension in his shoulders. Reacher turned again and glanced at the giant. He was twenty feet away, holding the wrench in his right fist, resting its weight in his left palm.

Reacher said, "You've got an office boy and a broken-down old jock with a big spanner. I'm not impressed."

"Maybe they have guns."

"They don't. They'd have them out already. No one waits to pull a gun."

"They could still do you considerable harm."

"I doubt it. The first eight you sent didn't do much."

"Are you really willing to try?"

"Are you? If it goes the wrong way, then you're definitely alone with me. And with your conscience. I'm here to visit the sick, and you want to have me beaten up? What kind of a Christian are you?"

"God guides my hand."

"In the direction you want to go anyway. I'd be more impressed if you picked up a message telling you to sell up and give all your money to the poor and go to Denver to care for the homeless."

Thurman said nothing.

Reacher said, "I'm going to the infirmary now. You are, too. Your choice whether you walk there or I carry you there in a bucket."

Thurman's shoulders slumped in an all-purpose sigh and shrug and he raised a palm to his two guys, one after the other, like he was telling a couple of dogs to stay. Then he set off walking, toward the line of cabins. Reacher walked at his side. They passed the security office, and Thurman's own office, and the three other offices Reacher had seen before on his tour, the one marked Operations, the one marked Purchasing, the last marked Invoicing. They passed the first white-painted unit and stopped outside the second. Thurman heaved himself up the short flight of steps and opened the door. He went inside and Reacher followed.

It was a real sick bay. White walls, white linoleum floor, the smell of antiseptic, soft nightlights burning. There were sinks with lever taps, and medicine cabinets, and blood pressure cuffs, and sharp disposal cans on the walls. There was a rolling cart with a kidney-shaped steel dish on it. A stethoscope was curled in the dish.

There were four hospital cots. Three were empty, one was occupied, by the big deputy. He looked pretty bad. Pale, inert, listless. He looked smaller than before. His hair looked thinner. His eyes were open, dull and unfocused. His breathing was shallow and irregular. There was a medical chart clipped to the rail at the foot of his bed. Reacher used his thumb and tilted it horizontal and scanned it. Neat handwriting. Professional notations. The guy had a whole lot of things wrong with him. He had fever, fatigue, weakness, breathlessness, headaches, rashes, blisters, sores, chronic nausea and vomiting, diarrhea, dehydration, and signs of complex internal problems. Reacher dropped the chart back into position and asked, "You have a doctor working here?"

Thurman said, "A trained paramedic."

"Is that enough?"

"Usually."

"For this guy?"

"We're doing the best we can."

Reacher stepped alongside the bed and looked down. The guy's skin was yellow. Jaundice, or the nightlight reflected off the walls. Reacher asked him, "Can you talk?"

Thurman said, "He's not very coherent. But we're hoping he'll get better."

The big deputy rolled his head from one side to the other. Tried to speak, but got hung up with a dry tongue in a dry mouth. He smacked his lips and breathed hard and started again. He looked straight up at Reacher and his eyes focused and glittered and he said, "The . . ." And then he paused for breath and blinked and started over, apparently with a new thought. A new subject. He said, haltingly, "You did this to me."

"Not entirely," Reacher said.

The guy rolled his head again, away and back, and gasped once, and said, "No, the . . ." And then he stopped again, fighting for breath, his voice reduced to a meaningless rasp. Thurman grabbed Reacher's elbow and pulled him back and said, "We need to leave now. We're tiring him."

Reacher said, "He needs to be in a proper hospital."

"That's the paramedic's decision. I trust my people. I hire the best talent I can find."

"Did this guy work with TCE?"

Thurman paused a beat. "What do you know about TCE?"

"A little. It's a poison."

"No, it's a degreaser. It's a standard industrial product."

"Whatever. Did this guy work with it?"

"No. And those that do are well protected."

"So what's wrong with him?"

"You should know. Like he said, you did this to him."

"You don't get symptoms like these from a fistfight."

"I heard it was more than a fistfight. Do you ever stop to reflect on the damage you cause? Maybe you ruptured something inside of him. His spleen, perhaps."

Reacher closed his eyes. Saw the barroom again, the dim light, the tense silent people, the air thick with raised dust and the smell of fear and conflict. *He stepped in and jabbed hard and caught the guy low down in the side, below the ribs, above the waist, two hundred and fifty pounds of weight punched through the blunt end of a chair leg into nothing but soft tissue.* He opened his eyes again and said, "All the more reason to get him checked out properly."

Thurman nodded. "I'll have him taken to the hospital in Halfway tomorrow. If that's what it takes, so that you can move on with a clear conscience."

"My conscience is already clear," Reacher said. "If people leave me alone, I leave them alone. If they don't, what comes at them is their problem."

"Even if you overreact?"

"Compared to what? There were six of them. What were they going to do to me? Pat me on the cheek and send me on my way?"

"I don't know what their intentions were."

"You do," Reacher said. "Their intentions were your intentions. They were acting on your instructions."

"And I was acting on the instructions of a higher authority."

"I guess I'll have to take your word for that."

"You should join us. Come the Rapture, you don't want to be left behind."

"The Rapture?"

"People like me ascend to heaven. People like you stay here without us."

"Works for me," Reacher said. "Bring it on."

Thurman didn't answer that. Reacher took a last look at the guy in the bed and then stepped away and walked out the door, down the steps, back to the blazing arena. The foreman and the guy with the wrench stood where they had been before. They hadn't moved at all. Reacher heard Thurman close the infirmary door and clatter down the steps behind him. He moved on and felt Thurman follow him toward the gate. The guy with the wrench was looking beyond Reacher's shoulder, at Thurman, waiting for a sign, maybe hoping for a sign, slapping the free end of the wrench against his palm.

Reacher changed direction.

Headed straight for the guy.

He stopped a yard away and stood directly face-to-face and looked him in the eye and said, "You're in my way."

The guy glanced in Thurman's direction and

waited. Reacher said, "Have a little self-respect. You don't owe that old fool anything."

The guy said, "I don't?"

"Not a thing," Reacher said. "None of you does. He owes you. You all should wise up and take over. Organize. Have a revolution. You could lead it."

The guy said, "I don't think so."

Thurman called out, "Are you leaving now, Mr. Reacher?"

"Yes," Reacher said.

"Are you ever coming back?"

"No," Reacher lied. "I'm done here."

"Do I have your word?"

"You heard me."

The giant glanced beyond Reacher's shoulder again, hope in his eyes. But Thurman must have shaken his head or given some other kind of a negative instruction, because the guy just paused a beat and then stepped aside, one long sideways pace. Reacher walked on, back to the sick deputy's truck. It was where he had left it, with all its windows intact.

47

From the plant to the Hope town line was fifteen miles by road, but Reacher made it into a twenty-mile excursion by looping around to the north, through the scrub. He figured that the townsfolk would have reorganized fairly fast, and there was no obvious way of winning the consequent twin confrontations at both ends of Main Street. So he avoided them altogether. He hammered the deputy's old truck across the rough ground and navigated by the glow of the fire to his right. It looked to be going strong. In his experience brick buildings always burned well. The contents went first, and then the floors and the ceilings, and then the roof, with the outer walls holding up and forming a tall chimney to enhance the air flow. And when the walls finally went, the collapse blasted sparks and embers all over the place, to start new fires. Sometimes a whole city block could be taken out by one cigarette and one book of matches.

He skirted the town on a radius he judged to be about four miles and then he shadowed the road back east a hundred yards out in the dirt. When the clock in his head hit midnight he figured he was less than a mile short of the line. He veered right and bounced up onto the tarred pebbles and finished the trip like a normal driver. He thumped over the line and Hope's thick blacktop made the ride go suddenly quiet.

Vaughan was waiting a hundred yards ahead.

She was parked on the left shoulder with her lights off. He slowed and held his arm out his window in a reassuring wave. She put her arm out her own window, hand extended, fingers spread, an answering gesture. Or a traffic signal. He coasted and feathered the brakes and the steering and came to a stop with his fingertips touching hers. To him the contact felt one-third like a mission-accomplished high-five, one-third like an expression of relief to be out of the lions' den again, and one-third just plain good. He didn't know what it felt like to her. She gave no indication. But she left her hand there a second longer than she needed to.

"Whose truck?" she asked.

"The senior deputy's," Reacher said. "His name is Underwood. He's very sick."

"With what?"

"He said I did it to him."

"Did you?"

"I gave a sick man a couple of contusions, which I don't feel great about. But I didn't give him diarrhea or blisters or sores and I didn't make his hair fall out."

"So is it TCE?"

"Thurman said not."

"You believe him?"

"Not necessarily."

Vaughan held up a plastic bottle of water.

Reacher said, "I'm not thirsty."

"Good," Vaughan said. "This is a sample. Tap water, from my kitchen. I called a friend of a friend of David's. He knows a guy who works at the state lab in Colorado Springs. He told me to take this in for testing. And to find out how much TCE Thurman actually uses."

"The tank holds five thousand gallons."

"But how often does it get used up and refilled?"

"I don't know."

"How can we find out?"

"There's a purchasing office, probably full of paperwork."

"Can we get in there?"

"Maybe."

Vaughan said, "Go dump that truck back over the line. I'll drive you to town. We'll take a doughnut break."

So Reacher steered the truck backward into the sand and left it there, keys in. Way behind him he could see a faint red glow on the horizon. Despair was still on fire. He didn't say anything about it. He just walked forward and crossed the line again and climbed in next to Vaughan.

"You smell of cigarettes," she said.

"I found one," he said. "I smoked a half-inch, for old times' sake."

"They give you cancer, too."

"I heard that. You believe it?"

"Yes," she said. "I do, absolutely."

She took off east, at a moderate speed, one hand on the wheel and the other in her lap. He asked her, "How's your day going?"

"A gum wrapper blew across the street in front of me. Right there in my headlights. Violation of the anti-littering ordinance. That's about as exciting as it gets in Hope."

"Did you call Denver? About Maria?"

She nodded.

"The old man picked her up," she said. "By the hardware store. He confirmed her name. He knew a lot about her. They talked for half an hour."

"Half an hour? How? It's less than a twenty-minute drive."

"He didn't let her out in Despair. She wanted to go to the MP base."

They got to the diner at twenty minutes past midnight. The college-girl waitress was on duty. She smiled when she saw them walk in together, as if some kind of a long-delayed but pleasant inevitability had finally taken place. She looked to be about twenty years old, but she was grinning away like a smug old matchmaker from an ancient village. Reacher felt like there was a secret he wasn't privy to. He wasn't sure that Vaughan understood it either.

They sat opposite each other in the back booth. They didn't order doughnuts. Reacher ordered coffee and Vaughan ordered juice, a blend of three exotic fruits, none of which Reacher had ever encountered before.

"You're very healthy," he said.

"I try."

"Is your husband in the hospital? With cancer, from smoking?"

She shook her head.

"No," she said. "He isn't."

Their drinks arrived and they sipped them in silence for a moment and then Reacher asked, "Did the old guy know why Maria wanted to go to the MPs?"

"She didn't tell him. But it's a weird destination, isn't it?"

"Very," Reacher said. "It's an active-service forward operating base. Visitors wouldn't be permitted. Not even if she knew one of the grunts. Not even if one of the grunts was her brother or her sister."

"Combat MPs use women grunts?"

"Plenty."

"So maybe she's one of them. Maybe she was reporting back on duty, after furlough."

"Then why would she have booked two more nights in the motel and left all her stuff there?"

"I don't know. Maybe she was just checking something."

"She's too small for a combat MP."

"They have a minimum size?"

"The army always has had, overall. These days, I'm not sure what it is. But even if she squeezed in, they'd put her somewhere else, covertly."

"You sure?"

"No question. Plus she was too quiet and timid. She wasn't military."

"So what did she want from the MPs? And why isn't she back yet?"

"Did the old guy actually see her get in?"

"Sure," Vaughan said. "He waited, like an old-fashioned gentleman."

"Therefore a better question would be, if they let her in, what did they want from her?"

Vaughan said, "Something to do with espionage."

Reacher shook his head. "I was wrong about that. They're not worried about espionage. They'd have the plant buttoned up, east and west, probably with a presence inside, or at least on the gates."

"So why are they there?"

"They're guarding the truck route. Which means they're worried about theft, of something that would need a truck to haul away. Something heavy, too heavy for a regular car."

"Something too heavy for a small plane, then."

Reacher nodded. "But that plane is involved somehow. This morning I was barging around and therefore they had to shut down the secret operation for a spell, and tonight the plane didn't fly. I didn't hear it, and I found it later, right there in its hangar."

"You think it only flies when they've been working on the military stuff?"

"I know for sure it didn't when they hadn't been, so maybe the obverse is true, too."

"Carrying something? In or out?"

"Maybe both. Like trading."

"Secrets?"

"Maybe."

"People? Like Lucy Anderson's husband?"

Reacher drained his mug. Shook his head. "I can't make that work. There's a logic problem with it. Almost mathematical."

"Try me," Vaughan said. "I did four years of college."

"How long have you got?"

"I'd love to catch whoever dropped the gum wrapper. But I could put that on the back burner, if you like."

Reacher smiled. "There are three things going on over there. The military contract, plus something else, plus something else again."

"OK," Vaughan said. She moved the saltshaker, the pepper shaker, and the sugar shaker to the center of the table. "Three things."

Reacher moved the saltshaker to one side, immediately. "The military contract is what it is. Nothing controversial. Nothing to worry about, except the possibility that someone might steal something heavy. And that's the MPs' problem. They're straddling the road, they've got six Humvees, they've got thirty miles of empty space for a running battle, they can stop any truck they need to. No special vigilance required from the townspeople. No reason for the townspeople to get excited at all."

"But?"

Reacher cupped his hands and put his left around the pepper shaker and his right around the sugar shaker. "But the townspeople *are* excited about something. *All* of them. They *are* vigilant. Today they all turned out in defense of something."

"What something?"

"I have no clue." He held up the sugar shaker, in his right hand. "But it's the bigger of the two unknowns. Because everyone is involved in it. Let's call it the right hand, as in the right hand doesn't know what the left is doing."

"What's the left hand?"

Reacher held up the pepper shaker, in his left hand. "It's smaller. It involves a subset of the population. A small, special subgroup. Everyone knows about the sugar, most *don't* know about the pepper, a few know about both the sugar *and* the pepper."

"And we don't know about either."

"But we will."

"How does this relate to Lucy Anderson's husband not being taken out by plane?"

Reacher held up the sugar shaker. A large glass item, in his right hand. "Thurman flies the plane. Thurman is the town boss. Thurman directs the larger unknown. It couldn't happen any other way. And if the Anderson guy had been a part of it, everyone would have been aware. Including the town cops and Judge Gardner. Thurman would have made sure of that. Therefore Lucy Anderson would not have been arrested, and she would not have been thrown out as a vagrant."

"So Thurman's doing something, and everyone is helping, but a few are also working on something else behind his back?"

Reacher nodded. "And that something the few are working on behind his back involves these young guys."

"And the young guys either get through or they

don't, depending on who they bump into first, the many right-hand people or the few left-hand people."

"Exactly. And there's a new one now. Name of Rogers, just arrested, but I didn't see him."

"Rogers? I've heard that name before."

"Where?"

"I don't know."

"Wherever, he was one of the unlucky ones."

"The odds will always be against them."

"Exactly."

"Which was Ramirez's problem."

"No, Ramirez didn't bump into anyone," Reacher said. "I checked the records. He was neither arrested nor helped."

"Why? What made him different?"

"Great question," Reacher said.

"What's the answer?"

"I don't know."

48

The clock in Reacher's head hit one in the morning and the clock on the diner's wall followed it a minute later. Vaughan looked at her watch and said, "I better get back in the saddle."

Reacher said, "OK."

"Go get some sleep."

"OK."

"Will you come with me to Colorado Springs? To the lab, with the water sample?"

"When?"

"Tomorrow, today, whatever it is now."

"I don't know anything about water."

"That's why we're going to the lab."

"What time?"

"Leave at ten?"

"That's early for you."

"I don't sleep anyway. And this is the end of my pattern. I'm off duty for four nights now. Ten on, four off. And we should leave early because it's a long ride, there and back."

"Still trying to keep me out of trouble? Even on your downtime?"

"I've given up on keeping you out of trouble."

"Then why?"

Vaughan said, "Because I'd like your company. That's all."

She put four bucks on the table for her juice. She put the salt and the pepper and the sugar back where they belonged. Then she slid out of the booth and walked away and pushed through the door and headed for her car.

Reacher showered and was in bed by two o'clock in the morning. He slept dreamlessly and woke up at eight. He showered again and walked the length of the town to the hardware store. He spent five minutes looking at ladders on the sidewalk, and then he went inside and found the racks of pants and shirts and chose a new one of each. This time he went for darker colors and a different brand. Prewashed, and therefore softer. Less durable in the long term, but he wasn't interested in the long term.

He changed in his motel room and left his old stuff folded on the floor next to the trash can. Maybe the maid had a needy male relative his size. Maybe she would know how to launder things so they came out at least marginally flexible. He stepped out of his room and saw that Maria's bathroom light was on. He walked to the office. The clerk was on her stool. Behind her shoulder, the hook for Maria's room had no key on it. The clerk saw him looking and said, "She came back this morning."

He asked, "What time?"

"Very early. About six."

"Did you see how she got here?"

The woman looked both ways and lowered her voice and said, "In an armored car. With a soldier."

"An armored car?"

"Like you see on the news."

Reacher said, "A Humvee."

The woman nodded. "Like a jeep. But with a roof. The soldier didn't stay. Which I'm glad about. I'm no prude, but I couldn't permit a thing like that. Not here."

"Don't worry," Reacher said. "She already has a boyfriend."

Or had, he thought.

The woman said, "She's too young to be fooling around with soldiers."

"Is there an age limit?"

"There ought to be."

Reacher paid his bill and walked back down the row, doing the math. According to the old man's telephone testimony, he had let Maria out at the MP base around eight-thirty the previous morning. She had arrived back in a Humvee at six. The Humvee wouldn't have detoured around the Interstates. It would have come straight through Despair, which was a thirty-minute drive, max. Therefore she had been held for twenty-one hours. Therefore her problem was outside of the FOB's local jurisdiction. She had been locked in a room and her story had been passed up the chain of command. Phone tag, voice mails, secure telexes. Maybe a conference call. Eventually, a decision taken elsewhere, release, the offer of a ride home.

Sympathy, but no help.

No help about what?

He stopped outside her door and listened. The shower wasn't running. He waited one minute in case she was toweling off and a second minute in case she was dressing. Then he knocked. A third minute later she opened the door. Her hair was slick with water. The weight gave it an extra inch of length. She was dressed in jeans and a blue T-shirt. No shoes. Her feet were tiny, like a child's. Her toes were straight. She had been raised by conscientious parents, who had cared about appropriate footwear.

"You OK?" he asked her, which was a dumb question. She didn't look OK. She looked small and tired and lost and bewildered.

She didn't answer.

He said, "You went to the MP base, asking about Raphael."

She nodded.

He said, "You thought they could help you, but they didn't."

She nodded.

He said, "They told you it was Despair PD business."

She didn't answer.

He said, "Maybe I could help you. Or maybe the Hope PD could. You want to tell me what it's all about?"

She said nothing.

He said, "I can't help you unless I understand the problem."

She shook her head.

"I can't tell you," she said. "I can't tell anyone."

The way she said the word *can't* was definitive. Not surly or angry or moody or plaintive, but calm, considered, mature, and ultimately just plain informative. As if she had looked at a whole bunch of options, and boiled them down to the only one that was viable. As if a world of trouble was surely inevitable if she opened her mouth.

She couldn't tell anyone.

Simple as that.

"OK," Reacher said. "Hang in there."

He walked away, to the diner, and had breakfast.

He guessed Vaughan planned to pick him up at the motel, so at five to ten he was sitting in the plastic lawn chair outside his door. She showed up three minutes past the hour, in a plain black Crown Vic. Dull paint, worn by time and trouble. An unmarked squad car, like a detective would drive. She stopped close to him and buzzed the window down. He said, "Did you get promoted?"

"It's my watch commander's ride. He took pity on me and loaned it out. Since you got my truck smashed up."

"Did you find the litterbug?"

"No. And it's a serial crime now. I saw the silver foil later. Technically that's two separate offenses."

"Maria is back. The MPs brought her home early this morning."

"Is she saying anything?"

"Not a word." He got out of the chair and walked around the hood and slid in beside her. The car was very plain. Lots of black plastic, lots of mouse-fur upholstery of an indeterminate color. It felt like a beat-up rental. The front was full of police gear. Radios, a laptop on a bracket, a video camera on the dash, a hard-disc recorder, a red bubble light on a curly cord. But there was no security screen between the front and the rear, and therefore the seat was going to rack all the way back. It was going to be comfortable. Plenty of legroom. The water sample was on the rear seat. Vaughan was looking good. She was in old blue jeans and a white Oxford shirt, the neck open two buttons and the sleeves rolled to her elbows.

She said, "You've changed."

"In what way?"

"Your clothes, you idiot."

"New this morning," he said. "From the hardware store."

"Nicer than the last lot."

"Don't get attached to them. They'll be gone soon."

"What's the longest you ever wore a set of clothes?"

"Eight months," Reacher said. "Desert BDUs, during Gulf War One. Never took them off. We had all kinds of supply snafus. No spares, no pajamas."

"You were in the Gulf, the first time?"

"Beginning to end."

"How was it?"

"Hot."

Vaughan pulled out of the motel lot and headed north to First Street. Turned left, east, toward Kansas. Reacher said, "We're taking the long way around?"

"I think it would be better."

Reacher said, "Me too."

It was an obvious cop car and the roads were empty and Vaughan averaged ninety most of the way, charging head-on toward the mountains. Reacher knew Colorado Springs a little. Fort Carson was there, which was a major army presence, but it was really more of an Air Force town. Aside from that, it was a pleasant place. Scenery was pretty, the air was clean, it was often sunny, the view of Pikes Peak was usually spectacular. The downtown area was neat and compact. The state lab was in a stone government building. It was a satellite operation, an offshoot of the main facility in Denver, the capital. Water was a big deal all over Colorado. There wasn't much of it. Vaughan handed over her bottle and filled out a form and a guy wrapped the form around the bottle and secured it with a rubber band. Then he carried it away, ceremoniously, like that particular quart had the power to save the world, or destroy it. He came back and told Vaughan that she would be notified of the results by phone, and to please let the lab know some figures for Despair's total TCE consumption. He explained that the state used a rough rule-of-thumb formula, whereby a certain percentage of evaporation could be assumed, and a further percentage of absorption by the ground could be relied upon, so that what really mattered was how much was running off and how deep an aquifer was. The state knew the depth of Halfway County's aquifer to the inch, so the only variable would be the exact amount of TCE heading down toward it.

"What are the symptoms?" Vaughan asked. "If it's there already?"

The lab guy glanced at Reacher.

"Prostate cancer," he said. "That's the early warning. Men go first."

They got back in the car. Vaughan was distracted. A little vague. Reacher didn't know what was on her mind. She was a cop and a conscientious member of her community, but clearly she was worrying about more than a distant chemical threat to her water table. He wasn't sure why she had asked him to travel with her. They hadn't spoken much. He wasn't sure that his company was doing her any good at all.

She pulled out off the curb and drove a hundred yards on a tree-lined street and stopped at a light at a T-junction. Left was west and right was east. The light turned green and she didn't move. She just sat there, gripping the wheel, looking left, looking right, as if she couldn't choose. A guy honked behind her. She glanced in the mirror and then she glanced at Reacher.

She said, "Will you come with me to visit my husband?"

49

Vaughan turned left into the hills and then left again and headed south, following a sign for Pueblo. Years before, Reacher had traveled the same road. Fort Carson lay between Colorado Springs and Pueblo, south of one and north of the other, bulked a little ways west of the main drag.

"You OK with this?" Vaughan asked him.

"I'm fine with it."

"But?"

"It's an odd request," he said.

She didn't answer.

"And it's an odd word," he said. "You could have said, come and meet my husband. Or see him. But you said visit. And who gets visitors? You already told me he isn't in jail. Or in the hospital. So where is he? In a rooming house, working away from home? Permanently on duty somewhere? Locked in his sister's attic?"

"I didn't say he wasn't in the hospital," Vaughan said. "I said he didn't have cancer from smoking."

She forked right, away from an I-25 on-ramp, and used a state four-lane that seemed way too wide for the traffic it was getting. She drove a mile between green hills and turned left through a grove of pines on a worn gray road that had no center line. There was no wire and no painted sign, but Reacher was sure the land on both sides was owned by the army. He knew there were thousands of spare acres beyond the northern tip of Fort Carson, requisitioned decades ago at the height of Hot or Cold War fever, and never really used for much. And what he was seeing out the window looked exactly like Department of Defense property. It looked the same everywhere. Nature, made uniform. A little sullen, a little halfhearted, somewhat beaten down, neither raw nor developed.

Vaughan slowed after another mile and made a right into a half-hidden driveway. She passed between two squat brick pillars. The bricks were smooth tan items and the mortar was yellow. Standard army issue, back in the middle fifties. The pillars had hinges but no gates. Twenty yards farther on was a modern billboard on thin metal legs. The billboard had some kind of a corporate logo and the words *Olympic TBI Center* on it. Twenty yards later another billboard said: *Authorized Personnel Only.* Twenty yards after that the driveway's shoulders had been mowed, but not recently. The mown section ran on straight for a hundred yards and led to a carriage circle in front of a group of low brick buildings. Army buildings, long ago deemed surplus to requirements and sold off. Reacher recognized the architecture. Brick and tile, green metal window casements, green tubular handrails, radiused corners built back when chamfered edges had looked like the future. In the center of the carriage circle was a round patch of weedy dirt, where once a CO would have been proud of a rose garden. The change of ownership was confirmed by a repeat of the first billboard, next to the main entrance hall: the corporate logo, plus *Olympic TBI Center* again.

A section of lawn on the right had been hacked out and replaced by gravel. There were five cars on it, all of them with local plates, none of them new or clean. Vaughan parked the Crown Vic on the end of the line and shut it down, first the shifter, then the brake, then the key, a slow and deliberate sequence. She sat back in her seat and dropped her hands to her lap.

"Ready?" she asked.

"For what?" he said.

She didn't answer. Just opened her door and swiveled on the sticky mouse-fur seat and climbed out. Reacher did the same on his side. They walked together to the entrance. Three steps up, through the doors, onto the kind of mottled green tile floor Reacher had walked a thousand times before. The place was recognizably mid-fifties U.S. Army. It felt abandoned and run-down and there were new mandated smoke detectors sloppily wired through exposed plastic conduits, but otherwise it couldn't have changed much. There was an oak hutch on the right, where once a busy sergeant would have sat. Now it was occupied by a mess of what looked like medical case notes and a civilian in a gray sweatshirt. He was a thin sullen man of about forty. He had unwashed black hair worn a little too long. He said, "Hello, Mrs. Vaughan." Nothing more. No warmth in his voice. No enthusiasm.

Vaughan nodded but didn't look at the guy or reply. She just walked to the back of the hall and turned into a large room that in the old days might have served any one of a number of different purposes. It might have been a waiting room, or a reception lounge, or an officers' club. Now it was different. It was dirty and badly maintained. Stained walls, dull floor, dust all over it. Cobwebs on the ceiling. It smelled faintly of antiseptic and urine. It had big red waist-high panic buttons wired through more plastic conduit. It was completely empty, except for two men strapped into wheelchairs. Both men were young, both were entirely slack and still, both had open mouths, both had empty gazes focused a thousand miles in front of them.

Both had shaved heads, and misshapen skulls, and wicked scars.

Reacher stood still.

Looked at the panic buttons.

Thought back to the medical files.

He was in a clinic.

He looked at the guys in the wheelchairs.

He was in a residential home.

He looked at the dust and the dirt.

He was in a dumping ground.

He thought back to the initials on the billboard.

TBI.

Traumatic Brain Injury.

Vaughan had moved on, into a corridor. He caught up with her, halfway along its length.

"Your husband had an accident?" he said.

"Not exactly," she said.

"Then what?"

"Figure it out."

Reacher stopped again.

Both men were young.

An old army building, mothballed and then reused.

"War wounds," he said. "Your husband is military. He went to Iraq."

Vaughan nodded as she walked.

"National Guard," she said. "His second tour. They extended his deployment. Didn't armor his Humvee. He was blown up by an IED in Ramadi."

She turned into another corridor. It was dirty. Dust balls had collected against the baseboards. Some were peppered with mouse droppings. The lightbulbs were dim, to save money on electricity. Some were out and had not been changed, to save money on labor.

Reacher asked, "Is this a VA facility?"

Vaughan shook her head.

"Private contractor," she said. "Political connections. A sweetheart deal. Free real estate and big appropriations."

She stopped at a dull green door. No doubt fifty years earlier it had been painted by a private soldier, in a color and in a manner specified by the Pentagon, with materials drawn from a quartermaster's stores. Then the private soldier's workmanship had been inspected by an NCO, and the NCO's approval had been validated by an officer's. Since then the door had received no further attention. It had dulled and faded and gotten battered and scratched. Now it had a wax pencil scrawl on it: *D. R. Vaughan,* and a string of digits that might have been his service number, or his case number.

"Ready?" Vaughan asked.

"When you are," Reacher said.

"I'm never ready," she said.

She turned the handle and opened the door.

50

David Robert Vaughan's room was a twelve-foot cube, painted dark green below a narrow cream waist-high band, and light green above. It was warm. It had a small sooty window. It had a green metal cabinet and a green metal footlocker. The footlocker was open and held a single pair of clean pajamas. The cabinet was stacked with file folders and oversized brown envelopes. The envelopes were old and torn and frayed and held X-ray films.

The room had a bed. It was a narrow hospital cot with locked wheels and a hand-wound tilting mechanism that raised the head at an angle. It was set to a forty-five-degree slope. In it, under a tented sheet, leaning back in repose like he was relaxing, was a guy Reacher took to be David Robert Vaughan himself. He was a compact, narrow-shouldered man. The tented sheet made it hard to estimate his size. Maybe five-ten, maybe a hundred and eighty pounds. His skin was pink. He had blond stubble on his chin and his cheeks. He had a straight nose and blue eyes. His eyes were wide open.

Part of his skull was missing.

A saucer-sized piece of bone wasn't there. It left a

wide hole above his forehead. Like he had been wearing a small cap at a jaunty angle, and someone had cut all around the edge of it with a saw.

His brain was protruding.

It swelled out like an inflated balloon, dark and purple and corrugated. It looked dry and angry. It was draped with a thin man-made membrane that stuck to the shaved skin around the hole. Like Saran Wrap.

Vaughan said, "Hello, David."

There was no response from the guy in the bed. Four IV lines snaked down toward him and disappeared under the tented sheet. They were fed from four clear plastic bags hung high on chromium stands next to the bed. A colostomy line and a urinary catheter led away to bottles mounted on a low cart parked under the bed. A breathing tube was taped to his cheek. It curved neatly into his mouth. It was connected to a small respirator that hissed and blew with a slow, regular rhythm. There was a clock on the wall above the respirator. Original army issue, from way back. White Bakelite rim, white face, black hands, a firm, quiet, mechanical tick once a second.

Vaughan said, "David, I brought a friend to see you."

No response. And there never would be, Reacher guessed. The guy in the bed was completely inert. Not asleep, not awake. Not anything.

Vaughan bent and kissed her husband on the forehead.

Then she stepped over to the cabinet and tugged an X-ray envelope out of the pile. It was marked *Vaughan, D. R.* in faded ink. It was creased and furred. It had been handled many times. She pulled the film out of the envelope and held it up against the light from the window. It was a composite image that showed her husband's head from four different directions. Front, right side, back, left side. White skull, blurred gray brain matter, a matrix of bright pinpoints scattered all through it.

"Iraq's signature injury," Vaughan said. "Blast damage to the human brain. Severe physical trauma. Compression, decompression, twisting, shearing, tearing, impact with the wall of the skull, penetration by shrapnel. David got it all. His skull was shattered, and they cut the worst of it away. That was supposed to be a good thing. It relieves the pressure. They give them a plastic plate later, when the swelling goes down. But David's swelling never went down."

She put the film back in the envelope, and shuffled the envelope back into the pile. She pulled another one out. It was a chest film. White ribs, gray organs, a blinding shape that was clearly someone else's wristwatch, and small bright pinpoints that looked like drops of liquid.

"That's why I don't wear my wedding band," Vaughan said. "He wanted to take it with him, on a chain around his neck. The heat melted it and the blast drove it into his lungs."

She put the film back in the stack.

"He wore it for good luck," she said.

She butted the paperwork into a neat pile and moved to the foot of the bed. Reacher asked, "What was he?"

"Infantry, assigned to the First Armored Division."

"And this was IED versus Humvee?"

She nodded. "An improvised explosive device against a tin can. He might as well have been on foot in his bathrobe. I don't know why they call them *improvised.* They seem pretty damn professional to me."

"When was this?"

"Almost two years ago."

The respirator hissed on.

Reacher asked, "What was his day job?"

"He was a mechanic. For farm equipment, mostly."

The clock ticked, relentlessly.

Reacher asked, "What's the prognosis?"

Vaughan said, "At first it was reasonable, in theory. They thought he would be confused and uncoordinated, you know, and perhaps a little unstable and aggressive, and certainly lacking all his basic life and motor skills."

"So you moved house," Reacher said. "You were thinking about a wheelchair. You bought a one-story and took the door off the living room. You put three chairs in the kitchen, not four. To leave a space."

She nodded. "I wanted to be ready. But he never woke up. The swelling never went away."

"Why not?"

"Make a fist."

"A what?"

"Make a fist and hold it up."

Reacher made a fist and held it up.

Vaughan said, "OK, your forearm is your spinal cord and your fist is a bump on the end called your brain stem. Some places in the animal kingdom, that's as good as it gets. But humans grew brains. Imagine I scooped out a pumpkin and fitted it over your fist. That's your brain. Imagine the pumpkin goo was kind of bonded with your skin. This is how it was explained to me. I could hit the pumpkin or you could shake it a little and you'd be OK. But imagine suddenly twisting your wrist, very violently. What's going to happen?"

"The bond is going to shear," Reacher said. "The pumpkin goo is going to unstick from my skin."

Vaughan nodded again. "That's what happened to David's head. A shearing injury. The very worst kind. His brain stem is OK but the rest of his brain doesn't even know it's there. It doesn't know there's a problem."

"Will the bond re-form?"

"Never. That just doesn't happen. Brains have spare capacity, but neuron cells can't regenerate. This is all he will ever be. He's like a brain-damaged lizard. He's got the IQ of a goldfish. He can't move and he can't see and he can't hear and he can't think."

Reacher said nothing.

Vaughan said, "Battlefield medicine is very good now. He was stable and in Germany within thirteen hours. In Korea or Vietnam he would have died at the scene, no question."

She moved to the head of the bed and laid her hand on her husband's cheek, very gently, very tenderly. Said, "We think his spinal cord is severed too, as far as we can tell. But that doesn't really matter now, does it?"

The respirator hissed and the clock ticked and the IV lines made tiny liquid sounds and Vaughan stood quietly and then she said, "You don't shave very often, do you?"

"Sometimes," Reacher said.

"But you know how?"

"I learned at my daddy's knee."

"Will you shave David?"

"Don't the orderlies do that?"

"They should, but they don't. And I like him to look decent. It seems like the least I can do." She took a supermarket carrier bag out of the green metal cabinet. It held men's toiletries. Shaving gel, a half-used pack of disposable razors, soap, a washcloth. Reacher found a bathroom across the hall and stepped back and forth with the wet cloth, soaping the guy's face, rinsing it, wetting it again. He smoothed blue gel over the guy's chin and cheeks and lathered it with his fingertips and then set about using the razor. It was difficult. A completely instinctive sequence of actions when applied to himself became awkward on a third party. Especially on a third party who had a breathing tube in his mouth and a large part of his skull missing.

While he worked with the razor, Vaughan cleaned the room. She had a second supermarket bag in the cabinet that held cloths and sprays and a dustpan and brush. She stretched high and bent low and went through the whole twelve-foot cube very thoroughly. Her husband stared on at a point miles beyond the ceiling and the respirator hissed and blew. Reacher finished up and Vaughan stopped a minute later and stood back and looked.

"Good work," she said.

"You too. Although you shouldn't have to do that yourself."

"I know."

They repacked the supermarket bags and put them away in the cabinet. Reacher asked, "How often do you come?"

"Not very often," Vaughan said. "It's a Zen thing, really. If I visit and he doesn't know I've visited, have I really visited at all? It's self-indulgent to come here just to make myself feel like a good wife. So I prefer to visit him in my memory. He's much more real there."

"How long were you married?"

"We're still married."

"I'm sorry. How long?"

"Twelve years. Eight together, then he spent two in Iraq, and the last two have been like this."

"How old is he?"

"Thirty-four. He could live another sixty years. Me too."

"Were you happy?"

"Yes and no, like everyone."

"What are you going to do?"

"Now?"

"Long term."

"I don't know. People say I should move on. And maybe I should. Maybe I should accept destiny, like Zeno. Like a true Stoic. I feel like that, sometimes. But then I panic and get defensive. I feel, first they do this to him, and now I should divorce him? But he wouldn't know anyway. So it's back to the Zen thing. What do you think I should do?"

"I think you should take a walk," Reacher said. "Right now. Alone. Walking by yourself is always good. Get some fresh air. See some trees. I'll bring the car and pick you up before you hit the four-lane."

"What are you going to do?"

"I'll find some way to pass the time."

51

Vaughan said goodbye to her husband and she and Reacher walked back along the dirty corridors and through the dismal lounge to the entrance hall. The guy in the gray sweatshirt said, "Goodbye, Mrs. Vaughan." They walked out to the carriage circle and headed for the car. Reacher leaned against its flank and Vaughan kept on going. He waited until she was small in the distance and then he pushed off the car and headed back to the entrance. Up the steps, in the door. He crossed to the hutch and asked, "Who's in charge here?"

The guy in the gray sweatshirt said, "I am, I guess. I'm the shift supervisor."

Reacher asked, "How many patients here?"

"Seventeen," the guy said.

"Who are they?"

"Just patients, man. Whatever they send us."

"You run this place according to a manual?"

"Sure. It's a bureaucracy, like everywhere."

"You got a copy of the manual available?"

"Somewhere."

"You want to show me the part where it says it's

OK to keep the rooms dirty and have mouse shit in the corridors?"

The guy blinked and swallowed and said, "There's no point *cleaning,* man. They wouldn't *know.* How could they? This is the vegetable patch."

"Is that what you call it?"

"It's what it *is,* man."

"Wrong answer," Reacher said. "This is not the vegetable patch. This is a veterans' clinic. And you're a piece of shit."

"Hey, lighten up, dude. What's it to you?"

"David Robert Vaughan is my brother."

"Really?"

"All veterans are my brothers."

"He's brain dead, man."

"Are you?"

"No."

"Then listen up. And listen very carefully. A person less fortunate than yourself deserves the best you can give. Because of duty, and honor, and service. You understand those words? You should do your job right, and you should do it well, simply because you can, without looking for notice or reward. The people here deserve your best, and I'm damn sure their relatives deserve it."

"Who are you anyway?"

"I'm a concerned citizen," Reacher said. "With a number of options. I could embarrass your corporate parent, I could call the newspapers or the TV, I could come in here with a hidden camera, I could get you fired. But I don't do stuff like that. I offer personal choices instead, face-to-face. You want to know what your choice is?"

"What?"

"Do what I tell you, with a cheery smile."

"Or?"

"Or become patient number eighteen."

The guy went pale.

Reacher said, "Stand up."

"What?"

"On your feet. Now."

"What?"

Reacher said, "Stand up, now, or I'll make it so you never stand up again."

The guy paused a beat and got to his feet.

"At attention," Reacher said. "Feet together, shoulders back, head up, gaze level, arms straight, hands by your sides, thumbs in line with the seams of your pants." Some officers of his acquaintance had barked and yelled and shouted. He had always found it more effective to speak low and quiet, enunciating clearly and precisely as if to an idiot child, bearing down with an icy stare. That way he had found the implied menace to be unmistakable. Calm, patient voice, huge physique. The dissonance was striking. It was a case of whatever worked. It had worked then, and it was working now. The guy in the sweatshirt was swallowing hard and blinking and standing in a rough approximation of parade-ground order.

Reacher said, "Your patients are not just whatever they send you. Your patients are people. They served their country with honor and distinction. They deserve your utmost care and respect."

The guy said nothing.

Reacher said, "This place is a disgrace. It's filthy and chaotic. So listen up. You're going to get off your skinny ass and you're going to organize your people and you're going to get it cleaned up. Starting right now. I'm going to come back, maybe tomorrow, maybe next week, maybe next month, and if I can't see my face in the floor I'm going to turn you upside down and use you like a mop. Then I'm going to kick your ass so hard your colon is going to get tangled up in your teeth. Are we clear?"

The guy paused and shuffled and blinked. Then he said, "OK."

"With a cheery smile," Reacher said.

The guy forced a smile.

"Bigger," Reacher said.

The guy forced dry lips over dry teeth.

"That's good," Reacher said. "And you're going to get a haircut, and every day you're going to shower, and every time Mrs. Vaughan comes by you're going to stand up and welcome her warmly and you're going to personally escort her to her husband's room, and her husband's room is going to be clean, and her husband is going to be shaved, and the window is going to be sparkling, and the room is going to be full of sunbeams, and the floor is going to be so shiny Mrs. Vaughan is going to be in serious danger of slipping on it and hurting herself. Are we clear?"

"OK."

"Are we clear?"

"Yes."

"Completely?"

"Yes."

"Crystal?"

"Yes."

"Yes what?"

"Yes. Sir."

"You've got sixty seconds to get started, or I'll break your arm."

The guy made a phone call while still standing and then used a walkie-talkie and fifty seconds later there were three guys in the hallway. Dead on sixty seconds a fourth guy joined them. A minute later they had buckets and mops out of a maintenance closet and a minute after that the buckets were full of water and all five guys were casting about, as if facing an immense and unfamiliar task. Reacher left them to it. He walked back to the car and set off in pursuit of Vaughan.

He caught up with her a mile down the DoD road. She slid in next to him and he drove on, retracing their route, through the pines, through the hills. She said, "Thank you for coming."

"No problem," he said.

"You know why I wanted you to?"

"Yes."

"Tell me."

"You wanted someone to understand why you live like you live and do what you do."

"And?"

"You wanted someone to understand why it's OK to do what you're going to do next."

"Which is what?"

"Which is entirely up to you. And either way is good with me."

She said, "I lied to you before."

He said, "I know."

"Do you?"

He nodded at the wheel. "You knew about Thurman's military contract. And the MP base. The Pentagon told you all about them, and the Halfway PD, too. Makes sense that way. I bet it's right there in your department phone book, in your desk drawer, *M* for military police."

"It is."

"But you didn't want to talk about it, which means that it's not just any old military scrap getting recycled there."

"Isn't it?"

Reacher shook his head. "It's combat wrecks from Iraq. Has to be. Hence the New Jersey plates on some of the incoming trucks. From the port facilities there. Why would they bypass Pennsylvania and Indiana for regular scrap? And why would they put regular scrap in closed shipping containers? Because Thurman's place is a specialist operation. Secret, miles from nowhere."

"I'm sorry."

"Don't be. I understand. You didn't want to talk about it. You didn't even want to think about it. That's why you tried to stop me from ever going there. Get over it, you said. Move on. There's nothing to see."

"There are blown-up Humvees there," she said.

"They're like monuments to me. Like shrines. To the people who died. Or nearly died."

Then she said, "And to the people who should have died."

They drove on, across the low slopes of the mountains, back to I-70, back toward the long loop near the Kansas line. Reacher said, "It doesn't explain Thurman's taste for secrecy."

Vaughan said, "Maybe it's a respect thing with him. Maybe he sees them as shrines, too."

"Did he ever serve?"

"I don't think so."

"Did he lose a family member?"

"I don't think so."

"Anyone sign up from Despair?"

"Not that I heard."

"So it's not likely to be respect. And it doesn't explain the MPs, either. What's to steal? A Humvee is a car, basically. Armor is plain steel sheet, when it's fitted at all. An M60 wouldn't survive any kind of a blast."

Vaughan said nothing.

Reacher said, "And it doesn't explain the airplane."

Vaughan didn't answer.

Reacher said, "And nothing explains all these young guys."

"So you're going to stick around?"

He nodded at the wheel.

"For a spell," he said. "Because I think something

is about to happen. That crowd impressed me. Would they have that much passion for the beginning of something? Or the middle of something? I don't think so. I think they were all stirred up because they're heading for the end of something."

52

They hit Hope at five in the afternoon. The sun was low. Reacher pulled off First Street and headed down to Third, to the motel. He stopped outside the office. Vaughan looked at him inquiringly and he said, "Something I should have done before."

They went in together. The nosy clerk was at the counter. Behind her, three keys were missing from their hooks. Reacher's own, for room twelve, plus Maria's, room eight, plus one for the woman with the large underwear, room four.

Reacher said, "Tell me about the woman in room four."

The clerk looked at him and paused a second, like she was gathering her thoughts, like she was under pressure to assemble an accurate capsule biography. Like she was in court, on the witness stand.

"She's from California," she said. "She's been here five days. She paid cash for a week."

Reacher said, "Anything else?"

"She's a fuller-figured person."

"Age?"

"Young. Maybe twenty-five or -six."

"What's her name?"

The clerk said, "Mrs. Rogers."

Back in the car Vaughan said, "Another one. But a weird one. Her husband wasn't arrested until yesterday, but she's been here five whole days? What does that mean?"

Reacher said, "It means our hypothesis is correct. My guess is they were on the road together up until five days ago, he found the right people in Despair and went into hiding, she came directly here to wait it out, then he got flushed out by the mass mobilization yesterday and bumped into the wrong people and got picked up. The whole town was turned upside down. Every rock was turned over. He was noticed."

"So where is he now?"

"He wasn't in a cell. So maybe he got back with the right people again."

Vaughan said, "I knew I had heard the name. His wife came in with the supermarket delivery guy. He drives in from Topeka, Kansas, every few days. He gave her a ride. He mentioned it to me. He told me her name."

"Truck drivers check in with you?"

"Small towns. No secrets. Maria came in the same way. That's how I knew about her."

"How did Lucy Anderson come in?"

Vaughan paused a beat.

"I don't know," she said. "I never heard of her before the Despair PD dumped her at the line. She wasn't here before."

"So she came in from the west."

"I guess some of them do. Some from the east, some from the west."

"Which raises a question, doesn't it? Maria came in from the east, from Kansas, but she asked the old guy in the green car to let her out at the MP base west of Despair. How did she even know it was there?"

"Maybe Lucy Anderson told her. She would have seen it."

"I don't think they talked at all."

"Then maybe Ramirez told her about it. Maybe on the phone to Topeka. He came in from the west and saw it."

"But why would he notice it? Why would he care? Why would it be a topic of conversation with his girlfriend?"

"I don't know."

Reacher asked, "Is your watch commander a nice guy?"

"Why?"

"Because he better be. We need to borrow his car again."

"When?"

"Later tonight."

"Later than what?"

"Than whatever."

"How much later?"

"Eight hours from now."

Vaughan said, "Eight hours is good."

Reacher said, "First we're going shopping."

They got to the hardware store just as it was closing. The old guy in the brown coat was clearing his sidewalk display. He had wheeled the leaf blowers inside and was starting in on the wheelbarrows. Reacher went in and bought a slim flashlight and two batteries and a two-foot wrecking bar from the old guy's wife. Then he went back out and bought the trick stepladder that opened to eight different positions. For storage or transport it folded into a neat package about four feet long and a foot and a half wide. It was made of aluminum and plastic and was very light. It fit easily on the Crown Vic's rear bench.

Vaughan invited him over for dinner, at eight o'clock. She was very formal about it. She said she needed the intervening two hours to prepare. Reacher spent the time in his room. He took a nap, and then he shaved and showered and cleaned his teeth. And dressed. His clothes were new, but his underwear was past its prime, so he ditched it. He put on his pants and his shirt and raked his fingers through his hair and checked the result in the mirror and deemed it acceptable. He had no real opinion about his appearance. It was what it was. He couldn't change it. Some people liked it, and some people didn't.

Fifty yards from Vaughan's house, he couldn't see the watch commander's car. Either it was in the driveway, or Vaughan had given it back. Or gotten an emergency call. Or changed her plans for the evening. Then from thirty yards away, he saw the car right there on the curb. A hole in the darkness. Dull glass. Black paint, matte with age. Invisible in the gloom.

Perfect.

He walked through the plantings on her stepping-stone path and touched the bell. *The average delay at a suburban door in the middle of the evening, about twenty seconds.* Vaughan got there in nine flat. She was in a black knee-length sleeveless A-line dress, and black low-heel shoes, like ballet slippers. She was freshly showered. She looked young and full of energy.

She looked stunning.

He said, "Hello."

She said, "Come in."

The kitchen was full of candlelight. The table was set with two chairs and two places and an open bottle of wine and two glasses. Aromas were coming from the stove. Two appetizers were standing on the counter. Lobster meat, avocado, pink grapefruit segments, on a bed of lettuce.

She said, "The main course isn't ready. I screwed up the timing. It's something I haven't made for a while."

"Three years," Reacher said.

"Longer," she said.

"You look great," he said.

"Do I?"

"The prettiest view in Colorado."

"Better than Pikes Peak?"

"Considerably. You should be on the front of the guide book."

"You're flattering me."

"Not really."

She said, "You look good, too."

"That's flattery for sure."

"No, you clean up well."

"I try my best."

She asked, "Should we be doing this?"

He said, "I think so."

"Is it fair to David?"

"David never came back. He never lived here. He doesn't know."

"I want to see your scar again."

"Because you're wishing David had come back with one. Instead of what he got."

"I guess."

Reacher said, "We were both lucky. I know soldiers. I've been around them all my life. They fear grotesque wounds. That's all. Amputations, mutilations, burns. I'm lucky because I didn't get one, and David is lucky because he doesn't know he did."

Vaughan said nothing.

Reacher said, "And we're both lucky because we both met you."

Vaughan said, "Show me the scar."

Reacher unbuttoned his shirt and slipped it off. Vaughan hesitated a second and then touched the ridged skin, very gently. Her fingertips were cool and smooth. They burned him, like electricity.

"What was it?" she asked.

"A truck bomb in Beirut."

"Shrapnel?"

"Part of a man who was standing closer."

"That's awful."

"For him. Not for me. Metal might have killed me."

"Was it worth it?"

Reacher said, "No. Of course not. It hasn't been worth it for a long time."

"How long a time?"

"Since 1945."

"Did David know that?"

"Yes," Reacher said. "He knew. I know soldiers. There's nothing more realistic than a soldier. You can try, but you can't bullshit them. Not even for a minute."

"But they keep on showing up."

"Yes, they do. They keep on showing up."

"Why?"

"I don't know. Never have."

"How long were you in the hospital?"

"A few weeks, that's all."

"As bad a place as David is in?"

"Much worse."

"Why are the hospitals so bad?"

"Because deep down to the army a wounded soldier that can't fight anymore is garbage. So we depend on civilians, and civilians don't care either."

Vaughan put her hand flat against his scar and then slid it around his back. She did the same with her other hand, on the other side. She hugged his waist and held the flat of her cheek against his chest. Then she raised her head and craned her neck and he bent down and kissed her. She tasted of warmth and wine and toothpaste. She smelled like soap and clean skin and delicate fragrance. Her hair was soft. Her eyes were closed. He ran his tongue along the row of unfamiliar teeth and found her tongue. He cradled her head with one hand and put the other low on her back.

A long, long kiss.

She came up for air.

"We should do this," she said.

"We are doing it," he said.

"I mean, it's OK to do this."

"I think so," he said again. He could feel the end of her zipper with the little finger of his right hand. The little finger of his left hand was down on the swell of her ass.

"Because you're moving on," she said.

"Two days," he said. "Three, max."

"No complications," she said. "Not like it might be permanent."

"I can't do permanent," he said.

He bent and kissed her again. Moved his hand and caught the tag of her zipper and pulled it down. She was naked under the dress. Warm, and soft, and smooth, and lithe, and fragrant. He stooped and scooped her up, one arm under her knees and the other under her shoulders. He carried her down the hallway, to where he imagined the bedrooms must be, kissing her all the way. Two doors. Two rooms. One smelled unused, one smelled like her. He carried her in and put her down and her dress slipped from her shoulders and fell. They kissed some more and her hands tore at the button on his pants. A minute later they were in her bed.

Afterward, they ate, first the appetizer, then pork cooked with apples and spices and brown sugar and white wine. For dessert, they went back to bed. At midnight, they showered together. Then they dressed, Reacher in his pants and shirt, Vaughan in black jeans and a black sweater and black sneakers and a slim black leather belt.

Nothing else.

"No gun?" Reacher asked.

"I don't carry my gun off duty," she said.

"OK," he said.

At one o'clock, they went out.

53

Vaughan drove. She insisted on it. It was her watch commander's car. Reacher was happy to let her. She was a better driver than him. Much better. Her panic one-eighty had impressed him. Backward to forward, at full speed. He doubted if he could have done it. He figured if he had been driving the mob would have caught them and torn them apart.

"Won't they be there again?" Vaughan asked.

"Possible," he said. "But I doubt it. It's late, on the second night. And I told Thurman I wouldn't be back. I don't think it will be like yesterday."

"Why would Thurman believe you?"

"He's religious. He's accustomed to believing things that comfort him."

"We should have planned to take the long way around."

"I'm glad we didn't. It would have taken four hours. It wouldn't have left time for dinner."

She smiled and they took off, north to First Street, west toward Despair. There was thick cloud in the sky. No moon. No stars. Pitch black. Perfect. They thumped over the line and a mile before the top of the rise Reacher said, "It's time to go stealthy. Turn all the lights off."

Vaughan clicked the headlights off and the world went dark and she braked hard.

"I can't see anything," she said.

"Use the video camera," he said. "Use the night vision."

"What?"

"Like a video game," he said. "Watch the computer screen, not the windshield."

"Will that work?"

"It's how tank drivers do it."

She tapped keys and the laptop screen lit up and then stabilized into a pale green picture of the landscape ahead. Green scrub on either side, vivid boulders, a bright ribbon of road spearing into the distance. She took her foot off the brake and crawled forward, her head turned, staring at the thermal image, not the reality. At first she steered uncertainly, her hand-eye coordination disrupted. She drifted left and right and overcorrected. Then she settled in and got the hang of the new technique. She did a quarter-mile perfectly straight, and then she sped up and did the next quarter a little faster, somewhere between twenty and thirty.

"It's killing me not to glance ahead," she said. "It's so automatic."

"This is good," Reacher said. "Stay slow." He figured that at twenty or thirty there would be almost no engine noise. Just a low purr, and a soft burble from the pipes. There would be surface noise at any speed, from the tires on the grit, but that would get better closer to town. He leaned left and put his head on her shoulder and watched the screen. The landscape reeled itself in, silent and green and ghostly. The camera had no human reactions. It was just a dumb unblinking eye. It didn't glance left or right or up or down or change focus. They came over the rise and the screen filled with blank cold sky for a second and then the nose of the car dipped down again and they saw the next nine miles laid out in front of them. Green scrub, scattered rocks glowing lighter, the ribbon of road, a tiny flare of heat on the horizon where the embers of the police station were still warm.

Reacher glanced ahead through the windshield a couple of times, but without headlights there was nothing to see. Nothing at all. Just darkness. Which meant that anyone waiting far ahead in the distance wasn't seeing anything either. Not yet anyway. He recalled walking back to Hope, stepping over the line, not seeing Vaughan's cruiser at all. And that was a newer car, shinier, with white doors and polished reflectors in the light bar on the roof. He hadn't seen it. But she had seen him. *I saw you half a mile away,* she had said. *A little green speck.* He had seen himself on the screen afterward, a luminous sliver in the dark, getting bigger, coming closer.

Very fancy, he had said.

Homeland Security money, she had replied. *Got to spend it on something.*

He stared at the screen, watching for little green specks. The car prowled onward, slow and steady, like a black submarine loose in deep water. Two miles. Four. Still nothing ahead. Six miles. Eight. Nothing to see, nothing to hear, except the idling motor and the squelching tires and Vaughan's tense breathing as she gripped the wheel and squinted sideways at the laptop screen.

"We must be getting close," she whispered.

He nodded, on her shoulder. The screen showed buildings maybe a mile ahead. The gas station hut, slightly warmer than its surroundings. The dry goods store, with daytime heat trapped in its brick walls. A background glow from the downtown blocks. A pale blur in the air a little ways south and west, above where the police station had been.

No little green specks.

He said, "This is where they were yesterday."

She said, "So where are they now?"

She slowed a little and drifted onward. The screen held steady. Geography and architecture, nothing more. Nothing moving.

"Human nature," Reacher said. "They got all pumped up yesterday and thought they'd gotten rid of us. They don't have the stamina to do it all again."

"There could be one or two out and about."

"Possible."

"They'll call ahead and warn the plant."

"That's OK," Reacher said. "We're not going to the plant. Not yet anyway."

They drifted on, slow and dark and silent. The vacant lot and the abandoned motor court barely showed up on the screen. Thermally they were just parts of the landscape. The gas station and the household goods store shone brighter. Beyond them the other blocks glowed mid-green. There were window-sized patches of brighter color, and heat was leaking from roofs with imperfect insulation. But there were no pinpoints of light. No little green specks. No crowds, no small groups of shuffling people, no lone sentries.

Not dead ahead anyway.

The camera's fixed angle was useless against the cross-streets. It showed their mouths to a depth of about five feet. That was all. Reacher stared sideways into the darkness as they rolled past each opening. Saw nothing. No flashlights, no match flares, no lighter sparks, no cigarette coals glowing red. The tire noise had dropped away to almost nothing. Main Street was worn down to the tar. No more pebbles. Vaughan was holding her breath. Her foot was feather light on the pedal. The car rolled onward, a little faster than walking, a lot slower than running.

Two green specks stepped out ahead.

They were maybe a quarter of a mile away, at the west end of Main Street. Two figures, emerging from a cross-street. A foot patrol. Vaughan braked gently and came to a stop, halfway through town. Six blocks behind her, six ahead.

"Can they see us?" she whispered.

"I think they're facing away," Reacher said.

"Suppose they're not?"

"They can't see us."

"There are probably more behind us."

Reacher turned and stared through the rear window. Saw nothing. Just pitch black night. He said,

"We can't see them, they can't see us. Laws of physics."

The screen lit up with a white flare. Cone-shaped. Moving. Sweeping.

"Flashlight," Reacher said.

"They'll see us."

"We're too far away. And I think they're shining it west."

Then they weren't. The screen showed the beam turning through a complete circle, flat and level, like a lighthouse. Its heat burned the screen dead white as it passed. Its light lit up the night mist like fog.

Vaughan asked, "Did they see us?"

Reacher watched the screen. Thought about the reflectors in the Crown Vic's headlights. Polished metal, like cats' eyes. He said, "Whoever they are, they're not moving. I don't think they have enough candlepower."

"What do we do?"

"We wait."

They waited two minutes, then three, then five. The idling engine whispered. The flashlight beam snapped off. The image on the laptop screen collapsed back to two narrow vertical specks, distant, green, barely moving. There was nothing to see through the rear window. Just empty darkness.

Vaughan said, "We can't stay here."

Reacher said, "We have to."

The green specks moved, from the center of the screen to the left-hand edge. Slow, blurred, a ghost trail of luminescence following behind them. Then they disappeared, into a cross-street. The screen stabilized. Geography, and architecture.

"Foot patrol," Reacher said. "Heading downtown. Maybe worried about fires."

"Fires?" Vaughan said.

"Their police station burned down last night."

"Did you have something to do with that?"

"Everything," Reacher said.

"You're a maniac."

"Their problem. They're messing with the wrong guy. We should get going."

"Now?"

"Let's get past them while their backs are turned."

Vaughan feathered the gas and the car rolled forward. One block. Two. The screen held steady. Geography, and architecture. Nothing more. The tires were quiet on the battered surface.

"Faster," Reacher said.

Vaughan sped up. Twenty miles an hour. Thirty. At forty the car set up a generalized *whoosh* from the engine and the exhaust and the tires and the air. It seemed painfully loud. But it generated no reaction. Reacher stared left and right into the downtown streets and saw nothing at all. Just black voids. Vaughan gripped the wheel and held her breath and stared at the laptop screen and ten seconds later they were through the town and in open country on the other side.

Four minutes after that, they were approaching the metal plant.

54

The thermal image showed the sky above the plant to be lurid with heat. It was coming off the dormant furnaces and crucibles in waves as big as solar flares. The metal wall was warm. It showed up as a continuous horizontal band of green. It was much brighter at the southern end. Much hotter around the secret compound. It glowed like crazy on the laptop screen.

"Some junkyard," Reacher said.

"They've been working hard in there," Vaughan said. "Unfortunately."

The acres of parking seemed to be all empty. The personnel gate seemed to be closed. Reacher didn't look at it directly. He was getting better information below the visible spectrum, down in the infrared.

Vaughan said, "No sentries?"

Reacher said, "They trust the wall. As they should. It's a great wall."

They drove on, slow and dark and silent, past the lot, past the north end of the plant, onto the truck route. Fifty yards later, they stopped. The Tahoes' beaten tracks showed up on the screen, almost imperceptibly lighter than the surrounding scrub. Compacted dirt, no microscopic air holes, therefore no ventilation, therefore slightly slower to cool at the end of the day. Reacher pointed and Vaughan turned the wheel and bumped down off the blacktop. She stared at the screen and got lined up with the ruts. The car bucked and bounced across the uneven ground. She followed the giant figure 8. The camera's dumb eye showed nothing ahead except gray-green desert. Then it picked up the fieldstone wall. The residential compound. The stones had trapped some daytime heat. The wall showed up as a low speckled band, like a snake, fifty yards to the right, low and fluid and infinitely long.

Vaughan circled the compound in the Tahoes' tracks, almost all the way around, to a point Reacher judged to be directly behind the airplane barn. They parked and shut down and Reacher switched the interior light to the off position and they opened their doors and climbed out. It was pitch dark. The air felt fresh and cold. The clock in his head showed one-thirty in the morning.

Perfect.

They walked fifty yards to the fieldstone wall. They climbed it easily and dropped down on the other side. The back of the airplane barn was directly ahead of them, huge, looming, darker than the sky. They headed straight for it, past cypress trees and over stony ground. The barn was standing dark and empty. The plane was out. Reacher listened hard. Heard nothing. He signaled and Vaughan came up alongside him.

"Step one," he whispered. "We just verified that when they work by day, the plane flies by night."

Vaughan asked, "What's step two?"

"We verify whether they're bringing stuff in, or taking stuff out, or both."

"By watching?"

"You bet."

"How long have we got?"

"About half an hour."

They stepped into the barn. It was vast and pitch dark. It smelled of oil and gasoline and wood treated with creosote. The floor was beaten dirt. Most of the space was completely empty, ready to receive the returning plane. They felt their way around the walls. Vaughan risked a peek with the flashlight. She clamped its head in her palm and reduced its light to a dull red glow. There were shelves on the walls, loaded with gas cans and quarts of oil and small components boxed up in cardboard. Oil filters, maybe, and air filters. Service items. In the center of the back wall was a horizontal drum wrapped with thin steel cable. The drum was set in a complex floor-mounted bracket and had an electric motor bolted to its axle. A winch. To its right the walls were lined with more shelves. There were spare tires. More components. The whole place felt halfway between tidy and chaotic. It was a workspace, nothing more. There were no obvious hiding places. And there were arc lights faintly visible, high above them in the rafters. If they were turned on, the space would be as bright as day.

Vaughan turned off the flashlight.

"No good," she said.

Reacher nodded in the dark. Led the way back out of the barn, to the taxiway, which was a broad strip of dirt beaten and graded the same as the runway. Either side of it were patches of cultivated garden a hundred yards square, spiky silver bushes and tall slender trees set in gravel. Xeriscaping, near enough to the barn for a reasonable view, far enough away that light spill would fall short. Reacher pointed and whispered, "We'll take one each. Hunker down and don't move until I call you. The runway lights will come on behind you, but don't worry about them. They're set to shine flat, north and south."

She nodded and he went left and she went right. She was invisible in the gloom after three paces. He crawled his way to the garden's center and lay down on his front with bushes either side of him and a tree towering over him. Ahead at an angle he had a good oblique view into the barn. He guessed Vaughan would have a complementary view from the other direction. Together they had the whole thing covered. He pressed himself into the ground and waited.

He heard the plane at five after two in the morning. The single engine, distant, lonely, far away, feathering and blipping. He pictured the landing light as he had seen it before, hanging in the sky, hopping a little, heading down. The sound grew closer but quieter, as Thurman found his glide path and backed off the power. The runway lights came on. They were brighter than Reacher had expected. He felt suddenly vulnerable. He could see his own shadow ahead of him, tangled up with the shadows of the leaves all around him. He craned his neck and looked for Vaughan. Couldn't see her. The engine noise grew louder. Then the hangar lights came on. They were very bright. They threw a hard edge of shadow from the barn's roof that came within six feet of him. He looked ahead and saw the giant from the metal plant standing in the barn, his hand on a light switch, a huge shadow thrown out beyond him, almost close enough for Reacher to touch. Nine hundred yards away to his right the plane's engine blipped and sputtered and he heard a rush of air and felt a tiny thump through the ground as the wheels touched down. The engine noise dropped to a rough idle as the plane coasted and then it ramped back up to a roar as the plane taxied. Reacher heard it coming in behind him, unbearably loud. The ground shook and trembled. The plane came in between the two garden areas and the noise thundered and the propeller wash blasted dust off the ground. It slowed and darted right on its unstable wheelbase and the engine revved hard and it turned a tight circle and came to rest in front of its barn, facing outward. It rocked and shuddered for a second and then the engine shut down and the exhaust popped twice and the propeller jerked to a stop.

Silence came back, like a blanket.

The runway lights died.

Reacher watched.

The plane's right-hand door opened and Thurman eased himself out onto the wing step. Big, bulky, stiff, awkward. He was still in his wool suit. He climbed down and stood for a second and then walked away toward the house.

He was carrying nothing.

No bag, no valise, no briefcase, no kind of a package.

Nothing.

He stepped beyond the light spill and disappeared. The giant from the metal plant hauled the steel cable out of the barn and hooked it to an eye below the tail plane. He walked back to the winch and hit a button and the electric motor whined and the plane was pulled slowly backward into the barn. It stopped in its parked position and the giant unhooked the cable and rewound the winch all the way. Then he squeezed around the wing tip and killed the lights and walked away into the darkness.

Carrying nothing.

He had opened no compartments or cubbies, he had checked no holds or nacelles, and he had retrieved nothing from the cabin.

Reacher waited twenty long minutes, for safety's sake. He had never blundered into trouble through impatience, and he never planned to. When he was sure all was quiet he crawled out from the planted area and crossed the taxiway and called softly to Vaughan. He couldn't see her. She was well concealed. She came up from the darkness at his feet and hugged him briefly. They walked to the darkened barn and ducked under the Piper's wing and regrouped next to the fuselage.

Vaughan said, "So now we know. They're taking stuff out, not in."

Reacher said, "But what, and to where? What kind of range does this thing have?".

"With full tanks? Around seven or eight hundred miles. The state cops had a plane like this, once. It's a question of how fast you fly and how hard you climb."

"What would be normal?"

"A little over half-power might get you eight hundred miles at a hundred and twenty-five knots."

"He's gone seven hours every night. Give him an hour on the ground, call it six hours in the air, three there, three back, that's a radius of three hundred and seventy-five miles. That's a circle nearly four hundred thousand square miles in area."

"That's a lot of real estate."

"Can we tell anything from the vector he comes in on?"

Vaughan shook her head. "He has to line up with the runway and land into the wind."

"There's no big tank of gas here. Therefore he refuels at the other end. Therefore he goes where you can buy gas at ten or eleven at night."

"Which is a lot of places," Vaughan said. "Municipal airfields, flying clubs."

Reacher nodded. Pictured a map in his head and thought: *Wyoming, South Dakota, Nebraska, Kansas, part of Oklahoma, part of Texas, New Mexico, the northeast corner of Arizona, Utah*. Always assuming Thurman didn't just fly an hour each way and spend five at dinner somewhere close by in Colorado itself. He said, "We're going to have to ask him."

"Think he'll tell us?"

"Eventually."

They ducked back under the wing and retraced their steps behind the barn to the wall. A minute later they were back in the car, following the ghostly green image of the Tahoes' ruts counterclockwise, all the way around the metal plant to the place where Reacher had decided to break in.

55

The white metal wall was blazing hot in the south and cooler in the north. Vaughan followed it around and stopped halfway along its northern stretch. Then she pulled a tight left and bounced out of the ruts and nosed slowly head-on toward the wall and stopped with her front bumper almost touching it. The front half of the hood was directly below the wall's horizontal cylinder. The base of the windshield was about five feet down and two feet out from the cylinder's maximum bulge.

Reacher got out and dragged the stepladder off the rear bench. He laid it on the ground and unfolded it and adjusted it into an upside-down L-shape. Then he estimated by eye and relaxed the angle a little beyond ninety degrees and locked all the joints. He lifted it high. He jammed the feet in the gutter at the base of the Crown Vic's windshield, where the hood's lip overlapped the wipers. He let it fall forward, gently. It hit the wall with a soft metallic noise, aluminum on painted steel. The long leg of the L came to rest almost vertical. The short leg lay on top of the cylinder, almost horizontal.

"Back up about a foot," he whispered.

Vaughan moved the car and the base of the ladder pulled outward to a kinder angle and the top fell forward by a corresponding degree and ended up perfectly flat.

"I love hardware stores," Reacher said.

Vaughan said, "I thought this kind of wall was supposed to be impregnable."

"We're not over it yet."

"But we're close."

"Normally they come with guard towers and searchlights, to make sure people don't bring cars and ladders."

Vaughan shut the engine down and jammed the parking brake on tight. The laptop screen turned itself off and they were forced back to the visible spectrum, which didn't contain anything very visible. Just darkness. Vaughan carried the flashlight and Reacher took the wrecking bar from the trunk. He levered himself up onto the hood and crouched under the swell of the cylinder. He stepped forward to the base of the windshield and turned again and started to climb the ladder. He carried the wrecking bar in his left hand and gripped the upper rungs with his right. The aluminum squirmed against the steel and set up a weird harmonic in the hollows of the wall. He slowed down to quiet the noise and made it to the angle and leaned forward and crawled along the short horizontal leg of the L on his hands and knees. He shuffled off sideways and lay like a starfish on the cylinder's top surface. Six feet in diameter, almost nineteen feet in circumference, effectively flat enough to be feasible, but still curved enough to be dangerous. And the white paint was slick and shiny. He raised his head cautiously and looked around.

He was six feet from where he wanted to be.

The pyramid of old oil drums was barely visible in the dark, two yards to the west. Its top tier was about eight feet south and eighteen inches down from the top of the wall. He swam forward and grabbed the ladder again. It shifted sideways toward him. No resistance. He called down, "Get on the bottom rung."

The ladder straightened under Vaughan's weight. He hauled himself toward it and clambered over it and turned around and lay down again on the other side. Now he was exactly where he wanted to be. He called, "Come on up."

He saw the ladder flex and sway and bounce a little and the strange harmonic keening started up again. Then Vaughan's head came into view. She paused and got her bearings and made it over the angle and climbed off and lay down in the place he had just vacated, uneasy and spread-eagled. He handed her the wrecking bar and hauled the ladder up sideways, awkwardly, crossing and uncrossing his hands until he had the thing approximately balanced on top of the curve. He glanced right, into the arena, and tugged the ladder a little closer to him and then fed it down on the other side of the wall until the short leg of the L came to rest on an oil drum two tiers down from the top. The long leg came to rest at a gentle slope, like a bridge.

"I love hardware stores," he said again.

"I love solid ground," Vaughan said.

He took the wrecking bar back from her and

stretched forward and got both hands on the ladder rails. He jerked downward, hard, to make sure it was seated tight. Then he supported all his weight with his arms, like he was chinning a bar, and let his legs slide off the cylinder. He kicked and struggled until he got his feet on the ladder. Then he climbed down, backward, his ass in the air where the slope was gentle, in a more normal position after the angle. He stepped off onto the oil drum and glanced around. Nothing to see. He held his end of the ladder steady and called up to Vaughan, "Your turn."

She came down the same way he had, backward, butt high like a monkey, then more or less vertically after the turn, ending up standing on the drum between his outstretched arms, which were still on the ladder. He left them there for a minute and then he moved and said, "Now it's easy. Like stairs."

They clambered down the pyramid. The empty drums boomed softly. They stepped off onto the sticky dirt and crunched out into the open.

"This way," Reacher said.

They covered the quarter-mile to the vehicle gate in less than five minutes. The white Tahoes were parked close together near one end of it and there was a line of five flat-bed semis near the other. No tractor units attached. Just the trailers, jacked up at their fronts on their skinny parking legs. Four were facing outward, toward the gate. They were loaded with steel bars. Product, ready to go. The fifth was facing inward, toward the plant itself. It was loaded with a closed shipping container, dark in color, maybe blue, with the words *CHINA LINES* stenciled on it. Scrap, incoming. Reacher glanced at it and passed it by and headed toward the line of offices. Vaughan walked with him. They ignored the security hut, and Thurman's own office, and Operations, and Purchasing, and Invoicing, and the first white-painted infirmary unit. They stopped outside the second. Vaughan said, "Visiting the sick again?"

Reacher nodded. "He might talk, without Thurman here."

"The door might be locked."

Reacher raised the wrecking bar.

"I have a key," he said.

But the door wasn't locked. And the sick deputy wasn't talking. The sick deputy was dead.

The guy was still tucked tight under the sheet, but he had taken his last breath some hours previously. That was clear. And maybe he had taken it alone. He looked untended. His skin was cold and set and waxy. His eyes were clouded and open. His hair was thin and messy, like he had been tossing on the pillow, listlessly, looking for companionship or comfort. His chart had not been added to or amended since the last time Reacher had seen it. The long list of symptoms and complaints was still there, unresolved and apparently undiagnosed.

"TCE?" Vaughan said.

"Possible," Reacher said.

We're doing the best we can, Thurman had said.

We're hoping he'll get better. I'll have him taken to the hospital in Halfway tomorrow.

Bastard, Reacher thought.

"This could happen in Hope," Vaughan said. "We need the data for Colorado Springs. For the lab."

"That's why we're here," Reacher said.

They stood by the bedside for a moment longer and then they backed out. They closed the door gently, as if it would make a difference to the guy, and headed down the steps and then up the line to the office marked Purchasing. Its door was secured with a padlock through a hasp. The padlock was strong and the hasp was strong but the screws securing the hasp to the jamb were weak. They yielded to little more than the weight of the wrecking bar alone. They pulled out of the wood frame and fell to the ground and the door sagged open an inch. Vaughan turned the flashlight on and hid its beam in her palm. She led the way inside. Reacher followed and closed the door and propped a chair against it.

There were three desks inside and three phones and a whole wall of file cabinets, three drawers high, maybe forty inches tall. A hundred and forty cubic feet of purchase orders, according to Reacher's automatic calculation.

"Where do we start?" Vaughan whispered.

"Try *T* for TCE."

The T drawers were about four-fifths of the way along the array, as common sense and the alphabet dictated they should be. They were crammed with papers. But none of the papers referred to trichloroethylene. Everything was filed according to supplier name.

The T drawers were all about corporations called Tri-State and Thomas and Tomkins and Tribune. Tri-State had renewed a fire insurance policy eight months previously, Thomas was a telecommunications company that had supplied four new cell phones three months previously, Tomkins had put tires on two front-loaders six months ago, and Tribune delivered binding wire on a two-week schedule. All essential activity for the metal plant's operation, no doubt, but none of it chemical in nature.

"I'll start at *A*," Vaughan said.

"And I'll start at *Z*," Reacher said. "I'll see you at *M* or *N*, if not before."

Vaughan was faster than Reacher. She had the flashlight. He had to rely on stray beams spilling from the other end of the array. Some things were obviously irrelevant. Anything potentially questionable, he had to haul it out and peer at it closely. It was slow work. The clock in his head ticked around, relentlessly. He started to worry about the dawn. It wasn't far away. At one point he found something ordered in the thousands of gallons, but on close inspection it was only gasoline and diesel fuel. The supplier was Western Energy of Wyoming and the purchaser was Thurman Metals of Despair, Colorado. He crammed the paper back in place and moved left to the *V* drawers. The first file he pulled was for medical supplies. Saline solution, IV bags, IV stands, miscellaneous requisites. Small quantities, enough for a small facility.

The supplier was Vernon Medical of Houston, Texas.

The purchaser was Olympic Medical of Despair, Colorado.

Reacher held the paper out to Vaughan. An official purchase order, on an official company letterhead, complete with the same corporate logo they had seen twice on the billboards south of Colorado Springs. Main office address, inside the metal plant, two cabins down.

"Thurman owns Olympic," Reacher said. "Where your husband is."

Vaughan was quiet for a long moment. Then she said, "I don't think I like that."

Reacher said, "I wouldn't either."

"I should get him out of there."

"Or get Thurman out of there."

"How?"

"Keep digging."

They got back to work. Reacher got through *V*, and *U*, and skipped *T* because they had already checked it. He learned that Thurman's oxyacetylene supplier was Utah Gases and his kerosene supplier was Union City Fuels. He found no reference to trichloroethylene. He was opening the last of the S drawers when Vaughan said, "Got it."

"Kearny Chemical of New Jersey," she said. "TCE purchases going back seven years."

She lifted the whole file cradle out of the drawer and shone the flashlight on it and riffed through the papers with her thumb. Reacher saw the word trichloroethylene repeated over and over, jumping around from line to line like a kid's badly drawn flip cartoon.

"Take the whole thing," he said. "We'll add up the quantities later."

Vaughan jammed the file under her arm and pushed the drawer shut with her hip. Reacher moved the chair and opened the door and they stepped out together to the dark. Reacher stopped and used the flashlight and found the fallen screws and pushed them back into their holes with his thumb. They held loosely and made the lock look untouched. Then he followed Vaughan as she retraced their steps, past Operations, past Thurman's digs, past the security office. She waited for him and they dodged around the China Lines container together and headed out into open space.

Then Reacher stopped again.

Turned around.

"Flashlight," he said.

Vaughan gave up the flashlight and he switched it on and played the beam across the side of the container. It loomed up, huge and unreal in the sudden light, high on its trailer like it was suspended in midair. It was forty feet long, corrugated, boxy, metal. Completely standard in every way. It had *CHINA LINES* painted on it in large letters, dirty white, and a vertical row of Chinese characters, plus a series of ID numbers and codes stenciled low in one corner.

Plus a word, handwritten in capitals, in chalk.

The chalk was faded, as if it had been applied long ago at the other end of a voyage of many thousands of miles.

The word looked like *CARS*.

Reacher stepped closer. The business end of the

container had a double door, secured in the usual way with four foot-long levers that drove four sturdy bolts that ran the whole height of the container and socketed home in the box sections top and bottom. The levers were all in the closed position. Three were merely slotted into their brackets, but the fourth was secured with a padlock and guaranteed by a tell-tale plastic tag.

Reacher said, “This is an incoming delivery.”

Vaughan said, “I guess. It’s facing inward.”

“I want to see what’s inside.”

“Why?”

“I’m curious.”

“There are cars inside. Every junkyard has cars.”

He nodded in the dark. “I’ve seen them come in. From neighboring states, tied down on open flat-beds. Not locked in closed containers.”

Vaughan was quiet for a beat. “You think this is army stuff from Iraq?”

“It’s possible.”

“I don’t want to see. It might be Humvees. They’re basically cars. You said so yourself.”

He nodded again. “They are basically cars. But no one ever calls them cars. Certainly not the people who loaded this thing.”

“If it’s from Iraq.”

“Yes, if.”

“I don’t want to see.”

“I do.”

“We need to get going. It’s late. Or early.”

“I’ll be quick,” he said. “Don’t watch, if you don’t want to.”

She stepped away, far enough into the darkness that he couldn't see her anymore. He held the flashlight in his teeth and stretched up tall and jammed the tongue of the wrecking bar through the padlock's hoop. Counted *one two* and on *three* he jerked down with all his strength.

No result.

Working way above his head was reducing his leverage. He got his toes on the ledge where the box was reinforced at the bottom and grabbed the vertical bolt and hauled himself up to where he could tackle the problem face-to-face. He got the wrecking bar back in place and tried again. *One, two, jerk.*

No result.

Case-hardened steel, cold rolled, thick and heavy. A fine padlock. He wished he had bought a three-foot bar. Or a six-foot pry bar. He thought about finding some chain and hooking a Tahoe up to it. The keys were probably in. But the chain would break before the padlock. He mused on it and let the frustration build. Then he jammed the wrecking bar home for a third try. *One. Two.* On *three* he jerked downward with all the force in his frame and jumped off his ledge so that his whole bodyweight reinforced the blow. A two-fisted punch, backed up by two hundred and fifty pounds of moving mass.

The padlock broke.

He ended up sprawled in the dirt. Curved fragments of metal hit him in the head and the shoulder. The wrecking bar clanged off the ledge and caught him in the foot. He didn't care. He climbed back up and broke the tag and smacked the levers out of their slots and opened the doors. Metal squealed. He lit up the flashlight and took a look inside.

Cars.

The restlessness of a long sea voyage had shifted them neatly to the right side of the container. There were four of them, two piled on two, longitudinally. Strange makes, strange models. Dusty, sandblasted, pastel colors.

They were grievously damaged. They were opened like cans, ripped, peeled, smashed, twisted. They had holes through their sheet metal the size of telephone poles.

They had pale rectangular license plates covered with neat Arabic numbers. Off-white backgrounds, delicate backward hooks and curls, black diamond-shaped dots.

Reacher turned in the doorway and called into the darkness, "No Humvees." He heard light footsteps and Vaughan appeared in the gloom. He leaned down and took her hand and pulled her up. She stood with him and followed the flashlight beam as he played it around.

"From Iraq?" she asked.

He nodded. "Civilian vehicles."

"Suicide bombers?" she asked.

"They'd be blown up worse than this. There wouldn't be anything left at all."

"Insurgents, then," she said. "Maybe they didn't stop at the roadblocks."

"Why bring them here?"

"I don't know."

"Roadblocks are defended with machine guns.

These things were hit by something else entirely. Just look at the damage."

"What did it?"

"Cannon fire, maybe. Some kind of big shells. Or wire-guided missiles."

"Ground or air?"

"Ground, I think. The trajectories look like they were pretty flat."

"Artillery versus sedans?" Vaughan said. "That's kind of extreme."

"You bet it is," Reacher said. "Exactly what the hell is going on over there?"

They closed the container and Reacher scratched around in the sand with the flashlight until he found the shattered padlock. He threw the separate pieces far into the distance. Then they hiked the quarter-mile back to the oil drum pyramid and scaled the wall in the opposite direction. Out, not in. It was just as difficult. The construction was perfectly symmetrical. But they got over. They climbed down and stepped off onto the Crown Vic's hood and slid back to solid ground. Reacher folded the ladder and packed it in the rear seat. Vaughan put the captured Kearny Chemical file in the trunk, under the mat.

She asked, "Can we take the long way home? I don't want to go through Despair again."

Reacher said, "We're not going home."

56

They found Despair's old road and followed it west to the truck route. They turned their headlights on a mile later. Four miles after that they passed the MP base, close to four o'clock in the morning. There were two guys in the guard shack. The orange nightlight lit their faces from below. Vaughan didn't slow but Reacher waved anyway. The two guys didn't wave back.

Vaughan asked, "Where to?"

"Where the old road forks. We're going to pull over there."

"Why?"

"We're going to watch the traffic. I'm working on a theory."

"What theory?"

"I can't tell you. I might be wrong, and then you wouldn't respect me anymore. And I like it better when a woman respects me in the morning."

Thirty minutes later Vaughan bumped down off the new blacktop and U-turned in the mouth of the old road and backed up on the shoulder. When the sun came up they would have a view a mile both ways. They would be far from inconspicuous, but also far from suspicious. Crown Vics were parked on strategic bends all over America, all day every day.

They cracked their windows to let some air in and reclined their seats and went to sleep. Two hours, Reacher figured, before there would be anything to see.

Reacher woke up when the first rays of the morning sun hit the left-hand corner of the windshield. Vaughan stayed asleep. She was small enough to have turned in her seat. Her cheek was pressed against the mouse fur. Her knees were up and her hands were pressed together between them. She looked peaceful.

The first truck to pass them by was heading east toward Despair. It was a flat-bed semi with Nevada plates on both ends. It was loaded with a tangle of rusted-out junk. Washing machines, tumble dryers, bicycle frames, bent rebar, road signposts all folded and looped out of shape by accidents. The truck thundered by with its exhaust cackling on the overrun as it coasted through the bend. Then it was gone, in a long tail of battered air and dancing dust.

Ten minutes later a second truck blew by, an identical flat-bed doing sixty, from Montana, heaped with wrecked cars. Its tires whined loud and Vaughan woke up and glanced ahead at it and asked, "How's your theory doing?"

Reacher said, "Nothing to support it yet. But also nothing to disprove it."

"Good morning."

"To you, too."

"Sleep long?"

"Long enough."

The next truck was also heading east, an ugly ten-wheel army vehicle with two guys in the cab and a green box on the back, a standardized NATO payload hauler built in Oshkosh, Wisconsin, and about as pretty as an old pair of dungarees. It wasn't small, but it was smaller than the preceding semis. And it was slower. It barreled through the curve at about fifty miles an hour and left less of a turbulent wake.

"Resupply," Reacher said. "For the MP base. Beans, bullets, and bandages, probably from Carson."

"Does that help?"

"It helps the MPs. The beans anyway. I don't suppose they're using many bullets or bandages."

"I meant, does it help with your theory?"

"No."

Next up was a semi coming west, out of Despair. The bed was loaded with steel bars. A dense, heavy load. The tractor unit's engine was roaring. The exhaust note was a deep bellow and black smoke was pouring from the stack.

Vaughan said, "One of the four we saw last night."

Reacher nodded. "The other three will be right behind it. The business day has started."

"By now they know we broke into that container."

"They know somebody did."

"What will they do about it?"

"Nothing."

The second of the outgoing semis appeared on the

horizon. Then the third. Before the fourth showed up another incoming truck blew by. A container truck. A blue China Lines container on it. Heavy, by the way the tires stressed and whined.

New Jersey plates.

Vaughan said, "Combat wrecks."

Reacher nodded and said nothing. The truck disappeared in the morning haze and the fourth outgoing load passed it. Then the dust settled and the world went quiet again. Vaughan arched her back and stretched, perfectly straight from her heels to her shoulders.

"I feel good," she said.

"You deserve to."

"I needed you to know about David."

"You don't have to explain," Reacher said. He was turned in his seat, watching the western horizon a mile away. He could see a small shape, wobbling in the haze. A truck, far away. Small, because of the distance. Square, and rigid. A box truck, tan-colored.

He said, "Pay attention now."

The truck took a minute to cover the mile and then it roared past. Two axles, plain, boxy. Tan paint. No logo on it. No writing of any kind.

It had Canadian plates, from Ontario.

"Prediction," Reacher said. "We're going to see that truck heading out again within about ninety minutes."

"Why wouldn't we? It'll unload and go home."

"Unload what?"

"Whatever is in it."

"Which would be what?"

"Scrap metal."

"From where?"

"Ontario's biggest city is Toronto," Vaughan said. "So from Toronto, according to the law of averages."

Reacher nodded. "Route 401 in Canada, I-94 around Detroit, I-75 out of Toledo, I-70 all the way over here. That's a long distance."

"Relatively."

"Especially considering that Canada probably has steel mills all its own. I know for sure they're thick on the ground around Detroit and all over Indiana, which is practically next door. So why haul ass all the way out here?"

"Because Thurman's place is a specialist operation. You said so yourself."

"Canada's army is three men and a dog. They probably keep their stuff forever."

Vaughan said, "Combat wrecks."

Reacher said, "Canada isn't fighting in Iraq. Canadians had more sense."

"So what was in that truck?"

"My guess is nothing at all."

Plenty more trucks passed by in both directions, but they were all uninteresting. Semi trailers from Nebraska, Wyoming, Utah, Washington State, and California, loaded with crushed cars and bales of crushed steel and rusted industrial hulks that might once have been boilers or locomotives or parts of ships. Reacher looked at them as they passed and then looked away. He kept his focus on the eastern horizon and the clock in his head. Vaughan got out and brought the captured file from under the mat in the trunk. She took the papers out of the cardboard cradle and turned them over and squared them on her knee. Licked her thumb and started with the oldest page first. It was dated a little less than seven years previously. It was a purchase order for five thousand gallons of trichloroethylene, to be delivered prepaid by Kearny Chemical to Thurman Metals. The second-oldest page was identical. As was the third. The fourth fell into the following calendar year.

Vaughan said, "Fifteen thousand gallons in the first year. Is that a lot?"

"I don't know," Reacher said. "We'll have to let the state lab be the judge."

The second year of orders came out the same. Fifteen thousand gallons. Then the third year jumped way up, to five separate orders for a total of twenty-five thousand gallons. A refill every seventy-some days. An increase in consumption of close to sixty-seven percent.

Vaughan said, "The start of major combat operations. The first wrecks."

The fourth year held steady at twenty-five thousand gallons.

The fifth year matched it exactly.

"David's year," Vaughan said. "His Humvee was rinsed with some of those gallons. What was left of it."

The sixth year she looked at jumped again. Total of six orders. Total of thirty thousand gallons. Iraq, getting worse. A twenty percent increase. And the current year looked set to exceed even that. There were already six orders in, and the year still had a whole quarter to run. Then Vaughan paused and looked at the six pages again, one by one, side by side, and she said, "No, one of these is different."

Reacher asked, "Different how?"

"One of the orders isn't for trichloroethylene. And it isn't in gallons. It's in tons, for something called trinitrotoluene. Thurman bought twenty tons of it."

"When?"

"Three months ago. Maybe they misfiled it."

"From Kearny?"

"Yes."

"Then it isn't misfiled."

"Maybe it's another kind of degreaser."

"It isn't."

"You heard of it?"

"Everyone has heard of it. It was invented in 1863 in Germany, for use as a yellow dye."

"I never heard of it," Vaughan said. "I don't like yellow."

"A few years later they realized it decomposes in an exothermic manner."

"What does that mean?"

"It explodes."

Vaughan said nothing.

"Trichloroethylene is called TCE," Reacher said. "Trinitrotoluene is called TNT."

"I've heard of *that*."

"Everyone has heard of it."

"Thurman bought twenty tons of dynamite? Why?"

"Dynamite is different. It's nitroglycerine soaked

into wood pulp and molded into cylinders wrapped in paper. TNT is a specific chemical compound. A yellow solid. Much more stable. Therefore much more useful."

"OK, but why did he buy it?"

"I don't know. Maybe he busts things up with it. It melts easily, and pours. That's how they get it into shell casings and bombs and shaped charges. Maybe he uses it like a liquid and forces it between seams he can't cut. He was boasting to me about his advanced techniques."

"I never heard any explosions."

"You wouldn't. You're twenty miles from the plant. And maybe they're small and controlled."

"Is it a solvent, when it's liquid?"

"I'm not sure. It's a reagent, that's all I know. Carbon, hydrogen, nitrogen, and oxygen. Some complicated formula, lots of sixes and threes and twos."

Vaughan riffled back through the pages she had already examined.

"Whatever, he never bought any before," she said. "It's something new."

Reacher glanced ahead through the windshield. Saw the tan box truck heading back toward them. It was less than a mile away. He took the red bubble light off the dash and held it in his hand.

"Stand by," he said. "We're going to stop that truck."

"We can't," Vaughan said. "We don't have jurisdiction here."

"The driver doesn't know that. He's Canadian."

57

Vaughan was a cop from a small quiet town, but she handled the traffic stop beautifully. She started the car when the truck was still a quarter-mile away and put it in gear. Then she waited for the truck to pass and pulled out of the old road onto the new and settled in its wake. She hung back a hundred yards, to be clearly visible in its mirrors. Reacher opened his window and clamped the bubble light on the roof. Vaughan hit a switch and the light started flashing. She hit another switch and her siren quacked twice.

Nothing happened for ten long seconds.

Vaughan smiled.

"Here it comes," she said. "The *Who, me?* moment."

The truck started to slow. The driver lifted off and the cab pitched down a degree as weight and momentum settled on the front axle. Vaughan moved up fifty yards and drifted left to the crown of the road. The truck put its turn signal on. It rolled ahead and then braked hard and aimed for a spot where the shoulder was wide. Vaughan skipped past and tucked in again and the two vehicles came to a stop, nose-to-tail in the middle of nowhere, forty miles of empty road behind them and more than that ahead.

She said, "A search would be illegal."

Reacher said, "I know. Just tell the guy to sit tight, five minutes. We'll wave him on when we're done."

"With what?"

"We're going to take a photograph."

Vaughan got out and cop-walked to the driver's window. She spoke for a moment, then walked back. Reacher said, "Back up on the other shoulder, at right angles. We need to see the whole truck, side-on with the camera."

Vaughan checked ahead and behind and jockeyed forward and back and then reversed across the blacktop in a wide curve and came to rest sideways on the opposite shoulder, with the front of her car pointed dead-center at the side of the truck. It was a plain, simple vehicle. A stubby hood, a cab, twin rails running back from it with a box body bolted on. The box had alloy skin and was corrugated every foot for strength and rigidity. Tan paint, no writing.

Reacher said, "Camera."

Vaughan hit laptop keys and the screen lit up with a picture of the truck.

Reacher said, "We need to see the thermal image."

Vaughan said, "I don't know if it works in the daytime." She hit more keys and the screen blazed white. No detail, no definition. Everything was hot.

Reacher said, "Turn down the sensitivity."

She toggled keys and the screen dimmed. Ahead through the windshield the real-time view stayed unchanged but the image on the laptop screen faded to nothing and then came back ghostly green. Vaughan played around until the road surface and the background scrub showed up as a baseline gray, barely visible. The truck itself glowed a hundred shades of green. The hood was warm, with a bright center where the engine was. The exhaust pipe was a vivid line, with green gases shimmering out the end in clouds. The rear differential was hot and the tires were warm. The cab was warm, a generalized green block with a slight highlight where the driver was sitting and waiting.

The box body was cold at the rear. It stayed cold until it suddenly got warmer three-quarters of the way forward. A section five feet long directly behind the cab was glowing bright.

Reacher said, "Take it down some more."

Vaughan tapped a key until the tires went gray and merged with the road. She kept on going until the grays went black and the picture simplified to just five disembodied elements in just two shades of green. The engine, hot. The exhaust system, hot. The differential case, warm. The cab, warm.

The first five feet of the box body, warm.

Vaughan said, "It reminds me of the wall around the metal plant. Hotter at one end than the other."

Reacher nodded. Stuck his arm out the window, waved the driver onward, and peeled the bubble light off the roof. The truck lurched as the gears caught and it pulled across the rumble strip and got straight in the traffic lane and lumbered slowly away, first gear, then second, then third. The laptop screen showed a vivid plume of hot exhaust that swelled and swirled into a lime-green cloud before cooling and dissipating and falling away into blackness.

Vaughan asked, "What did we just see?"

"A truck on its way to Canada."

"That's all?"

"You saw what I saw."

"Is this part of your theory?"

"Pretty much all of it."

"Want to tell me about it?"

"Later."

"Than what?"

"When it's safely across the border."

"Why then?"

"Because I don't want to put you in a difficult position."

"Why would it?"

"Because you're a cop."

"Now you're trying to keep *me* out of trouble?"

Reacher said, "I'm trying to keep everybody out of trouble."

They turned around and drove back to where the old road forked. They bumped down off the new blacktop and this time they kept on going, between the two ruined farms, all the way to Halfway township. First stop was the coffee shop, for a late breakfast. Second stop was a Holiday Inn, where they rented a bland beige room and showered and made love and went to sleep. They woke up at four, and did all the same things in reverse order, like a film run backward. They made love again, showered again, checked out of the hotel, and headed back to the coffee shop for an early dinner. By five-thirty they were on the road again, heading east, back toward Despair.

Vaughan drove. The setting sun was behind her, bright in her mirror. It put a glowing rectangle of light on her face. The truck route was reasonably busy in both directions. The metal plant ahead was still sucking stuff in and spitting it out again. Reacher watched the license plates. He saw representatives from all of Colorado's neighboring states, plus a container truck from New Jersey, heading outward, presumably empty, and a flat-bed semi from Idaho heading inward, groaning under a load of rusted steel sheet.

He thought: *license plates.*

He said, "I was in the Gulf the first time around."

Vaughan nodded. "You wore the same BDUs every day for eight months. In the heat. Which is a delightful image. I felt bad enough putting these clothes back on."

"We spent most of the time in Saudi and Kuwait, of course. But there were a few covert trips into Iraq itself."

"And?"

"I remember their license plates being silver. But the ones we saw last night in the container were off-white."

"Maybe they changed them since then."

"Maybe. But maybe they didn't. Maybe they had other things to worry about."

"You think those weren't Iraqi cars?"

"I think Iran uses off-white plates."

"So what are you saying? We're fighting in Iran and nobody knows? That's not possible."

"We were fighting in Cambodia in the seventies and nobody knew. But I think it's more likely there's a bunch of Iranians heading west to Iraq to join in the fun every day. Maybe like commuting to a job. Maybe we're stopping them at the border crossings. With artillery."

"That's very dangerous."

"For the passengers, for sure."

"For the world," Vaughan said.

They passed the MP base just before six-fifteen. Neat, quiet, still, six parked Humvees, four guys in the guard shack. All in order, and recently resupplied.

For what?

They slowed for the last five miles and tried to time it right. Traffic had died away to nothing. The plant was closed. The lights were off. Presumably the last stragglers were heading home, to the east. Presumably the Tahoes were parked for the night. Vaughan made the left onto Despair's old road and then found the ruts in the gathering gloom and followed them like she had the night before, through the throat of the figure 8 and all the way to the spot behind the airplane barn. She parked there and went to pull the key but Reacher put his hand on her wrist and said, "I have to do this part alone."

Vaughan said, "Why?"

"Because this has to be face-to-face. And the

whole deal here is that you're permanent and I'm not. You're a cop from the next town, with a lot of years ahead of you. You can't go trespassing and breaking and entering all over the neighborhood."

"I already have."

"But nobody knew. Which made it OK. This time it won't be OK."

"You're shutting me out?"

"Wait on the road. Any hassle, take off for home. I'll make my own way back."

He left the ladder and the wrecking bar and the flashlight where they were, in the car. But he took the captured switchblades with him. He put one in each pocket, just in case.

Then he hiked the fifty yards through the scrub and climbed the fieldstone wall.

58

It was still too light to make any sense out of hiding. Reacher just leaned against the barn's board wall, near the front corner, outside, on the blind side, away from the house. He could smell the plane. Cold metal, oil, unburned hydrocarbons from the tanks. The clock in his head showed one minute before seven in the evening.

He heard footsteps at one minute past.

Long strides, a heavy tread. The big guy from the plant, hustling. Lights came on in the barn. A bright rectangle of glare spilled forward, shadowed with wings and propeller blades.

Then nothing, for two minutes.

Then more footsteps. Slower. A shorter stride. An older man with good shoes, overweight, battling stiffness and limping with joint pain.

Reacher took a breath and stepped around the corner of the barn, into the light.

The big guy from the plant was standing behind the Piper's wing, just waiting, like some kind of a servant or a butler. Thurman was on the path leading from the house. He was dressed in his wool suit. He was wearing a white shirt and a blue tie.

He was carrying a small cardboard carton.

The carton was about the size of a six-pack of beer. There was no writing on it. The top flaps were folded shut, one under the other. It wasn't heavy. Thurman was carrying it two-handed; out in front of his body, reverentially, but without strain. He stopped dead on the path but didn't speak. Reacher watched him try to find something to say, and then watched him give up. So he filled the silence himself. He said, "Good evening, folks."

Thurman said, "You told me you were leaving."

"I changed my mind."

"You're trespassing."

"Probably."

"You need to leave now."

"I've heard that before."

"I meant it before, and I mean it now."

"I'll leave when I've seen what's in that box."

"Why do you want to know?"

"Because I'm curious about what part of Uncle Sam's property you're smuggling out of here every night."

The big guy from the plant squeezed around the tip of the Piper's wing and stepped out of the barn and put himself between Reacher and Thurman, closer to Thurman than Reacher. Two against one, explicitly. Thurman looked beyond the big guy's shoulder directly at Reacher and said, "You're intruding." Which struck Reacher as an odd choice of word. *Interfering, trespassing, butting in,* he would have expected.

"Intruding on what?" he asked.

The big guy asked his boss, "You want me to throw him out?"

Reacher saw Thurman thinking about his answer. There was debate in his face, some kind of a long-range calculus that went far beyond the possible positive or negative outcome of a two-minute brawl in front of an airplane hangar. Like the old guy was playing a long game, and thinking eight moves ahead.

Reacher said, "What's in the box?"

The big guy said, "Shall I get rid of him?"

Thurman said, "No, let him stay."

Reacher said, "What's in the box?"

Thurman said, "Not Uncle Sam's property. God's property."

"God brings you metal?"

"Not metal."

Thurman stood still for a second. Then he stepped around his underling, still carrying the box two-handed out in front of him, like a wise man bearing a gift. He knelt and laid it at Reacher's feet, and then stood up and backed away again. Reacher looked down. Theoretically the box might be booby-trapped, or he might get hit on the head while he crouched down next to it. But he felt either thing was unlikely. The instructors at Rucker had said: *be skeptical, but not too skeptical*. Too much skepticism led to paranoia and paralysis.

Reacher knelt next to the box.

Unlaced the criss-crossed flaps.

Raised them.

The box held crumpled newspaper, with a small plastic jar nested in it. The jar was a standard medical item, sterile, almost clear, with a screw lid. A sample jar, for urine or other bodily fluids. Reacher had seen many of them.

The jar was a quarter full with black powder.

The powder was coarser than talc, finer than salt.

Reacher asked, "What is it?"

Thurman said, "Ash."

"From where?"

"Come with me and find out."

"Come with you?"

"Fly with me tonight. I have nothing to hide. And I'm a patient man. I don't mind proving my innocence, over and over and over again, if I have to."

The big guy helped Thurman up onto the wing and watched as he folded himself in through the small door. Then he passed the box up. Thurman took it and laid it on a rear seat. The big guy stood back and let Reacher climb up by himself. Reacher ducked low and led with his legs and made it into the co-pilot's seat. He slammed the door and squirmed around until he was as comfortable as he was ever going to get, and then he buckled his harness. Beside him Thurman buckled his and hit a bunch of switches. Dials lit up and pumps whirred and the whole airframe tensed and hummed. Then Thurman hit the starter button and the exhaust coughed and the propeller blade jerked around a quarter of the way and then the engine caught with a roar and the prop spun up and the cabin filled with loud noise and furious vibration. The plane lurched forward, uncertain, earthbound, darting slightly left and right. It waddled forward out of the hangar. Dust blew up all over the place. The plane moved on, down the taxiway, the prop turning fast, the wheels turning slow. Reacher watched Thurman's hands. He was operating the controls the same way an old guy drives a car, leaning back in his seat, casual, familiar, automatic, using the kind of short abbreviated movements born of long habit.

The taxiway led through two clumsy turns to the north end of the runway. The lights were on. Thurman got centered on the graded strip and hit the power and the vibration leached forward out of the cabin into the engine and the wheels started thumping faster below. Reacher turned and saw the cardboard carton slide backward on the seat and nestle against the back cushion. He glanced ahead and saw lit dirt below and rushing darkness above. Then the plane went light and the nose lifted. The plane clawed its way into the night sky and climbed and turned and Reacher looked down and saw first the runway lights go off and then the hangar lights. Without them, there was little to see. The wall around the metal plant was faintly visible, a huge white rectangle in the gloaming.

The plane climbed hard for a minute and then leveled off and Reacher was dumped forward in his seat against his harness straps. He looked over at the dash and saw the altimeter reading two thousand feet. Airspeed was a little over a hundred and twenty. The compass reading was southeast. Fuel was more than half-full. Trim was good. The artificial horizon was level. There were plenty of green lights, and no reds.

Thurman saw him checking and asked, "Are you afraid of flying, Mr. Reacher?"

Reacher said, "No."

The engine was loud and the vibration was setting up a lot of buzzes and rattles. Wind was howling around the screens and whistling in through cracks. Altogether the little Piper reminded Reacher of the kind of old cars people used as taxis at suburban railroad stations. Sagging, worn out, clunky, but capable of making it through the ride. Maybe.

He asked, "Where are we going?"

"You'll see."

Reacher watched the compass. It was holding steady on south and east. There was an LED window below the compass with two green numbers showing. A GPS readout, latitude and longitude. They were below the fortieth parallel and more than a hundred degrees west. Both numbers were ticking downward, slowly and in step. South and east, at a modest speed. He called up maps in his mind. Empty land ahead, the corner of Colorado, the corner of Kansas, the Oklahoma panhandle. Then the compass swung a little farther south, and Reacher realized that Thurman had been skirting the airspace around Colorado Springs. An Air Force town, probably a little trigger-happy. Better to give it a wide berth.

Thurman kept the height at two thousand feet and the speed at a hundred and a quarter and the compass stayed a little south of southeast. Reacher consulted his mental maps again and figured that if they didn't land or change course they were going to exit Colorado just left of the state's bottom right-hand corner. The time readout on the dash showed seventeen minutes past seven in the evening, which was two minutes fast. Reacher thought about Vaughan, alone in her car. She would have heard the plane take off. She would be wondering why he hadn't come back over the wall.

Thurman said, "You broke into a container last night."

Reacher said, "Did I?"

"It's a fair guess. Who else would have?"

Reacher said nothing.

Thurman said, "You saw the cars."

"Did I?"

"Let's assume so, like intelligent men."

"Why do they bring them to you?"

"There are some things any government feels it politic to conceal."

"What do you do with them?"

"The same thing we do with the wrecks towed off I-70. We recycle them. Steel is a wonderful thing, Mr. Reacher. It goes around and around. Peugeots and Toyotas from the Gulf might once have been Fords and Chevrolets from Detroit, and they in turn might once have been Rolls-Royces from England or Holdens from Australia. Or bicycles or refrigerators. Some steel is new, of course, but surprisingly little of it. Recycling is where the action is."

"And the bottom line."

"Naturally."

"So why don't you buy yourself a better plane?"

"You don't like this one?"

"Not much," Reacher said.

They flew on. There was nothing but darkness ahead, relieved occasionally by tiny clusters of yellow light far below. Hamlets, farms, gas stations. At one point Reacher saw brighter lights in the distance to the left and the right. Lamar, probably, and La Junta. Small towns, made larger by comparison with the emptiness all around them. Sometimes cars were visible on roads, tiny cones of blue light crawling slowly.

Reacher asked, "How is Underwood doing? The deputy?"

Thurman paused a moment. Then he said, "He passed on."

"In the hospital?"

"Before we could get him there."

"Will there be an autopsy?"

"He has no next of kin to request one."

"Did you call the coroner?"

"No need. He was old, he got sick, he died."

"He was about forty."

"Ashes to ashes, dust to dust. It's in store for all of us."

"You don't sound very concerned."

"A good Christian has nothing to fear in death. And I own a town, Mr. Reacher. I see births and deaths all the time. One door closes, another opens."

Thurman leaned back, his gut between him and the stick, his hands held low. The engine held fast on a mid-range roar and the whole plane shivered with vibration and bucked occasionally on rough air. The latitude number counted down slowly, and the longitude number slower still. Reacher closed his eyes. Flight time to the state line would be about seventy or eighty minutes. He figured they weren't going to land in Colorado itself. There wasn't much left of it. Just empty grassland. He figured they were going to Oklahoma, or Texas.

They flew on. The air got steadily worse. Reacher opened his eyes. Downdrafts dropped them into troughs like a stone. Then updrafts hurled them back up again. They were sideswiped by gusts of wind. Not like in a big commercial Boeing. No juddering vibration and bouncing wings. No implacable forward motion. Just violent physical displacement, like a pinball caught between bumpers. There was no storm outside. No rain, no lightning. No thunderheads. Just roiling evening thermals coming up off the plains in giant waves, invisible, compressing, decompressing, making solid walls and empty voids. Thurman held the stick loosely and let the plane buck and dive. Reacher moved in his seat and smoothed the harness straps over his shoulders.

Thurman said, "You *are* afraid of flying."

"Flying is fine," Reacher said. "Crashing is another story."

"An old joke."

"For a reason."

Thurman started jerking the stick and hammering the rudder. The plane rose and fell sharply and smashed from side to side. At first Reacher thought they were seeking smoother air. Then he realized Thurman was deliberately making things worse. He was diving where the downdrafts were sucking anyway and climbing with the updrafts. He was turning into the side winds and taking them like roundhouse punches. The plane was hammering all over the sky. It was being tossed around like the insignificant piece of junk it was.

Thurman said, "This is why you need to get your life in order. The end could come at any time. Maybe sooner than you expect."

Reacher said nothing.

Thurman said, "I could end it for you now. I could roll and stall and power dive. Two thousand feet, we'd hit the deck at three hundred miles an hour. The wings would come off first. The crater would be ten feet deep."

Reacher said, "Go right ahead."

"You mean that?"

"I dare you."

An updraft hit and the plane was thrown upward and then the decompression wave came in and the lift under the wings dropped away to a negative value and the plane fell again. Thurman dropped the nose and hit the throttle and the engine screamed and the Piper tilted into a forty-five-degree power dive. The artificial horizon on the dash lit up red and a warning siren sounded. It was barely audible over the scream of the engine and the battering airflow. Then Thurman pulled out of the dive. He jerked the nose up. The airframe groaned as the main spar stressed and the plane curved level and then rose again through air that was momentarily calmer.

Reacher said, "Chicken."

Thurman said, "I have nothing to fear."

"So why pull out?"

"When I die, I'm going to a better place."

"I thought the big guy got to make that decision, not you."

"I've been a faithful servant."

"So go for it. Go to a better place, right now. I dare you."

Reacher said nothing. Thurman flew on, straight and level, through air that was calming down. Two thousand feet, a hundred and twenty-five knots, south of southeast.

"Chicken," Reacher said again. "Phony."

Thurman said, "God wants me to complete my task."

"What, he told you that in the last two minutes?"

"I think you're an atheist."

"We're all atheists. You don't believe in Zeus or Thor or Neptune or Augustus Caesar or Mars or Venus or Sun Ra. You reject a thousand gods. Why should it bother you if someone else rejects a thousand and one?"

Thurman didn't answer.

Reacher said, "Just remember, it was you who was afraid to die, not me."

They flew on, twenty more minutes. The air went still and quiet. Reacher closed his eyes again. Then dead-on an hour and a quarter total elapsed time Thurman moved in his seat. Reacher opened his eyes. Thurman hit a couple of switches and fired up his radio and held the stick with his knees and clamped a headset over his ears. The headset had a microphone on a boom that came off the left-hand earpiece. Thurman flicked it with his fingernail and said, "It's me, on approach." Reacher heard a muffled crackling reply and far below in the distance saw lights come on. Red and white runway lights, he assumed, but they were so far away they looked like a tiny pink pinpoint. Thurman started a long slow descent. Not very smooth. The plane was too small and light for finesse. It jerked and dropped and leveled and dropped again. Laterally it was nervous. It darted left, darted right. The pink pinpoint jumped around below them and drew closer and resolved into twin lines of red and white. The lines looked short. The plane wobbled and stumbled in the air and dipped low and then settled on a shallow path all the way down. The runway lights rushed up to meet it and started blurring past, left and right. For a second Reacher thought Thurman had left it too late, but then the wheels touched down and bounced once and settled back and Thurman cut the power and the plane rolled to a walk with half the runway still ahead of it. The engine note changed to a deep roar and the walk picked up to taxiing speed and Thurman jerked left off the runway and drove a hundred yards to a deserted apron. Reacher could see the vague outlines of brick buildings in the middle distance. He saw a vehicle approaching, headlights on. Big, dark, bulky.

A Humvee.

Camouflage paint.

The Humvee parked twenty feet from the Piper and the doors opened and two guys climbed out.

Battledress uniform, woodland pattern.

Soldiers.

59

Reacher sat for a moment in the sudden silence with his ears ringing and then he opened the Piper's door and climbed out to the wing. Thurman passed him the cardboard carton. Reacher took it one-handed and slid down to the tarmac. The two soldiers snapped to attention and threw salutes and stood there like a ceremonial detail, expectantly. Thurman climbed down behind Reacher and took the box from him. One of the soldiers stepped forward. Thurman bowed slightly and offered the box. The soldier bowed slightly and took it and turned on his heel and slow-marched back to the Humvee. His partner fell in behind him, line astern. Thurman followed them. Reacher followed Thurman.

The soldiers stowed the box in the Humvee's load bed and then climbed in the front. Reacher and Thurman got in the back. Big vehicle, small seats, well separated by the massive transmission tunnel. A diesel engine. They turned a tight circle on the apron and drove toward a building that stood alone in a patch of lawn. Lights were on in two ground floor windows. The Humvee parked and the soldiers retrieved the box from the load bed and slow-marched it into the building. A minute later they came back out again without it.

Thurman said, "Job done, for tonight, at least."

Reacher asked, "What was in the jar?"

"People," Thurman said. "Men, maybe women. We scrape them off the metal. When there's been a fire, that's all that's left of them. Soot, baked onto steel. We scrape it off and collect it in twists of paper, and then we put the day's gleanings into jars. It's as close as we can get to giving them a proper burial."

"Where are we?"

"Fort Shaw, Oklahoma. Up in the panhandle. They deal with recovered remains here. Among other things. They're associated with the identification laboratory in Hawaii."

"You come here every night?"

"As often as necessary. Which is most nights, sadly."

"What happens now?"

"They give me dinner, and they gas up my plane."

The soldiers climbed back into the front seats and the Humvee turned again and drove a hundred yards to the main cluster of buildings. A fifties army base, one of thousands in the world. Brick, green paint, whitewashed curbs, swept blacktop. Reacher had never been there before. Had never even heard of it. The Humvee parked by a side door that had a sign that said it led to the Officers' Club. Thurman turned to Reacher and said, "I won't ask you to join me for dinner. They'll have set just one place, and it would embarrass them."

Reacher nodded. He knew how to find food on

post. Probably better food than Thurman would be eating in the O Club.

"I'll be OK," he said. "And thanks for asking."

Thurman climbed out and disappeared through the O Club door. The grunts in the front of the Humvee craned around, unsure about what to do next. They were both privates first class, probably stationed permanently in the States. Maybe they had a little Germany time under their belts, but nothing else of significance. No Korea time. No desert time, certainly. They didn't have the look. Reacher said, "Remember wearing diapers, when you were two years old?"

The driver said, "Sir, not specifically, sir."

"Back then I was a major in the MPs. So I'm going to take a stroll now, and you don't need to worry about it. If you want to worry about it, I'll dig out your CO and we'll do the brother officer thing, and he'll OK it and you'll look stupid. How does that sound?"

The guy wasn't totally derelict. Not totally dumb. He asked, "Sir, what unit, and where?"

Reacher said, "110th MP. HQ was in Rock Creek, Virginia."

The guy nodded. "It still is. The 110th is still in business."

"I certainly hope so."

"Sir, you have a pleasant evening. Chow in the mess until ten, if you're interested."

"Thanks, soldier," Reacher said. He climbed out and the Humvee drove away and left him. He stood still for a moment in the sharp night air and then set out walking to the standalone building. Its original purpose was unclear to him. No reason to have a physically separated building unless it held infectious patients or explosives, and it didn't look like either a hospital or an armory. Hospitals were bigger and armories were stronger.

He went in the front door and found himself in a small square hallway with stairs ahead of him and doors either side. The upstairs windows had been dark. The lit windows had been on the ground floor. *If in doubt, turn left* was his motto. So he tried the left-hand door and came up empty. An administrative office, lights blazing, nobody in it. He stepped back to the hallway and tried the right-hand door. Found a medic with the rank of captain at a desk, with Thurman's jar in front of him. The guy was young for a captain, but medics got promoted fast. They were usually two steps ahead of everyone else.

"Help you?" the guy said.

"I flew in with Thurman. I was curious about his jar."

"Curious how?"

"Is it what he says it is?"

"Are you authorized to know?"

"I used to be. I was an MP. I did some forensic medicine with Nash Newman, who was probably your ultimate boss back when you were a second lieutenant. Unless he had retired already. He's probably retired now."

The guy nodded. "He is retired now. But I heard of him."

"So are there human remains in the jar?"

"Probably. Almost certainly, in fact."

"Carbon?"

"No carbon," the guy said. "In a hot fire all the carbon is driven off as carbon dioxide. What's left of a person after cremation are oxides of potassium, sodium, iron, calcium, maybe a little magnesium, all inorganic."

"And that's what's in the jar?"

The guy nodded again. "Entirely consistent with burned human flesh and bone."

"What do you do with it?"

"We send it to the Central Identification Laboratory in Hawaii."

"And what do they do with it?"

"Nothing," the guy said. "There's no DNA in it. It's just soot, basically. The whole thing is an embarrassment, really. But Thurman keeps on showing up. He's a sentimental old guy. We can't turn him away, obviously. So we stage a sweet little ceremony and accept whatever he brings. Can't trash it afterward, either. Wouldn't be respectful. So we move it off our desks onto Hawaii's. I imagine they stick it in a closet and forget all about it."

"I'm sure they do. Does Thurman tell you where it comes from?"

"Iraq, obviously."

"But what kind of vehicles?"

"Does it matter?"

"I would say so."

"We don't get those details."

Reacher asked, "What was this building originally?"

"A VD clinic," the medic said.

"You got a phone I could use?"

The guy pointed to a console on his desk.

"Have at it," he said.

Reacher dialed 411 upside down and got the number for David Robert Vaughan, Fifth Street, Hope, Colorado. He said the number once under his breath to memorize it and then dialed it.

No answer.

He put the phone back in the cradle and asked, "Where's the mess?"

"Follow your nose," the medic said. Which was good advice. Reacher walked back to the main cluster and circled until he smelled the aroma of fried food coming out of a powerful extraction vent. The vent came through the wall of a low lean-to addition to a larger square one-story building. The mess kitchen, and the mess. Reacher went in and got a few questioning looks but no direct challenges. He got in line and picked up a cheeseburger the size of a softball, plus fries, plus beans, plus a mug of coffee. The burger was excellent, which was normal for the army. Mess cooks were in savage competition to produce the best patty. The coffee was excellent, too. A unique standardized blend, in Reacher's opinion the best in the world. He had been drinking it all his life. The fries were fair and the beans were adequate. All in all, probably better than the limp piece of grilled fish the officers were getting.

He took more coffee and sat in an armchair and read the army papers. He figured the two PFCs would come get him when Thurman was ready to leave. They would drive their guests out to the flight line and salute smartly and finish their little show in style, just after midnight. Taxiing, takeoff, the climb, then ninety minutes in the air. That would get them back to Despair by two, which seemed to be the normal schedule. Three hours' worth of free aviation fuel, plus a free four-hour dinner. Not bad, in exchange for a quarter-full jar of soot. *A born-again-Christian American and a businessman* was how Thurman had described himself. Whatever kind of a Christian he was, he was a useful businessman. That was for damn sure.

The mess kitchen closed. Reacher finished the papers and dozed. The PFCs never showed. At twelve-ten in the morning Reacher woke up and heard the Piper's engine in the distance and by the time the sound registered in his mind it was revving hard. By the time he made it outside the little white plane was on the runway. He stood and watched as it lifted off and disappeared into the darkness above.

60

The Humvee came back from the flight line and the two PFCs got out and nodded to Reacher like nothing was wrong. Reacher said, "I was supposed to be on that plane."

The driver said, "No sir, Mr. Thurman told us you had a one-way ticket tonight. He told us you were heading south from here, on business of your own. He told us you were all done in Colorado."

Reacher said, "Shit." He thought back to Thurman, in front of the airplane barn. The deliberate pause. *Debate in his face, some kind of a long-range calculus, like he was playing a long game, thinking eight moves ahead.*

Fly with me tonight.

I won't ask you to join me for dinner.

Reacher shook his head. He was ninety minutes' flying time from where he needed to be, in the middle of the night, in the middle of nowhere, with no airplane.

Outwitted by a seventy-year-old preacher.

Dumb.

And tense.

I think they were all stirred up because they're heading for the end of something.

What, he had no idea.

When, he had no clue.

He checked the map in his head. There were no highways in the Oklahoma panhandle. None at all. Just a thin red tracery of state four-lanes and county two-lanes. He glanced at the Humvee and at the PFCs and said, "You guys want to drive me out to a road?"

"Which road?"

"Any road that gets traffic more than once an hour."

"You could try 287. That goes south."

"I need to go north. Back to Colorado. Thurman wasn't entirely frank with you."

"287 goes north, too. All the way up to I-70."

"How far is that?"

"Sir, I believe it's dead-on two hundred miles."

Hitchhiking had gotten more and more difficult in the ten years since Reacher left the army. Drivers were less generous, more afraid. The West was sometimes better than the East, which helped. Day was always better than night, which didn't. The Humvee from Fort Shaw let him out at twelve-forty-five, and it was a quarter past one in the morning before he saw his first northbound vehicle, a Ford F150 that didn't even slow down to take a look. It just blew past. Ten minutes later an old Chevy Blazer did the same thing. Reacher blamed the movies. They made people scared of strangers. Although in reality most movies had the passing strangers messed up by the locals, not the other way around. Weird inbred families that hunted people for sport. But mostly Reacher blamed himself. He knew he was no kind of an attractive roadside proposition. *Look at yourself. What do you see?* Maria from San Diego was the kind of person that got rides easily. Sweet, small, unthreatening, needy. Vaughan would do OK, too. Hulks six-five in height were a riskier bet.

At ten of two a dark Toyota pick-up at least slowed and took a look before passing by, which was progress of a sort. Five after two, a twenty-year-old Cadillac swept past. It had an out-of-tune motor and a collapsed rear suspension and an old woman low down behind the wheel. White hair, thin neck. What Reacher privately called a Q-tip. Not a likely prospect. Then at a quarter past two an old Suburban heaved into view. In Reacher's experience new Suburbans were driven by uptight assholes, but old models were plain utilitarian vehicles often driven by plain utilitarian people. Their bulk often implied a kind of no-nonsense self-confidence on the part of their owners. The kind of self-confidence that said strangers weren't necessarily a problem.

The best hope so far.

Reacher stepped off the shoulder and put one foot in the traffic lane. Cocked his thumb in a way that suggested need, but not desperation.

The Suburban's brights came on.

It slowed.

It stopped altogether fifteen feet short of where

Reacher was standing. A smart move. It gave the guy behind the wheel a chance to look over his potential passenger without the kind of social pressure that face-to-face proximity would imply. Reacher couldn't see the driver. Too much dazzle from the headlights.

A decision was made. The headlights died back to low beam and the truck rolled forward and stopped again. The window came down. The driver was a fat red-faced man. He was clinging to the wheel like he would fall out of his chair if he didn't. He said, "Where are you headed?" His voice was slurred.

Reacher said, "North into Colorado. I'm trying to get to a place called Hope."

"Never heard of it."

"Me neither, until a few days ago."

"How far away?"

"Maybe four hours."

"Is it on the way to Denver?"

"It would be a slight detour."

"Are you an honest man?"

Reacher said, "Usually."

"Are you a good driver?"

"Not really."

"Are you drunk?"

Reacher said, "Not even a little bit."

The guy said, "Well, I am. A lot. So you drive to wherever it is you want to go, keep me out of trouble, let me sleep it off, and then point me toward Denver, OK?"

Reacher said, "Deal."

Hitchhiking usually carried with it the promise of random personal encounters and conversations made more intense by the certainty that their durations would necessarily be limited. Not this time. The florid guy heaved himself over into the passenger seat and collapsed its back against a worn mechanism and went straight to sleep without another word. He snored and bubbled far back in his throat and he thrashed restlessly. According to the smell of his breath he had been drinking bourbon all evening. A lot of bourbon, probably with bourbon chasers. He was still going to be illegal when he woke up in four hours' time and pressed on to Denver.

Not Reacher's problem.

The Suburban was old and worn and grimy. Its total elapsed mileage was displayed in a window below the center of the speedometer in LED figures like a cheap watch. A lot of figures, starting with a two. The motor wasn't in great shape. It still had power but it had a lot of weight to haul and it didn't want to go much faster than sixty miles an hour. There was a cell phone on the center console. It was switched off. Reacher glanced at his sleeping passenger and switched it on. It wouldn't spark up. No charge in the battery. There was a charger plugged into the cigarette lighter. Reacher steered with his knees and traced the free end of the wire and shoved it into a hole on the bottom of the phone. Tried the switch again. The phone came on with a tinkly little tune. The sleeping guy just snored on.

The phone showed no service. The middle of nowhere.

The road narrowed from four lanes to two. Reacher drove on. Five miles ahead he could see a pair of red tail lights. Small lights, set low, widely spaced. Moving north a little slower than the Suburban. The speed differential was maybe five miles an hour, which meant it took sixty whole minutes to close the gap. The lights were on a U-Haul truck. It was cruising at about fifty-five. When Reacher came up behind it, it sped up to a steady sixty. Reacher pulled out and tried to pass, but the Suburban wouldn't accelerate. It bogged down at about sixty-two, which would have put Reacher on the wrong side of the road for a long, long time. Maybe forever. So he eased off and tucked in behind the truck and battled the frustration of having to drive just a little slower than he wanted to. The cell phone was still showing no service. There was nothing to see behind. Nothing to see to the sides. The world was dark and empty. Thirty feet ahead, the U-Haul's back panel was lit up bright by the Suburban's headlights. It was like a rolling billboard. An advertisement. It had a picture of three trucks parked side by side at an angle: small, medium, and large. Each was shown in U-Haul's distinctive orange and white colors. Each had *U-Haul* painted on its front. Each promised an automatic transmission, a gentle ride, a low deck, air conditioning, and cloth seats. A price of nineteen dollars and ninety-five cents was advertised in large figures. Reacher eased the Suburban closer to check the fine print. The bargain price was for in-town use of a small truck for one day, mileage extra, subject to contract terms. Reacher eased off again and fell back.

U-Haul.

You haul. We don't. Independence, self-reliance, initiative.

In general Reacher didn't care for the corruption of written language. *U* for *you, EZ* for *easy, hi* for *high, lo* for *low*. He had spent many years in school learning to read and spell and he wanted to feel that there had been some point to it. But he couldn't get too worked up about *U-Haul*. What was the alternative? *Self-Drive Trucks?* Too clunky. Too generic. No kind of a catchy business name. He followed thirty feet behind the bright rolling billboard and the triple U-Haul logos blurred together and filled his field of view.

U *for* you.

Then he thought: You *for* U.

You did this to me.

To assume makes an ass out of u and me.

He checked the phone again.

No signal. They were in the middle of the Comanche National Grassland. Like being way out at sea. The closest cell tower was probably in Lamar, which was about an hour ahead.

The drunk guy slept noisily and Reacher followed the wallowing U-Haul truck for sixty solid minutes. Lamar showed up ahead as a faint glow on the horizon. Probably not more than a couple of streetlights, but in contrast to the black grassland all around it felt like a destination. There was a small municipal airfield to the west. And there was cell coverage. Reacher glanced down and saw two bars showing on the phone's signal strength meter. He dialed Vaughan's home number from memory.

No answer.

He clicked off and dialed information. Asked for the Hope PD. Let the phone company connect him. He figured his sleeping passenger could spring for the convenience. He heard the ring tone and then there was a click and more ring tone. Automatic call forwarding, he guessed. The Hope PD building wasn't manned at night. Vaughan had mentioned a day guy, but no night guy. Incoming calls would be rerouted out straight to the nighttime prowl car. To a cell provided by the department, or to a personal cell. Ten nights out of fourteen it would be Vaughan answering. But not tonight. She was off duty. It would be another officer out there chasing gum wrappers. Maybe a deputy.

A voice in his ear said, "Hope PD."

Reacher said, "I need to talk to Officer Vaughan."

The guy in the passenger seat stirred, but didn't wake up.

The voice in Reacher's ear said, "Officer Vaughan is off duty tonight."

Reacher said, "I know. But I need her cell number."

"I can't give that to you."

"Then call it yourself and ask her to call me back on this number."

"I might wake her."

"You won't."

Silence.

Reacher said, "This is important. And be quick. I'll be heading out of range in a minute."

He clicked off. The town of Lamar loomed up ahead. Low dark buildings, a tall water tower, a lit-up gas station. The U-Haul pulled off for fuel. Reacher checked the Suburban's gauge. Half-full. A big tank. But a thirsty motor and many miles to go. He followed the U-Haul to the pumps. Unplugged the phone. It showed decent battery and marginal reception. He put it in his shirt pocket.

The pumps were operational but the pay booth was closed up and dark. The guy from the U-Haul poked a credit card into a slot on the pump and pulled it out again. Reacher used his ATM card and did the same thing. The pump started up and Reacher selected regular unleaded and watched in horror as the numbers flicked around. Gas was expensive. That was for damn sure. More than three bucks for a gallon. The last time he had filled a car, the price had been a dollar. He nodded to the U-Haul guy, who nodded back. The U-Haul guy was a youngish well-built man with long hair. He was wearing a tight black short-sleeve shirt with a clerical collar. Some kind of a minister of religion. Probably played the guitar.

The phone rang in Reacher's pocket. He left the nozzle wedged in the filler neck and turned away and answered. The Hope cop said, "Vaughan didn't pick up her cell."

Reacher said, "Try your radio. She's out in the watch commander's car."

"Where?"

"I'm not sure."

"Why is she out in the watch commander's car?"

"Long story."

"You're the guy she's been hanging with?"

"Just call her."

"She's married, you know."

"I know. Now call her."

The guy stayed on the line and Reacher heard him get on the radio. A call sign, a code, a request for an immediate response, all repeated once, and then again. Then the sound of dead air. Buzzing, crackling, the heterodyne whine of nighttime interference from high in the ionosphere. Plenty of random noise.

But nothing else.

No reply from Vaughan.

61

Reacher got out of the gas station ahead of the minister in the U-Haul and headed north as fast as the old Suburban would go. The drunk guy slept on next to him. He was leaking alcohol through his pores. Reacher cracked a window. The night air kept him awake and sober and the whistle masked the snoring. Cell coverage died eight miles north of Lamar. Reacher guessed it wouldn't come back until they got close to the I-70 corridor, which was two hours ahead. It was four-thirty in the morning. ETA in Hope, around dawn. A five-hour delay, which was an inconvenience, but maybe not a disaster.

Then the Suburban's engine blew.

Reacher was no kind of an automotive expert. He didn't see it coming. He saw the temperature needle nudge upward a tick, and thought nothing of it. Just stress and strain, he figured, because of the long fast cruise. But the needle didn't stop moving. It went all the way up into the red zone and didn't stop until it was hard against the peg. The motor lost power and a hot wet smell came in through the vents. Then there was a muffled thump under the hood and strings of tan emulsion blew out of the ventilation slots in front of the windshield and spattered all over the glass. The motor died altogether and the Suburban slowed hard. Reacher steered to the shoulder and coasted to a stop.

Not good, he thought.

The drunk guy slept on.

Reacher got out in the darkness and headed around to the front of the hood. He used the flats of his hands to bounce some glow from the headlight beams back onto the car. He saw steam. And sticky tan sludge leaking from every crevice. Thick, and foamy. A mixture of engine oil and cooling water. Blown head gaskets. Total breakdown. Repairable, but not without hundreds of dollars and a week in the shop.

Not good.

Half a mile south he could see the U-Haul's lights coming his way. He stepped around to the passenger door and leaned in over the sleeping guy and found a pen and an old service invoice in the glove compartment. He turned the invoice over and wrote: *You need to buy a new car. I borrowed your cell phone. Will mail it back.* He signed the note: *Your hitchhiker.* He took the Suburban's registration for the guy's address and folded it into his pocket. Then he ran fifty feet south and stepped into the traffic lane and held his arms high and waited to flag the U-Haul down. It picked him up in its headlights about fifty yards out. Reacher waved his arms above his head. The universal distress signal. The U-Haul's headlights flicked to bright. The truck slowed, like Reacher knew it would. A lonely road, and a disabled vehicle and a stranded driver, both of them at least fleetingly familiar to the Good Samaritan behind the wheel.

The U-Haul came to rest a yard in front of Reacher, halfway on the shoulder. The window came down and the guy in the dog collar stuck his head out.

"Need help?" he said. Then he smiled, wide and wholesome. "Dumb question, I guess."

"I need a ride," Reacher said. "The engine blew."

"Want me to take a look?"

Reacher said, "No." He didn't want the minister to see the drunk guy. From a distance he was out of sight on the reclined seat, below the window line. Close up, he was big and obvious. Abandoning a broken-down truck in the middle of nowhere was one thing. Abandoning a comatose passenger was another. "No point, believe me. I'll have to send a tow truck. Or set fire to the damn thing."

"I'm headed north to Yuma. You're welcome to join me, for all or part of the way."

Reacher nodded. Called up the map in his head. The Yuma road crossed the Hope road about two hours ahead. The same road he had come in on originally, with the old guy in the green Grand Marquis. He would need to find a third ride, for the final western leg. His ETA was now about ten in the morning, with luck. He said, "Thanks. I'll jump out about halfway to Yuma."

The guy in the dog collar smiled his wholesome smile again and said, "Hop in."

The U-Haul was a full-sized pick-up frame overwhelmed by a box body a little longer and wider and a lot taller than a pick-up's load bed. It sagged and wallowed and the extra weight and aerodynamic resistance made it slow. It struggled up close to sixty miles an hour and stayed there. Wouldn't go any faster. Inside it smelled of warm exhaust fumes and hot oil and plastic. But the seat was cloth, as advertised, and reasonably comfortable. Reacher had to fight to stay awake. He wanted to be good company. He didn't want to replicate the drunk guy's manners.

He asked, "What are you hauling?"

The guy in the collar said, "Used furniture. Donations. We run a mission in Yuma."

"We?"

"Our church."

"What kind of a mission?"

"We help the homeless and the needy."

"What kind of a church?"

"We're Anglicans, plain vanilla, middle of the road."

"Do you play the guitar?"

The guy smiled again. "We try to be inclusive."

"Where I'm going, there's an End Times Church."

The minister shook his head. "An End Times congregation, maybe. It's not a recognized denomination."

"What do you know about them?"

"Have you read the Book of Revelation?"

Reacher said, "I've heard of it."

The minister said, "Its correct title is The Revelation of Saint John the Divine. Most of the original is lost, of course. It was written either in Ancient

Hebrew or Aramaic, and copied by hand many times, and then translated into Koine Greek, and copied by hand many times, and then translated into Latin, and copied by hand many times, and then translated into Elizabethan English and printed, with opportunities for error and confusion at every single stage. Now it reads like a bad acid trip. I suspect it always did. Possibly all the translations and all the copying actually improved it."

"What does it say?"

"Your guess is as good as mine."

"Are you serious?"

"Some of our homeless people make more sense."

"What do people think it says?"

"Broadly, the righteous ascend to heaven, the unholy are left on earth and are visited by various colorful plagues and disasters, Christ returns to battle the Antichrist in an Armageddon scenario, and no one winds up very happy."

"Is that the same as the Rapture?"

"The Rapture is the ascending part. The plagues and the fighting are separate. They come afterward."

"When is all this supposed to happen?"

"It's perpetually imminent, apparently."

Reacher thought back to Thurman's smug little speech in the metal plant. *There are signs,* he had said. *And the possibility of precipitating events.*

Reacher asked, "What would be the trigger?"

"I'm not sure there's a trigger, as such. Presumably a large element of divine will would be involved. One would certainly hope so."

"Pre-echoes, then? Ways to know it's coming?"

The minister shrugged at the wheel. "End Times people read the Bible like other people listen to Beatles records backward. There's something about a red calf being born in the Holy Land. End Times enthusiasts are real keen on that part. They comb through ranches, looking for cattle a little more auburn than usual. They ship pairs to Israel, hoping they'll breed a perfect redhead. They want to get things started. That's another key characteristic. They can't wait. Because they're all awfully sure they'll be among the righteous. Which makes them self-righteous, actually. Most people accept that who gets saved is God's decision, not man's. It's a form of snobbery, really. They think they're better than the rest of us."

"That's it? Red calves?"

"Most enthusiasts believe that a major war in the Middle East is absolutely necessary, which is why they've been so unhappy about Iraq. Apparently what's happening there isn't bad enough for them."

"You sound skeptical."

The guy smiled again.

"Of course I'm skeptical," he said. "I'm an Anglican."

There was no more conversation after that, either theological or secular. Reacher was too tired and the guy behind the wheel was too deep into night-driving survival mode, where nothing existed except the part of the road ahead that his headlights showed him. His eyes were wedged open and he was sitting forward, as if he knew that to relax would be fatal. Reacher stayed awake, too. He knew the Hope road wouldn't be signposted and it wasn't exactly a major highway. The guy behind the wheel wouldn't spot it on his own.

It arrived exactly two hours into the trip, a lumpy two-lane crossing their path at an exact right angle. It had stop signs, and the main north-south drag didn't. By the time Reacher called it and the minister reacted and the U-Haul's overmatched brakes did their job they were two hundred yards past it. Reacher got out and waved the truck away and waited until its lights and its noise were gone. Then he walked back through the dark empty vastness. Predawn was happening way to the east, over Kansas or Missouri. Colorado was still pitch black. There was no cell phone signal.

No traffic, either.

Reacher took up station on the west side of the junction, standing on the shoulder close to the traffic lane. East-west drivers would have to pause at the stop sign opposite, and they would get a good look at him twenty yards ahead. But there were no east-west drivers. Not for the first ten minutes. Then the first fifteen, then the first twenty. A lone car came north, trailing the U-Haul by twenty miles, but it didn't turn off. It just blasted onward. An SUV came south, and slowed, ready to turn, but it turned east, away from Hope. Its lights grew small and faint and then they disappeared.

It was cold. There was a wind coming out of the east, and it was moving rain clouds into the sky.

Reacher turned his collar up and crossed his arms over his chest and trapped his hands under his biceps for warmth. Cloudy diffused streaks of pink and purple lit up the far horizon. A new day, empty, innocent, as yet unsullied. Maybe a good day. Maybe a bad day. Maybe the last day. *The end is near,* Thurman's church had promised. Maybe a meteorite the size of a moon was hurtling closer. Maybe governments had suppressed the news. Maybe rebels were right then forcing the locks on an old Ukrainian silo. Maybe in a research lab somewhere a flask had cracked or a glove had torn or a mask had leaked.

Or maybe not. Reacher stamped his feet and ducked his face into his shoulder. His nose was cold. When he looked up again he saw headlights in the east. Bright, widely spaced, far enough away that they seemed to be static. A large vehicle. A truck. Possibly a semi trailer. Coming straight toward him, with the new dawn behind it.

Four possibilities. One, it would arrive at the junction and turn right and head north. Two, it would arrive at the junction and turn left and head south. Three, it would pause at the stop sign and then continue west without picking him up. Four, it would pause and cross the main drag and then pause again to let him climb aboard.

Chances of a happy ending, twenty-five percent. Or less, if it was a corporate vehicle with a no-passenger policy because of insurance hassles.

Reacher waited.

When the truck was a quarter-mile away he saw that it was a big rigid panel van, painted white. When it was three hundred yards away he saw that it had a refrigerator unit mounted on top. Fresh food delivery, which would have reduced the odds of a happy outcome if it hadn't been for the stop signs. Food drivers usually didn't like to stop. They had schedules to keep, and stopping a big truck and then getting it back up to speed could rob a guy of measurable minutes. But the stop signs meant he had to slow anyway.

Reacher waited.

He heard the guy lift off two hundred yards short of the junction. Heard the hiss of brakes. He raised his hand high, thumb extended. *I need a ride.* Then he raised both arms and waved. The distress semaphore. *I* really *need a ride.*

The truck stopped at the line on the east side of the junction. Neither one of its direction indicators was flashing. A good sign. There was no traffic north or south, so it moved on again immediately, diesel roaring, gears grinding, heading west across the main drag, straight toward Reacher. It accelerated. The driver looked down. The truck kept on moving.

Then it slowed again.

The air brakes hissed loud and the springs squealed and the truck came to a stop with the cab forty feet west of the junction and the rear fender a yard out of the north-south traffic lane. Reacher turned and jogged back and climbed up on the step. The window came down and the driver peered out from seven feet south. He was a short, wiry man, incongruously small in the huge cab. He said, "It's going to rain."

Reacher said, "That's the least of my problems. My car broke down."

The guy at the wheel said, "My first stop is Hope."

Reacher said, "You're the supermarket guy. From Topeka."

"I left there at four this morning. You want to ride along?"

"Hope is where I'm headed."

"So quit stalling and climb aboard."

Dawn chased the truck all the way west, and overtook it inside thirty minutes. The world lit up cloudy and pale gold and the supermarket guy killed his headlights and sat back and relaxed. He drove the same way Thurman had flown his plane, with small efficient movements and his hands held low. Reacher asked him if he often carried passengers and he said that about one morning in five he found someone looking for a ride. Reacher said he had met a couple of women who had ridden with him.

"Tourists," the guy said.

"More than that," Reacher said.

"You think?"

"I know."

"How much?"

"All of it."

"How?"

"I figured it out."

The guy nodded at the wheel.

"Wives and girlfriends," he said. "Looking to be

close by while their husbands and boyfriends pass through the state."

"Understandable," Reacher said. "It's a tense time for them."

"So you know what their husbands and boyfriends are?"

"Yes," Reacher said. "I do."

"And?"

"And nothing. Not my business."

"You're not going to tell anyone?"

"There's a cop called Vaughan," Reacher said. "I'm going to have to tell her. She has a right to know. She's involved, two ways around."

"I know her. She's not going to be happy."

Reacher said, "Maybe she will be, maybe she won't be."

"I'm not involved," the guy said. "I'm just a fellow traveler."

"You are involved," Reacher said. "We're all involved."

Then he checked his borrowed cell phone again. No signal.

There was nothing on the radio, either. The supermarket guy hit a button that scanned the whole AM spectrum from end to end, and he came up with nothing. Just static. A giant continent, mostly empty. The truck hammered on, bouncing and swaying on the rough surface. Reacher asked, "Where does Despair get its food?"

"I don't know," the guy said. "And I don't care."

"Ever been there?"

"Once. Just to take a look. And once was enough."

"Why do people stay there?"

"I don't know. Inertia, maybe."

"Are there jobs elsewhere?"

"Plenty. They could head west to Halfway. Lots of jobs there. Or Denver. That place is expanding, for sure. Hell, they could come east to Topeka. We're growing like crazy. Nice houses, great schools, good wages, right there for the taking. This is the land of opportunity."

Reacher nodded and checked his cell phone again. No signal.

They made it to Hope just before ten in the morning. The place looked calm and quiet and unchanged. Clouds were massing overhead and it was cold. Reacher got out on First Street and stood for a moment. His cell phone showed good signal. But he didn't dial. He walked down to Fifth and turned east. From fifty yards away he saw that there was nothing parked on the curb outside Vaughan's house. No cruiser, no black Crown Vic. Nothing at all. He walked on, to get an angle and check the driveway.

The old blue Chevy pick-up was in the driveway. It was parked nose-in, tight to the garage door. It had glass in its windows again. The glass was still labeled with paper barcodes and it was crisp and clear except where it was smeared in places with wax and handprints. It looked very new against the faded old paint. The ladder and the wrecking bar and the flashlight were in the load bed. Reacher walked up the stepping-stone path to the door and rang the bell. He heard it sound inside the house. The neighborhood was still and silent. He stood on the step for thirty long seconds and then the door opened.

Vaughan looked out at him and said, "Hello."

62

Vaughan was dressed in the same black clothes she had worn the night before. She looked still and calm and composed. And a little distant. A little preoccupied. Reacher said, "I was worried about you."

Vaughan said, "Were you?"

"I tried to call you twice. Here, and in the car. Where were you?"

"Here and there. You better come in."

The kitchen looked just the same as before. Neat, clean, decorated, three chairs at the table. There was a glass of water on the counter and coffee in the machine.

Reacher said, "I'm sorry I didn't get right back."

"Don't apologize to me."

"What's wrong?"

"You want coffee?"

"After you tell me what's wrong."

"Nothing is wrong."

"Like hell."

"OK, we shouldn't have done what we did the night before last."

"Which part?"

"You know which part. You took advantage. I

started to feel bad about it. So when you didn't come back with the plane I switched off my phone and my radio and drove out to Colorado Springs and told David all about it."

"In the middle of the night?"

Vaughan shrugged. "They let me in. They were very nice about it, actually. They treated me very well."

"And what did David say?"

"That's cruel."

Reacher shook his head. "It isn't cruel. It's a simple question."

"What's your point?"

"That David no longer exists. Not as you knew him. Not in any meaningful sense. And that you've got a choice to make. And it's not a new choice. There have been mass casualties from the Civil War onward. There have been tens of thousands of men in David's position over more than a century. And therefore there have been tens of thousands of women in your position."

"And?"

"They all made a choice."

"David still exists."

"In your memory. Not in the world."

"He's not dead."

"He's not alive, either."

Vaughan said nothing. Just turned away and took a fine china mug from a cupboard and filled it with coffee from the machine. She handed the mug to Reacher and asked, "What was in Thurman's little box?"

"You saw the box?"

"I was over the wall ten seconds after you. Did you really think I was going to wait in the car?"

"I didn't see you."

"That was the plan. But I saw you. I saw the whole thing. *Fly with me tonight?* He ditched you somewhere, didn't he?"

Reacher nodded. "Fort Shaw, Oklahoma. An army base."

"You fell for it."

"I sure did."

"You're not as smart as you think."

"I never claimed to be smart."

"What was in the box?"

"A plastic jar."

"What was in the jar?"

"Soot," Reacher said. "People, after a fire. They scrape it off the metal."

Vaughan sat down at her table.

"That's terrible," she said.

"Worse than terrible," Reacher said. "Complicated."

"How?"

Reacher sat down opposite her.

"You can breathe easy," he said. "There are no wrecked Humvees at the plant. They go someplace else."

"How do you know?"

"Because Humvees don't burn like that. Mostly they bust open and people spill out."

Vaughan nodded. "David wasn't burned."

Reacher said, "Only tanks burn like that. No way out of a burning tank. Soot is all that's left."

"I see."

Reacher said nothing.

"But how is that complicated?" she asked.

"It's the first in a series of conclusions. Like a logical chain reaction. We're using main battle tanks over there. Which isn't a huge surprise, I guess. But we're losing some, which *is* a huge surprise. We always expected to lose a few, to the Soviets. But we sure as hell didn't expect to lose any to a bunch of ragtag terrorists with improvised explosive devices. In less than four years they've figured out how to make shaped charges good enough to take out main battle tanks belonging to the U.S. Army. That doesn't help our PR very much. I'm real glad the Cold War is over. The Red Army would be helpless with laughter. No wonder the Pentagon ships the wrecks in sealed containers to a secret location."

Vaughan got up and walked over to her counter and picked up her glass of water. She emptied it in the sink and refilled it from a bottle in her refrigerator. Took a sip.

"I got a call this morning," she said. "From the state lab. My tap water sample was very close to five parts per billion TCE. Borderline acceptable, but it's going to get a lot worse if Thurman keeps on using as much of the stuff as he uses now."

"He might stop," Reacher said.

"Why would he?"

"That's the final conclusion in the chain. We're not there yet. And it's only tentative."

"So what was the second conclusion?"

"What does Thurman do with the wrecked tanks?"

"He recycles the steel."

"Why would the Pentagon deploy MPs to guard recycled steel?"

"I don't know."

"The Pentagon wouldn't. Nobody cares about steel. The MPs are there to guard something else."

"Like what?"

"Only one possibility. A main battle tank's front and side armor includes a thick layer of depleted uranium. It's a byproduct from enriching natural uranium for nuclear reactors. It's an incredibly strong and dense metal. Absolutely ideal for armor plate. So the second conclusion is that Thurman is a uranium specialist. And that's what the MPs are there for. Because depleted uranium is toxic and somewhat radioactive. It's the kind of thing you want to keep track of."

"How toxic? How radioactive?"

"Tank crews don't get sick from sitting behind it. But after a blast or an explosion, if it turns to dust or fragments or vapor, you can get very sick from breathing it, or by being hit by shrapnel made of it. That's why they bring the wrecks back to the States. And that's what the MPs are worried about, even here. Terrorists could steal it and break it up into small jagged pieces and pack them into an explosive device. It would make a perfect dirty bomb."

"It's heavy."

"Incredibly."

"They'd need a truck to steal it. Like you said."

"A big truck."

Reacher sipped his coffee and Vaughan sipped her water and said, "They're cutting it up at the plant.

With hammers and torches. That must make dust and fragments and vapor. No wonder everyone looks sick."

Reacher nodded.

"The deputy died from it," he said. "All those symptoms? Hair loss, nausea and vomiting, diarrhea, blisters, sores, dehydration, organ failure? That wasn't old age or TCE. It was radiation poisoning."

"Are you sure?"

Reacher nodded again. "Very sure. Because he told me so. From his deathbed he said *The,* and then he stopped, and then he started again. He said, *You did this to me.* I thought it was a new sentence. I thought he was accusing me. But it was really all the same sentence. He was pausing for breath, that's all. He was saying, *The U did this to me.* Like some kind of a plea, or an explanation, or maybe a warning. He was using the chemical symbol for uranium. Metalworkers' slang, I guess. He was saying, *The uranium did this to me.*"

Vaughan said, "The air at the plant must be thick with it. And we were right there."

Reacher said, "Remember the way the wall glowed? On the infrared camera? It wasn't hot. It was radioactive."

63

Vaughan sipped her bottled water and stared into space, adjusting to a new situation that was in some ways better than she had imagined, and in some ways worse. She asked, "Why do you say there are no Humvees there?"

Reacher said, "Because the Pentagon specializes. Like I told you. It always has, and it always will. The plant in Despair is about uranium recycling. That's all. Humvees go somewhere else. Somewhere cheaper. Because they're easy. They're just cars."

"They send cars to Despair, too. We saw them. In the container. From Iraq or Iran."

Reacher nodded.

"Exactly," he said. "Which is the third conclusion. They sent those cars to Despair for a reason."

"Which was what?"

"Only one logical possibility. Depleted uranium isn't just for armor. They make artillery shells and tank shells out of it, too. Because it's incredibly hard and dense."

"So?"

"So the third conclusion is that those cars were hit with ammunition made from depleted uranium.

They're tainted, so they have to be processed appropriately. And they have to be hidden away. Because we're using tanks and DU shells against thin-skinned civilian vehicles. That's overkill. That's *very* bad PR. Thurman said there are some things any government feels it politic to conceal, and he was right."

"What the hell is happening over there?"

Reacher said, "Your guess is as good as mine."

Vaughan raised her glass halfway and stopped. She looked at it like she was having second thoughts about ingesting anything and put it back down on the table. She said, "Tell me what you know about dirty bombs."

"They're the same as clean bombs," Reacher said. "Except they're dirty. A bomb detonates and creates a massive spherical pressure wave that knocks things over and pulps anything soft, like people, and small fragments of the casing are flung outward on the wave like bullets, which does further damage. That effect can be enhanced by packing extra shrapnel inside the casing around the explosive charge, like nails or ball bearings. A dirty bomb uses contaminated metal for the extra shrapnel, usually radioactive waste."

"How bad is the result?"

"That's debatable. With depleted uranium, the powdered oxides after a high-temperature explosion are certainly bad news. There are fertility issues, miscarriages, and birth defects. Most people think the radiation itself isn't really a huge problem. Except that, like I said, it's debatable. Nobody really knows for sure. Which is the exact problem. Because you can bet your ass everyone will err on the side of caution. Which multiplies the effect, psychologically. It's classic asymmetric warfare. If a dirty bomb goes off in a city, the city will be abandoned, whether it needs to be or not."

"How big would the bomb need to be?"

"The bigger the better."

"How much uranium would they need to steal?"

"The more the merrier."

Vaughan said, "I think they're already stealing it. That truck we photographed? The front of the load compartment was glowing just like the wall."

Reacher shook his head.

"No," he said. "That was something else entirely."

64

Reacher said, "Walk to town with me. To the motel."

Vaughan said, "I don't know if I want to be seen with you. Especially at the motel. People are talking."

"But not in a bad way."

"I'm not so sure."

"Whatever, I'll be gone tomorrow. So let them talk for one more day."

"Tomorrow?"

"Maybe earlier. I might need to stick around to make a phone call. Apart from that, I'm done here."

"Who do you need to call?"

"Just a number. I don't think anyone will answer."

"What about all this other stuff going on?"

"So far all we've got is the Pentagon washing its dirty linen in private. That's not a crime."

"What's at the motel?"

"I'm guessing we'll find room four is empty."

They walked together through the damp late-morning air, two blocks north from Fifth Street to Third, and then three blocks west to the motel. They bypassed the office and headed on down the row. Room four's door was standing open. There was a maid's cart parked outside. The bed was stripped and the bathroom towels were dumped in a pile on the floor. The closets were empty. The maid had a vacuum cleaner going.

Vaughan said, "Mrs. Rogers is gone."

Reacher nodded. "Now let's find out when and how."

They backtracked to the office. The clerk was on her stool behind the counter. Room four's key was back on its hook. Now only two keys were missing. Reacher's own, for room twelve, and Maria's, for room eight.

The clerk slid off her stool and stood with her hands spread on the counter. Attentive, and helpful. Reacher glanced at the phone beside her and asked, "Did Mrs. Rogers get a call?"

The clerk nodded. "Six o'clock last night."

"Good news?"

"She seemed very happy."

"What then?"

"She checked out."

"And went where?"

"She called a cab to take her to Burlington."

"What's in Burlington?"

"Mostly the airport bus to Denver."

Reacher nodded. "Thanks for your help."

"Is anything wrong?"

"That depends on your point of view."

Reacher was hungry and he needed more coffee, so he led Vaughan another block north and another block west to the diner. The place was practically empty. Too late for breakfast, too early for lunch. Reacher stood for a second and then slid into the booth that Lucy Anderson had used the night he had met her. Vaughan sat across from him, where Lucy had sat. The waitress delivered ice water and silverware. They ordered coffee, and then Vaughan asked, "What exactly is going on?"

"All those young guys," Reacher said. "What did they have in common?"

"I don't know."

"They were young, and they were guys."

"And?"

"They were from California."

"So?"

"And the only white one we saw had a hell of a tan."

"So?"

Reacher said, "I sat right here with Lucy Anderson. She was cautious and a little wary, but basically we were getting along. She asked to see my wallet, to check I wasn't an investigator. Then later I said I had been a cop, and she panicked. I put two and two together and figured her husband was a fugitive. The more she thought about it, the more worried she got. She was very hostile the next day."

"Figures."

"Then I caught a glimpse of her husband in Despair and went back to check the rooming house where he was staying. It was empty, but it was very clean."

"Is that important?"

"Crucial," Reacher said. "Then I saw Lucy again, after her husband had moved on. She said they have lawyers. She talked about people in her position. She sounded like she was part of something organized. I said I could follow her to her husband and she said it wouldn't do me any good."

The waitress came over with the coffee. Two mugs, two spoons, a Bunn flask full of a brand-new brew. She poured and walked away and Reacher sniffed the steam and took a sip.

"But I was misremembering all along," he said. "I didn't tell Lucy Anderson that I had been a cop. I told her I had been a *military* cop. That's why she panicked. And that's why the rooming house was so clean. It was like a barracks ready for inspection. Old habits die hard. The people passing through it were all soldiers. Lucy thought I was tracking them."

Vaughan said, "Deserters."

Reacher nodded. "That's why the Anderson guy had such a great tan. He had been in Iraq. But he didn't want to go back."

"Where is he now?"

"Canada," Reacher said. "That's why Lucy wasn't worried about me following her. It wouldn't do me any good. No jurisdiction. It's a sovereign nation, and they're offering asylum up there."

"The truck," Vaughan said. "It was from Ontario."

Reacher nodded. "Like a taxi service. The glow on the camera wasn't stolen uranium. It was Mrs. Rogers's husband in a hidden compartment. Body heat, like the driver. The shade of green was the same."

65

Vaughan sat still and quiet for a long time. The waitress came back and refilled Reacher's mug twice. Vaughan didn't touch hers.

She asked, "What was the California connection?"

Reacher said, "Some kind of an anti-war activist group out there must be running an escape line. Maybe local service families are involved. They figured out a system. They sent guys up here with legitimate metal deliveries, and then their Canadian friends took them north over the border. There was a couple at the Despair hotel seven months ago, from California. A buck gets ten they were the organizers, recruiting sympathizers. And the sympathizers policed the whole thing. They busted your truck's windows. They thought I was getting too nosy, and they were trying to move me on."

Vaughan pushed her mug out of the way and moved the salt and the pepper and the sugar in front of her. She put them in a neat line. She straightened her index finger and jabbed at the pepper shaker. Moved it out of place. Jabbed at it again, and knocked it over.

"A small subgroup," she said. "The few left-hand

people, working behind Thurman's back. Helping deserters."

Reacher said nothing.

Vaughan asked, "Do you know who they are?"

"No idea."

"I want to find out."

"Why?"

"Because I want to have them arrested. I want to call the FBI with a list of names."

"OK."

"Well, don't you want to?"

Reacher said, "No, I don't."

Vaughan was too civilized and too small town to have the fight in the diner. She just threw money on the table and stalked out. Reacher followed her, like he knew he was supposed to. She headed toward the quieter area on the edge of town, or toward the motel again, or toward the police station. Reacher wasn't sure which. Either she wanted solitude, or to demand phone records from the motel clerk, or to be in front of her computer. She was walking fast, in a fury, but Reacher caught her easily. He fell in beside her and matched her pace for pace and waited for her to speak.

She said, "You knew about this yesterday."

He said, "Since the day before."

"How?"

"The same way I figured the patients in David's hospital were military. They were all young men."

"You waited until that truck was over the border before you told me."

"Yes, I did."

"Why?"

"I didn't want you to have it stopped."

"Why not?"

"I wanted Rogers to get away."

Vaughan stopped walking. "For God's sake, you were a military cop."

Reacher nodded. "Thirteen years."

"You hunted guys like Rogers."

"Yes, I did."

"And now you've gone over to the dark side?"

Reacher said nothing.

Vaughan said, "Did you know Rogers?"

"Never heard of him. But I knew ten thousand just like him."

Vaughan started walking again. Reacher kept pace. She stopped fifty yards short of the motel. Outside the police station. The brick façade looked cold in the gray light. The neat aluminum letters looked colder.

"They had a duty," Vaughan said. "You had a duty. David *did* his duty. They should do theirs, and you should do yours."

Reacher said nothing.

"Soldiers should go where they're told," she said. "They should follow orders. They don't get to choose. And you swore an oath. You should obey it. They're traitors to their country. They're cowards. And you are, too. I can't believe I slept with you. You're *nothing*. You're disgusting. You make my skin crawl."

Reacher said, "Duty is a house of cards."

"What the hell does that mean?"

"I went where they told me. I followed orders. I did everything they asked, and I watched ten thousand guys do the same. And we were happy to, deep down. I mean, we bitched and pissed and moaned, like soldiers always do. But we bought the deal. Because duty is a transaction, Vaughan. It's a two-way street. We owe them, they owe us. And what they owe us is a solemn promise to risk our lives and limbs if and only if there's a damn good reason. Most of the time they're wrong anyway, but we like to feel some kind of good faith somewhere. At least a little bit. And that's all gone now. Now it's all about political vanity and electioneering. That's all. And guys know that. You can try, but you can't bullshit a soldier. *They* blew it, not us. They pulled out the big card at the bottom of the house and the whole thing fell down. And guys like Anderson and Rogers are over there watching their friends getting killed and maimed and they're thinking, Why? Why should we do this shit?"

"And you think going AWOL is the answer?"

"I think the answer is for civilians to get off their fat asses and vote the bums out. They should exercise control. That's *their* duty. That's the next-biggest card at the bottom of the house. But that's gone, too. So don't talk to me about AWOL. Why should the grunts on the ground be the only ones who *don't* go AWOL? What kind of a two-way street is that?"

"You served thirteen years and you support deserters?"

"I understand their decision. Precisely because I served those thirteen years. I had the good times. I wish they could have had them, too. I loved the army. And I hate what happened to it. I feel the same as I would if I had a sister and she married a creep. Should she keep her marriage vows? To a point, sure, but no further."

"If you were in now, would you have deserted?"

Reacher shook his head. "I don't think I would have been brave enough."

"It takes courage?"

"For most guys, more than you would think."

"People don't want to hear that their loved ones died for no good reason."

"I know. But that doesn't change the truth."

"I hate you."

"No, you don't," Reacher said. "You hate the politicians, and the commanders, and the voters, and the Pentagon." Then he said, "And you hate that David didn't go AWOL after his first tour."

Vaughan turned and faced the street. Held still. Closed her eyes. She stood like that for a long time, pale, a small tremble in her lower lip. Then she spoke. Just a whisper. She said, "I asked him to. I begged him. I said we could start again anywhere he wanted, anywhere in the world. I said we could change our names, anything. But he wouldn't agree. Stupid, stupid man."

Then she cried, right there on the street, outside her place of work. Her knees buckled and she staggered a step and Reacher caught her and held her tight. Her tears soaked his shirt. Her body trembled. She wrapped her arms around him. She crushed her face into his chest. She wailed and cried for her shattered life, her broken dreams, the telephone call two years before, the chaplain's visit to her door, the X-rays, the filthy hospitals, the unstoppable hiss of the respirator.

Afterward they walked up and down the block together, aimlessly, just to be moving. The sky was gray with low cloud and the air smelled like rain was on the way. Vaughan wiped her face on Reacher's shirt tail and ran her fingers through her hair. She blinked her eyes clear and swallowed and took deep breaths. They ended up outside the police station again and Reacher saw her gaze trace the line of twenty aluminum letters fixed to the brick. *Hope Police Department.* She said, "Why didn't Raphael Ramirez make it?"

Reacher said, "Because Ramirez was different."

66

Reacher said, "One phone call from your desk will explain it. We might as well go ahead and make it. Since we're right here anyway. Maria has waited long enough."

Vaughan said, "One call to who?"

"The MPs west of Despair. You were briefed about them, they'll have been briefed about you. Therefore they'll cooperate."

"What do I ask them?"

"Ask them to fax Ramirez's summary file. They'll say, Who? You'll tell them, Bullshit, you know Maria was just there, so you know they know who he is. And tell them we know Maria was there for twenty-one hours, which is enough time for them to have gotten all the paperwork in the world."

"What are we going to find?"

"My guess is Ramirez was in prison two weeks ago."

The Hope Police Department's fax machine was a boxy old product standing alone on a rolling cart. It had been square and graceless to start with, and now it was grubby and worn. But it worked. Eleven minutes after Vaughan finished her call it sparked up and started whirring and sucked a blank page out of the feeder tray and fed it back out with writing on it.

Not much writing. It was a bare-bones summary. Very little result for twenty-one hours of bureaucratic pestering. But that was explained by the fact that it had been the army doing the asking and the Marines doing the answering. Inter-service cooperation wasn't usually very cooperative.

Raphael Ramirez had been a private in the Marine Corps. At the age of eighteen he had been deployed to Iraq. At the age of nineteen he had served a second deployment. At the age of twenty he had gone AWOL ahead of a third deployment. He had gone on the run but had been arrested five days later in Los Angeles and locked up awaiting court-martial back at Pendleton.

Date of arrest, three weeks previously.

Reacher said, "Let's go find Maria."

They found her in her motel room. Her bed had a dent where she had been sitting, staying warm, saving energy, passing time, enduring. She answered the door tentatively, as if she was certain that all news would be bad. There was nothing in Reacher's face to change her mind. He and Vaughan led her outside and sat her in the plastic lawn chair under her bathroom window. Reacher took room nine's chair and Vaughan took room seven's. They dragged them over and positioned them and made a tight little triangle on the concrete apron.

Reacher said, "Raphael was a Marine."

Maria nodded. Said nothing.

Reacher said, "He had been to Iraq twice. He didn't want to go back a third time. So nearly four weeks ago he went on the run. He headed up to LA. Maybe he had friends there. Did he call you?"

Maria said nothing.

Vaughan said, "You're not in trouble, Maria. Nobody's going to get you for anything."

Maria said, "He called most days."

Reacher asked, "How was he?"

"Scared. Scared to death. Scared of being AWOL, scared of going back."

"What happened in Iraq?"

"To him? Not much, really. But he saw things. He said the people we were supposed to be helping were killing us, and we were killing the people we were supposed to be helping. Everybody was killing everybody else. In bad ways. It was driving him crazy."

"So he ran. And he called most days."

Maria nodded.

Reacher said, "But then he didn't call, for two or three days. Is that right?"

"He lost his cell phone. He was moving a lot. To stay safe. Then he got a new phone."

"How did he sound on the new phone?"

"Still scared. Very worried. Even worse."

"Then what?"

"He called to say he had found some people. Or some people had found him. They were going to get him to Canada. Through a place called Despair, in Colorado. He said I should come here, to Hope, and wait for his call. Then I should join him in Canada."

"Did he call from Despair?"

"No."

"Why did you go to the MPs?"

"To ask if they had found him and arrested him. I was worried. But they said they had never heard of him. They were army, he was Marine Corps."

"And so you came back here to wait some more."

Maria nodded.

Reacher said, "It wasn't exactly like that. He was arrested in LA. The Marines caught up with him. He didn't lose his phone. He was in jail for two or three days."

"He didn't tell me that."

"He wasn't allowed to."

"Did he break out again?"

Reacher shook his head. "My guess is he made a deal. The Marine Corps offered him a choice. Five years in Leavenworth, or go undercover to bust the escape line that ran from California all the way to Canada. Names, addresses, descriptions, techniques, routes, all that kind of stuff. He agreed, and they drove him back to LA and turned him loose. That's why the MPs didn't respond. They found out what was going on and were told to stonewall you."

"So where is Raphael now? Why doesn't he call?"

Reacher said, "My father was a Marine. Marines have a code. Did Raphael tell you about it?"

Maria said, "Unit, corps, God, country."

Reacher nodded. "It's a list of their loyalties, in priority order. Raphael's primary loyalty was to his unit. His company, in fact. Really just a handful of guys. Guys like him."

"I don't understand."

"I think he agreed to the deal but couldn't carry it through. He couldn't betray guys just like him. I think he rode up to Despair but didn't call in to the Marines. I think he hung around on the edge of town and stayed out of sight, because he was conflicted. He didn't want to know who was involved, because he was afraid he might have to give them away later. He hung out for days, agonizing. He got thirsty and hungry. He started hallucinating and decided to walk over to Hope, and find you, and get out some other way."

"So where is he?"

"He didn't make it, Maria. He collapsed halfway. He died."

"But where is his body?"

"The people in Despair took care of it."

"I see."

Then for the second time in an hour Reacher watched a woman cry. Vaughan held her and Reacher said, "He was a good man, Maria. He was just a kid who couldn't take any more. And in the end he didn't betray what he believed in." He said those things over and over again, in different orders, and with different emphases, but they didn't help.

Maria was all cried out after twenty minutes and Vaughan led her back inside. Then she joined Reacher again and they walked away together. She asked, "How did you know?"

Reacher said, "No other rational explanation."

"Did he really do what you said? Agonized and then sacrificed himself?"

"Marines are good at self-sacrifice. On the other hand maybe he double-crossed the Corps from the get-go. Maybe he planned all along to head straight to Hope and grab Maria and disappear."

"It doesn't take four days to walk from Despair to Hope."

"No," Reacher said. "It doesn't."

"So he probably did the right thing."

"I hope that was Maria's impression."

"Do you think he told them about the people in California?"

"I don't know."

"This will carry on if he didn't."

"You say that like it's a bad thing."

"It could get out of hand."

"You could make a couple of calls. They're in the hotel register in Despair, name and address. You could check and see who they are, and whether they're still around, or whether they've disappeared into federal custody."

"I'm sorry about what I said before."

"Don't worry about it."

They walked on, and then Reacher said, "And you weren't wrong, when you did what you did the night before last. Otherwise whoever killed David killed you too. You want to give them that? Because I don't. I want you to have a life."

"That sounds like the beginnings of a farewell speech."

"Does it?"

"Why stay? The Pentagon is washing its dirty linen in private, which isn't a crime. And we seem to have decided this other thing isn't a crime either."

"There's one more thing on my mind," Reacher said.

67

Reacher and Vaughan walked back to the diner, where Reacher ate for the first time since the burger he had scored in the Fort Shaw mess the night before. He topped up his caffeine level with four mugs of coffee and when he had finished he said, "We need to go see those MPs. Now you've established contact we might get away with a face-to-face meeting."

Vaughan said, "We're going to drive through Despair again?"

Reacher shook his head. "Let's take your truck and go cross-country."

They peeled the paper barcodes off the new glass and Vaughan fetched paper towels and Windex from her kitchen and they wiped the wax and the handprints off the screen. Then they set off, early in the afternoon. Vaughan took the wheel. They drove five miles west on Hope's road and risked another nine on Despair's. The air was clear and the mountains were visible ahead, first invitingly close and then impossibly distant. Three miles before Despair's first vacant lot they slowed and bumped down off the road, onto the scrub, and started a long loop to the north. They kept the town on their left, on a three-mile radius. It was just a blur in the distance. Not possible to tell if it was guarded by mobs or sentries, or abandoned altogether.

It was slow going across the open land. Undergrowth scraped along the underside and low bushes slapped at their flanks. The ladder and the wrecking bar in the load bed bounced and rattled. The flashlight rolled from side to side. Occasionally they found dry washes and followed them through looping meanders at a higher speed. Then it was back to picking their way around table rocks bigger than the Chevy itself and keeping the sun centered on the top rail of the windshield. Four times they drove into natural corrals and had to back up and start over. After an hour the town fell away behind them and the plant showed up ahead on the left. The wall glowed white in the sun. The parking lot looked empty. No cars. There was no smoke rising from the plant. No sparks, no noise. No activity at all.

Reacher said, "What day is it?"

Vaughan said, "It's a regular workday."

"Not a holiday?"

"No."

"So where is everybody?"

They steered left and narrowed the gap between themselves and the plant. The Chevy was raising a healthy dust plume in the air behind it. It would be visible to a casual observer. But there were no casual observers. They slowed and stopped two miles out and waited. Five minutes. Ten. Then fifteen. No circulating Tahoes came around.

Vaughan asked, "What exactly is on your mind?"

"I like to be able to explain things to myself," Reacher said.

"What can't you explain?"

"The way they were so desperate to keep people out. The way they shut down the secret compound for the day just because I was barging around within half a mile of it. The way they found Ramirez's body and dealt with it so fast and efficiently. It was no surprise to them. It's like they set themselves up to be constantly vigilant for intruders. To expect them, even. And they worked out procedures in advance for dealing with them. And everyone in town is involved. The first day I showed up, even the waitress in the restaurant knew exactly what to do. Why would they go to those lengths?"

"They're playing ball with the Pentagon. Keeping private things private."

"Maybe. But I'm not sure. Certainly the Pentagon wouldn't ask for that. Despair is already in the middle of nowhere and the plant is three miles out of town and the bad stuff happens in a walled-off compound inside it. That's good enough for the Pentagon. They wouldn't ask local people to go to bat for them. Because they trust walls and distance and geography, not people."

"Maybe Thurman asked the people himself."

"I'm sure he did. I'm certain of it. But why? On behalf of the Pentagon, or for some other reason of his own?"

"Like what?"

"Only one logical possibility. Actually, an illogical

possibility. Or a logical impossibility. One word from the MPs and we'll know. If they talk to us at all."

"What word?"

"Either yes or no."

There were four guys in the guard shack, which seemed to be their usual daytime deployment. Overkill, in Reacher's opinion, which meant the post was most likely commanded by a lieutenant, not a sergeant. A sergeant would have had two in the shack and the other two either resting up with the others or out on mobile patrol in a Humvee, depending on the perceived threat assessment. But officers had to sign off on fuel requisitions, which would nix the mobile Humvee, and officers didn't like men sitting around with nothing to do, which is why the shack was overcrowded. But Reacher didn't expect the grunts to be unhappy about it. Or about anything. They had been in Iraq, and now they weren't. The only question in his mind was whether their officer had been in Iraq with them. If he had, he might be reasonable. If he hadn't, he might be a royal pain in the ass.

Vaughan drove past the base and U-turned and came back and parked facing the right way, tight on the shoulder, close to but not blocking the gate. Like she would outside a fire station. Respectful. Unwilling to put a foot wrong in the dance that had to be coming.

Two guys came out of the guard shack immediately. They were the same two Reacher had seen before. Morgan, the bespectacled specialist with the squint lines, and his partner, the silent private first class. Reacher kept his hands clearly visible and slid out of the truck. Vaughan did the same thing on her side. She introduced herself by name, and as an officer with the Hope PD. Morgan saluted her, in a way Reacher knew meant the MPs had run her plate the first time around, despite his best efforts, and that they had found out what her husband had been, and what he was now.

Which will help, he thought.

Then Morgan turned and looked straight at him.

"Sir?" he said.

"I was an MP myself," Reacher said. "I did your lieutenant's job about a million years ago."

"Sir, which unit?"

"The 110th."

"Rock Creek, Virginia," Morgan said. A statement, not a question.

Reacher said, "I went there a couple of times, to get my ass kicked. The rest of the time, I was on the road."

"On the road where?"

"Everywhere you've ever been, and about a hundred other places."

"Sir, that's interesting, but I'm going to have to ask you to move your vehicle."

"At ease, Corporal. We'll move it as soon as we've talked to your lieutenant."

"On what subject, sir?"

"That's between him and us," Reacher said.

"Sir, I can't justify disturbing him on that basis."

"Move along, soldier. I've read the manual, too.

Let's skip a few pages, to where you've already determined that this is important."

"Is this about the missing Marine private?"

"Much more interesting."

"Sir, it would help me to have fuller particulars."

"It would help you to have a million dollars and a date with Miss America, too. But what are the chances, soldier?"

Five minutes later Reacher and Vaughan were inside the wire, inside one of the six green metal buildings, face-to-face across a desk with a one-striper called Connor. He was a small lean man. He was maybe twenty-six years old. He had been to Iraq. That was for sure. His BDUs were beat up and sandblasted and his cheekbones were burned shiny. He looked competent, and probably was. He was still alive, and he wasn't in disgrace. In fact he was probably headed for a captain's rank, pending paperwork. Medals too, maybe. He asked, "Is this an official visit from the Hope PD?"

Vaughan said, "Yes."

"You're both members of the department?"

Vaughan said, "Mr. Reacher is a civilian adviser."

"So how can I help?"

Reacher said, "Long story short, we know about the DU salvage at Thurman's plant."

Connor said, "That bothers me a little."

Reacher said, "It bothers us a little, too. Homeland Security rules require us to maintain a register of chemically sensitive sites within twenty miles." He said it as if it was true, which it might have been. Anything was possible, with Homeland Security. "We should have been told."

"You're more than twenty miles from the plant."

"Twenty exactly to downtown," Reacher said. "Only fifteen to the town limit."

"It's classified," Connor said. "You can't put it in a register."

Reacher nodded. "We understand that. But we should have been made aware of it, privately."

"Sounds like you are aware of it."

"But now we want to verify some details. Once bitten, twice shy."

"Then you need to speak to the Department of Defense."

"Better if we don't. They'll wonder how we got wind of it. Your guys talking will be their first guess."

"My guys don't talk."

"I believe you. But do you want to take a chance on the Pentagon believing you?"

Connor said, "What details?"

"We think we're entitled to know when and how the scrap DU gets transported out, and what route is used."

"Worried about it rolling down First Street?"

"You bet."

"Well, it doesn't."

"It all goes west?"

Connor said, "It goes nowhere."

Vaughan said, "What do you mean?"

"You guys aren't the only ones with your panties in a wad. Colorado's pretty uptight. They want to close the Interstate and use an armed convoy. Which they can't contemplate on a regular basis. Once every five years is what they're thinking."

"How long ago did the first convoy leave?"

"It didn't. The first convoy will happen about two years from now."

Reacher said, "So right now they're stockpiling the stuff at the plant?"

Connor nodded. "The steel moves out, the DU stays."

"How much have they got there?"

"As of right now, maybe twenty tons."

"Have you seen it?"

Connor shook his head. "Thurman reports monthly by mail."

"You like that?"

"What's not to like?"

"The guy is sitting on a mountain of dangerous stuff."

"And? What could he possibly do with it?"

68

Reacher and Vaughan got back in the truck and Vaughan said, "Was that answer a yes or a no?"

"Both," Reacher said. "No, it doesn't get moved out, yes, it's all still there."

"Is that a good both or a bad both?"

Reacher ducked his head and looked up through the screen. The sun was a dull glow behind the cloud, but it was still way above the horizon.

"Four hours until dark," he said. "We've got time for a considered decision."

"It's going to rain."

"Probably."

"Which will wash more TCE into the aquifer."

"Probably."

"We're not going to sit here until dark, in the rain."

"No, we're not. We're going to the Holiday Inn in Halfway again."

"Only if we get separate rooms."

"Shut up, Vaughan. We're going to get the same room we got before, and we're going to do all the same things."

The same room was not available, but they got one just like it. Same size, same décor, same colors. Indistinguishable. They did all the same things in it. Showered, went to bed, made love. Vaughan was a little reserved at first, but got into it later. Afterward she said that David had been better in bed. Reacher wasn't offended. She needed to believe it. And it was probably true.

They lay in the rucked sheets and Vaughan explored Reacher's scars. She had small hands. The bullet hole in his chest was too big for the tip of her little finger. Her ring finger fitted it better. Every woman he had been naked with was fascinated by it, except the woman he had gotten it for. She had preferred to forget. The rain started after an hour. It was heavy. It drummed on the hotel's roof and sheeted against the window. A cozy feeling, in Reacher's opinion. He liked being inside, in bed, listening to rain. After an hour Vaughan got up and went to shower. Reacher stayed in bed and leafed through the Bible that the Gideons had left in the nightstand.

Vaughan came back and asked, "Why does it matter?"

"Why does what matter?"

"That Thurman is stockpiling depleted uranium?"

Reacher said, "I don't like the combination. He's got twenty tons of radioactive waste and twenty tons of TNT. He's an End Times enthusiast. I spoke to a minister last night. He said that End Times people can't wait to get things started. Thurman himself said there might be precipitating events on the way. He said it kind of smugly, like he secretly knew it was true. And the whole town seems to be waiting for something to happen."

"Thurman can't start the Armageddon. It'll happen when it happens."

"These people are fanatics. They seem to think they can nudge things along. They're trying to breed red cows in Israel."

"How would that help?"

"Don't ask me."

"Cows aren't dangerous."

"Another requirement seems to be a major war in the Middle East."

"We've already got one."

"Not major enough."

"How could it be worse?"

"Lots of ways."

"Personally I don't see any."

"Suppose another country joined in?"

"They'd be crazy to."

"Suppose someone fired the first shot for them?"

"How would they?"

Reacher said, "Suppose a dirty bomb went off in Manhattan or D.C. or Chicago. What would we do?"

"According to you, we'd evacuate the city."

"And then?"

"We'd investigate."

Reacher nodded. "We'd have people in hazmat suits crawling all over the wreckage. What would they find?"

"Evidence."

"For sure. They'd identify the materials involved. Suppose they found TNT and depleted uranium?"

"They'd make a list of possible sources."

"Correct. Everyone in the world can buy TNT, but DU is rarer. It's a byproduct of an enrichment process that occurs in maybe twenty places."

"Nuclear powers."

"Exactly."

"A list of twenty suspects wouldn't help."

"Exactly," Reacher said again. "And the intended victim isn't going to stand up and take responsibility, because the intended victim didn't know anything about anything in the first place. But suppose we were nudged in the preferred direction?"

"How?"

"Remember Oklahoma City? The Federal Building? That was a big explosion, but they knew it was a Ryder truck. Within hours. They're great at putting tiny fragments together."

"But presumably one uranium fragment is like another."

"But suppose you were a state-sponsored terrorist from overseas. You'd want maximum bang for the buck. So if you didn't have quite enough uranium when you were building your bomb, you might use other stuff to pack it out."

"What other stuff?"

"Maybe pieces of wrecked cars," Reacher said.

Vaughan said nothing.

Reacher said, "Suppose the guys in the hazmat suits found fragments of Peugeots and Toyotas sold only in certain markets. Suppose they found fragments of Iranian license plates."

Vaughan was quiet for a moment, working it out.

"Iran is working with uranium. They're boasting about it."

"There you go," Reacher said. "What would happen next?"

"We'd make certain assumptions."

"And?"

"We'd attack Iran."

"And after that?"

"Iran would attack Israel, Israel would retaliate, everyone would be fighting."

"Precipitating events," Reacher said.

"That's insane."

"These are people that believe red cows signal the end of the world."

"These are people who care enough to make sure ash gets a proper burial."

"Exactly. Because by anyone's standards that's a meaningless gesture. Maybe it's just camouflage. To make sure no one looks at them too closely."

"We have no evidence."

"We have an End Times nutcase with technical expertise and twenty tons of TNT and twenty tons of DU and four Iranian cars and a limitless supply of shipping containers, some of which were last seen in the Middle East."

Vaughan said, "You think it's possible?"

"Anything is possible."

"But no judge in America would sign off on a search warrant. Not with what we've got. It's not even circumstantial. It's just a crazy theory."

Reacher said, "I'm not looking for a search warrant. I'm waiting for dark."

Darkness came two hours later. With it came doubts from Vaughan. She said, "If you're really serious about this, you should call the State Police. Or the FBI."

Reacher said, "I would have to give my name. I don't like to do that."

"Then talk to that MP lieutenant. He already knows your name. And it's his bag after all."

"He's looking at medals and a promotion. He won't want to rock the boat."

It was still raining. A steady, hard downpour.

Vaughan said, "You're not a one-man justice department."

"What's on your mind?"

"Apart from legalities?"

"Yes, apart from those."

"I don't want you to go there. Because of the radiation."

"It won't hurt me."

"OK, *I* don't want to go there. You said there were fertility issues and birth defects."

"You're not pregnant."

"I hope."

"Me too."

"But these things can linger. I might want children one day."

That's progress, Reacher thought. He said, "It's the dust that's the problem. And this rain will damp it down. And you don't have to come in. Just drive me there."

They left thirty minutes later. Halfway was a small place but it took a long time to get out of it. People were driving cautiously, like they usually did in storms in places that were normally dry. The roads were running with water, like rivers. Vaughan put her wipers on high. They batted back and forth, furiously. She found the turn east and took it. Within a minute the old Chevy was the only car on the road. The only car for miles around. Rain battered the windshield and drummed on the roof.

"This is good," Reacher said.

"You think?"

"Everyone will be indoors. We'll have the place to ourselves."

They passed the MP post thirty minutes later. There were still four guys in the guard shack. They were dressed in rain capes. Their orange nightlight was on. It made a thousand dull jewels from the raindrops on the windows.

Vaughan asked, "Will Thurman fly in this weather?"

Reacher said, "He doesn't need to. They weren't working today."

They drove on. Up ahead they saw a horizontal sliver of blue light. The plant, lit up. Much smaller than before. Like it had moved ten miles south, toward the horizon. But as they got closer they saw that it hadn't moved. The glow was smaller because only the farthest quarter was illuminated. The secret compound.

Vaughan said, "Well, they're working now."

"Good," Reacher said. "Maybe they left the gates open."

They hadn't. The personnel gate and the main vehicle gate were both closed. The bulk of the plant was dark. Nearly a mile beyond it the secret compound was bright and distant and tempting.

Vaughan said, "Are you sure about this?"

Reacher said, "Absolutely."

"OK, where?"

"Same place as before."

The Tahoes' beaten ruts were soft and full of water. The little Chevy spun its wheels and fishtailed and clawed its way forward. Vaughan found the right place. Reacher said, "Back it in." The wheels spun and the truck bumped up out of the ruts and Vaughan stopped it with its tailgate well under the curve of the metal cylinder, which put its rear window about where the base of the Crown Vic's windshield had been.

"Good luck," she said. "And be careful."

"Don't worry," Reacher said. "My biggest risk will be pneumonia."

He got out into the rain and was soaked to the skin even before he got his stuff out of the load bed. He knelt in the mud beside the truck and adjusted the ladder to the relaxed L-shape that had worked before. He put the flashlight in one pocket and hooked the crook of the wrecking bar in the other. Then he lifted the ladder vertically into the back of the pick-up and jammed its feet into the right angle between the load bed floor and the back wall of the cab. He let it fall forward and the short leg of the L came down flat on top of the cylinder, aluminum against steel, a strange harmonic *clonk* that sounded twice, once immediately and then once again whole seconds later, as if the impact had raced all around the miles of hollow wall and come back stronger.

Reacher climbed into the load bed. Rain lashed the metal and bounced up to his knees. It drummed on the steel cylinder above his head and sheeted down off the bulge of its maximum curvature like a thin waterfall. Reacher stepped sideways and up and started climbing. Rain hammered his back. Gravity pulled the wrecking bar vertical and it hit every tread on the ladder. Steel against aluminum against steel. The harmonics came back, a weird metallic keening modulated by the thrash of the rain. He made it over the angle of the L and stopped. The cylinder was covered in shiny paint and the paint was slick with running water. Maneuvering had been hard before. Now it was going to be very difficult.

He fumbled the flashlight out of his pocket and switched it on. He held it between his teeth and watched the water and picked the spot where half of it was sluicing one way and half the other. The geometric dead-center of the cylinder. The continental divide. He lined up with it and eased off the ladder and sat down. An uneasy feeling. Wet cotton on wet paint. Insecure. No friction. Water was dripping off him and threatening to float him away like an aquaplaning tire.

He sat still for a long moment. He needed to twist from the waist and lift the ladder and reverse it. But he couldn't move. The slightest turn would unstick him. Newton's Law of Motion. Every action has an equal and opposite reaction. If he twisted his upper body to the left, the torque would spin his lower body to the right, and he would slide right off the cylinder. *An effective design, derived from prison research.*

Fourteen feet to the ground. He could survive a controlled fall, if he didn't land on a tangle of jagged scrap. But without the ladder on the inside it wasn't clear how he would ever get out again.

Perhaps the gates had simpler switches on the inside. No combination locks.

Perhaps he could improvise a ladder out of scrap metal. Perhaps he could learn to weld, and build one.

Or perhaps not.

He thought: *I'll worry about all that later.*

He sat for a moment more in the rain and then nudged himself forward and rolled over onto his stomach as he slid and his palms squealed against the wet metal and the wrecking bar thumped and banged and then ninety degrees past top dead-center he was free-falling through empty air, one split second, and two, and three.

He hit the ground a whole lot later than he thought he would. But there was no scrap metal under him and his knees were bent and he went down in a heap and rolled one way and the wrecking bar went the other. The flashlight spun away. The breath was knocked out of him. But that was all. He sat up and a fast mental inventory revealed no physical damage, beyond mud and grease and oil all over his clothes, from the sticky earth.

He got to his feet and wiped his hands on his pants. Found the flashlight. It was a yard away, still burning bright. He carried it in one hand and the wrecking bar in the other and stood for a moment behind the pyramid of old oil drums. Then he stepped out and set off walking, south and west. Dark shapes loomed up at him. Cranes, gantries, crushers, crucibles, piles of metal. Beyond them the distant inner compound was still lit up.

The lights made a T shape.

A very shallow T. The crossbar was a blazing blue line half a mile long. Above it light spill haloed in the wet air. Below it the T shape's vertical stroke was very short. Maybe fourteen feet tall. That was all. Maybe thirty feet wide. A very squat foundation for such a long horizontal line.

But it was there.

The inner gate was open.

An invitation. A trap, almost certainly. *Like moths to a flame.* Reacher looked at it for a long moment and then slogged onward. The flashlight beam showed rainbow puddles everywhere. Oil and grease, floating. Rain was washing down through the sand and capillary action was pulling waste back to the surface. Walking was difficult. Within ten paces Reacher's shoes were carrying pounds of sticky mud. He was getting taller with every step. Every time the flashlight showed him a pile of old I-beams or a tangle of old rebar he stopped and scraped his soles. He was wetter than if he had fallen into a swimming pool. His hair was plastered to his head and water was running into his eyes.

Ahead he could see the white security Tahoes, blurred and ghostly in the darkness. They were parked side by side to the left of the main vehicle gate. Three hundred yards away. He headed straight for them. The trip took him seven minutes. Half-speed, because of the soft ground. When he got there, he turned right and checked the vehicle gate. No luck. On the inside it had the same gray box as on the outside. The same keypad. The same three-million-plus combinations. He turned away from it and tracked along the wall and walked past the security office, and Thurman's office, and the operations office. He stopped outside Purchasing. Scraped his shoes and climbed the steps and used his fingernails to pull the screws out of the padlock hasp. The door sagged open. He went inside.

He headed straight for the row of file cabinets. Aimed toward the right-hand end. Opened the *T* drawer. Pulled the Thomas file. The telecoms company. The cell phone supplier. Clipped to the back of the original purchase order was a thick wad of paper. The contracts, the details, the anytime minutes, the taxes, the fees, the rebates, the makes, the models. And the numbers. He tore off the sheet with the numbers and folded it into his pants pocket. Then he headed back out to the rain.

Close to one mile and forty minutes later he was approaching the inner gate.

69

The inner gate was still open. The inner compound was still blazing with light. Up close, the light was painfully bright. It spilled out in a solid bar the width of the opening and spread and widened like a lighthouse beam that reached a hundred yards.

Reacher hugged the wall and approached from the right. He stopped in the last foot of shadow and listened hard. Heard nothing over the pelting rain. He waited one slow minute and then stepped into the light. His shadow moved behind him, fifty feet long.

No reaction.

He walked in, fast and casual. No alternative. He was as lit up and vulnerable as a stripper on a stage. The ground under his feet was rutted with deep grooves. He was up to his ankles in water. Ahead on the left was the first artful pile of shipping containers. They were stacked in an open V, point outward. To their right and thirty feet farther away was a second V. He aimed for the gap between them. Stepped through, and found himself alone in an arena within an arena within an arena.

Altogether there were eight stacks of shipping containers arranged in a giant circle. They hid an area of maybe thirty acres. The thirty acres held cranes and gantries and crushers, and parked backhoes and bulldozers, and carts and dollies and trailers loaded with smaller pieces of equipment. Coils of baling wire, cutting torches, gas bottles, air hammers, high pressure spray hoses, hand tools. All grimy and battered and well used. Here and there leather welders' aprons and dark goggles were dumped in piles.

Apart from the industrial infrastructure, there were two items of interest.

The first, on the right, was a mountain of wrecked main battle tanks.

The mountain was maybe thirty feet high and fifty across at the base. It looked like an elephants' graveyard, from a grotesque prehistoric nightmare. Bent gun barrels reared up, like giant tusks or ribs. Turret assemblies were dumped and stacked haphazardly, characteristically low and wide and flat, peeled open like cans. Humped engine covers were stacked on their ends, like plates in a rack, some of them torn and shattered. Side skirts were everywhere, some of them ripped like foil. Parts of stripped hulls were tangled in the wreckage. Some of them had been taken apart by Thurman's men. Most of them had been taken apart much farther away, by different people using different methods. That was clear. There were traces of desert camouflage paint in some places. But not many. Most of the metal was scorched dull black. It looked cold in the blue light and it glistened in the rain, but Reacher felt he could see smoke still rising off it, and hear men still screaming under it.

He turned away. Looked left.

The second item of interest was a hundred yards east.

It was an eighteen-wheel semi truck.

A big rig. Ready to roll. A tractor, a trailer, a blue forty-foot China Lines container on the trailer. The tractor was a huge square Peterbilt. Old, but well maintained. The trailer was a skeletal flat-bed. The container looked like every container Reacher had ever seen. He walked toward it, a hundred yards, two minutes through mud and water. He circled the rig. The Peterbilt tractor was impressive. A fine paint job, an air filter the size of an oil drum, bunk beds behind the front seats, twin chrome smokestacks, a forest of antennas, a dozen mirrors the size of dinner plates. The container looked mundane and shabby in comparison. Dull paint, faded lettering, a few dings and dents. It was clamped tight to the trailer. It had a double door, secured with the same four foot-long levers and the same four long bolts that he had seen before. The levers were all in the closed position.

There were no padlocks.

No plastic tell-tale tags.

Reacher put the wrecking bar in one hand and pulled himself up with the other and got a precarious slippery foothold on the container's bottom ledge. Got his free hand on the nearest lever and pushed it up.

It wouldn't move.

It was welded to its bracket. An inch-long worm of metal had been melted into the gap. The three other levers were the same. And the doors had been welded to each other and to their frames. A neat patient sequence of spot welds had been applied, six inches apart, their bright newness hidden by flicks of dirty blue paint. Reacher juggled the wrecking bar and jammed the flat of the tongue into the space between two welds and pushed hard.

No result. Impossible. Like trying to lift a car with a nail file.

He climbed down, and looked again at the trailer clamps. They were turned tight. And welded.

He dropped the wrecking bar and walked away. He covered the whole of the hidden area, and the whole of the no-man's-land that lay beyond the stacks of piled containers, and the whole length of the perimeter track inside the wall. A long walk. It took him more than an hour. He came back to the inner circle the other way. From the side opposite the inner gates. They were two hundred yards away.

And they were closing.

70

The gates were motorized. Driven by electricity. That was Reacher's first absurd conclusion. They were moving slowly, but smoothly. A consistent speed. Too smooth and too consistent for manual operation. Relentless, at about a foot a second. They were already at a right angle to the wall. Each gate was fifteen feet wide. Five yards. The total remaining arc of travel for each of them was therefore about eight yards.

Twenty-four seconds.

They were two hundred yards away. No problem for a college sprinter on a track. Debatable for a college sprinter in six inches of mud. Completely impossible for Reacher. But still he started forward involuntarily, and then slowed as the arithmetic reality hit him.

He stopped altogether when he saw four figures walk in through the closing gap.

He recognized them immediately, by their size and shape and posture and movement. On the right was Thurman. On the left was the giant with the wrench. In the middle was the plant foreman. He was pushing Vaughan in front of him. The three men were walking easily. They were dressed in yellow slickers and sou'wester hats and rubber boots. Vaughan had no protection against the weather. She was soaked to the skin. Her hair was plastered against her head. She was stumbling, as if every few paces she was getting a shove in the back.

They all kept on coming.

Reacher started walking again.

The gates closed, with a metallic *clang* that sounded twice, first in real time and then again as an echo. The echo died, and Reacher heard a solenoid open and a bolt shoot home, a loud precise sound like a single shot from a distant rifle.

The four figures kept on coming.

Reacher kept on walking.

They met in the center of the hidden space. Thurman and his men stopped. They stood still five feet short of an imaginary line that ran between the pile of wrecked tanks and the eighteen-wheeler. Reacher stopped five feet on the other side. Vaughan kept on going. She picked her way through the mud and made it to Reacher's side and turned around. Put a hand on his arm.

Two against three.

Thurman called, "What are you doing here?"

Reacher could hear the rain beating against the slickers. Three guys, three sets of shoulders, three hats, stiff plastic material.

He said, "I'm looking around."

"At what?"

"At what you've got here."

Thurman said, "I'm losing patience."

Reacher said, "What's in the truck?"

"What kind of incredible arrogance makes you think you're entitled to an answer to that question?"

"No kind of arrogance," Reacher said. "Just the law of the jungle. You answer, I leave. You don't, I don't."

Thurman said, "My tolerance for you is nearly exhausted."

"What's in the truck?"

Thurman breathed in, breathed out. Glanced to his right, at his foreman, and then beyond the foreman at the giant with the wrench. He looked at Vaughan, and then back at Reacher. Reacher said, "What's in the truck?"

Thurman said, "There are gifts in the truck."

"What kind?"

"Clothes, blankets, medical supplies, eyeglasses, prosthetic limbs, dried and powdered foodstuffs, purified water, antibiotics, vitamins, sheets of construction-grade plywood. Things like that."

"Where from?"

"They were bought with tithes from the people of Despair."

"Why?"

"Because Jesus said, it is more blessed to give than to receive."

"Who are the gifts for?"

"Afghanistan. For refugees and displaced persons and those living in poverty."

"Why is the container welded shut?"

"Because it has a long and perilous journey ahead of it, through many countries and many tribal areas where warlords routinely steal. And padlocks on shipping containers can be broken. As you well know."

"Why put it all together here? In secret?"

"Because Jesus said, when you give alms, do not let your left hand know what your right hand is doing, so that your alms may be in secret. We follow scripture here, Mr. Reacher. As should you."

"Why turn out the whole town in defense of a truckful of gifts?"

"Because we believe that charity should know neither race nor creed. We give to Muslims. And not everyone in America is happy with that policy. Some feel that we should give only to fellow Christians. An element of militancy has entered the debate. Although in fact it was the prophet Muhammad himself who said a man's first charity should be to his own family. Not Jesus. Jesus said whatever you wish that men would do to you, do so to them. He said love your enemies and pray for those who persecute you, so that you may be sons of your father who is in heaven."

Reacher said, "Where are the cars from Iran?"

"The what?"

"The cars from Iran."

Thurman said, "Melted down and shipped out."

"Where is the TNT?"

"The what?"

"You bought twenty tons of TNT from Kearny Chemical. Three months ago."

Thurman smiled.

"Oh, that," he said. "It was a mistake. A typo. A coding error. A new girl in the office was one number off, on Kearny's order form. We got TNT instead of TCE. They're adjacent in Kearny's inventory. If you were a chemist, you'd understand why. We sent it back immediately, on the same truck. Didn't even unload. If you had troubled yourself to break into Invoicing as well as Purchasing, you would have seen our application for a credit."

"Where is the uranium?"

"The what?"

"You pulled twenty tons of depleted uranium out of these tanks. And I just walked all over this compound and I didn't see it."

"You're standing on it."

Vaughan looked down. Reacher looked down.

Thurman said, "It's buried. I take security extremely seriously. It could be stolen and used in a dirty bomb. The state is reluctant to let the army move it. So I keep it in the ground."

Reacher said, "I don't see signs of digging."

"It's the rain. Everything is churned up."

Reacher said nothing.

Thurman said, "Satisfied?"

Reacher said nothing. He glanced right, at the eighteen-wheeler. Left, at the parked backhoe. Down, at the ground. The rain splashed in puddles all around and thrashed against the slickers ten feet away.

"Satisfied?" Thurman asked again.

Reacher said, "I might be. After I've made a phone call."

"What phone call?"

"I think you know."

"I don't, actually."

Reacher said nothing.

Thurman said, "But anyway, this is not the right time for phone calls."

Reacher said, “Not the right place either. I'll wait until I get back to town. Or back to Hope. Or Kansas.”

Thurman turned and glanced at the gate. Turned back. Reacher nodded. Said, “Suddenly you want to check on what numbers I know.”

“I don't know what you're talking about.”

“I think you do.”

“Tell me.”

“No.”

“I want some courtesy and respect.”

“And I want to hit a grand slam at Yankee Stadium. I think both of us are going to be disappointed.”

Thurman said, “Turn out your pockets.”

Reacher said, “Worried about those numbers? Maybe I memorized them.”

“Turn out your pockets.”

“Make me.”

Thurman went still and his eyes narrowed and debate crossed his face, the same kind of long-range calculus that Reacher had seen before, in front of the airplane hangar. The long game, eight moves ahead. Thurman spent a second or two on it and then he stepped back, abruptly, and raised his right arm. His plastic sleeve came out into the downpour and made noise. He waved his two employees forward. They took two long strides and stopped again. The plant foreman kept his hands loose at his sides and the big guy slapped the wrench in and out of his palm, wet metal on wet skin.

Reacher said, “Not a fair fight.”

Thurman said, “You should have thought about that before.”

Reacher said, "Not fair to them. They've been cutting uranium. They're sick."

"They'll take their chances."

"Like Underwood did?"

"Underwood was a fool. I give them respirators. Underwood was too lazy to keep his on."

"Did these guys wear theirs?"

"They don't work in here. They're perfectly healthy."

Reacher glanced at the foreman, and then at the giant. Asked, "Is that right? You don't work in here?"

Both guys shook their heads.

Reacher asked, "Are you healthy?"

Both guys nodded.

Reacher asked, "You want that state of affairs to last more than the next two minutes?"

Both guys smiled, and moved a step closer.

Vaughan said, "Just do it, Reacher. Turn out your pockets."

"Still looking out for me?"

"It's two against one. And one of them is the same size as you and the other one is bigger."

"Two against two," Reacher said. "You're here."

"I'm no use. Let's just suck it up and move on."

Reacher shook his head and said, "What's in my pockets is my business."

The two guys took another step. The foreman was on Reacher's right and the big guy was on his left. Both of them close, but not within touching distance. The rain on their clothing was loud. Water was running out of Reacher's hair into his eyes.

He said, "You know we don't have to do this. We could walk out of here friends."

The foreman said, "I don't think so."

"Then you won't walk out of here at all."

"Brave talk."

Reacher said nothing.

The foreman glanced across at the big guy.

He said, "Let's do it."

Get your retaliation in first.

Reacher feinted left, toward the giant. The big guy rocked back, surprised, and the foreman rocked forward, toward the action. Momentum, moving west. A perfect little ballet. Reacher planted his heel very carefully in the mud and jerked the other way, to his right, to the east, and smashed the foreman in the stomach with his elbow. A five-hundred-pound collision. One guy moving left, one guy moving right, an elbow the size of a pineapple moving fast. The stomach is high in the midsection. Behind it lies the celiac plexus, the largest autonomic nerve center in the abdominal cavity. Sometimes called the solar plexus. A heavy blow can shut the whole thing down. Result, great pain and diaphragm spasms. Consequence, a fall to the ground and a desperate struggle to breathe.

The foreman went down.

He fell facefirst into a foot-wide rut filled with water. Reacher kicked him in the side to roll him out of it. He didn't want the guy to drown. He stepped over the writhing form into clear air and glanced around through the bright blue light. Thurman had backed off twenty feet. Vaughan was rooted to the spot. The big guy was crouched eight feet away, holding his wrench like a clean-up hitter waiting on a high fastball.

Reacher kept his eyes on the big guy's eyes and said, "Vaughan, step away. This guy is going to start swinging. He could hit you by mistake." But he sensed Vaughan wasn't moving. So he danced away east, dragging the fight with him. The big guy followed, big feet in rubber boots splashing awkwardly through standing water. Reacher dodged north, toward Thurman. Thurman backed off again, keeping his distance. Reacher stopped. The big guy wound up for a swing. The huge wrench slashed horizontal, at shoulder height. Reacher stepped back a pace and the wrench missed and its wild momentum carried the big guy through a complete circle.

Reacher backed off another pace.

The big guy followed.

Reacher stopped.

The big guy swung.

Reacher stepped back.

Thirty acres. Reacher wasn't fast and he wasn't nimble but he was a lot more mobile than anyone who outweighed him by a hundred pounds. And he had the kind of natural stamina that came from being exactly what he was born to be. He wasn't on the downside of twenty years of weight rooms and steroids. Unlike his opponent. The big guy was breathing hard and every missed swing was jacking his fury and his adrenaline rush all the way up to carelessness. Reacher kept on moving and stopping and dodging and stopping again. Eventually the big guy learned. With his fifth swing he aimed for a spot three feet behind Reacher's back.

Reacher saw it coming in the guy's crazed eyes and dodged the other way. Forward. The wrench hissed through empty air and Reacher rolled around the guy's spinning back and bent his knees and smashed his elbow up into the guy's kidney. Then he stepped away, two paces, three, and stood still and shook his arms loose and rolled his shoulders. The big guy turned. His back looked stiff and his knees were weakening. He charged and swung and missed and Reacher dodged away.

Like a bullfight. Except the big guy's IQ was marginally higher than a bull's. After a dozen fruitless swings he recognized that his tactics were futile. He sent the wrench spinning away into the marshy ground and got ready to charge. Reacher smiled. Because by then the damage was done. The guy was panting and staggering a little. The violent exertions and the adrenaline overload had spent him. He was going to lose. He didn't know it. But Reacher knew it.

And Thurman knew it.

Thurman was hurrying back toward the gate. Hurrying, but slowly. An old man, a heavy coat, awkward footwear, mud on the ground. Reacher called, "Vaughan, don't let him leave. He has to stay here." He saw her move in the corner of his eye. A small soaked figure, darting north. Then he saw the giant launch himself. A crazed lunge, across fifteen feet of distance. Three hundred and fifty pounds, coming on like a train. Reacher felt small and static by comparison. The guy might have been fast on a football field but he was slow now. His boots churned in the liquid mud. No grip. No traction. He came in on a flailing run and Reacher feinted left and stepped right and tripped him. The guy splashed down in the water and slid a full yard and Reacher turned away and was hit in the back by what felt like a truck. He went down hard and got a mouthful of mud and reflexively rolled away and jacked himself back up and dodged and missed a punch from the plant foreman by about an inch and a half.

Two against one again.

Inefficient.

The foreman launched another big roundhouse swing and Reacher swatted it away and saw the giant struggling to get up. His hands and knees were scrabbling and sliding in the mud. Fifty feet north Vaughan had hold of Thurman's collar. He was struggling to get free. Maybe winning. Then the foreman swung again and Reacher moved and the foreman's fist glanced off his shoulder. But not before stinging a bruise from where he had been hit before, in the bar.

Which hurt.

OK, no more Mr. Nice Guy.

Reacher planted his back heel in the mud and leaned in and launched a flurry of heavy punches, a fast deadly rhythm, four blows, right, left, right, left, *one* to the gut, *two* to the jaw, *three* to the head, and *four,* a crushing uppercut under the chin, like he was his demented five-year-old self all over again, but five times heavier and eight times more experienced. The foreman was already on his way down when the uppercut landed. It lifted him back up and then dropped him like the earth had opened up. Reacher spun away and lined up and kicked the scrabbling giant in the head, like he was punting a football, instep against ear. The impact pinwheeled the guy's body a whole two feet and dropped him back in the mud.

The foreman lay still.

The giant lay still.

Game over.

Reacher checked his hands for broken bones and found none. He stood still and got his breathing under control and glanced north through the light. Thurman had broken free of Vaughan's grasp and was heading for the gate again, slipping and sliding and twisting and turning to fend her off. His hat was gone. His hair was wet and wild. Reacher set off in their direction. Paused to collect the giant wrench from where it had fallen. He hefted it up and carried it on his shoulder like an ax. He trudged onward, heavily. A slow-motion chase. He caught Vaughan ten yards from the gate and passed her and clamped a hand on Thurman's shoulder and pressed downward. The old guy folded up and went down on his knees. Reacher moved onward, to the gate. He found the little gray box. Flipped the lid. Saw the keypad. Swung the wrench and smashed it to splinters. Hit it again. And again. It fell out of its housing in small broken pieces. A small metal chassis hung up on thin trailing wires. Reacher chopped downward with the wrench until the wires tore and ruptured and the chassis fell to the ground.

Thurman was still on his knees. He said, "What are you doing? Now we can't get out of here."

"Wrong," Reacher said. "You can't, but we can."

"How?"

"Wait and see."

"It's not possible."

"Would you have given me the combination?"

"Never."

"So what's the difference?"

Vaughan said, "Reacher, what the hell is in your pockets?"

"Lots of things," Reacher said. "Things we're going to need."

71

Reacher trudged through the mud and rolled Thurman's men into what medics called the recovery position. On their sides, arms splayed, necks at a natural angle, one leg straight and the other knee drawn up. No danger of choking. A slight danger of drowning, if the puddles didn't stop filling. The rain was still hard. It thrashed against their slickers and drummed on the sides of their boots.

Thurman poked and prodded at the shattered box where the keypad had been. No result. The gates stayed closed. He gave up and slipped and slid back to the center of the hidden area. Reacher and Vaughan fought their way across to the eighteen-wheeler. It was just standing there, shut down and silent and oblivious.

Vaughan said, "You really think this is a bomb?"

Reacher said, "Don't you?"

"Thurman was mighty plausible. About the gifts for Afghanistan."

"He's a preacher. It's his job to be plausible."

"What if you're wrong?"

"What if I'm right?"

"How much damage could it do?"

"If they built it right I wouldn't want to be within three miles of it when it goes off."

"Three *miles*?"

"Twenty tons of TNT, twenty tons of shrapnel. It won't be pretty."

"How do we get out of here?"

"Where's your truck?"

"Where we left it. They ambushed me. Opened the outer gate and drove me through the plant in Thurman's SUV. It's parked the other side of the inner gate. Which you just made sure will never open again."

"No big deal."

"You can't climb the wall."

"But you can," Reacher said.

They talked for five fast minutes about what to do and how to do it. Knives, welds, the average size and thickness of a car's roof panel, canvas straps, knots, trailer hitches, four-wheel-drive, low-range gearing. Thurman was pacing aimlessly a hundred yards away. They left him there and headed through the mud to the wall. They picked a spot ten feet left of the gate. Reacher took the two switchblades out of his pocket and handed them to Vaughan. Then he stood with his back to the wall, directly underneath the maximum radius of the horizontal cylinder above. Rain sheeted off it and soaked his head and shoulders. He bent down and curled his left palm and made a stirrup. Vaughan lined up directly in front of him, facing him, and put her right foot in the stirrup. He took her weight and she balanced with her wrists on his shoulders and straightened her leg and boosted herself up. He cupped his right hand under her left foot. She stood upright in his palms and her weight fell forward and her belt buckle hit him in the forehead.

"Sorry," she said.

"Nothing we haven't done before," he said, muffled.

"I'm ready," she said.

Reacher was six feet five inches tall and had long arms. In modest motel rooms he could put his palms flat on an eight-foot ceiling. Vaughan was about five feet four. Arms raised, she could probably stretch just shy of seven feet. Total, nearly fifteen feet. And the wall was only fourteen feet high.

He lifted. Like starting a bicep curl with a free weights bar loaded with a hundred and twenty pounds. Easy, except that his hands were turned in at an unnatural angle. And his footing was insecure, and Vaughan wasn't a free weights bar. She wasn't rigid and she was wobbling and struggling to balance.

"Ready?" he called.

"Wait one," she said.

He felt her weight move in his hands, left to right, right to left, shifting, equalizing, preparing.

"Now go," she said.

He did four things. He boosted her sharply upward, used her momentary weightlessness to shift his hands flat under her shoes, stepped forward half a pace, and locked his arms straight.

She fell forward and met the bulge of the cylinder

with the flats of her forearms. The hollow metal construction boomed once, then again, much delayed.

"OK?" he called.

"I'm there," she said.

He felt her go up on tiptoes in his palms. Felt her reach up and straighten her arms. According to his best guess her hands should right then have been all the way up on the cylinder's top dead-center. He heard the first switchblade pop open. He swiveled his hands a little and gripped her toes. For stability. She was going to need it. He moved out another few inches. By then she should have been resting with her belly against the metal curve. Rain was streaming down all over him. He heard her stab downward with the knife. The wall clanged and boomed.

"Won't go through," she called.

"Harder," he called back.

She stabbed again. Her whole body jerked and he dodged and danced underneath her, keeping her balanced. Like acrobats in a circus. The wall boomed.

"No good," she called.

"Harder," he called.

She stabbed again. No boom. Just a little metallic clatter, then nothing.

"The blade broke," she called.

Reacher's arms were starting to ache.

"Try the other one," he called. "Be precise with the angle. Straight downward, OK?"

"The metal is too thick."

"It's not. It's from an old piece-of-shit Buick, probably. It's like aluminum foil. And that's a good Japanese blade. Hit it hard. Who do you hate?"

"The guy that pulled the trigger on David."

"He's inside the wall. His heart is the other side of the metal."

He heard the second switchblade open. Then there was silence for a second. Then a convulsive jerk through her legs and another dull boom through the metal.

A different boom.

"It's in," she called. "All the way."

"Pull on it," he called back.

He felt her take her weight on the wooden handle. He felt her twist as she wrapped both fists around it. He felt her feet pull up out of his hands. Then he felt them come back.

"It's slicing through," she called. "It's cutting the metal."

"It will," he called back. "It'll stop when it hits a weld."

He felt it stabilize a second later. Called, "Where is it?"

"Right at the top."

"Ready?"

"On three," she called. "One, two, *three.*"

She jerked herself upward and he helped as much as he could, fingertips and tiptoes, and then her weight was gone. He came down in a heap and rolled away in case she was coming down on top of him. But she wasn't. He got to his feet and walked away to get a better angle and saw her lying longitudinally on top of the cylinder, legs spread, both hands wrapped tight around the knife handle. She rested like that for a second and then shifted her weight and slid down the far side of the bulge, slowly at first, then faster, swinging around, still holding tight to the knife handle. He saw her clasped hands at the top of the curve, and then her weight started pulling the blade through the metal, fast at first where a track was already sliced and then slower as the blade bit through new metal. It would jam again at the next weld, which he figured was maybe five feet down the far side, allowing for the size of a typical car's roof panel, minus a folded flange at both sides for assembly purposes, which would be about a quarter of the way around the cylinder's circumference, which would mean she would be hanging off the wall at full stretch with about four feet of clear air under the soles of her shoes.

A survivable fall.

Probably.

He waited what seemed like an awful long time, and then he heard two hard thumps on the outside of the wall. They each sounded twice, once immediately and then again as the sound raced around the hollow circle and came back. He closed his eyes and smiled. Their agreed signal. Out, on her feet, no broken bones.

"Impressive," Thurman said, from ten yards away.

Reacher turned. The old guy was still hatless. His blow-dried waves were ruined. Ninety yards beyond him his two men were still down and inert.

Four minutes, Reacher thought.

Thurman said, "I could do what she did."

"In your dreams," Reacher said. "She's fit and agile. You're a fat old man. And who's going to boost you up? Real life is not like the movies. Your guys aren't going to wake up and shake their heads and get right to it. They're going to be puking and falling down for a week."

"Are you proud of that?"

"I gave them a choice."

"Your lady friend can't open the gate, you know. She doesn't have the combination."

"Have faith, Mr. Thurman. A few minutes from now you're going to see me ascend."

Reacher strained to hear sounds from the main compound, but the rain was too loud. It hissed in the puddles and pattered on the mud and clanged hard against the metal of the wall. So he just waited. He took up station six feet from the wall and a yard left of where Vaughan had gone over. Thurman backed off and watched.

Three minutes passed. Then four. Then without warning a long canvas strap snaked up and over the wall and the free end landed four feet to Reacher's right. The kind of thing used for tying down scrap cars to a flat-bed trailer. Vaughan had driven Thurman's Tahoe up to the security office and had found a strap of the right length in the pile near the door and had weighted its end by tying it around a scrap of pipe. He pictured her after the drive back, twenty feet away through the metal, swinging the strap like a cowgirl with a rope, building momentum, letting it go, watching it sail over.

Reacher grabbed the strap and freed the pipe and retied the end into a generous two-foot loop. He wrapped the canvas around his right hand and walked toward the wall. Kicked it twice and backed off a step and put his foot in the loop and waited. He pictured Vaughan securing the other end to the trailer hitch on Thurman's Tahoe, climbing into the driver's seat, selecting four-wheel-drive for maximum traction across the mud, selecting the low-range transfer case for delicate throttle control. He had been insistent about that. He didn't want his arms torn off at the shoulders when she hit the gas.

He waited. Then the strap went tight above him and started to quiver. The canvas around his hand wrapped tight. He pushed down into the loop with his sole. He saw the strap pull across the girth of the cylinder. No friction. Wet canvas on painted metal, slick with rain. The canvas stretched a little. Then he felt serious pressure under his foot and he lifted smoothly into the air. Slowly, maybe twelve inches a second. Less than a mile an hour. Idle speed, for the Tahoe's big V-8. He pictured Vaughan behind the wheel, concentrating hard, her foot like a feather on the pedal.

"Goodbye, Thurman," he said. "Looks like it's you that's getting left behind this time."

Then he looked up and got his left hand on the bulge of the cylinder and pushed back and hauled with his right to stop his wrapped knuckles crushing against the metal. His hips hit the maximum curve and he unwrapped his hand and hung on and let himself be pulled up to top dead-center. Then he dropped the strap and let the loop around his foot pull his legs up sideways and then he kicked free of the loop and came to rest spread-eagled on his stomach along the top of the wall. He jerked his hips and sent his legs down the far side and squealed his palms across ninety degrees of wet metal and pushed off and fell, two long split seconds. He hit the ground and fell on his back and knocked the wind out of himself. He rolled over and forced some air into his lungs and crawled up on his knees.

Vaughan had stopped Thurman's Tahoe twenty feet away. Reacher got to his feet and walked over to it and unhooked the strap from the trailer hitch. Then he climbed into the passenger seat and slammed the door.

"Thanks," he said.

"You OK?" she asked.

"Fine. You?"

"I feel like I did when I was a kid and I fell out of an apple tree. Scared, but a good scared." She changed to high-range gearing and took off fast. Two minutes later they were at the main vehicle gate. It was standing wide open.

"We should close it," Reacher said.

"Why?"

"To help contain the damage. If I'm right."

"Suppose you're not?"

"Maximum of five phone calls will prove it one way or the other."

"How do we close it? They don't seem to have any manual override."

They stopped just outside the gate and got out and walked over to the gray metal box on the wall. Reacher flipped the lid. One through nine, plus zero.

"Try six-six-one-three," he said.

Vaughan looked blank but stepped up and raised her index finger. Pressed six, six, one, three, neat and rapid. There was silence for a second and then motors whined and the gates started closing. A foot a second, wheels rumbling along tracks. Vaughan asked, "How did you know?"

"Most codes are four figures," Reacher said. "ATM cards, things like that. People are used to four-figure codes."

"Why those four figures?"

"Lucky guess," Reacher said. "Revelation is the sixty-sixth book in the King James Bible. Chapter one, verse three says the time is at hand. Which seems to be Thurman's favorite part."

"So we could have gotten out without climbing."

"If we had, they could have, too. I want them in there. So I had to smash the lock."

"Where to now?"

"The hotel in Despair. The first phone call is one that you get to make."

72

They abandoned Thurman's Tahoe next to where Vaughan's old Chevy was waiting. They transferred between vehicles and bumped through the deserted parking lot and found the road. Three miles later they were in downtown Despair. It was still raining. The streets and the sidewalks were dark and wet and completely deserted. The middle of the night, in the middle of nowhere. They threaded through the cross-streets and pulled up outside the hotel. The façade was as blank and gloomy as before. The street door was closed but not locked. Inside the place looked just the same. The empty dining room on the left, the deserted bar on the right, the untended reception desk dead ahead. The register on the desk, the large square leather book. Easy to grab, easy to swivel around, easy to open, easy to read. Reacher put his fingertip under the last registered guests, the couple from California, from seven months previously. He tilted the book, so that Vaughan had a clear view of their names and addresses.

"Call them in," he said. "And if they're helping the deserters, do whatever your conscience tells you to."

"If?"

"I think they might be into something else."

Vaughan made the call from her cell and they sat in faded armchairs and waited for the call back. Vaughan said, "Gifts are a perfectly plausible explanation. Churches send foreign aid all the time. Volunteers, too. They're usually good people."

"No argument from me," Reacher said. "But my whole life has been about the people that aren't usual. The exceptions."

"Why are you so convinced?"

"The welding."

"Locks can be broken."

"The container was welded to the trailer. And that's not how containers get shipped. They get lifted off and put on boats. By cranes. That's the whole point of containers. The welding suggests they don't mean for that container to leave the country."

Vaughan's phone rang. A three-minute wait. From a cop's perspective, the upside of all the Homeland Security hoopla. Agencies talked, computers were linked, databases were shared. She answered and listened, four long minutes. Then she thanked her caller and clicked off.

"Can't rule out the AWOL involvement," she said.

"Because?" Reacher asked.

"They're listed as activists. And activists can be into all kinds of things."

"What kind of activists?"

"Religious conservatives."

"What kind?"

"They run something called the Church of the Apocalypse in LA."

"The Apocalypse is a part of the End Times story," Reacher said.

Vaughan said nothing.

Reacher said, "Maybe they came here to recruit Thurman as a brother activist. Maybe they recognized his special potential."

"They wouldn't have stayed in this hotel. They'd have been guests in his house."

"Not the first time. He didn't know them yet. The second time, maybe. And the third and the fourth, maybe the fifth and the sixth. Depends how hard they had to work to convince him. There's a four-month gap between their first visit and when he ordered the TNT from Kearny."

"He said that was a bureaucratic error."

"Did you believe him?"

Vaughan didn't answer.

"Four phone calls," Reacher said. "That's all it's going to take."

They drove west to the edge of town. Three miles away through the rainy darkness they could see the plant's lights, faint and blue and distant, blurred by the rain on the windshield, a fragmented sepulchral glow way out in the middle of nowhere. Empty space all around it. They parked on a curb facing out of town, level with the last of the buildings. Reacher eased his butt off the seat and took the cell phone he had borrowed out of his pocket. Then he took out the sheet of paper he had taken from the purchasing office. The new cell phone numbers. The paper was wet and soggy and he had to peel apart the folds very carefully.

"Ready?" he asked.

Vaughan said, "I don't understand."

He dialed the third number down. Heard ring tone in his ear, twice, four times, six times, eight. Then the call was answered. A muttered greeting, in a voice he recognized. A man's voice, fairly normal in tone and timbre, but a little dazed, and muffled twice, first by coming from a huge chest cavity, and again by the cellular circuitry.

The big guy, from the plant.

Reacher said, "How are you? Been awake long?"

The guy said, "Go to hell."

Reacher said, "Maybe I will, maybe I won't. I'm not sure about the likelihood of things like that. You guys are the theologians, not me."

No reply.

Reacher asked, "Is your buddy awake, too?"

No reply.

Reacher said, "I'll call him and see for myself."

He clicked off and dialed the second number on the list. It rang eight times and the plant foreman answered.

Reacher said, "Sorry, wrong number."

He clicked off.

Vaughan asked, "What exactly are you doing?"

"How did the insurgents hurt David?"

"With a roadside bomb."

"Detonated how?"

"Remotely, I assume."

Reacher nodded. "Probably by radio, from the

nearest ridge line. So if Thurman *has* built a bomb, how will he detonate it?"

"The same way."

"But not from the nearest hill. He'll probably want a lot more distance than that. He'll probably want to be out of state somewhere. Maybe at home here in Colorado, or in his damn church. Which would take a very powerful radio. In fact, he'd probably have to build one himself, to be sure of reliability. Which is a lot of work. So my guess is he decided to use one that someone else already built. Someone like Verizon or T-Mobile or Cingular."

"Cell phone?"

Reacher nodded again. "It's the best way. The phone companies spend a lot of time and money building reliable networks. Look at their commercials. They're proud of the fact that you can call anywhere from anywhere. Some of them even give you free long distance."

"And the number is on that list?"

"It would make sense," Reacher said. "Two things happened at the same time, three months ago. Thurman ordered twenty tons of TNT, and four new cell phones. Sounds like a plan to me. He already had everything else he needed. My guess is he kept one phone for himself, and gave two to his inner circle, so they could have secure communications between themselves, separate from anything else they were doing. And my guess is the fourth phone is buried in the heart of that container, with the ringer wired to a primer circuit. The ringer on a cell phone puts out a decent little voltage. Maybe they fitted a standby battery, and maybe they connected an external antenna. Maybe one of those antennas on the Peterbilt was a cell antenna from Radio Shack, wired back to the trailer."

"And you're going to call that number?"

Reacher said, "Soon."

He dialed the first number on the list. It rang, and then Thurman answered, fast and impatient, like he had been waiting for the call. Reacher asked, "You guys over the wall yet?"

Thurman said, "We're still here. Why are you calling us?"

"You starting to see a pattern?"

"The last phone was Underwood's. He's dead, so he won't answer. So there's no point calling it."

Reacher said, "OK."

"How long are you going to keep us here?"

"Just a minute more," Reacher said. He clicked off and laid the phone on the Chevy's dash. Stared out through the windshield.

Vaughan said, "You can't do this. It would be murder."

Reacher said, "Live by the sword, die by the sword. Thurman should know that quotation better than anyone. It's from the Bible. Matthew, chapter twenty-six, verse fifty-two. Slightly paraphrased. Also, they have sown the wind, and they shall reap the whirlwind. Hosea, chapter eight, verse seven. I'm sick of people who claim to live by the scriptures cherry-picking the parts they find convenient, and ignoring all the rest."

"You could be completely wrong about him."

"Then there's no problem. Gifts don't explode. We've got nothing to lose."

"But you might be right."

"In which case he shouldn't have lied to me. He should have confessed. I would have let him take his chance in court."

"I don't believe you."

"We'll never know now."

"He doesn't seem worried enough."

"He's used to saying things and having people believe him. And he told me he's not afraid of dying. He told me he's going to a better place."

"You're not a one-man justice department."

"He's no better than whoever blew up David's Humvee. Worse, even. David was a combatant, at least. And out on the open road. Thurman is going to have that thing driven to a city somewhere. With children and old people all around. Thousands of them. And more thousands maybe not quite close enough. He's going to put thousands more people in your situation."

Vaughan said nothing.

"And for what?" Reacher said. "For some stupid, deluded fantasy."

Vaughan said nothing.

Reacher checked the final number. Entered it into his phone. Held the phone flat on his palm and held it out to Vaughan.

"Your choice," he said. "Green button to make the call, red button to cancel it."

Vaughan didn't move for a moment. Then she took her hand off the wheel. Folded three fingers and her thumb. Held her index finger out straight. It was small, neat, elegant, and damp, and it had a trimmed nail. She held it still, close to the phone's LED window.

Then she moved it.

She pressed the green button.

Nothing happened. Not at first. Reacher wasn't surprised. He knew a little about cell phone technology. He had read a long article, in a trade publication abandoned on an airplane. Press the green button, and the phone in your hand sends a request by radio to the nearest cell tower, called a base transceiver station by the people who put it there. The phone says: *Hey, I want to make a call.* The base transceiver station forwards the plea to the nearest base station controller, by microwave if the bean counters got their way during the planning phase, or by fiber optic cable if the engineers got theirs. The base station controller bundles all the near-simultaneous requests it can find and moves them on to the closest mobile switching center, where the serious action starts.

Maybe at this point a ring tone starts up in your earpiece. But it means nothing. It's a placebo. It's there to reassure you. So far you're not even close to connected.

The mobile switching center identifies the destination phone. Checks if it's switched on, that it's not busy, that it's not set to call divert. Speech channels are limited in number, and therefore expensive to operate. You don't get near one unless there's a viable chance of an answer.

If all is well, a speech channel clicks in. It extends first from your local mobile switching center to its distant opposite number. Maybe by fiber optics, maybe by microwave, maybe by satellite if the distance is great. Then the distant mobile switching center hits up its closest base station controller, which hits up its closest base transceiver station, which emits a radio blast to the phone you're looking for, an 850 megahertz or a 1.9 gigahertz pulse surfing on a perfect spherical wavefront close to the speed of light. A nanosecond later, the circuit is complete. The tone in your ear morphs from phony to real and the target phone starts its urgent ringing.

Total time lag, an average of seven whole seconds.

Vaughan took her finger back and stared forward out the windshield. The Chevy's engine was still running and the wipers were still beating back and forth. The windshield smeared in perfect arcs. There was still a little protective wax on the glass.

Two seconds.

"Nothing," Vaughan said.

Reacher said, "Wait."

Four seconds.

Five.

They stared into the distance. The blue arena lights hung and shimmered in the wet air, pale and misty, fractured by intervening raindrops like twinkling starlight.

Six seconds.

Seven.

Then: The silent horizon lit up with an immense white flash that filled the windshield and bloomed instantly higher and wider. The rain all around turned to steam as the air superheated and jets of white vapor speared up and out in every direction like a hundred thousand rockets had launched simultaneously. The vapor was followed by a halo of black soot that punched instantly from a tight cap to a raging black hemisphere a mile high and a mile wide. It rolled and tore and folded back on itself and was pierced by violent trails of steam as supersonic white-hot shrapnel flung through it at more than fifteen thousand miles an hour.

No sound. Not then. Just blinding light and silence.

In still air the sound would have taken fourteen seconds to arrive from three miles away. But the air wasn't still. It was moving fast in a massive compression wave. The wave carried the sound with it. It arrived three seconds after the light. The truck rocked back against the brake and the air roared with the rolling violence of the explosion, first a crisp deafening *crump* and then a banshee screaming from the shrapnel in the air and an otherworldly pelting sound as a million blasted fragments obliterated everything in their path and fell to earth and tore up the scrub and boiled and hissed where they lay. Then the decompression wave blew in the other way as air rushed back to fill the vacuum, and the truck rocked again, and the black cloud was pulverized to nothing by the violent wind, and then there was nothing to see except tongues of random flame and spouts of drifting steam, and nothing to hear except the steady patter of shrapnel falling back to earth from three miles up, and after ten long seconds there was not even that, just the patient rain on the Chevy's roof.

73

Vaughan called out the whole of the Hope PD for crowd control. Within thirty minutes she had all four of her deputies and her brother officer and her watch commander and the desk guy all lined up on the western edge of Despair's last block. Nobody was allowed through. The state cops showed up next. Within an hour they had three cars there. Five more showed up within the next four hours. They had taken the long way around. Everyone knew there had been uranium at the plant. The state cops confirmed that the MPs had the road blocked to the west, on a five-mile perimeter. It was close to dawn and they were already stopping incoming trucks.

Dawn came and the rain finally stopped and the sky turned hard blue and the air turned crystal clear. *Like nerves after pain,* Reacher had read once, in a poem. The morning was too cool to raise steam off the soaked ground. The mountains looked a thousand miles away, but every detail was visible. Their rocky outcrops, their pine forests, their tree lines, their snow channels. Reacher borrowed a pair of binoculars from Vaughan's watch commander and climbed to the third floor of the last building to the west. He struggled with a jammed window and crouched and put his elbows on the sill and focused into the distance.

Not much to see.

The white metal wall was gone. Just a few rags and tatters of shredded metal remained, blown and tumbled hundreds of yards in every direction. The plant itself was mostly a black smoking pit, with cranes and gantries knocked over and smashed and bent. Crushers had been toppled off their concrete pads. Anything smaller had been smashed to pieces too small to reliably identify. The office buildings were gone entirely. Thurman's residential compound had been obliterated. The house had been smashed to matchwood. The fieldstone wall was a horizontal rock field spread south and west like grains of spilled salt on a table. The plantings were all gone. Occasional foot-high stumps were all that was left of the trees. The airplane barn had been demolished. No sign of the Piper.

Immense damage.

Better here than somewhere else, Reacher thought.

He came downstairs to a changed situation. Federal agencies had arrived. Gossip was flowing. Air Force radar in Colorado Springs had detected metal fifteen thousand feet up. It had hung there for a long second before falling back to earth. Radiation-sniffing drone planes had been dispatched and were closing in on wide circular paths. The rain was seen as a mercy. DU dust was believed to be strongly hygroscopic. Nothing bad would drift. Every contractor within a hundred miles, in Colorado and Nebraska and Kansas, had been contacted. A hurricane fence nearly nineteen miles long was needed. The site was going to be fenced off forever, on a three-mile radius. The fence was going to be hung with biohazard signs every six feet. The agencies already owned the signs, but not the wire.

No hard information was volunteered by the townsfolk. No hard questions were asked by the agencies. The word on everyone's lips was *accident. An accident at the plant.* It was second nature, a part of the hardscrabble culture. An accident at the mill, an accident at the mine. Consistent with history. If the agencies had doubts, they knew better than to voice them. The Pentagon had begun to stonewall even before the last fragments had cooled.

State officials arrived, with contingency plans. Food and water was to be trucked in. Buses were to be laid on, for job searches in neighboring towns. Special welfare would be provided, for the first six months. Transitional help of every kind would be afforded. After that, any stragglers would be strictly on their own.

First Reacher and then Vaughan were pushed steadily east by the official activity. By the middle of the afternoon they were sitting together in the Chevy outside the dry goods store, with nothing more to do. They took one last look to the west and then set off down the road toward Hope.

They went to Vaughan's house, and showered, and dressed again. Vaughan said, "David's hospital is going to fold."

"Someone else will step in," Reacher said. "Someone better."

"I'm not going to abandon him."

"I don't think you should."

"Even though he won't know."

"He knew beforehand. And it was important to him."

"You think so?"

"I know so. I know soldiers."

Reacher took the borrowed phone out of his pocket and dropped it on the bed. Followed it with the registration, from the old Suburban's glove box. Asked Vaughan to mail both things back, with no return address on the package. She said, "That sounds like the start of a farewell speech."

"It is," Reacher said. "And the middle, and the end."

They hugged, a little formally, like two strangers who shared many secrets. Then Reacher left. He walked down her winding path, and walked four blocks north to First Street. He got a ride very easily. A stream of vehicles was heading east, emergency workers, journalists, men in suits in plain sedans, contractors. The excitement had made them friendly. There was a real community spirit. Reacher rode with a post-hole digger from Kansas who had signed up to dig some of the sixteen thousand holes necessary for the new fence. The guy was cheerful. He was looking at months of steady work.

Reacher got out in Sharon Springs, where there was a good road south. He figured San Diego was about a thousand miles away, or more, if he followed some detours.

ABOUT THE AUTHOR

LEE CHILD is the author of twelve Jack Reacher thrillers, including the *New York Times* bestsellers *Persuader, The Enemy, One Shot,* which has been optioned for a major motion picture by Paramount Pictures, *The Hard Way,* and *Bad Luck and Trouble*. His debut, *Killing Floor,* won both the Anthony and the Barry awards for Best First Mystery. Foreign rights in the Reacher series have sold in forty territories. Child, a native of England and a former television director, lives in New York City, where he is at work on his thirteenth Reacher thriller, *Gone Tomorrow*.